Bad Guys Beware

An Alaska Mystery

Large Print Edition

Carole Gibb

Bad Guys Beware: An Alaska Mystery with Crime Reporter Kit Finnegan

Quickread Press
Seattle, Washington, USA

ISBN 978-0-9858878-5-8

Cover design by Gery Rudolph

For my parents

Mary Lou Healy and John Robert Healy

1

Kit Finnegan told herself to ignore the bald guy with the sunglasses and just enjoy her victory. She was the proud quarter-drop champion at an indoor games festival held annually in her hometown of Nipntuck, in Southeast Alaska. Well, maybe proud wasn't quite the word, considering how she'd won.

The quarter-drop competition involved clamping a quarter between one's thighs, duckwalking ten yards, and dropping the quarter into a shot glass positioned on the floor.

Aside from being well coordinated, Kit was short, which meant her quarter didn't have very far to drop. But she didn't take the prize for aiming her quarter true. Without thinking ahead she'd worn a skirt, and when she unclamped her legs to drop the quarter nothing happened—it stayed stuck to her sweaty thigh. The crowd in the Sea Shanty pub erupted in raucous laughter.

Focused on winning, she gave a determined hop, and when it still didn't let go the crowd lost it even more.

The judges, who kept breaking into laughter, awarded her the prize, which included the quarter, the shot glass, and a handful of jukebox tokens.

And now, waiting to order a victory beer at the crowded bar, Kit was doing her best to forget about the guy wearing sunglasses. He was short and bowlegged, with a shiny dome, and he was wearing shades—on a rainy Sunday afternoon in a dim pub. There was something menacing about him. She felt it.

Then she sighed. The problem wasn't with the bald guy and his sunglasses, it was with her. Nipntuck had been annoyingly peaceful lately. Without a crime story to investigate for the newspaper, she got twitchy and started to see suspicious characters behind every pair of sunglasses. The guy with the shades was either trying to be movie-star cool or he was just hung over, Kit told herself, nothing more.

She caught Big Pat's eye and made a show

of clutching at her throat to indicate that she was parched. Her brother Pat owned the Sea Shanty and was tending bar. He slid a cold pint into her waiting palm.

Before taking a sip, she asked, "Did I hear right? You've added one last event?"

Pat said. "Yep. An impromptu song-writing contest. And the prize is a good one."

"What's the prize?"

"Three hundred cash plus I'm throwing in the stuffed moose head on the wall."

The moose head was extremely popular with the patrons. It was cross-eyed, which gave it personality, and to the islanders of Nipntuck, personality was gold. It trumped both money and looks. "That's going to spark some competition," she said.

"My plan exactly," he grinned. "Rebecca signed up, bragging that she was bursting with song ideas." He pointed. "But I don't think it's going so well."

Kit turned and spied her friend toward the back of the bar. Rebecca was staring off into space, frowning deeply and tapping a pencil against her cheek. Kit, a writer herself, knew that look of pained concentration.

She started over to offer some solace, and noticed the bald guy with the sunglasses again. He was against the wall, right behind Rebecca's table. Although positive she'd never met him, something about him was familiar. He noticed her gaze and turned away with a jerk. Watching him retreat through the crowd, Kit felt her gut churn as if her body knew something her mind didn't. She told herself to quit with the paranoia.

Rebecca's table held a dozen bar napkins covered with desperate-looking doodles. She saw Kit and threw down her pencil. "I need to drop out."

Kit patted her on the shoulder. "The competition would have crushed you anyway. First prize is a wad of cash, plus the stuffed moose head off the wall."

"The moose with the crossed eyes?" Rebecca whooped in excitement. "We are *not* dropping out!" She yanked Kit into the chair beside her and grabbed up her pencil. "We are doing this."

"We?!" Kit asked.

After chewing on her lip for a minute, Rebecca said, "I know, let's write a song about

Jean-Philippe!"

Kit said flatly, "I hate Jean-Philippe."

"Excellent," said Rebecca. "Just start with the word . . . 'you' . . . and see what comes next."

The cash would be nice. Kit took a gulp of beer and thought about her ex. The idea of him made her scowl, but suddenly she found herself grinning. In a syrupy voice, she sang, "You . . . look so good to me . . ." then her voice went flat, "when the lights are out."

Rebecca, laughing, wrote it down.

Sweetly, Kit sang, "You enter the room and my heart leaps . . ." her eyes narrowed, "for cover!"

Inspired, Rebecca sang, "We always have the best time when we are . . ." Kit jumped in, "apart."

Rebecca wrote it down and then sang, "I'm sure in my heart you're the one . . ."

". . . who needs counseling," Kit quickly stated.

Rebecca gushed, "I'll never leave you . . ."

Kit snapped her fingers and said, "alone with my purse!"

"Sister!" Rebecca shouted at the same

time, and they laughed.

The master of ceremonies tapped the mike twice and announced that the contest was about to begin.

"One more would be good," Rebecca said. She thought for a moment, then sang, "The day we met was the *best* day . . ."

Kit didn't hesitate. "To have dumped you!"

~~~

Doug Quinn—his friends just called him Quinn—didn't mind air travel, but the descent into Nipntuck seemed less like air travel and more like an act of daring. The jet had to brush very close to a row of steep coastal mountains in an airspace thick with floatplanes, and far too many dive-bombing eagles. The eagles were big enough to stutter a jet engine, and they had been known to.

When they landed on the island with a double bump and screech of wheels, the palatable tension in the passenger cabin relaxed and a smattering of applause broke out.

Waiting to disembark, Quinn thought back over the phone call that had brought him to Nipntuck on this drizzly Sunday.

Two days before he'd been out on his deck in Fairbanks, enjoying the evening sun on his face, when his cell phone rang. The number was preceded by a 907 area code—a call from within the state, but the rest of the number was unfamiliar.

The caller introduced himself as Marcus Holland. "I run SeaLab, a renewable energy research firm based in Southeast Alaska, on Nipntuck Island."

"I've heard of SeaLab." Quinn had been to the island a few times to see an old friend and get in some sportfishing. "You specialize in tidal power."

"That's correct. I apologize for calling out of the blue like this, but I was friends with your father, and last year he mentioned certain . . . covert work you did when you lived back in D.C."

This drew a laugh from Quinn. "Knowing my father, he probably made it sound more exciting than it was. I provided logistical support to the intelligence community on occasion. That's honestly all it was."

"He did happen to describe a few . . . dicey situations you handled well."

Quinn laughed again. "Driving on D.C.'s Beltway is a dicey situation. So is buying a woman a drink. But what can I do for you?"

Marcus said, "I could use some assistance for a week or two, if you're available. I have a security-related issue here at SeaLab." He paused.

Quinn had just completed a contract with Homeland Security, working for a division called the Arctic Guard. He had some paperwork to do, but his schedule was open after that. He asked Marcus to tell him more.

"I'll pay your travel expenses and advance you seventy-five hundred dollars. Another seventy-five hundred will be yours upon completion of the job. If there are unexpected delays or hazards, I'll compensate accordingly."

"What do you need done?" The pay was along the lines of what Quinn liked to make and sometimes did.

Marcus cleared his throat. "I'd like to lay it out for you in person. This particular assignment may require some . . . delicacy."

Quinn considered this. "Security work" could mean anything, and being a strongly built six-two he was frequently offered the kind that involved using his fists—the kind he made it a point to avoid. Security work that demanded delicacy, though, that sounded like an interesting prospect.

So now it was Sunday and he'd come to Nipntuck to meet with Marcus Holland. The plan was to dine downtown aboard the company yacht, the *Blue Sea*, while discussing the job. The energy scientist had told him to come hungry; there would be a big seafood dinner waiting for him.

He grabbed his duffel bag from the airport's single, creaky luggage carousel and went to rent a car.

Nipntuck was on an island with only seventy-seven miles of paved road, and no bridges connecting it to anywhere else. Quinn had found the supply of rental cars more than adequate when he'd visited before so he hadn't made a reservation. But it turned out that all rental cars and taxis were engaged due to some weekend event called Pubfest.

The festival was just winding down, the counter clerk told him; he'd have his choice of cars in an hour. But Quinn said he couldn't wait and the clerk directed him two blocks south to the Rent-a-Wreck place.

There was one car left on the lot, and when he saw it, Quinn understood why it was still there. The thing looked like some crazy person's bad idea. The bubble top of a VW Bug had been welded onto the body of a station wagon, and the tires looked like they'd been borrowed from a motorcycle. A Mercedes hood ornament was glued sloppily on the front.

"You're joking, right?" he asked.

"It's a Rent-a-Wreck," the guy told him. "Take it or leave it."

The car, Quinn discovered, took on a bad shimmy any time he went over forty. He cruised along slowly, not at all bothered by the moderate pace, considering the view.

On his left loomed a mountain carpeted in steep old-growth forest. To his right the vista opened dramatically onto a huge saltwater bay. Rocks everywhere slashed the bay's surface and the surge from the gulf broke against them, spraying and boiling restlessly. Quinn had heard these jagged rocks were the inspiration for the name Nipntuck. Running from storms on the Gulf, mariners had to beat their way through a quarter mile of them before reaching the harbor. In the days before electronic chart programs and depth sounders, it had been a nip and tuck race.

He reached downtown, swung into the harbor, parked, grabbed his bag, and descended the ramp that led down to the docks. Marcus had given him the choice of a hotel or the yacht for lodging and he'd gladly chosen the yacht.

He passed salty-looking people on the docks loading supplies, making repairs, and shooting the breeze. He came to the C float, turned right, and found the *Blue Sea* in its slip.

The boat was well kept. White tie-up lines lay coiled precisely on deck, and despite the gray weather the deeply polished brightwork threw off glints of light.

He knocked and called out a hello, but no one stirred inside. The door was unlocked, so he stuck his head inside and called again but got no response. *Odd*, he thought. Where was Marcus? And where was the seafood dinner he'd been promised? He was famished.

He left Marcus a phone message saying

he was at the *Blue Sea*, ready to meet. *And eat*, he thought, making himself comfortable in a deck chair under the boat's awning.

He liked being around boats and this harbor was buzzing with them. About half were pleasure craft and the rest were working boats—commercial fishing vessels, freight barges, and charter boats.

A boxy plywood houseboat came chugging around the breakwater. After several botched attempts, it finally bumped into its slip next to the *Blue Sea*. A set of homemade chimes—a dozen cowbells mixed in with copper plumbing pipes—clanged aggressively from its awning.

He liked being around boats except ones with annoying chimes. The grating noise, plus his empty stomach, launched him out of his chair. He started pacing.

After the initial phone call from the scientist, Quinn had checked out the SeaLab website. A banner across the top explained that the site was under construction, and below that ran an announcement that SeaLab would hold an "unveiling" the following weekend. The media and the general public were invited to join Marcus Holland as he revealed an innovation that would, the website claimed, "radically reshape the way we meet our energy needs, individually, and also as a country."

The security job, Quinn figured, would be related to SeaLab's mysterious innovation. He was impatient to learn more about it, but for that to happen, Marcus needed to show.

Another fifteen minutes passed, and he decided to go wait at a restaurant. He left his bag on deck along with his business card and a note to Marcus that he'd gone for a bite.

Close to the harbor, a pub called the Sea Shanty caught his eye. The place was hopping, which surprised him since it was nearly eight on a Sunday night. Then he saw a poster and realized this was the site of Pubfest. The formal festivities had ended but plenty of revelers remained.

He began working his way through a plate of Dungeness crab legs, thinking that if the job turned out to be some flaky deal he'd pass politely, but stick around for a few days. He knew two people who lived on Nipntuck island. One of them, his oldest friend Nate, would surely be up for some sportfishing.

His thoughts turned to the other person he knew on the island, his former fiancée, Allie. After their engagement ended, she had relocated to Nipntuck to be with her new man. When he agreed to come see Marcus Holland about this job, Quinn had pretended to feel no flicker of hope that he might cross paths with her here. But the flicker was there.

He hadn't been able to even look at another woman since Allie broke things off with him eight months ago. If he did run into her maybe it would help, somehow. Maybe he could orchestrate a better closing scene than the highly unsatisfactory one they'd had. Maybe then he could move on.

"Sir?" His waitress stood beside the table, smiling. She was so tall her thighs were practically at eye level. She picked up his plate to take away the empty crab shells. "Anything else?"

Impulsively, he asked, "A date?"

Maybe he didn't even need to see Allie. Maybe all he needed to move on was a change of scenery, and a beautiful waitress.

She waggled her hand and the substantial

diamond on her ring finger winked at him. Widening her smile, she said, "Thanks, though."

Quinn was glad he asked. He'd been frozen in the heart department these past eight months, but it was coming back to him now, how much he enjoyed courtship. He considered it a grand thing, right up there with long legs.

A young friend had spent the last many months trying to convince him that people didn't really date anymore, that instead they "hooked up," or "hung out." But he was a man who loved to take a woman out—open doors for her, make her laugh out loud, find out what they might have in common.

Lost in thought, he didn't notice his old friend Nate Farley walking up. "What's with the dopey expression?" Nate asked, plopping down into the booth.

Quinn indicated the waitress across the bar. "In and out of love in thirty seconds."

"Safer that way," Nate murmured.

"I'm in town for all of an hour," Quinn said, "and somehow you manage to find me."

"I have spies everywhere. What brings

you to town?"

"First, I want to hear about the black eyes." Nate's cherublike face sported not one, but two purple ringers.

"I moved in with a woman who neglected to tell me about her on-again, off-again fisherman boyfriend. He came to shore unexpectedly."

Quinn said, "Does he have at least one black eye now?" Though on the chunky side, Nate was deceptively quick with his fists.

"It wasn't like that. She and I were in bed and the guy burst in on us. She grabbed for the covers and accidentally elbowed me here." Nate pointed to the bridge of his nose. "The guy was ripping mad but couldn't hit me because I was already out cold. By the time I woke up, they were 'on again.' He brought her ten pounds of black-cod collars, for Pete's sake. There's no competing with that."

Quinn laughed. Nate was a computer consultant, which put him at a disadvantage in a community where fish greased the wheels.

The waitress saw Nate and, without having to ask, came over with a dark beer, a bowl of salmon chowder, and a small loaf of sourdough bread.

"Spies," Quinn snorted. "You're a regular here."

Nate grinned. "This joint used to be a pinball place. The guy who bought it, Big Pat, went through a long, painful remodel. Everything that could go wrong did go wrong. But the troubles he suffered built up all this customer loyalty—or at least, sympathy—before the place even opened. So when it finally did open, people stampeded in here to celebrate and now it's become the go-to spot. I missed Pubfest—had to work—but everyone's saying it was a gas." He took a long taste of his beer and smacked his lips. "So what's your story? Why are you here?"

Quinn told him about the job offer and how Marcus Holland, so far, was a no-show for their meeting. He asked if Nate had heard about SeaLab's unveiling in a week.

Nate, busy eating, just shook his head.

"According to their website, SeaLab's innovation will 'radically reshape the way the country meets its energy needs.'"

Nate raised a fist, and through a mouthful of food, said, "Yeah! Bring it on."

Quinn said, "So what sort of energy breakthrough would do this?"

Nate chewed for a minute, and said, "This country's power distribution system pretty much sucks. We could use a breakthrough there, for sure. But that's hardly news to you. You're the dude from D.C., remember?"

"For the last few years, I've been wandering around in the Arctic, remember?"

Quinn probably knew as much as Nate, but Nate could ferret information out of unusual sources, and was astute—and often entertaining—in his analysis of said information.

Nate said, "I heard from a fairly reliable source that the brownouts and blackouts happening across the country—even the ones seemingly caused by storms—are frequently caused by bad guys probing parts of the grid, tampering with how it works, testing different ways it can be disabled."

Quinn nodded. "When I was in D.C., there was some talk around that."

"Talk isn't what we need," Nate scowled. "Someone messing with our electrical grid is bad news. Think about it—a terrorist strike on that front, everything would go tits up. Gas pumps wouldn't work without electricity. Traffic lights. Grocery stores couldn't ring up your purchases. Banks? Forget it. Your computer at the office? Your cell phone? No juice, man. We'd be fucked." Nate said this loudly, and the lady in the next booth turned and gave him a stern look. He leaned in, "The psychological effect would be the worst because our most basic needs are dependent on a steady supply of electricity. Having the plug pulled ultimately means being in the dark, being unable to communicate with the people you love, being unable to get food, water, heat—"

To steer things closer to the original subject, Quinn jumped in, "So what kind of breakthrough would address it?"

"Well, there are these supercapacitor thingy-dingies."

"Thingy-dingies," Quinn repeated.

"Yeah. I'm talking nanotech, man."

He started tossing out words like nanomeadows, air batteries, and buckyballs, until Quinn interrupted. "Give it to me in plain terms," he said, "and I'll buy your dinner."

"I'm not up on this stuff, truth be told," Nate said, "but under particular circumstances a material like carbon, for instance, will behave completely unlike itself. The electrons do a dance and arrange themselves into new sorts of materials. We're talking something that may only be one molecule thick, but it can be layered or reproduced on a grand scale so that, voilà, you get your super-duper useful thingy-dingies."

"Okay . . ." Quinn said slowly. "But SeaLab's working on tidal power, something that involves huge turbines. Isn't it doubtful they would also be into this kind of gee-whiz molecular stuff? You're talking opposite ends of the spectrum."

"True," Nate said. "I brought up nanotech mostly because I think it's cool, not because I think SeaLab's doing it."

Quinn laughed and said, "So, if SeaLab was working on something major would you know about it?"

"Not necessarily. Their lab is offshore, on a small island twelve miles away from here, so they've stayed pretty much off the radar." He shrugged. "Our country does need to change the way it meets its energy needs. SeaLab is right about that, anyway." He dropped his spoon in his bowl, leaned back and gave his stomach a two-handed, much-satisfied pat.

Quinn studied the purple rings decorating his friend's eyes. "So where are you staying, now that your girlfriend's back with her fisherman?"

"I'm in between places. Where are *you* staying?"

Oh no, Quinn thought. He hadn't expected Nate to be homeless or he wouldn't have brought it up. "On SeaLab's yacht," he said slowly.

"The *Blue Sea*? I know it—it's a beaut."

Quinn pretended not to notice the soulful look Nate was sending his way. The last time Nate visited him in Fairbanks, he'd started a grease fire, and the time before that he'd accidentally left a fish in Quinn's car trunk. During a heat wave. He wasn't an ideal houseguest.

Nate said, "I can bunk there with you. I'll help you with information gathering."

"I'll ask Marcus about it." He flagged down their waitress to pay. "What are you up to now?"

Nate said he had to go collect payment from a client.

Like half the people in Nipntuck, he didn't bother owning a car so Quinn offered him a ride.

"It's only a few blocks, but sure," he replied. "We can take the long way and scope out women."

Quinn looked pointedly at the glob of chowder forming a crust on his friend's collar. "You repel women."

Nate looked down, lifted his shirt to his mouth, and got most of the glob off. "Only the ones I meet."

In the harbor parking lot, though, Nate changed his mind about the ride. He gave a hoot of laughter when he saw the Rent-a-Wreck, and said, "Talk about repelling women! Thanks, but I'll walk." He punched Quinn's shoulder. "See you soon."

2

~~~~~~

Back at the yacht, Quinn found no sign of Marcus. He was about to look up the scientist's home address when he heard a sudden clattering of footsteps and a tall blonde woman, dressed in a form-fitting dress and high heels, ran past on the dock shouting, "Jetsam! Jetsam!"

She spotted Quinn and pointed frantically at a tiny bump in the water. "My kitten! She fell in!"

He ran with her to the end of the C float. She called the kitten, but it was confused and just kept turning in circles. Then a current began moving it away from them. "Oh no!" The woman turned an imploring look on Quinn. "Can you get her?"

He hadn't even considered it, but when she asked, he tore off his coat and, after only the slightest hesitation, jumped in.

"Ahhgghh!" he yelled. The water was unbelievably cold.

The kitten was about ten yards from him, its face mostly two round eyes. It tried to swim back toward him, but made no headway against the current. In a few strokes he closed the gap and reached out a hand. The scared creature didn't hesitate; it scaled him and sat on top of his head, claws digging into his skull.

Feeling slightly ridiculous and very cold, he swam a gentle breaststroke back to the woman. She plucked the kitten off his scalp, and he pulled himself out onto the float.

"Wow," she breathed. "That was heroic! Thank you so much!" Her expression changed to concern. "You must be freezing."

He told her he had a change of clothes over on the *Blue Sea*, and she walked with him back toward the yacht. "I'm Rebecca Zachau."

"Doug Quinn. Everyone calls me Quinn."

"After you change, will you stop over? I want to give you a little gift, to thank you for your help." She gestured past the plywood boat. "My boat's the *Valiant*.

"Sure," he said.

"It's the boat with the cross-eyed moose head on deck."

He laughed and she laughed too, explaining, "It's a prize I won this afternoon at Pubfest."

Quinn changed clothes and found Rebecca's boat. After pausing to admire the cross-eyed moose, he tapped on the *Valiant's* scarred wooden door.

"Come on in," she called.

He had to bend sideways to clear the door frame. He went down three steps into her cabin, and once inside, because the ceiling didn't make six feet, he still couldn't straighten up.

Smiling, Rebecca pointed to a chair. "Have a seat, before you get a kink in your neck."

He spotted a small dog curled under the table and tensed. He disliked dogs, and they always seemed to return the sentiment, but at least this one was sound asleep. Rebecca was shining her warm smile on him, so he ignored the dog and sat down.

Teasingly, he said, "You dress exceptionally well for a boater." She was, in fact, dressed beautifully.

"A guy from work is taking me to dinner. A last-minute invitation—but he said to dress up because he's taking me to Silvers."

Moving around him, she reached into a cubby near the door and pulled out a small jar. It was labeled Nagoonberry Jelly.

To Quinn, this was no small token of thanks. Nagoonberries were a delicacy found only in certain places along Alaska's southeast coast. They resembled raspberries but had a singular sweetness all of their own.

She placed the jar in his hands. "Thank you for saving Jetsam."

He took the gift with a smile, observing that Jetsam was well-named.

"It's a theme around here. I named her Jetsam because my dog," she pointed under the table, "is named Flotsam. I found the poor boy washed up on the beach six months ago, nearly dead. He either fell overboard or someone tried to drown him. He's all recovered, except for being stone-deaf."

She moved to peer out a small porthole, apparently to see if her date was approaching. Quinn expected to get the boot, but instead, she squeezed back past him to sit in the cabin's only other seat and said, "I made the jam myself. Well, actually, my mom stayed with me on the phone, coaching me as I made it. So how do you like the *Blue Sea*? Isn't that the most beautiful boat? I've always thought it would be a great place to have a dinner party. Does it go very fast?"

He was impressed by how little breath she needed between sentences. "I just arrived from Fairbanks and was supposed to meet Marcus Holland on the *Blue Sea*, but he's late. Have you seen him around?"

"Not since Friday." Seeing Quinn's confused look, she added, "Oh! I work at SeaLab; he's my boss." She jumped up to look out the porthole again. "You've checked with Elise? She keeps pretty good track of him." Before Quinn could reply, she said, "I'm sure he just forgot what day it is; he does that. Honestly, he is so funny. He'll come up and look at me through his thick glasses—they make his eyes look real big, you know? And he'll say, 'Young lady, you're one of our top researchers, aren't you?' He's, like, grinning at me, and I say, 'I try to be, sir!' And he says, 'Well, I have a trick question for you.'

And then he asks me what day it is. And he truly needs me to tell him, because he works all hours and then falls asleep on his office couch. He'll wake and see the wall clock says ten-fifteen—it's one of those round clocks with big black numbers—and because it's summer, with all the daylight, he isn't sure which ten-fifteen it is—morning or night! He has both the time and date on his computer, but the color on his screen makes it hard to read. I offered to change his desktop color, but he just said 'No, thank you! It's more fun to ask.'"

Quinn found himself charmed—by both this woman and her boss.

She said, "I'm sure he just forgot about your meeting. It's been super busy at work, you know, with the unveiling on Saturday."

"So SeaLab's about to go public with some important breakthrough?"

"Yes—and don't ask me what it is because I don't even know myself! Marcus has everybody working on pieces of this cool project, but he's working on the centerpiece that ties everything together. He says that Saturday's unveiling is going to rock our socks." She laughed. "He really said 'rock our socks.'" She got up to peer out the porthole again. "But truthfully, I think we're about to—oh! I can see my date. He's across the harbor, just coming down the ramp!"

Quinn followed her out on deck, and as he stepped off the boat, Rebecca said, "I'm going on a daybreak run tomorrow with my friend Kit. We always treat ourselves to chocolate croissants and a pot of coffee, afterward. If you're awake, around six, you're welcome to stop on over."

He said he would, and wished her a nice evening. On his way back to the *Blue Sea*, he passed a man wearing a fine Italian suit. He appeared distracted and didn't seem to notice Quinn. *Gotta be her date.* A second later, he heard the man call out in a warm voice, "Rebecca."

He could imagine the way Rebecca's apple-cheeked beauty would shine next to the guy's lean handsomeness. Some people looked good together and those two would.

Quinn returned to the *Blue Sea* and found it still empty. He decided to take his cue from Rebecca, who hadn't seemed concerned about

Marcus. What she'd said about the scientist's tendency to lose track of time made him feel less inclined to worry.

Waiting on the yacht was pleasant enough. He called up the web on his mobile phone and searched for SeaLab's name in the news. He figured there would be some coverage concerning the unveiling, which was less than a week away. He was surprised to see no mention of it.

He saw a few articles that mentioned Marcus. He'd served on several community boards, and had funded a school science fair. Just before Quinn closed out his browser, one less-typical story caught his eye. It shed no light on SeaLab's upcoming event, but it was interesting nonetheless. Marcus had a grown son show up on his doorstep last year—a son he didn't know he had.

Quinn scanned the story. Almost thirty years ago, Marcus Holland had been teaching at Stanford University when, without any warning, his girlfriend broke up with him and moved away. It turns out that she'd become pregnant. Marcus didn't know about the pregnancy, or that she gave their child up for adoption. Years later, the grown son finally tracked down his biological mother and she told him where to find his father.

In the article, Marcus said he was overjoyed to learn he had a son. "I can't believe my good fortune, because Turner is taller than me and can reach things on the top shelf at the lab," he joked in the article. "It's a problem that's been plaguing me for years."

A noise on deck made Quinn turn expectantly, but instead of Marcus, it was Nate. He swung open the door and tossed a ziplock bag at Quinn. "My client paid me in fish. Try some." Then he reached down, took a hold of a big black garbage bag, and stepped inside, waving a big bottle of Chimay Blue Réserve. The black bag contained Nate's belongings, Quinn realized, and the fish and Chimay were bribes.

He bit into a piece of smoked king salmon and couldn't keep from groaning with pleasure. Nate opened the beer, poured a glass, and handed it to Quinn. Quinn wasn't much of a drinker but he liked this particular ale, and Nate knew it.

"Okay," Quinn said. "Marcus probably

won't object if you sleep here for a night or two."

Nate went to stow his bags, and Quinn stepped out on deck.

He noted with relief that the chimes on the plywood houseboat had stilled their racket. There wasn't the slightest chop in the harbor, nor was there a breeze. The night was almost eerily still.

He tipped his head back to study the black sky. Many things can make a man late, but why didn't Marcus phone with some word of explanation? Quinn's internal alarm was starting to sound. First thing in the morning, he decided, he'd go pound on some doors.

~~~

It was just after four and barely light out, when Quinn shot out of bed. Someone outside was screaming. He ran from his stateroom and crashed into Nate, who was also sprinting to respond.

The cries came from the direction of Rebecca's boat. For a split second Quinn thought the kitten had gone for another swim, but he realized the screams were too primal for that. He vaulted over the *Blue Sea*'s rail and ran past the plywood boat. A petite woman on the dock beside Rebecca's boat was screaming and hauling on a line that hung into the water between the boat and the dock. A bag of spilled croissants lay at her feet.

When he saw the reason for her hysteria, Quinn believed for a brief second that he was having a nightmare. Rebecca was underwater, her bloodless face tilted up toward the surface. A line circled her neck and ran up to the rail of her boat. Her hair, drawn by the current, fanned to one side as if blowing in a wind.

He leapt to the woman's side to help, and then Nate was beside them helping as well.

"Shit," Nate said tearfully. Quinn saw it, too. A lead weight, the size of a cannonball, had been lashed around Rebecca's white ankles.

Working together, they lifted her onto the dock.

She wore white flannel pajamas with tiny blue flowers, and this small, heartbreaking fact gave Quinn that nightmare sensation all over again.

3

Kit threw herself on Rebecca and began CPR as soon as they had her out of the water and onto the dock. She used her full strength, both palms on Becca's chest, arms stiff, pressing again and again. She was trained in the mechanics of CPR, having worked on boats since she was small, but she'd never had to use it. With all her might she pressed, stopping briefly after thirty compressions to allow one of the men, who was poised and waiting, to breathe twice into Rebecca's unresponsive mouth.

She pressed on, never breaking her rhythm, shaking her head no when one of the men offered to spell her. But Rebecca remained deathly still. It seemed to go on forever, and then the medical technicians arrived. Only then did she realize she'd been yelling at

Rebecca, pleading with her to live.

She slumped on the dock, nauseous and numb, while the technicians went swiftly to work. One of them shocked Rebecca with a defibrillator, while another continued with CPR. A third med-tech readied an IV. He held Rebecca's wrist, and looking at her watch, asked Kit what time Rebecca had been found. Kit was able to see that the watch had stopped at two-fifty-five. In a hoarse whisper, she told him she'd found Rebecca at four.

She started to turn her face away, overcome by the implications, but suddenly the medic on the defibrillator spoke. "There's a pulse!" he said urgently, and Kit felt her own heart leap.

The technicians scrambled, preparing to fly Rebecca by helicopter to Juneau, where the hospital was equipped to handle cold-water drowning cases. Kit said she wanted to go, but the paramedics said there wasn't room for her in the chopper and asked her to remain behind to talk with the police. They rushed Rebecca away on a stretcher, and the crowd of bystanders slowly dispersed.

Damp with sweat, Kit was now so cold

that she couldn't stop shuddering. The two men had also been instructed to wait for the police, and the larger man, noticing Kit's tremors, found a blanket and put it around her shoulders. She pulled the blanket close, and the thought that she'd been holding at bay until this moment hit her. *Dear God, who did this?* She pressed her hands to her face. *What twisted individual could hurt Rebecca like this?*

Her head felt strange, her thinking sluggish. *Keep moving*, she commanded herself, aware that shock was threatening to overtake her. She needed to take a look around inside Rebecca's boat. Climbing aboard, she felt a stab of grief when she saw the moose head on deck.

Inside the pilothouse, the dog was under the table growling, but he stopped when he saw it was her. Rebecca's yellow kitten gave a plaintive little mewl from where she lay on the bunk. The only other sound was Rebecca's Mickey Mouse alarm clock ticking away.

Nothing seemed disturbed or out of place until Kit's eyes fell on the tiny galley table. And what she saw made her gasp. On the cleared surface, obviously meant to be seen, was half a page torn from a notebook. Written in Rebecca's handwriting were the words: *I'm so very, very sorry—please forgive me. ~ Rebecca*

Kit stood shaking her head. *That cannot be a suicide note.*

She and Rebecca had been friends for only a year. But one of Becca's characteristics— it was probably her strongest feature—was that she unfailingly looked on the bright side of life.

Dazed, she looked around the boat, and her eyes landed on a pair of nylon stockings hung to dry on a tiny wire over the boat's oil stove. She reached out and touched them. They were still damp, as were the bristles of the toothbrush propped in a glass over the sink. The bed was unmade and there was a book lying near the pillow. It was one she'd loaned Rebecca—*The Princess Bride*, a sweet, funny, uplifting tale.

Her confusion was growing, but now, mixed in with it was fright, and something that resembled outrage. *I don't know how to explain the note*, she thought, *but I do know a person doesn't wash her stockings, brush her teeth, climb into bed with a good book, and then think,*

'Oh, right, I forgot to kill myself.'

A tap sounded on the side of the pilothouse. The sound made her jerk around, but it was just one of the men outside, telling her a cop was finally coming.

It should have been reassuring that the police had arrived, but it wasn't. Nipntuck, a fishing enclave surrounded by wilderness, had an abundance of medical emergencies, so its med-techs were well-trained. By contrast, there was hardly any crime, so cop jobs were cushy gigs that got filled by friends of the police chief.

Kit knew everyone on the police force from her job as crime reporter for the *Nipntuck News*. She stepped out on deck and saw who was approaching, and her heart dropped. It was Ollie, the cop on the force with the most seniority and the least ambition.

He sauntered up, nodded at the two men and asked her, "You here for the paper?"

She said no, she was Rebecca's friend. He didn't ask what had happened. He asked her to spell Rebecca's last name. She told him it was Zachau and spelled it. He carefully wrote it down in his notebook, then gestured to the other two and asked their names and dates of birth. They were Quinn and Nate, Kit learned; both were twenty-nine, older than her by six years.

"There's a note inside," she said, her throat tight. Ollie nodded, pulled a pack of gum from his windbreaker, took a stick and slowly unwrapped it. She continued, "It looks like a suicide note, but things don't add up."

"Uh-huh."

She told him what she'd seen on the boat. He chewed his gum and just looked at her. "And here's something you should know." She pointed to the line hanging off the rail of the *Valiant*. "Rebecca can't tie knots."

They all looked at the thick rope. One end had been cut away from Rebecca's neck by the medics. The other circled the rail in a perfect bowline.

Ollie gave a sympathetic nod and offered her a stick of gum. She wanted to knock the gum from his hand and yell, "Do something!"

She was already close to losing it, when a horrifying thought struck. *The news that Becca survived is surely spreading around town. Her attacker will know that she's been resuscitated, and could try to hurt her again.*

She told Ollie this, and his blank expression told her he wasn't following her logic. Or, rather, he refused to believe it. She insisted, "You have to get her some protection!"

He muttered something about suicides being a sad thing and climbed aboard the *Valiant.*

Kit's throat start to close in panic. *He's determined to call this a suicide, to make things easy for himself.*

Quinn stepped alongside her. "You're right. People are going to talk about her being revived. Even if the rescue professionals don't, the bystanders will." At this, Kit's throat tightened further. Then he said, "I'll call a contact in Juneau to arrange protection for her over there."

Kit stared at him, thinking, *who is this guy?*

He turned away and made a brief phone call, none of which she caught. He hung up and said quietly, "Rebecca has just been admitted. She now has the pseudonym Mary Brown. A private security guard will be posted outside her door. Your name and mine have been cleared, but otherwise, her case is on information lockdown. Apparently Juneau's hospital is one of the best in the nation for cold-water drowning cases, so there's good reason to believe she's going to make it. We can call back in fifteen or twenty minutes and they'll be able to tell us more about her condition."

The pilothouse door swung open and Ollie appeared on the *Valiant*'s deck holding a piece of paper. He stuffed it into his breast pocket and walked over to the moose head. He stood looking at it, pursing his lips.

"Was that Rebecca's note he just put in his *pocket*?" Quinn asked Kit. "No evidence bag?"

She nodded and in a blink, Quinn had vaulted over the railing of the *Valiant* and was at Ollie's side. The cop took an involuntary step backward and dropped his hand to the gun he wore on his belt.

In a terse voice, Quinn told Ollie that he had met Rebecca the night before and she had not been in the least suicidal. "She was about to go on a date to Silvers Restaurant with a man from work. I don't have a name, but I can describe the guy."

"That's not necessary," Ollie said. He

stepped around Quinn, climbed off the *Valiant*, and addressed Kit, "I guess we need to notify her family. You feel like doing that?"

"*What?*"

He shrugged. "We're swamped over at the station."

Kit knew Rebecca's mom lived on an island called Saluda off the northwest coast of Alaska, nearly as far from Nipntuck as one could get and still be in the state. Despite the distance, mother and daughter were very close, staying in constant touch through letters and phone calls. It horrified Kit to think Ollie might be the one to tell Rebecca's mom anything about this terrible event.

"I'll do it." She wouldn't be able to tell the poor woman what happened, but she could at least promise to find out.

Without another word, Ollie left.

Watching him go, Quinn said, "*What the hell?*"

His disbelief told Kit he wasn't a local, whereas Nate's resigned expression implied that he was. She expected him to enlighten Quinn, but instead, Nate just turned and spat into the water as though he tasted bile.

Quinn asked Kit, "The note . . . what did it say?"

"*I'm so very, very sorry—please forgive me.* And she signed it."

"Did it look like her handwriting?"

"It did. And it's the way she talks, too." Blinking back tears, she added, "I'm always telling her to quit with the superlatives." Suddenly, she remembered what Quinn had told Ollie. "You said someone took Rebecca to dinner at Silvers last night?"

Quinn described him: a co-worker, tall, well-dressed.

She shook her head, perplexed. Rebecca always had guys after her, and she flirted with several at work, but this didn't sound like anybody she'd talked about before.

~~~

Quinn waited on the deck of the *Valiant* while Kit went inside to find a number for Rebecca's mother. He looked around for anything out of place, but the only thing he noticed was confirmation that Rebecca couldn't tie knots. A tarp over some fuel jugs was secured with twine, looped and relooped together into unrecognizable clumps where there should have been knots. Normally it would have been funny, something he might have teased Rebecca about given a few more days to become friends, but now the sight just made him ache.

Nate, looking glassy-eyed and pale, offered to go pick up some hot coffee. Quinn could see he wanted a task to occupy his mind and agreed it was a good idea.

A moment later, Kit stepped out of the *Valiant*'s pilothouse cradling Rebecca's dog. "Rebecca lost her phone at Pubfest, I just remembered. I'll get her mom's number from information, but I'm having trouble remembering her last name. Her first name is Bev. Becca started calling her that when she turned twelve, and her mom just laughed and went along with it.

"So Bev's last name isn't the same as Rebecca's?"

Kit shook her head. "Becca got her dad's last name, and Bev kept her maiden name."

She climbed over the rail to set the dog down on the dock. He squatted and peed.

Then he looked up at them and wagged his tail once.

Quinn had never seen an uglier dog. His muzzle was squashed as if he'd run smack into a cement wall. Bulging eyes and crusty nostrils didn't improve the picture. And his legs were bowed as though overburdened by the weight of his ungainly head.

"What is it?" he asked.

"He's probably part boxer—that could be where he got his adorable face—and maybe part terrier." Suddenly her voice caught. "I know someone who will watch the kitten, but I have no idea what to do with Flotsam. I can't have pets where I live." She looked at Quinn. "Could you watch him?"

Quinn despised dogs. He broke out in a sweat around the damn things, positive that they were about to bite him. It wasn't logical. He knew that, but his sweat glands didn't.

"Please? Just temporarily?"

He coughed and gestured over toward the *Blue Sea*. "I'm staying over on that spotless yacht. I couldn't impose . . ." He sounded like a heel, and he knew it.

"The *Blue Sea*?" She brightened. "Oh,

Marcus knows Flotsam, and loves him."

Damn, Quinn thought, *just like a small town*.

She looked up at him through her lashes and added in a small, hopeful voice, "He knows a trick."

"I'm not so good with dogs."

She just kept looking at him, eyes wide and pleading. Quinn wished she would just understand, and not make him confess the whole truth. They stood there awkwardly until finally he had no choice but to tell her. He took a breath and said, "I'm afraid of dogs." There. Now she had to understand.

Her mouth opened in surprise. "But you're so . . . big," she said, "and he's so small."

He'd shared this embarrassing secret with her, and she says this? He felt himself breaking out in a sweat just trying to avoid breaking out in a sweat. "Alright," he heard himself say, "but you have to walk him, and everything else a person does with a dog."

"I will," she said quickly. Then she snapped her fingers. "Rebecca's mom, now I remember. Bev Watterson is her name."

He called the Juneau hospital to make sure Beverly Watterson was allowed through the security screen they'd erected around Rebecca, then he gave Kit the phone to speak with a doctor about Rebecca's condition.

The doctor said Rebecca was still unconscious but was showing strong vital signs. He asked what Kit knew of the mammalian diving reflex, and Kit said very little, except that she'd grown up hearing that people who were sometimes believed dead from drowning were in fact not dead, and CPR should be done until all hope was completely gone.

The doctor said that was correct, and explained that the body's reaction to going in cold water was to go into a special survival state. A couple of important things happened, the heartbeat slowed substantially, and vasoconstriction occurred, directing blood to critical areas—the lungs, heart and brain.

"We're estimating, based on Rebecca's stopped watch, that she was submerged for an hour. If true, her condition seems very favorable compared to what one would expect from a person submerged that long. The cold water temperature and her age were positive factors. But it's also possible she wasn't even conscious when she was submerged. She had chafing from the rope on her neck, and her ankles, but not much, suggesting there might not have been any struggle. The calmer a person is when they're submerged, the better their chances. Carbon dioxide forms when energy is burned, and a struggle before submersion means less oxygen and more carbon dioxide in the blood.

"Your arriving on the scene and performing CPR when you did, Kit, was very fortunate. And one more factor worked in her favor. Drowning victims experience laryngospasm, a reflex which closes off the airway to the lungs. The spasm can relax after a certain amount of time and allow water into the lungs, but fortunately, Rebecca's airway stayed closed. No water got in.

Kit was afraid to ask but knew she had to. "So what's the . . ." She forced the words out, her voice a whisper, "what about brain damage?"

The doctor said it was too soon to tell.

~~~

Kit felt the need to steady her nerves before making the call to Rebecca's mom, and realized a short walk might help. She promised to come back and settle the dog on the yacht afterward.

Quinn offered to walk with her, but she declined. She wanted to go somewhere close by, but away from people. Her eyes landed on the breakwater. It was an L-shaped rock wall extending out from shore to provide some protection for the boats tied in the harbor. She scrambled up onto its uneven top and walked to the end.

It had started to rain, but she barely noticed. Absentmindedly, she tugged the hood of her jacket up and stood watching the bay. It varied from day to day, depending on the weather, but today there were no breakers, just a slow surge rolling in from the wide Gulf. It pushed a lump of water high against the rocks, then withdrew. She watched its hypnotic swelling, trying to breathe slow and deep along with the surge, and finally, she felt ready.

She dialed Bev's number, but got a busy signal. Normally one of the most annoying sounds on the planet, Kit was relieved when she heard it, knowing it granted Bev Watterson a few more minutes of normalcy before she heard the awful news.

She started to tuck her phone back into her pocket, but took it back out. She needed to call Gerald Walsh and ask his help determining what had happened to Rebecca.

Walsh was a state trooper, a stern, large-bellied bachelor in his fifties, who was an old family friend. He didn't answer, and his outgoing message stated that he was out of cell phone range for the next several days. She remembered now that his recent case, a high-profile robbery homicide, had taken him to a remote area south of Nipntuck.

She left him a message to call her as soon as possible and hung up quickly. The prospect of talking to Walsh was calming; not being able to reach him made her feel shaky and alone.

From an early age she'd formed a bond with Walsh that, at first glance, didn't make much sense. She was the only girl in a family with seven boys and had worked in fishing off and on since she was eight. She had more than enough males in her life. But this man, her senior by almost thirty years, had a particular brand of perceptiveness that gave him insight into things about her no one else seemed to understand.

Case in point: he wasn't in the least surprised when she'd quit fishing to take over the crime beat for the *Nipntuck News*.

She loved to chase fish, and Nipntuck barely had any crime, so the job change wasn't a logical leap, and it certainly earned her less money. Nobody got it, except Walsh. He understood her passion for unraveling crime, for chasing down the what and why of deviant human behavior. He recognized it in her because he had it, too.

Her phone rang and because her hands were chilled by rain she accidentally hung up on the caller. Thinking by some miracle it was Walsh, she checked the number, but it wasn't him. It was her editor who had called. Seeing this, her heart lurched. She was missing a deadline at work! Aside from crime reporting, she also wrote the business roundup, a regular feature in Nipntuck's Monday paper.

She began to run. It was odd, but as she leapt off the end of the breakwater onto the pavement, she could almost hear Rebecca, who always looked on the bright side of things, saying to her, *hey—at least you're dressed for running.*

4

Quinn went back to the *Blue Sea* and got there just as Nate showed up with three coffees and a couple of meatball sandwiches. He passed on Nate's offer of a sandwich, shrugged on his sport coat, and said he was going to find Marcus.

SeaLab's downtown office building was locked—not something Quinn expected to find at ten-thirty on a Monday morning. No cars in the lot, either.

He decided it was time to visit the scientist's residence. Outside of the downtown area, the island's main road was a two-lane highway that extended along the coast on both ends of town, six miles north and twelve miles to the south. It had a name but everyone just called it the road. The house was four miles out on the north spur, on a rocky jut of land overlooking the bay.

A gray Cadillac Seville was parked in the circular drive. Quinn pulled in behind the Seville and jogged through the rain to the porch where he rang the doorbell. After a long wait, the door opened to reveal a gaunt woman who looked to be around fifty.

"Yes?" she asked. Her eyes flicked past him to take in his beleaguered Rent-a-Wreck parked behind the Seville. A pencil-line eyebrow lifted, and it was not in admiration.

"Mrs. Holland?"

She gave a slight nod.

"My name's Quinn. I was supposed to meet your husband downtown yesterday." He dug for a business card and handed it to her. "Is he here by any chance?"

"What were you meeting about?" she countered.

"Some work he needed done."

Her eyes traveled over him, taking in his size, and then she said, "Come in."

She led the way to a sitting room and went straight to a wet bar. "Sit." She gestured to an antique cane chair.

He gave the frail chair his weight, but did

so slowly, keeping an ear cocked for the sound
of splintering.

"Drink?" she said.

He considered for a moment. "If there's
coffee . . ."

"There isn't." She picked up a tall glass,
"I'm having a highball. You?"

A highball before noon, he thought, *sure, you
betcha.* "Thanks, no," he said.

Ignoring the tongs, she used her fingers
to throw one, and then a second hunk of
ice into the glass. She poured from an open
bottle, and with a swirl of her glass, turned
and said, "Marcus hasn't been seen for days.
Apparently he's missing."

Quinn was surprised by her words, and
even more so by her tone—she sounded
bored. "Have you called the police?"

She angled onto a walnut sofa that looked
as uncomfortable as his cane chair. Instead
of answering, or even acknowledging
his question, she tipped back her drink,
swallowed, and asked, "What kind of work
do you do, Quinn?"

"Odd jobs." He said this automatically,
thinking, *her husband has disappeared and she*

wants to chitchat?

"What kind of odd jobs?"

Her eyes were starting to creep him out. Their yellowish cast made him wonder if she had a touch of jaundice. And the room gave off a strange feeling, as well. Though expensively furnished, it felt as though nobody lived there.

He said, "Mrs. Holland, do you have any idea where Marcus is?"

She waved her hand unconcernedly, "I have no idea."

Progress, he thought grimly, *she answered a question.* He asked her again if she'd contacted the police, and this time she answered—with a snort. Having seen for himself how useless Ollie was, he decided to let that subject rest.

"Mrs. Holland, can you think of anyone who might want to harm your husband?"

"Me," she said with another snort, and quickly tossed back another slug of her drink.

"Meaning what?" he asked, keeping his voice mild.

"Call me Georgette. You look uncomfortable in that chair." She patted the cushion beside her and her voice changed to a husky rasp. "Want to come sit over here?"

He stood up. "I'll let myself out."

"Fine," she waved her hand dismissively, "be a party pooper."

When Quinn got back downtown, he was relieved to see several cars parked in front of the SeaLab building.

Finally. He pulled into the lot. *I'll get some answers.*

~~~

Kit raced into the Nipntuck News building. Gasping from her six-block sprint, she hurried past the reception desk, shoved through the glass doors marked EDITORIAL DEPARTMENT and made a beeline to her desk.

Twenty-three minutes later, she had whipped up the copy for the business roundup and had emailed it to Billings, her editor. It wasn't pretty, but it would suffice. She then picked up her phone to call a friend she knew, a cat-lover, who agreed to collect Rebecca's kitten and keep her indefinitely.

She hung up and leaned back to stare at the ceiling without seeing it. She wanted, with equal fervor, a shoulder massage, a bowl of ice cream, a nap, and someone strong to hold her and tell her that Rebecca was going to be okay. Shock kept washing over her, intermixed with moments that almost felt normal, as if Rebecca had not been attacked.

An assistant editor popped around the corner, startling her. "Did you hear," he asked, "about the woman in the harbor this morning?"

Her heart flipped nervously. "What did you hear?"

"That someone drowned or almost drowned; nobody seems to know which. Billings wants you to find out what happened—did she die or not—and write it up, pronto."

She said, "I don't think the family has been notified yet." Her temples were pounding and she rubbed them, hoping that she just looked tired, instead of insanely distraught.

"Just say what happened but mention no names. It's so close to deadline there's only room for a small blurb anyway."

Her stomach began to heave with stress. It was her job to deliver truth to the newspaper's readers. But she strongly suspected Rebecca's life was in danger. There was a way to deflect some of that danger, but it meant compromising her duty to tell the truth.

She took a deep breath and typed up the blurb, stating that a young woman had drowned in the harbor that morning and the police had found a suicide note. Further details, including the woman's name, were being withheld until the family could be notified.

Those bystanders in the harbor would trust the *Nipntuck News* as an authoritative source and believe that Rebecca had ultimately not survived. More importantly, her attacker would read it and believe Rebecca had died. Kit proofread the copy, and with a grim set to her jaw, emailed it to her editor.

She left her desk and slipped into a rarely used conference room. Leaving the light off, she took a seat at the large oval table. The call to Bev was next. She hoped she'd get through it without crying. She dialed the number and got that busy signal again. Tears began to well up as she thought, *Bev, please free up the phone and let me get through. Rebecca needs you.*

The conference room wall held a map of Alaska. She rose and studied it. When her finger found Saluda, her heart fell. The island, off the northwestern coast of Alaska, was even farther out in the Bering Sea than she'd realized. On an island that far offshore, weather often kept a person from leaving, sometimes for days, and, in rare cases, even weeks. *I need to get word to her, so she can start making arrangements.*

She grabbed an Alaska phone book off the bookshelf, intending to find someone in Saluda who could help her convey this urgent message. She called the Saluda mercantile first, then the city hall and the school, and when all the numbers gave the same busy signal, she finally understood it was not a busy signal at all.

Saluda was tied in with Alaska's phone system using what Rebecca had called "some funky microwave technology." Kit had no idea how it worked, only that it frequently did not.

She called ACC, the statewide phone company, and felt her stomach tighten with irritation when she got a recording instructing her to leave a message. *You'd think the phone company, at least, would have a live person answering the phone.*

She left a message and then leaned her forehead down against her crossed arms on the table, trying to get her mind around the fact that someone had tried to kill Rebecca. The more she thought about it, the more deeply afraid she felt.

But then a sudden thought made her lift her head. The suicide note had done as Rebecca's attacker had intended; it had deflected any police investigation. Furthermore, the blurb in the newspaper would lead him to think that Becca had died. So he wouldn't be expecting trouble. In other words, he wouldn't be expecting *her.*

~~~

Quinn entered SeaLab's building and walked into a small, welcoming reception area with two wingback chairs and a cherry coffee table holding a spread of magazines. He stepped around a maintenance man on a ladder and approached an unoccupied receptionist's desk. In the far corner of the reception area a woman stood with her back to him, typing numbers into a postage machine.

Over her shoulder she said in a melodic voice, "Oh, hello. How can I help you?" She had on a creamy-hued business suit and a rose-colored silk scarf, and appeared to be in her early fifties. She walked toward him, moving in a way that showed she was both fit and graceful.

He introduced himself and said, "Mr. Holland had arranged to meet with me yesterday, but he missed the appointment."

She was Elise Carlson, she told him, sliding into her desk chair to scan an appointment book. "I'm so sorry. Marcus had to go out of town for the next few days."

"I came down from Fairbanks at his request. I'm surprised he didn't let me know his plans had changed."

Genuine apology shone in her eyes. "I notified everyone on this schedule, but I don't see your name, or I would have called to let you know." She made a wry face. "He still forgets to fill me in sometimes. I've only been pestering him now for twenty-two years." Her brows drew together. "What was your meeting about?"

"He wanted my help with a security problem but said he preferred to discuss the details in person. He didn't show up for our meeting yesterday, so this morning I went out to his house. His wife . . ." he hesitated, "seems to think he's missing."

Some expression crossed her face, embarrassment or perhaps something more like anxiety. She threw a glance at the maintenance man, tinkering with a light fixture, and then brought her eyes quickly back to Quinn.

"I must have misunderstood her," he said. *Considering she had been inebriated.* "Did you say he'll be back in a few days?"

Elise Carlson studied his face, threw another quick look at the maintenance man, and then said, "Why don't you follow me." She led the way down a short hall, stepped before a retinal scanner to gain entrance, and then led them into what he presumed was Marcus's office. Papers, books, and files lay everywhere.

She went to the desk and started looking through the mess. "I believe I saw your name jotted down somewhere. Marcus writes memos and forgets to actually give them to me. I tell him email would be quicker, but he says it's more fun to give me a hard time in person." She gave a laugh that seemed to catch in her throat.

While she searched, he admired a series of black-and-white photos mounted on the wall behind the desk. They were shots of a man—Marcus, he presumed—astride a classic BMW motorcycle, taken against breathtaking Nipntuck backdrops. One shot featured the rider in front of the glacier, another showed him backlit by a fuchsia sunset over Big Bear Bay, and the third photo had him pointing down to his motorcycle boot, which he'd planted in the road's muddy shoulder alongside a giant bear paw print. He wore a wide grin in all of them.

He heard Elise say in exasperation, "That man." Keeping her face turned away, she ruffled through the papers. Then suddenly Quinn saw her hands go up to cover her face.

"What is it?" he asked.

She dropped her hands, and he was startled to see she wore an expression of stark dismay. "Marcus is missing," she said. "But I'm not supposed to . . ." Her voice wavered. "Everything's so upside down . . ." She paused to compose herself. "May I take your business card? I'd like to find that memo, and then give you a call."

He pulled out his wallet and handed her his business card, which simply carried his name and contact information.

Suddenly they heard, "Elise!"

Two men entered the room. The one in front was obviously an executive, while the one on his heels looked like security. The one in front covered the distance quickly to stand before Quinn. Frowning, he said, "Can I help you with something?"

Quinn recognized him—it was Rebecca's date from the night before.

"Turner," Elise said, "I'm glad you're here."

Turner, he thought, Marcus's surprise son mentioned in the newspaper article.

Elise introduced the two men, giving Turner's last name as Davis, and then correcting herself with a smile, said, "I mean Holland, now." She explained that Quinn had been asked by Marcus to provide help with a security matter, and surprise flashed across Turner's face, replaced immediately by a smooth, unruffled expression.

Turner gestured to the man he'd entered with, who had stayed in the background. "We have plenty of security personnel."

Elise said, "I'm pretty sure I saw a memo concerning their arrangement, but I can't seem to locate it. I was thinking we might be able to use some help looking for—" Turner frowned. She cut herself short, hesitated, and then said, "with . . . our . . . latest concern."

Turner took Quinn's card from her, and in an amicable voice, said, "Perhaps we shouldn't let just anyone into our director's office. I'd like to suggest we move out to the reception area to finish this discussion."

She looked chagrined. "You're right . . . I'm . . ." she faltered.

Turner touched her shoulder. "It's fine," he said gently, and to Quinn he said, "Actually there isn't anything more to discuss. It's a bit awkward to fire someone I never hired, but please understand, we don't need your services."

The newspaper article had put Turner's age at twenty-nine, but he possessed a poise that made him seem older, Quinn noticed.

"Elise will show you out." Turner indicated

that Quinn should precede Elise out, but Quinn stayed where he was. A small muscle in Turner's jaw flexed.

Quinn said, "I recognize you now; we passed one another in the harbor last night."

The change of subject threw Turner. "What?" His eyes drilled into Quinn's and recognition gleamed. He gave a curt nod. "Now I remember."

"I have some bad news about your date. She was found this morning, drowned in the harbor."

"She drowned?" Turner stared at him blankly. "My God, what happened?"

"There was a suicide note," he said.

"I had no idea . . ." Lowering his eyes to the floor, Turner murmured, "She seemed a bit downcast, but I never guessed she was . . ." He shook his head.

Quinn added quietly, "Though it was made to look like suicide, it probably wasn't."

Turner's eyes met Quinn's, and his eyebrows went up. "What are you suggesting?"

Evenly, Quinn said, "What time did you and Rebecca part company?"

With a hint of impatience, Turner said,

"Excuse me?"

Slowly, Quinn said, "There seem to be some discrepancies . . ."

"Discrepancies," Turner interrupted in a flat voice. "Are you in law enforcement, Mr. Quinn?"

"I'm a concerned friend."

Turner said, "I'm sure you are, and of course you're upset. I'm upset as well. But I am under no obligation to have this conversation with you. Now, kindly leave these premises. I have to get back to work. And so does Elise."

Quinn didn't budge. The thick-necked man standing behind Turner didn't move a muscle, but Quinn could tell he wanted to. Elise touched his arm and said softly, "I'll show you out."

In the reception area, a young girl who barely looked old enough to be in high school was sitting at Elise's desk. "Suzie covers for me during lunch," Elise said. She picked up her purse and coat. "I'll walk out with you."

5

Kit exited the conference room and was almost back to her desk when she heard "Kit!" And again, "Kit!" The voice was heavily accented, French, so she actually heard: "Keeeet! Keeet!"

Jean-Philippe had been away on vacation, and she'd completely forgotten he was due back today.

She slowly swung around.

He stood behind her, smiling broadly and spreading his arms as if to say, "Here I am."

Without responding, she turned and aimed again for her desk.

"Wait!" He caught her by the arm and swung her around. His narrow face wore an injured look. "You don't even say, how was your trip? Not even one little how are you?"

His French accent, which she had thought

sexy, now seemed overblown and silly to her.

He lowered his voice and winked at her, "Or . . . maybe . . . Jean-Philippe, I missed you so much, I beat my pillow, weeping every night?"

In a low hiss, she said, "Miss you? Weep into my pillow! Not a chance!" She turned on her heel and stalked off, thinking, *if stupid could fly, that man would be a JET.*

She turned into the staff kitchen, needing a minute to collect herself. Nobody else was in there. She stood in front of the bulletin board, unseeing, and wished with all her heart that Kenny McPhee, her favorite coworker, hadn't left for that job with the *Seattle Times.*

McPhee got work with the paper in Seattle, and Jean-Philippe was hired to fill his position at the *Nipntuck News.* She'd worked extremely well with McPhee. They shared an eye-rolling attitude about their editor, gave each other story tips, and were never even *tempted* to sleep together. But when Jean-Philippe walked through those double glass doors, Kit could think of nothing *other* than sleeping with him.

She shuddered, remembering the last time she saw Jean-Philippe, right before he left for vacation. They were naked, talking idly in bed after making love, and he'd breezily mentioned something about a wife. *His* wife.

It was one of those moments a person never forgets. A blazing fury had filled her, and along with it, an overpowering revulsion. All she wanted was to get her skin covered and get away from him. Far, far away. She'd jumped away from the bed, but his hand snaked out, and he yanked her back. "Don't be mad! Ma chérie, come back to bed, let's be happy." She tried to pull away, but he hauled her on top of him and began bucking his hips and laughing his high-pitched laugh. She wrenched free of his grasp, reared up, and drove her elbow straight down into his solar plexus.

He howled with pain and outrage, and right then Kit understood that physical violence could, in certain cases, lead to profound satisfaction.

She had assumed he'd give her wide berth when he got back from vacation, but apparently he wasn't that smart.

Debbie, the paper's love advice columnist, strode into the kitchen, placed her cup of tea water in the microwave, and said, "Jean-Philippe is back, you saw?" The Frenchman had told everyone to pronounce his name "Zjhaawwn Feeleeep," but this woman, with her flat Midwestern accent, always said "Gene-Fill-up."

"Yeah," Kit said. The two of them watched the tea cup riding around in a slow circle through the window.

In a lowered voice, Debbie asked, "What happened with you two? Did he go away because of you?"

"No!" Kit was aghast. She thought no one knew about them. "He has a wife in Atlanta." *Oh no.* She couldn't believe she'd just blurted it out like that, and to this gossipy twit of all people.

"Wow, you'd never know," Debbie said. "Did she come back with him?"

"I don't know!" The microwave dinged, and Kit flung the door open. "Your tea's ready." Debbie took her tea and rushed out of the kitchen, eager to tell someone.

Kit forced herself out of the kitchen and was almost back to her desk when it dawned on her what she needed to do next, and quickly. Clara, her housemate, adored Rebecca. The news that she'd drowned in the harbor would be making its way around town. She had to get home and tell Clara what had really happened.

When she got to the house, the door to Clara's office was closed, so Kit knew she was with a client. The front room of their house featured a corduroy couch. It was, she believed, probably the most comfortable couch in existence. She crawled into its pudgy, burgundy folds and waited.

Clara ran two businesses from home. She designed costumes for the town's theater company, which was presently on summer vacation. And for her second business, she was a therapist of some sort.

The work seemed steady, whatever it was. Men—all her clients were men—flowed into her office and came back out looking happy and moving with a bounce in their step.

When asked what kind of therapy she offered, she just said in her sugary South Carolina drawl, "Why, the therapeutic kind, of course."

The only thing Kit ever heard coming

through the door was the murmur of voices, which led her to believe Clara offered mental health counseling of some sort. So why didn't she just come out and say so? Tormented by curiosity, Kit had asked to schedule a "session," and Clara had blithely replied, "Oh honey, you don't need a session." Then she'd added, "Besides, I only see men."

Kit heard voices coming down the hall, and Clara entered the front room followed by a cheery young man with a crew cut. Prone on the couch, she peeked out from under the crook of her arm and decided he was probably a Coast Guard guy.

Clara walked him to the door, closed it softly behind him, and came to sit on the couch. She was thirty-three, ten years older than Kit, with thick auburn hair and a merry laugh that went perfectly with her boobs-spilling-out style of dress.

"Hey, sweetie pie," she said, patting Kit on the thigh. Then she took a closer look. "What's the matter?"

Kit told her what had happened, forcing the words around the lump in her throat.

Clara took the news hard. "I can't believe it,"

she said tearfully. "Who would do this?"

"I don't know," Kit said. "But I'm going to find out."

~~~

Quinn and Elise stepped out of SeaLab's office to find the rain had paused. They both tilted their heads back to admire how the clouds had swirled aside enough to show the snowy top of Mt. Edge. When Quinn dropped his eyes, he saw a familiar look on Elise's face as she continued to gaze upward. He called it the "I Love Alaska" look. Different than the gaze of a visitor, it was a very personal look of awe and pleasure and gratitude, a moment's recognition that they lived in a stunningly beautiful place. And the sentiment wasn't just for newcomers like himself. He'd observed that old-time Alaskans still got that look, even after living in the state for twenty, thirty years.

Elise lowered her gaze and gave him a small smile. He said he'd like to buy her lunch.

With a nod, she said, "The Eat-n-Git is close by. The waitstaff is surly, but the food is good."

The diner was just down the block. The sign in the front window underlined Elise's warning about the staff's attitude. It said, "Sorry, we're open."

They took their seats, and Elise gave him an appraising look. "My instincts tell me you're someone I can trust, but Turner did have a valid concern. I should use more discretion."

A waitress walked up to their table and waved the coffee pot at their cups. They both said yes, and without a word she poured their coffees, rolled two creamers onto the table, and departed.

Elise, still giving him that appraising look, said, "What did Marcus say when he hired you?"

"He thought there was a security matter I might be able to address, one that needed careful handling."

"Careful handling," Elise frowned. "That's interesting. How did he find you? Not the yellow pages, I presume."

"Marcus knew my father. Dad worked in intelligence—we both lived in D.C. for a while, and he sent a few simple assignments my way."

"Such as?"

"Unexciting stuff. But it paid well."

His preference was to leave it at that. She appeared to understand this, and shifted topics. "What brought you to Alaska?"

"A nurse," Quinn smiled. "She was visiting D.C. on a work exchange. I went into the hospital for a minor injury, and she cast a spell on me. I followed her back to Fairbanks."

"And . . ."

"We've gone our separate ways, but the country up there has a hold of me now."

"And what do you do up there?"

"I've worked as a consultant, on and off, for Homeland Security's Arctic Guard, analyzing remote points of entry."

She nodded, seeming satisfied. "Now what's this about a woman you mentioned to Turner. Someone drowned?"

He was careful to use the past tense. "I . . . believe she worked at SeaLab. Her name was Rebecca."

"What?" Elise gasped.

The waitress appeared to take their order. He indicated that they needed more time, and with an exasperated noise, she turned and stomped off. To Elise he said, "I'm sorry to tell you the bad news."

She stared at him in disbelief. "What happened?"

He felt caution was wise, at least until he understood more, so he just told her the barest of details.

As he spoke, she tugged a tissue from her purse. "Oh no, that's . . . but she's . . . always so happy." She dabbed at her eyes. "But I don't know her—didn't know her—very well. I didn't even know she and Turner were going out." She suddenly looked stricken. "You told Turner it may not have been suicide?"

He hesitated. "It isn't clear what happened," he finally said. "The police are calling it a suicide, but there are some unanswered questions." Then he asked gently, "Perhaps we should order?"

She nodded and took a sip of her water.

After they ordered, he asked, "Turner is the son who showed up last year and surprised Marcus? He changed his last name from Davis to Holland?"

"Correct," she said.

"What's his role with the company?"

"Like me, Turner wears a number of hats. He's a resource when it comes to our legal needs. He oversees grounds security over on the island, plus he shares some limited cyber security duties with Marcus. He's really quite young to have so much responsibility. Oh, and we're grooming him to take over on marketing and communications. If you've seen our website, it's obvious we need help in that area."

"What are the hats you wear?"

"It's sort of a long answer," she gave him a smile. "Twenty years ago I started as executive secretary. Ten years ago, our office manager left to start her family, and I assumed her duties. Next, we found ourselves working with a terrifically inept finance officer, and by this time I'd earned both my CPA and my MBA, so Marcus let him go and named me chief financial officer. Oh, and until recently, I've been the personnel department and the website person as well."

"So you're the receptionist, the CFO, and a bunch of things in between," Quinn smiled, impressed.

"We're not a top-heavy enterprise, that's for certain," she smiled. "When you came into the office, you probably noticed how quiet everything is. I pretty much hold down the fort at our office here. The lab facility over on the island has a different atmosphere altogether. It's going sixteen, twenty hours a day, buzzing with people and creative energy. I make sure the money and materials flow so that Marcus and his team over there can focus on their work."

"Tell me about Marcus. What's going on with him?"

"Marcus . . ." she took a breath and let it out slowly, "Marcus has been missing since late Friday night. I apologize for not telling you the truth initially, but we're trying to keep his disappearance quiet."

"Why?"

"Marcus thought it best," she replied, "and I went along with it at first, but now I'm—"

"Excuse me—" he interrupted. "Did you say *Marcus* thought it best?"

~~~

Kit and Clara sat together on the couch. Clara, her eyes wet, said, "Rebecca shouldn't be alone. I'll take the ferry over to Juneau tomorrow." The state ferry traveled between Juneau and the surrounding island communities. It took longer than flying but was far more affordable.

She took Kit's hand and said, "Listen, I'm terrified that you'll get hurt, too. I understand that the police are no help, but what about your friend Walsh? Can't you ask him for help?"

"He's on a case down south, out of phone range. He'll call me back as soon as he hits the tarmac. In the meantime I have to do what I can." She swallowed back a lump in her throat. "I'm not sure what that is, though . . ." She straightened up. "Wait, I do know. Rebecca went on a date to Silvers last night, with someone from work." She got up from the couch.

"Where are you going?"

"To find out who took her out last night."

Clara looked pointedly at Kit's hands, which were shaking. "You need to eat lunch before you do anything else."

"The thought of food makes me feel ill."

"I'll make a big pan of halibut enchiladas, and keep them warm for you, no matter what time you get home."

Kit gave her a fast, tight hug before she left.

The receptionist, Elise, at SeaLab's downtown office, was someone Rebecca had talked about, so Kit wanted to start by asking her. The office was a short walk away. A girl was watching the front desk, and said Elise would be back from lunch soon.

She was about to go sit and wait but caught sight of a large yellow envelope under the girl's elbow. Scrawled on front was:

Rebecca Zachau's Employee File
For: Mr. Hamm

She pointed to the file and asked who Mr. Hamm was.

The girl looked down at the envelope. Plastic barrettes—one orange, one green—held her short hair back from either side of an uneven part. Shyly, she said Mr. Hamm had called and told her to make a copy of the file, but she didn't really know who anyone was. Elise, who knew everything, was the one to ask.

Kit sat perched on one of the wingback chairs, wishing Elise would hurry up with her lunch. She now had two questions to ask— which of Rebecca's coworkers had taken her to Silvers, and who was this Hamm?

The girl at the desk shifted restlessly in her chair and told Kit she'd be right back; she had to use the bathroom.

Right after she left, the door pushed open and in came a man. Kit blinked in shock, then hid her face quickly behind a magazine. It was the bald guy who had been wearing sunglasses at Friday's song contest at the Shanty.

He carried a gym bag and breathed loudly through his nose like he had a bad cold. He went directly to the desk and picked up the envelope. Kit watched over her magazine as he unwound the string that secured the envelope flap and pulled out Rebecca's file.

Now that he wasn't wearing sunglasses, Kit realized why he'd seemed familiar. She recognized him from a story that ran in the *Nipntuck News* several months ago. His name was Ted Connelly. He had tried to steal a six-pack of beer, but the merchant caught him red-handed. Connelly had head-butted the man—breaking his own nose with his poor aim—then he'd sprinted outside, yanked a woman from behind the wheel of a Subaru and leapt in to escape. But road salt had rusted the underbelly of the car so badly, its frail axle snapped under his weight. The police had to come and cut him out with torches.

Kit wasn't assigned to write up the initial incident, but she was assigned the follow-up, and then it turned out there was no follow-up. She had sat in the back of the courtroom and watched Connelly swagger out the door—case dismissed due to improper police procedure.

She'd sprinted back to the office to tell her editor she was going to write about police incompetence, but Billings told her no, leave that one alone; the police chief and the newspaper's owner were fishing pals. She started a file on the topic anyway.

With a grunt, Connelly closed the envelope and spun around. She stayed behind the magazine until he strode past her out the door, taking Rebecca's file with him. Then she jumped up to follow.

He walked several blocks before turning into Clausen's, Nipntuck's public steam bath.

Nearly every fishing town along Alaska's inhospitable coast had its steam bath, and Nipntuck was no exception. Warring factions of fishermen had built the town in the 1950s. This was back when big money could be made in fishing, but only by the toughest, smartest, and slyest. Those of Scandinavian descent had built the steam bath, and there, naked and sweaty, they'd bonded with one another and plotted ways to outfish their Irish-American competitors. Their competitors, with their Irish roots, were famously heat-intolerant. They built churches and did their bonding and plotting inside those cool, quiet walls.

Clausen's had two large communal sauna rooms, one for men and a separate one for women, but it also had private steam rooms as well. A friend had held a birthday spa party there, so Kit was familiar with the layout. She dashed up to the desk and asked to see the schedule for the private rooms, pretending that she wanted to sign up for an opening. She spotted, scrawled in the slot next to steam room number two, "Hamm & guest."

"Oh, never mind the private room," she told the clerk, and handed over her entry fee for the women's communal room.

For cover she grabbed a rolling cart with sodden towels and rolled it past the women's foyer. *Move fast, with assurance*, was her motto when going places she shouldn't.

She rolled the cart confidently into the men's area and found the private saunas after a quick jog to the left. She pressed her ear to door number two, but heard nothing. Her heart was pounding, and she wasn't sure what to do. She rapped on the door. There was no reply.

A steam room door down the hall swung open, and before the emerging men could see her, she slipped inside room number two. It was about twelve-foot square, and had three benches, like shelves, lining both the sides and back wall.

The top bench was so close to the ceiling that someone fit comfortably only by staying horizontal. Although comfort wasn't in the picture, really, that high up. The air up there was so fiery that few people braved that level. Given that the room was filled with steam, she was pretty sure she could go up there and eavesdrop. If she stayed completely still, she could probably escape detection. *No way*, she thought, and turned to make her escape. But the thought of Rebecca made her stop.

The burning air seared her nose and throat as she climbed up and pressed herself against the back wall. She'd just stopped moving when the door opened with a bang. She couldn't see the faces of the two men who came in. Their features were obscured by the steam but she could tell one of the men was taller and the other was shorter. The shorter one was Connelly. His breath rasping, he took the left bottom bench right by the door, while the taller man took the right.

Connelly made several grunts of satisfaction, while she held completely still, trying to ignore the fear crawling all over her skin. She was eavesdropping on a gorilla-shaped, violent-tempered man who was wearing no clothes, and the only thing separating them was ten feet of steam. *What was she thinking?*

It didn't help that she was one of those famously heat-intolerant Irish. Her clothes, hair, and skin were on fire. Her eyeballs were surely getting blisters. *Say something*, she begged the men silently, *I don't care if you talk about sports, boobs, or the stock market, just do something to take my mind off this heat.*

"I thought her file might tell us something," Connelly said, sounding defensive.

"Your job isn't to think." The other man spoke in a low, terse voice.

Kit presumed this was Hamm.

Connelly said sullenly, "So, you can't use the file, and yesterday, you told me to quit following her . . ."

A mixture of fear and curiosity gripped Kit. Connelly had been at the Shanty watching Rebecca. And today, he was trying to give her employee file to this man. *But why?*

Connelly whined, "Why won't you let me help?"

"You're helping with other things."

Kit's heart rate had been climbing, and now her head began to swim. She ground her jaws together to make herself stay alert.

"But what are we going to do about her?"

In a low voice, the other man said, "It's taken care of."

Despite the searing heat, Kit felt a chill ripple her skin.

"Fuck." Now Connelly sounded deflated. "I wanted to help. Like with Joan—"

"The matter's settled." The voice was commanding, curt. "We're done here. Let's go."

The door opened, and she felt a rush of cool air.

Hamm said he took care of Rebecca. Oh God! She had to identify him. She began to get down off the bench, but suddenly the entire room tilted. She went from dizzy, to out of control, to feeling nothing at all.

6

The waitress clattered the sandwich plates down in front of Elise and Quinn and was gone before they could ask for coffee refills. Ignoring the food and the fact that their orders were crossed, Quinn repeated his question. "*Marcus* wanted his disappearance kept quiet?"

Elise gave him a strained look. "He disappeared once before. He was gone for two days, but then he just showed up . . ." She picked up her plate and they switched orders. "He woke up on the *Blue Sea* . . . He had no idea where he'd been. No one saw him coming or going." She hesitated, looking uncomfortable, then continued. "He woke up smelling like a distillery, which unfortunately points to a relapse of some sort. He went through a bad drinking period years ago . . ."

"I'm assuming he went to the hospital?"

She nodded. "For privacy's sake, he flew down to Seattle. Turner went with him. But the doctors found nothing—"

Their waitress, coffee pot in hand, dropped the check on the table, even though they hadn't touched their food yet. She started to leave without pouring them any more coffee. The Eat-n-Git was aptly named, Quinn thought, calling her back. She splashed their cups half full and stomped off.

Elise continued, "We never found a satisfactory explanation, so we told ourselves it was an isolated incident. We did have one conversation about 'what if'—as in *what if it happens again*—and Marcus made himself very clear. If it happened again we had to cover for him. Turner would embark on a quiet search and once found, Marcus would pursue a treatment course. The awful thing is—" She stopped.

"Is what?" he prodded gently.

"There's some history around this whole thing that makes it especially painful." She gave him a look that was loaded with sadness. "Until about ten years ago, Marcus worked in a group of energy researchers commissioned by the U.S. government to address, confidentially, a particular energy challenge. His team members were people he respected, and the work mattered greatly to him. But then he . . . left the group."

"Why?"

Elise picked up her sandwich, and put it back down again. "This was a time of severe personal conflict for him. His wife . . ." she paused, and her cheeks turned red. "Anyway . . . his drinking took off. He left the group, but not before his reputation with the others became deeply damaged. He clawed his way out of that dark hole eight years ago and hasn't had a drink since. So now we're finally ready to build our team, and we've just begun discussions with several of his former team members. Once we hold the unveiling, we'll have no problem attracting top scientists from all over the world, if we want them, but these former colleagues are the ones Marcus wants. It's not just about growing the company; it's his chance to redeem himself."

Quinn took a moment to organize his thoughts. It bothered him that Marcus had disappeared, and then reappeared, without understanding where he'd been or what had really happened. How the hell could a person go on a drinking binge in Nipntuck and not be discovered? Then he realized that Nipntuck was a fishbowl, sure, but within just a few hundred steps in any direction, it became pure wilderness. He'd read in the Fairbanks newspaper last summer about an older guy with memory issues who went into the wilderness surrounding Nipntuck and disappeared for several days. Eventually the man worked his way out, miles from where he started, weak and hungry, but unharmed. So it was possible.

But it certainly wasn't the only possibility. He asked Elise whether they'd considered foul play.

Nodding, she said, "The doctors looked for neurological problems, but to rule out foul play we also had them test for drugs. They found nothing."

He pointed out that just going to see doctors in Seattle had created a time lapse. "The delay could have skewed the drug results."

"Maybe," she frowned, "but it was his idea to go to Seattle, so the time lapse was coincidental."

"Who might want to harm him?"

"We do have a . . . rival relationship with the energy consulting firm that moved here last year, ESI."

"Energy Systems Integrated?" He'd heard of it, but wasn't sure what the firm did.

"But," she said, "we more or less dismissed the possibility when the doctors found no trace of drugs. Plus, he was perfectly fine after he showed up, except for being confused about what had happened."

Quinn was curious about the rivalry with ESI, but wanted to pursue another thought first. "This unveiling on Saturday," he asked. "What can you tell me about that? The website alluded to it, but gave no concrete information."

She winced. "I know. That website is atrocious. We need to update it, but I keep getting frustrated with those little boxes . . . It's so annoying because they keep—" She seemed to notice she was going off-topic and made herself stop.

"What are you unveiling?"

"I'm under strict orders not to disclose anything specific about it."

"Why?"

"Patents," she said. "By the time we hold the unveiling, we expect to have everything locked in. But until then, we can't risk telling anyone anything they don't need to know. It may seem overly cautious, but we have our reasons."

He asked, "Is SeaLab's project related to what Marcus worked on ten years ago, with the group of scientists commissioned by the government? You said they were working on something confidential?"

She looked anxious. "I've already broken ranks by telling you Marcus is missing. I really can't talk about it, except to say that everything will be revealed next weekend."

He made a mental note to call someone he knew in D.C. who would tell him the skinny on that group—who the players were, what the focus had been ten years ago, and if it still existed. "What if Marcus doesn't show up by next Saturday?" he asked. "Can you hold the event without him?"

Distraught, she said, "Quinn, that's almost a week away." She picked up her coffee cup and put it back down with a clatter. Pressing the back of her hand to her cheek, she said, "It's good you're asking these questions, it's just . . ."

He said gently, "We'll find him. Tell me when he was last seen."

She pushed her sandwich away. It was mostly untouched. "He worked at our island facility Friday, until sometime after midnight. He left the island and brought his speedboat—he calls it the 'Toad'—back over to Nipntuck."

"The Toad?"

"It's fast. As he likes to say, 'it really hops.'" Elise managed a small smile. "And it's green."

"So did he make it back to his house that night?"

She shook her head. "No, but he rarely sleeps there. Mostly, he ends up sleeping on his couch over at the lab, but when he doesn't stay there, he'll stay on the company yacht, in the downtown harbor."

He nodded. "That's where he told me to bunk." He was about to mention he was letting Nate occupy a bunk there as well when she reached out and touched the back of his hand.

"Quinn, I want your help with a discreet search for Marcus, but I have to convince Turner to go for the idea. He's determined to honor his father's directive that we tell no one, but I'll point out to him you are already aware that Marcus is missing so we should let you help us."

She tugged her sleeve back to check her watch and looked startled. "Oh good grief! I forgot I have a dentist appointment. If I go now, I can still make it." She gave her watch a last look and added, "unfortunately."

Rising, she said, "Thank you for lunch. And for keeping everything we discussed confidential. I'll call you later this afternoon, once I speak with Turner."

~~~

Lucky for Kit, it wasn't long before someone found her. A man discovered her passed out, scooped her up and carried her to a nearby bench in the men's shower area, yelling for help. She opened her eyes to find herself surrounded by a circle of near-naked men.

Jungle dreams were something she had quite often, but they featured Tarzan-like men, wearing loincloths. The sight of white towels and several flabby bellies cleared up, right away, the thought that she might be dreaming.

Every inch of her clothing was soaked, as was her hair. Her body, but especially her face, felt like it had been torched. She was nauseous and blazingly thirsty.

There was some discussion about sending her to the hospital, and this scared her so much she almost fainted again. Hospitals and Kit did not get along. In fact, they freaked her out. She decided it was time to take charge, and doing her best to sound firm, announced she just needed some water. The words came out in a weak croak.

Four men jumped to get her some, and she drank thirstily. Then, before anyone thought to ask how she happened to be in that private men's sauna with all her clothes on, she announced, her voice stronger now, that she needed to pee.

They guarded the stall for her, and then a half-dozen towel-clad guys escorted her to the front lobby. There she encountered a manager who was adamant that she go to the hospital, and unfortunately, he wouldn't budge on it. For liability reasons, he insisted, and ordered her to take a seat while he called for the ambulance.

She understood completely, she said, the whole liability thing, sure. And the minute he turned his back, Kit got herself out of there.

~~~

After Elise left for her dentist appointment, Quinn got an evil glare from the waitress who clearly wanted him to "git." Ignoring her, he got out his phone and left a message with a knowledgeable friend in D.C., asking her to look into the nature of the classified work being done about ten years ago by Marcus Holland and some other energy scientists who were being quietly sponsored by the government.

He hung up and stared out the window. Elise seemed to think foul play could be ruled out, but he had a more suspicious mind than she. And she didn't know that Rebecca had been attacked. Telling her about Rebecca could prove useful, but it could also be a mistake. He trusted Nate completely, and Kit as well. He wanted to go slow when it came to sharing information with anyone else.

He called Nate, who answered after four rings. His tone indicated the he was in the middle of something.

"Got a minute?"

"Yeah."

"Marcus is missing. He has a history of binge drinking and that may be what's going on, or it may be something else entirely. I want to look at the possibility of foul play."

Nate said nothing.

"There's an energy consulting firm here that's some kind of rival to SeaLab, but I know nothing more than that. Can you look into it, when you get a chance? The outfit's called ESI."

He paused, thinking Nate would jump in with a mini-treatise on ESI, but he didn't. To Quinn this suggested he probably had client work on his mind.

"Also, anything you can dig up on SeaLab, including what their grounds security is like over on the island. Plus background information on Marcus and Georgette Holland, and Marcus's son Turner Holland, whose last name until recently was Davis." Quinn was about to give him Elise's name as well, but Nate uttered, "I'll get on it soon," and hung up.

Quinn left the Eat-n-Git and walked along Nipntuck's picturesque waterfront. Couples kept passing him, holding hands, moving with that loose-limbed, happy-in-love manner. He should have been thinking about Marcus, but he wasn't. The entire time he'd been in Nipntuck, in the back of his mind, he'd been thinking about a subject that now pressed forward, demanding that he face up to it. He wanted to see his former fiancée, Allie.

He'd asked his waitress out yesterday, which seemed to be a sign that he was no longer feeling frozen in the heart department. So if he was ready to move on, why try to see Allie? His motivation was not exactly clear. For closure? To torment himself? To beg her to come back? He hoped it was the first, and not the second or third.

Unable to resist any longer, he got out his phone and dialed her number. When he heard that silky voice invite him to leave a message, he almost hung up. But the tone beeped, and he swallowed and said, "Allie, it's me. I'm in town for a bit. Would love to see you. Call me." He disconnected, and felt instant regret, along with the fervent hope that she might call him back.

Turning back the way he'd come, he walked quickly, and forced his thoughts away from Allie. Georgette Holland had behaved oddly, and perhaps it was distress over her husband, but it sure didn't feel that way to Quinn. He decided to go have a second chat with her, armed as he was now with a bit more information.

He reached the Holland's residence, pulled in behind the silver Seville again, and his rental car announced his presence by backfiring twice, loud as a firecracker, before lapsing into a smoky silence. As he stepped out of the car, his cell phone rang. His chest contracted with hope, but it was Elise, not Allie.

"How was the dentist?" he asked.

"Horrid. I have a numb jaw, with a pounding headache on top of it. But thank you for asking." Then she sighed. "Quinn, I want to enlist your help, but Turner doesn't agree."

"That's unproductive," he said mildly.

"I know," Elise agreed. "But, like me, he's rattled by this, and is fearful of misstepping. He insists that we follow his father's instructions, without deviating, without involving an outsider." She sighed. "He says to give you a sincere thank-you, but no thank you. And asked me to make certain you're not offended."

"I'm not offended, but it seems you have the authority to engage my help without Turner's okay. He's well below you in the chain of command, right?"

"Not that far below, actually. Marcus made him an officer of the company, which is a lot of responsibility for someone so new on the scene, but yes, I do have more decision-making power. The thing is, I don't want to do anything to cause a rift between Turner and myself. We're in a crisis, and solidarity is important. If I could find that memo Marcus drafted about you, I might feel more inclined to insist, but . . ."

"I can try talking to Turner if you think it would help."

"I really don't. He's stubborn, a trait he shares with his father, unfortunately."

He heard his name called and looked to see Georgette Holland in the door to her house. She clutched a glass in one hand and was leaning on the door frame for extra support.

Elise was saying, "I want to reimburse you for the time you spent coming down here."

"We can settle up once Marcus reappears."

She sighed. "Thank you. It will be soon, I just know it."

"Let's hope. I'm going to stick around for a few days longer. Call me anytime, day or night, if you need to."

Elise thanked him once more, and they hung up.

Georgette Holland, in a loud voice, commanded Quinn to come inside. He watched her disappear from view, leaving the door open.

He went into the house and found her in the sitting room, already reclining on the walnut sofa, glass in hand. "What are you doing out in the drive?" Her words were blurry with alcohol. "I don't bite, you know." Her lips slid up in a smile Quinn thought looked grimly canine, and she gestured at an antique chair next to her. That seat looked even more frail than the cane chair he'd occupied on his first visit.

He remained standing while she eyed him over her drink. "Who were you talking to on the phone?"

"Elise," he said.

"What did she want?"

"I offered to help search for Marcus, but she declined."

"Well, *I* want your help." She announced this suddenly. "I want you to look for Marcus." Her bloodshot eyes were turned on him, but seemed unfocused. "I'm worried," she mumbled. "I haven't left the house since I heard."

What the hell made her suddenly care—or pretend to, he wondered. Then he was struck by a thought. If Georgette Holland enlisted him to look for Marcus, it wouldn't cause any rift between Elise and Turner.

He sat gingerly in the cane chair. "I'll see what I can learn."

"Whassss your fee?" she stared at him.

"I'll settle with Marcus when I find him, Mrs. Holland."

"You're a confident one." That grim smile

again. "Call me Georgette."

"Sure. When did you see Marcus last?"

"Last week sometime."

"Did he make it home Friday night?"

"No," she shrugged.

"What do you think is happening to him?"

She shrugged again and took a gulp of her drink.

"Do you think ESI is involved?"

"I have no idea." She sighed like she wished he would switch to a more interesting topic.

With her assent, he took a look around the house, starting in the front hallway. The entry table held no personal effects, his or hers. Opening the front closet, he rifled through a man's raincoat pockets, finding them empty. Next, he spent some moments glancing through drawers of the immaculate oak desk in what Georgette indicated was the study. He found nothing to shed light on Marcus's whereabouts, in fact, there was nothing to suggest the man's existence at all— no meaningful papers, no appointment book, nothing. "Does he even use this room?"

"He isn't home very much." She drew her mouth tight when she said this.

"Is there any luggage missing?"

"I doubt it."

"How does his typical day go?"

"No such thing," she waved her hand tiredly.

He pointed upstairs. "May I?"

"Feel free. But he's not up there, I already looked." She gave a sharp yap of a laugh.

There were several closed doors behind which he found spare bedrooms. The one open door led to the master bedroom suite where he could see no sign of Marcus save for a man's robe hanging on the bathroom door. A second bathroom down the hall contained a man's shaving kit, but it didn't look recently used.

He returned downstairs, found the kitchen equally unhelpful, and finished his survey by glancing into the laundry room. She came up behind him with her drink and stood uncomfortably close while tapping her fingers on the glass.

The last door he opened revealed a spacious garage with a sports car resting under a dust cloth. He lifted the edge of the cloth and gave an appreciative whistle. Crouched under the cloth was a sky blue BMW M6 convertible. It looked bored, sitting under there, he thought.

"His?" he asked.

"He never uses it. Says it's a young man's car."

Under different circumstances, he might have joked that he fit the description.

She brushed past him into the garage, pulled the dust cover off. "You can use it. The keys are in the coffee holder." Disdainfully, she added, "I saw what you drove up in."

He wondered if he'd fallen, slammed his head, and was dreaming this. He got in the car and turned the key. The throb of the cylinders sent a visceral warmth flooding through his body.

She pushed a button for the garage door and stood waiting for him to go, swirling her drink impatiently.

He lowered the window to tell her "I'll be back with a friend to pick that up." He nodded toward the rental car in her drive.

"Make it soon."

He eased the BMW out of the garage and onto the open road, heading away from town. Flying along the sinuous curves of the narrow highway, he concentrated on simply enjoying the ride. And that's when it struck him: Georgette had claimed she hadn't left the house since she heard Marcus was missing. But upon arriving he'd walked past the silver Seville—her car, he presumed—parked in the drive. The car's engine was ticking with that sound of a hot engine cooling.

He shook his head. His trip out there hadn't gleaned any more details about Marcus, but he'd confirmed a few things about Georgette Holland: that woman was definitely creepy, and her relationship with the truth was a loose one.

7

Back at the yacht, Quinn found Nate in the
front lounge, sitting, staring at his laptop.
He'd gathered rudimentary background
information on Marcus, Georgette, and
Turner, but was still working on the ESI
question. Quinn looked over the file that Nate
handed him. It listed birth dates, university
degrees, board appointments, family stats,
credit reports, and so on. The information
on Turner was noticeably thin, Nate said, but
he could dig deeper if Quinn wanted.

He said Turner was the one who took
Rebecca out to dinner, and Nate said he would
dig deeper, then. His voice was wooden, and
his face kept turning toward the window. He
looked sick, Quinn realized.

"Have you eaten today?"

Nate said he had had the two meatball

sandwiches earlier in the day. Then he admitted that the sandwiches had only stayed with him a short time.

"You should eat something, but something mild," Quinn said. "Let's go get an early dinner."

"Not hungry," Nate mumbled.

This was about Rebecca, Quinn knew, about being in the presence of violence. He understood now that Nate had been alone on the yacht all day, trying to work and feel normal, and failing. "Want to talk about it?"

"Not right now."

They heard a tap on the pilothouse door and Kit came in, her arms overflowing with Flotsam, his blanket, a bag of dog food, and two bowls. She set the dog down next to the stove in the corner, filled one bowl with water and one with food, and stood up to face the men.

Her face was extraordinarily pink, and her hair was plastered around her head. *Whatever she's been up to, she's been exerting herself*, Quinn thought.

In a rush, she told them about her unwelcome steam bath experience. He got her some water to drink and made her go slowly back over everything. She told them about Connelly's stolen six-pack incident, and his arrival at SeaLab to pick up Rebecca's employee file, then she repeated what she heard in the steam bath.

"The other guy, Hamm," Quinn said, "you didn't get a glimpse of him? Even an impression? Age or bearing?"

She shook her head. "I'm so mad at myself for passing out! I was so close to the guy, but I only heard his voice. There was something so . . . sinister about the way he said, 'It's been taken care of.'" She swallowed. "And then Connelly said, 'But I wanted to help. Like with Joan.'" Her voice cracking a little, she added, "I wonder who Joan is, and what they did to her."

Quinn took out his phone and did a search in the *Nipntuck News* archives, figuring there might be a photo to go with the article detailing the six-pack bust. But his search for Ted Connelly turned up no results.

"Something's screwy," Kit said. "It should be there." She reached up to tuck her hair behind her ear. Her hand shook, Quinn noticed.

Pushing herself up from the table, she declared, "I never did find out who took Rebecca out last night, so I need to get back to SeaLab's office before they close for the day."

Quinn said, "I found out. It was Turner Holland."

She studied him. "First, you're able to arrange protection for Rebecca over in Juneau with just a phone call, and now you can answer that question. Who are you?"

He said, "I need help retrieving a rental car a few miles out of town. If you and Nate want to come along, I'll explain what brought me to Nipntuck, and I'll also fill you in on my encounter with Turner."

He led them to the BMW, expecting a comment or two about the ride. But Nate just climbed silently into the backseat, giving more proof that he wasn't feeling like himself. Kit buckled herself into the front passenger seat, and when she said nothing about the car either, Quinn tried not to feel disappointed. Some women were into cars, and some weren't.

En route he explained to Kit his reason for

coming to Nipntuck, and then he described how Turner had reacted to the news about Rebecca.

"He said she was downcast!" Kit said. "That's bull . . . pucky!"

In the rearview mirror Quinn and Nate exchanged a look. *Bull pucky?* Quinn suppressed a smile, and went on to share what he'd learned from Elise at lunch, including what she revealed about Marcus's disappearances. "As you can probably imagine, this is privileged info—" A yellow Ferrari came around a curve, flashed past them and disappeared in the direction of town. "That was Turner," he said.

Kit twisted around to look. "Turn around! Follow him!"

They were in a series of blind S curves, so by the time they hit a straightaway with enough shoulder, there was no point in turning around. Kit pounded the back of the seat once, hard, in frustration, "What I would give for a pair of wings right now!"

He glanced at her. A spot of red bloomed in the middle of each fair cheek. Her black hair looked wavy and wild, and he had the urge to reach out and smooth it back from her face. She'd look good with wings, he thought.

He tugged his eyes back to the road and had to brake quickly or he would have gone right past Georgette's. He swung into the drive.

"That's what we're picking up?" she pointed.

"That's it. It needs to go back to the Rent-a-Wreck place near the airport."

"Who's driving what?"

Before he could answer, Kit showed him a quarter and said, "Heads, I drive the BMW."

Her eyes were fixed on him, and Quinn nodded dazedly, distracted by their color—an intense cobalt blue.

She thumbed the quarter up, and when it dropped into her waiting hand, she slapped it onto the back of her other hand and held it out for them to see. Nate leaned forward, showing some life, finally. It was heads up.

Smirking, Nate said, "We'll see you there, bud."

Quinn didn't want those two to pull away in the BMW together. "Ride with me," he returned, "be a pal." Nate scowled, but climbed out of the BMW.

Quinn held the BMW driver's side door open for Kit. She hopped in and belted up. Rolling down the window, she held up the quarter to show them: it was a trick quarter, with heads on both sides.

They watched her drive off, fishtailing a bit, then heard, "Quinn!"

Georgette stepped out the front door and came at them. "You're fired," she spat. Her breath was a sour blast in his face. She turned to go but paused to snarl, "Leave the BMW at the office lot downtown."

"What's going on?" In two strides he was in front of her. "Tell me."

She said nothing, just pushed past him to go inside. She closed the door with a loud thud.

He climbed into the car, and seeing Nate's questioning look, could only shrug. On the way back toward the airport he got out his phone to call Elise. "Maybe you can shed some light on a couple of curious developments. Georgette hired me to look for Marcus, claiming she was beside herself with worry about him."

"That is curious. She—" Elise cleared her

throat, "she doesn't tend to worry about him."

"Yeah, I picked up on that. Anyway, her lapse into being a concerned wife is over. She just fired me. Wouldn't give any explanation. And she was livid—apparently at me. I just saw Turner out this way, and I'm guessing he got her riled up about me, somehow. What the hell could he have said to her?"

"I have no idea," she sighed. "In any case, I have good news—you're rehired. I found the memo from Marcus."

Finally, Quinn thought, some information from the man himself.

He hit speakerphone so Nate could hear, and asked, "What's it say?"

She sounded tired. "That he wanted to hire you to provide a few weeks of security backup. And if you took the job, you'd be staying on the *Blue Sea*, and I was to cut you an advance check for seventy-five hundred dollars."

"What else?"

"Just that he would fill me in on more details once they were firmed up . . . but of course, he isn't here to do that . . ." her voice trailed off.

Although the memo failed to explain what Marcus wanted, at least it would put Turner's doubts to rest, Quinn thought. The ground had been shifting under his feet since he'd arrived in Nipntuck, and he was ready for that to stop.

"So you'll show Turner the memo, and we're good to go?"

"Well . . ." she paused. "One little hitch there . . ."

"What hitch?"

"I can't show Turner the memo."

So much for solid ground. "Talk to me, Elise."

"It's a security thing. The memo references confidential information . . ." She took a breath. "Turner believes he knows all there is to know about our project, but other than Marcus and myself, no one at SeaLab knows the full scope of it."

"You can't just block out the confidential information in the memo and show Turner the stuff about me?"

"Turner thinks he knows everything. He'll insist I tell him the rest and that I can't do. Pressure from him is not something I can cope with right now."

She sounded frustrated, which was exactly how he was starting to feel. "I need to concentrate on making things ready for the unveiling," she continued, "and he needs to concentrate on finding Marcus. So here's my suggestion: I'd like you to help look for Marcus, but I'd like you to try not to aggravate Turner."

Quinn was having trouble driving the Rent-a-Wreck with only one hand on the wheel. The car shimmied hardest on curves, and the road had a lot of them. He changed his grip on his phone and said, "But surely Turner will know if I'm around asking questions."

"Yes, I know. But there might be a way to avoid being in the same place as him at the same time. Oh!" Quinn heard what sounded like a slurp. "I'm drooling all over my phone. The dentist gave me a horse-sized dose of Novocain, and then proceeded to bumble around on the wrong side of my mouth until the hygienist intervened. He's new in town, and I'm a little worried because I didn't see any diplomas or licenses hung on his office wall."

"I hope you're joking."

"Nipntuck," she said, "is like an eddy in a

river that collects things. You'd be surprised how many charlatans end up here. Charlatans and geniuses, both."

When she said "genius," it reminded him. He glanced at Nate, who was following all this on speakerphone. He told Elise that he had a friend, Nate Farley, staying on the *Blue Sea* with him. She asked abruptly, "Does he know about the situation?"

"I can guarantee that he's trustworthy, and has helpful, ah, information-gathering skills."

She sounded peeved. "What's his name? Nate Farley?" Quinn hoped Nate's reputation would hold up to scrutiny, since she was obviously going to look into it. He heard another slurp, and she said, "Look, can we resume our talk tomorrow morning? You can join me while I walk the mall."

"Walk the mall?"

"You are spoiled, you know, by those dry summers you get in the Interior. Here, we use any covered space we can find, to get our exercise, even in the summer."

"Name the place and time."

"Glacier Mall, eight o'clock. It's small, with only a dozen shops, but there's a fountain and a common area that stretches out the loop we walk. There's a bunch of us who show up, five days a week, before the shops open."

"I'll bring my running shoes," he promised with a smile.

"You'd better."

"Before you go," he said. "Do you know a man named Connelly?"

"The name doesn't ring any bells with me."

"Or anyone named Hamm?"

"Fred Hamm. He works in grounds security at our lab, over on the island."

He was about to ask more about Hamm, but Elise said she had to go wipe her chin, and they signed off.

Nate had gone back to staring out the window again, Quinn noticed. To offer some diversion, he said, "I've had three bosses and been fired three times in twenty-four hours. Not bad, eh?"

"Shouldn't that leave you fired?" Troubled thoughts weren't enough to keep Nate's brain from finding the story problem Quinn's words presented.

Quinn thought for a minute. "You're right. I've been hired four times and only fired three.

Marcus hired me, then Turner fired me, but Elise hired me back over lunch. However, because of Turner's objections, Elise called and refired me, but Georgette hired me. Then, for reasons unknown, Georgette fired me, but Elise found the top-secret memo, which she can't talk about, and she hired me back."

Nate said, "So we still have our digs, but Georgette is taking the BMW back?"

"Yeah."

"Bummer."

"After we take care of the car, we'll get dinner," Quinn said. "You hungry yet?"

"Starved." A moment later Nate shifted in his seat. "Now that you brought it up, all I can think about is food." He wore a pained look. "Can't this thing go any faster?"

"It's floored."

Right then three pretty girls passed by in a Pinto. They were laughing and pointing at the shimmying wreck, which made Nate slump lower in his seat and let loose with a string of swear words. Sprinkled throughout were references to the BMW and to Kit—or rather, Kit's quarter. When Nate noticed Quinn's amused grin, he swore at him, too.

They pulled into the Rent-a-Wreck lot and saw Kit leaning against the BMW, eyes turned out over the water, arms crossed against the drizzle that had just begun. When they walked up to her, instead of some impish remark about the car, she gave Quinn a solemn look and said, "Maybe I shouldn't have done that. I hardly know you . . ." Her hand went to cover her heart. "But it was almost as though Becca was with me, urging me on." Her eyes welled up. "She knows I like to make mischief."

Before Quinn could react, Nate stepped forward and wrapped her in a hug, saying, "We thought it was funny."

"Really?" Her voice was muffled by his sweater.

Nate replied, "Well, Quinn was a little grouchy about it, but he's over that now." Kit made a sound, a half-laugh and half-sob, and Quinn gave Nate a disgusted look.

Nate held onto Kit, rocking her a little from side to side. Quinn's chest felt tight. He wished he'd been the one to step up and hold Kit.

After a moment she sighed deeply and

stepped back to look at both men. "The look on your faces when you saw the quarter . . ." She brushed quickly at her eyes, "Rebecca would be rolling on the ground right now." She smiled and held out the keys to Quinn. "The car drives like a dream."

And he'd thought she wasn't into cars. "Now the plan is to bring it downtown, and leave it at SeaLab's parking lot. You get a few more minutes behind the wheel, if you want."

She agreed gladly, and asked, "After we drop the car off, you guys want to come over for dinner? Fish enchiladas?"

"You are a goddess," Nate replied instantly.

8

Kit saw it happen all the time and found it comic. When men got around Clara they stood up straighter and talked in deeper voices. They said things to elicit her laugh— an easy task, because she loved to laugh, and she loved men. And that's exactly what happened with Quinn and Nate. Both of them unabashedly adored Clara the minute they entered her presence.

As promised, the fish enchiladas were warming in the oven. Right after they sat down to eat, Quinn's phone rang, and he excused himself to take the call outside. Kit filled her housemate in on all that had happened that afternoon, and Quinn joined them again just as she was telling Clara, "Now we just have to figure out who Hamm is."

Quinn said he'd learned that Hamm

worked in security over on SeaLab island.

"You seem to attract information," Kit said. "What is your secret?"

"My secret is to surround myself with knowledgeable women. Elise told me about Hamm."

"What about Connelly?" she asked, "Does he have ties to SeaLab, too?"

"Elise doesn't know who he is."

Nate barely joined the conversation. He kept sending Clara goofy grins while ploughing through his dinner—four enchiladas in all. It was somehow endearing, Kit realized, the way he ended up wearing globs of food on his sweater, and even managed to get a smear of sour cream in his hair.

~~~

They finished eating and went to sit in the front room. Quinn took the couch, Clara sat beside him, and Kit took a big cushy chair. Nate went straight to the beat-up La-Z-Boy, climbed in, sighed, belched, and closed his eyes.

Quinn said, "Nate."

His eyes opened.

"That phone call I took before dinner was

a friend in D.C. She told me about a group of scientists working covertly for the government. They call themselves ZAP, and Marcus used to be one of them. My contact found solid evidence that they are investigating ways to change the country's power infrastructure, to make it more resistant to attack."

"The grid," Nate said.

Quinn said, "Years ago, Marcus developed a drinking problem and was ousted from the group. He got himself back together and carried on working independently. Elise didn't want to confirm it outright, but I'm guessing that he's still working on that same issue."

Nate whistled. "So our sly little SeaLab may have come up with some hot new technology that's grid-related. That could explain why, when I tried to slip into their network, I found it unbelievably tight. Government-grade security, from the look of it. I wasn't able to do more than feel around the edges. It has a sort of fortress-feeling I've not encountered very often."

Quinn asked, "What's the story with ESI? Find out anything?"

Nate levered the chair upright and said,

"Do you want the official version or the truth?"

"Ah," Quinn said, "both."

"Officially, ESI's mission statement says they're 'dedicated to enhancing and extending the sustainability of our earth's energy resources.' In other words, ESI wants to be perceived as an eco-friendly energy R&D firm. But as the saying goes: follow the money, sonny. So I ignored the PR crap, and just asked the question: Who actually funds ESI? It turned out to be one hell of a convoluted trail—subsidiaries of subsidiaries of foreign-owned entities, some of them buried in divisions within shell companies, and so on—but finally I found out." He paused to look smug, while they waited, and then announced, "ESI is owned one hundred percent by the petroleum industry."

"The petroleum *industry*?" Kit said. "But the industry is made up of distinct companies, who also happen to be competitors."

"These companies each have a so-called cooperative research arm, each tagged with a different name, each tucked into a corner of an impossibly complex corporate structure.

But the money trail tells me they are all part of a quiet alliance, pursuing a common purpose."

She said, "And that would be . . . ?"

"Not sure," Nate said. "But I suspect the only green thing about it is that it has to do with money."

Quinn scratched his chin. "This is interesting. SeaLab might be working on something to revolutionize how electricity gets delivered, and perhaps generated. But that would affect the coal industry, if anything."

Clara rose. "Hold that thought! I want to bring out dessert, but I don't want to miss anything." Nate and Quinn both jumped up to help her in the kitchen.

After everyone was settled again, cradling their dishes of crème brûlée, the only sound for a few minutes was the occasional moan over the glorious taste of the dessert.

Nate was the first one to place his empty dish on the coffee table. Then he cleared his throat importantly and said, "I have a theory about the rivalry between SeaLab and ESI. What if it's a personal thing. The head honcho over at ESI, William Leetham, attended

Stanford at the same time as Marcus. They both held teaching positions there, so maybe they had to vie for funding, and notice from their mentors. And now, they're both in the private sector, so maybe the rivalry continues. You know—dick wagging, between guys.

Spooning up the last of his dessert, Quinn said, "That could be it."

Nate sat forward and looked at everyone. "Unless." He allowed a dramatic pause, "SeaLab has a secret project that's so big, so important, it's making the petroleum industry sweat."

Quinn asked, "Like what, smart guy?"

"What if they've developed some energy technology that not only promises to change our electricity picture, but might also displace gasoline and diesel, and maybe heating fuel, and natural gas as well." Nate shook his head in mock sorrow. "Those Big Oil barons would start feeling the pinch, man. Their profits would go from obscene to exorbitant. They'd have to start selling off those personally owned islands."

Kit chimed in. "And they'd be forced to give up their luxury submarines and trips to outer space. What a *shame* that'd be."

Quinn, smiling, laced his fingers behind his head. "Good work, Nate. In the morning, I'll ask Elise about it."

~~~

Kit's eyes kept being drawn to the way Quinn's shirt pulled tight against the muscles on his chest and arms. *Stop staring*, she ordered herself. She knew a lot of men who fished for a living and had extraordinary bodies because of it. Without a doubt though, this Quinn, whoever he was, got the prize for having the most gorgeous build she'd ever seen.

"Nate," Quinn said, "I need to get over to SeaLab island, and take a look around. Can you rent me a boat that'll get me there quickly?"

This snapped Kit's mind back on track. "I'll go too. That's where I'll find Hamm and Turner, and I want a word with both of them."

He started shaking his head. "Kit, we're talking about a situation that could be dangerous."

She folded her arms defiantly, and just

looked at him.

He tried again. "Look, it isn't like those guys will be eager to offer information."

"Do you know," she asked, sitting up straighter, "what I do for a living?"

He looked surprised by the question, and shook his head.

"I'm a reporter. An *investigative* reporter."

Clara piped up, "She wrote the article about the Holy Order of Tax-Evaders. All the papers ran the story, so you probably saw it up in Fairbanks."

"You broke that story?"

She said sharply, "You sound surprised."

Clara laughed and said, "Whatever you do, Quinn, don't mention her height. Or the fact that she looks seventeen."

Kit shot her an irritated look. Unless she was competing in the quarter-drop game, her size was a great annoyance to her.

Clara missed the look Kit gave her because she was staring at the ceiling, thinking. "The security over there is intense, Rebecca has talked about it. You'll get turned back by their security patrol before you even land at the dock."

Sitting forward, Kit said, "I know what we can do." She was thinking about Clara's closetful of theater costumes, including one very authentic-looking cop uniform. "You know that uniform you made for the play last year? That, combined with some good acting, could get us past security on the island."

Quinn said, "Turner has already met me, and knows I'm not a cop."

"It's a woman's uniform. A perfect fit for me."

Clara suffered a sudden coughing fit. Both men jumped up, and laughing at their own eager gallantry, race-walked one another to the kitchen to get her a glass of water.

While they were gone, Clara whispered, "I made that uniform for an actor who was over six feet, and weighed three hundred pounds."

"Shhhh," she whispered back. The guys returned, and once Clara had her glass of water, Kit declared, "Okay. We're going over to SeaLab island tomorrow."

Quinn tried one last time. "Impersonating an officer is illegal."

She narrowed her eyes at him, and held him in her gaze until he gave in.

"Alright," he said. "You and I will go over there together. But you have to let me pay you—" he held up a hand as she started to object, "that way I might have the illusion of being in charge. What do actors get for a day of work?"

"Oh, between four- and six-hundred," Clara spoke up.

Kit grabbed for Clara's glass of water. "They do not," she said, sputtering a little. "Not for one day!"

Clara said mildly, "It seems like this one should include a little hazard pay."

"Okay," he said. "Let's aim for tomorrow afternoon."

"I can rustle up a boat for you," Nate said.

"Good," Quinn said, "I meet with Elise in the morning. After that, we'll firm up our plan."

They exchanged numbers, and the two men got up to go.

Kit touched Nate's arm. "Do you mind taking Flotsam out onto the dock tonight for a short walk?"

"I'll take care of him," he said. "We bonded today."

After they left, Kit called the hospital in Juneau. The nurse said Rebecca's condition hadn't changed. "If something changes, will someone call me?" Kit asked, her voice faltering. The nurse assured her she was at the top of the list.

She sank into the couch beside Clara and they sat quietly, until Clara spoke up. "I have two pieces of not-great news."

Kit rubbed her forehead with her palm. "What's the first one?"

"I was going to ferry over to Juneau tomorrow, but I can't. You know how the ferryboat up north bumped that reef, and is now in drydock? To cover that route, ferries have been shifted around, so until further notice, we only get service to Juneau once a week. And, considering the second piece of news, I can't afford a last-minute plane ticket."

Kit raised a limp hand in a gesture for her to continue.

"The landlord sent us a letter. He's raising the rent."

Kit sat up in alarm. She and Clara were already in a rent bind—their third housemate, without warning, had just moved away. If they didn't find a replacement before the end of the month, they would have to ante up the extra rent.

"It's going up by one third. And he says it's effective the first of next month."

"But that's only ten days from now!" Kit couldn't believe the guy's gall. It's illegal to give us so little notice!"

Clara nodded. "I pointed that out to him. And you know what that awful man said? He'll give us thirty days, but he'll raise our rent by twice as much."

If there was ever a time that called for cussing, it was now, but Kit had instituted a swearing ban on herself. "That guy is a . . . worm!" she cried.

"He is," Clara agreed. "The worst worm, ever." She rose and gestured toward the kitchen. "I'll help with the dishes, and then I need to get busy making alterations on that cop costume."

They started on the dishes, and Clara said quietly, "I'm glad you brought those boys home for dinner. They cheered me up."

"Me too," Kit said. "By the way, I don't

want Quinn's money for posing as a cop tomorrow."

"You can always decline, but at least this way, your value has been acknowledged."

Kit paused to give her housemate an admiring look. "You come across all sugar and spice, but underneath, you are *wily*."

Clara smiled her best Mona Lisa smile. Then, softly, she said, "Quinn couldn't keep from looking at you."

Hearing this, Kit felt a rush of pleasure followed by an even stronger wave of guilt. It was only that morning they'd found Rebecca in the harbor. How could she feel pleasure at a time like this?

She blurted, "He's probably got a girlfriend," and studied the plate that she'd been scrubbing for a while. It was so clean it squeaked, as if in pain. Smiling, Clara lifted it out of her hands and dried it. In a small voice Kit added, "But maybe not."

She handed Clara the next plate to dry, and Clara, clearly amused by her distracted state, handed it back. "You forgot to wash this one, honey."

After the dishes were clean, Clara got

the cop uniform from her costume closet. Thinking about Kit's assertion that it would only fit a woman, they started giggling. The uniform was huge—it would have fit Quinn perfectly, in fact.

When she stopped laughing, Clara said, "It would be ten times faster to make you one from scratch, but I don't have the material." She sighed. "It is going to take me all night to tailor this monster down to fit you."

Kit didn't want to make Clara work all night on it. She tried to make her limbs look bigger while Clara appraised her.

"Ahh!" Kit said suddenly. "I have an idea."

~~~

When they got back to the *Blue Sea*, Quinn made the mistake of telling Nate that he had left a phone message for Allie.

Scowling, Nate said, "As in: *dark allie?*" His scowl deepened. "As in: don't *go* there?"

"I thought I'd call, just see how she is."

"You know how she is. You know better than anyone."

Quinn shrugged.

Nate snorted and said derisively, "Puppet

on a string."

"Shut up."

"She'll play you like a fish and pull you in close so she can watch your pain."

Annoyed, he said, "What is it, a puppet or a fish? Don't mix your metaphors, it makes you less credible." Nate just looked at him. Defensively, he added, "I don't have to go see her. I'll make that decision when she returns my call. If she even returns my call."

"You don't have to go see her."

"No, I don't."

"You didn't have to call her, but you did."

"Who made you my keeper?"

"You did!" Nate clutched his head. "You said—and I quote your exact words—'Don't let me get near that man-eating viper, no matter what.'"

"I said that?"

Nate shook his head. "I'm going to get it in writing next time. Notarized. Framed. I'll even hang it on the wall for you. I'll tell you what, I'll make a miniature copy and put it in a locket on a chain so you can wear it around your neck. Along with some garlic."

"There you go again. Viper or vampire—

make up your mind."

Nate snorted, "When are you going to learn?"

"You're overreacting."

"No, I mean it. Find a new way to suffer. This one's getting really old."

Quinn stood up and said, "Thanks, I'll try."

The bed in his stateroom was comfortable, but he couldn't sleep. He was agitated over Nate's comments, plus the damn pipe chimes on the boat next door were clanging, loudly. Lying there, the more he thought about those chimes, the more annoyed he got. The thing about a harbor, there was usually some wind, and with it came noises—rigging clanking, bumpers groaning, waves slapping. Who the hell needed chimes?

Flipping his blankets off, he got up, strode across the skinny float separating the two boats, and pounded on the plywood boat's door. No answer. The owner wasn't even there to enjoy his pretty chimes.

He considered tearing the damn things down and tossing them overboard, but instead went back to the *Blue Sea*, searched until he found some duct tape in a drawer, and a minute later he had silenced the obnoxious things.

His act did not go unnoticed: he heard a quiet cheer come from the dark deck of a nearby boat, and saw a cigarette glow from that direction, while a woman weaving along the next float also called out in a drunken slur, "You rule, Missster!"

And then, sweet peace finally settled over the harbor.

9

Like many bedrooms in the northern latitudes, Kit's room had custom-made blinds to keep out the relentless summer light, but she never used them. She welcomed the kiss of daylight on her eyelids, typically, and the free time it gave her before work.

Not this morning, though. She woke up around four and the minute she opened her eyes, the events of the previous day flooded over her. She lay there feeling fragile and sad, wishing she'd been granted a few more hours of oblivion.

She made herself get up and shower, then donned a raincoat and went out for a walk. Her legs took her over to the Sea Shanty where she used the hidden key to let herself in. She got the coffee machine going, sat at a table and pulled out her note pad.

She doodled aimlessly, letting her mind wander.

The day before, when she wrote the newspaper blurb stating that Rebecca had died, she did what she had to do. But it complicated things. It would be easier if she could go to Billings and say: "The woman who drowned in the harbor actually survived, but her attacker, who wants her dead, must not know."

She simply didn't trust her editor to keep it quiet. Once before, for a different reason, she had been forced to work around her boss, and it was starting to look like the same tactic might be necessary.

Last December, Billings ordered her not to pursue a particularly exciting lead, because he knew it involved some powerful people connected to the newspaper's owner. She couldn't leave the story alone. Her subsequent investigation led her to write the article headlined: "Busted: The Holy Order of Tax-Evaders."

It exposed a religious society formed by nine Nipntuck business and political leaders who faithfully flew up to Anchorage once a month—with their fishing poles, beer coolers, and mistresses—where they held "services." Under the auspices of their religious order, they gave themselves tax breaks that were, the judge ultimately said, astonishing in their creativity.

The Associated Press paid her nine-hundred smacks for the story and the *Anchorage News*, the *Fairbanks News-Miner*, the *Seattle Times*, plus a dozen smaller papers, plucked it off AP's wire and ran it.

The owner of the *Nipntuck News* was close pals with most of those implicated in the story, but his only choice was to give it prominent play, to avoid accusations of bias.

Kit's decision to chase the story had caused a terrible conflict in her at the time. Her conscience demanded she do it, but she felt fairly certain it would lose her the job at the Nipntuck News —a job she loved, and the only one like it in her hometown.

But then luck intervened.

The National Press Club named her top investigative reporter in the Northwest U.S. for that story, which meant that Billings didn't dare fire his star reporter—unless he wanted to raise eyebrows.

The funny part was, she never considered submitting the story for the award. Her pal McPhee, Jean-Philippe's predecessor, did it without her knowledge. When he filled out the submittal forms, he enlisted her older brother's help on questions concerning her writing credentials. Over frothy steins of beer, Big Pat had explained that except for one three-month journalism class taken through the state's distance-education program, Kit lacked formal training. Her most valuable experience came from a newspaper she started when she was twelve. Called *The Big Skinny,* it came out regularly for three years, except for the summer months when she was offshore commercial fishing. And people actually bought it.

Until she won the award, Big Pat liked to tease Kit that her journalism career peaked with *The Big Skinny* and went downhill from there. She was thinking about this and smiling when Big Pat himself came into the unlocked pub. He, too, was an early riser.

"I have something for you!" He went straight into the walk-in cooler and returned with a stuffed gallon ziplock bag. "You like halibut cheeks, right?" He was teasing. She loved them, and everybody knew it. She gasped when she saw what was in the bag. Usually a dozen or more halibut cheeks fit in a gallon bag, but this bag contained just one. The single cheek probably weighed at least three pounds.

"I jigged up a nice one yesterday."

"How big?" she gasped.

"Over three hundred pounds."

She squealed and threw her arms around him. It was a windfall fish, and it meant they'd all have a bounty of halibut to eat for some months.

"Hey," he said, stepping back. "I heard about Rebecca." His shoulders looked weighed down with sadness. "She's the last person I thought would commit suicide."

Kit hesitated, not sure whether to disclose what really happened. Pat could be trusted completely, but the fewer people informed, the safer Rebecca would be. Also, her brother would get in her face and insist that she not take matters into her own hands and wait until Walsh, their trooper friend, came back to town. He'd say he understood how hard it would be for her to wait and do nothing, but she must.

She did not want to have that conversation with him, so she held her tongue. He would be completely correct in his logic, except for one thing: it wouldn't be difficult for her to wait and do nothing. It would be impossible.

~~~

Quinn parked at the mall and climbed out of the Rent-a-Wreck. Elise was walking toward the main entrance, so he hustled to catch up.

He held the door open for her, and let another lady go in ahead of him, then looked for Elise. She was already off and walking, gesturing for him to catch up.

She wasn't just walking, she was speed walking. It was an activity he'd always thought looked funny, and now, he discovered it felt just the way it looked. It required pumping his arms and forcing his legs into a stride that was completely unnatural to him.

After they exchanged pleasantries, he dove right into his first question. "Yesterday you mentioned some sort of rivalry between ESI and SeaLab. Is it a personal thing between

Marcus and ESI's director, William Leetham?"

"There is some of that, but it's secondary. It mostly concerns our project. If ESI could learn the truth about what SeaLab has invented, they would do everything they could to stop us. That's the main reason we're so wed to secrecy."

"Why would Big Oil be concerned with SeaLab?"

She shot him a penetrating look. "Not many people are aware that ESI is with the petroleum industry."

"What's SeaLab working on?"

She looked at him and then away.

Frustrated, he said, "You need to confide in me. SeaLab's project could tie in with what's happening with Marcus."

She faltered slightly, and then recovered her step. "But why would ESI—or anyone— take Marcus just to have him show back up two days later? I mean . . . kidnapping? It's a huge risk."

"That's a good question," he said. "Now here's another one: If SeaLab's work has to do with the electrical grid, why the hell would the petroleum industry care?"

This made her eyes widen, so he knew he'd hit on something.

"Who mentioned anything about the electric grid?" she asked, on guard.

He sensed a flat-out lie might help move things along. "Marcus did."

She fell silent, apparently gathering her thoughts while Quinn took a moment to wonder why he wasn't getting the hang of the speed walking thing. He was no stranger to weight training, and ran at least twenty-five miles a week, most of them at a good clip. But this activity wasn't like walking and it wasn't like running. He couldn't seem to find the groove that Elise had.

She drew in a breath. "Alright. I'll explain what I can, so you'll see why ESI isn't likely to be involved in what's going on with Marcus. We have created some technology that will . . ." she paused, and then she started over. "The petroleum industry watches evolving technology very closely, and not because they're concerned citizens, believe me. Although they lack proof, ESI suspects that our technology could ultimately challenge the markets they currently monopolize. The truth is the petroleum industry could be obsolete in a matter of years. But you see—"

"Hold on," he interrupted. "Give me a minute to absorb what you just said."

He wanted to believe her. If SeaLab did have some amazing new technology to offer the world, the implications could be enormous. But a part of him worried that Elise, Marcus, Turner, the whole gang, could be suffering from some group delusion.

She saw the skepticism on his face. "I know what I'm telling you sounds crazy, given our size. But when a few smart people get together and refuse to do things the usual way, incredible things can happen."

He still wasn't convinced, but he nodded for her to go on. "Marcus, because of his drinking, was forced to disassociate from his colleagues some years ago. But splitting off was the best thing he could have done. That group of government scientists has floundered around, accomplishing very little over the years. The intent is there, but the bureaucracy, the infrastructure, the changing administrations, the bullshit, excuse me, all of it has bogged down their work. SeaLab, on the other hand, got a huge shot of financing when Marcus's father died. We've stayed on task, and we've stayed nimble."

They let a silence fall. He tried to form his next question, but was distracted by his right thigh, which kept threatening to cramp. He gave his leg an irritated shake.

"Is something wrong?" Elise asked with a smile.

"Nothing's wrong!" he said. "So . . . your point is . . ."

"Leetham is paid to ferret out and kill anything that might threaten profits for the petroleum industry. He knows what Marcus is capable of, so he's very nervous about what we're up to. He's trying to find out. He'll steal information, control patents, launch disinformation campaigns, buy up politicians, form cozy deals with other industry leaders . . . But what's happening to Marcus—it doesn't fit the profile. It's just not Leetham's style. That's the point I'm trying to make."

Without breaking her stride she glanced at her watch and said, "I'm sorry I don't have much more time. I need to get to work."

"I need your help with something. Can you keep Turner busy this afternoon, here on the main island in a dead cell range? Between, say, three and four? I want to take a look around over on SeaLab island."

She nodded. "I can ask him to meet me at the coffee shop by my house. There's no cell signal there because it's backed right up against Thunder Mountain."

"Who will be in charge of security at the island facility while Turner's meeting with you over here?"

"Stan Hamm."

Ah, thought Quinn. "So what's Hamm's story?"

"I don't know much about him. Our second-in-command guy had a boating accident, and Hamm stepped in."

Quinn wanted to talk to her about Hamm, but felt inclined to wait until he knew more. "Another question: How would you expect Marcus's office to look when he leaves?"

She thought for a moment. "He'd take his briefcase and his coat, of course."

"Does he clear his desk before he leaves or . . ."

"Oh no, he never tidies up. It always looks like a bomb went off in his office. Books and drawings everywhere, coffee rings all over the papers. You'll find his scummy coffee cup, half-filled with coffee, placed precariously on some uneven surface."

"Would he power down his desk computer?"

"Always. He leaves everything in a mess, but religiously turns his computer off and secures the door."

She had stopped by the mall entrance and was putting her coat on. "Keep me informed of your efforts, Quinn, and please share with me anything you find out, immediately."

Now that they'd stopped, Quinn noticed with annoyance his face was wet with sweat. Elise, looking fresh and relaxed, handed him a Kleenex so he could mop his forehead.

"I almost forgot." She pulled out an envelope with his name on it. "Here's your check for seventy-five hundred, as promised."

Taking it, he said, "One last question: Georgette invited me to use the BMW, but then rescinded the offer. Is there a company vehicle I could . . ."

She nodded. "I'm sure Marcus would be fine with you using the BMW. He doesn't drive the thing, but I keep hoping he'll come around."

"Why doesn't he drive it?"

"I got him the car, but I think it makes him sad, instead of happy."

"You bought him the car?"

"We have regular arguments about the salary he pays me. It's far more than I need." She smiled wryly. "So in a fit of pique, I bought him the car. He used to own a BMW motorcycle and always talked about how he and Georgette were going to take a road trip up the Alaska Highway."

She paused, and then said softly. "But when we get older, dreams like that can sort of . . . fade. He sold his bike and acted like it didn't matter, but I knew it did. So I thought if he had the car, maybe he would still do that road trip sometime. Not the way he pictured it, exactly, but he could still do it."

Quinn heard an inflection in her voice, and saw something unguarded in her expression. *She loves Marcus*, he thought with sudden certainty. *She loves him deeply.*

~~~

As soon as Kit got to work, she picked up the phone to call Billings. His office wasn't far from her desk, but his breath smelled like sour milk, so she preferred talking to him on the phone. While waiting for him to answer, she stretched her neck from side to side and stared across the newsroom at the rain pelting against the windows.

Billings came on the line, and she said, "I need to take unpaid leave, ah, starting tomorrow."

"Why?" he barked.

"Because I need to." He was silent and Kit matched his silence. She was going after this story, one way or the other. He could fire her if he wanted.

He hung up with a bang.

I'll take that as a yes, she thought and set her phone down gently.

The next thing on her list was reaching Rebecca's mom. She dialed the Saluda number—still no service—and left a second, terse-sounding message with the phone company. Then she gnawed on her lip, trying to decide what else she could do. She wished her trooper friend Walsh was in town. He'd help her figure something out.

Just thinking about Walsh gave her an idea. She looked up the number for the state troopers up in Nome. Nome was the regional hub for Alaska's central west coast, and if anyone could find a way to relay the message to Bev Watterson, it would be them. They were accustomed to dealing with this kind of thing.

She dialed and got a message machine. She didn't trust leaving the actual message for them to pass on to Bev, in case something got miscommunicated, so she gave her name and requested a call back on an urgent matter. She hung up, grateful that this unwelcome task would soon be in other hands.

She didn't see Jean-Philippe until he'd perched his skinny butt on the corner of her desk. He eyed her in a way he probably thought was seductive and said, "Keet, if you do two little favors for me, I will own you for life."

"Not own," she corrected, "Owe." How someone with his poor command of English could get hired at this newspaper mystified her. "And the answer is no."

He placed a sheet of paper in front of her. "This Chamber of Commerce meeting? Say you will cover it for me, please?"

She stared at him. He was just back from vacation, and unable to do the most basic task on his beat?

"Please," he moaned. He leaned toward her and tilted his head appraisingly. "You look beautiful in that blouse."

She glowered at him. "No."

"The second favor then, mi amour. The Press awards . . . they are in Seattle, in two days."

"I know that," she said, her voice cold. Of course, Billings had deemed it too expensive to fly her down to accept the award.

"My darling, I want to buy you a ticket to Seattle so you can go!"

Kit shook her head, confused. Last-minute tickets to Seattle were outrageously expensive. He was loaded—something to do with a family trust fund—but what was this about? She narrowed her eyes at him. "Why would this be a favor to you?"

He squirmed. "Ah, Keet, I cannot tell a lie.

My wife is here and I—"

"Here?" she looked around.

"No, not yet. I need to pick her up from the airport now, which is why I cannot cover this meeting. She has volunteered to do extra filing here this week, at this office, while she visits me. And . . . she's determined to . . . well . . . how would you say? Expose us?"

"Expose us?!" Kit laughed. "That's rich. There's nothing to expose."

His mouth went slack as he stared at her. "But you love me, don't you?"

"Quite the opposite. She's welcome to your sorry ass." She winced, remembering her vow to stop swearing. *Did ass count?*

He whipped out his wallet and pressed a credit card into her hand. "We have an understanding, then. It would be best if you left for Seattle today."

"What understanding! I'm not going to Seattle!"

"But why?" he cried.

Because I'm trying to chase down Rebecca's attacker. "The Cancer Society benefit is tomorrow night," she said, waving her hand at him to go away.

"Ooh," he twitched. "My wife insists she will accompany me to this dinner. She is very determined."

"Good luck with that." Tickets to the function were sold out.

He said, "If you go to Seattle, your ticket would be available."

She thrust the credit card back at him. "Dream on."

Before she could stop him, he slipped the card into her purse. "Alright, you little minx, go shopping when you get to Seattle."

He thinks I'm trying to up the ante! "No! Take it back," she told him. But he slid away, leaving the card with her.

10

Kit noticed the rain had quit and the gray clouds sat higher than they had for days. She put Jean-Philippe out of her mind and walked over to Silvers Restaurant, getting there just as the manager was unlocking the door.

"Excuse me, I'm Kit Finnegan, working on a story for the *Nipntuck News*. I have a couple of quick questions I need to ask."

"Go ahead," he said, jiggling the keys and giving them a twist.

"On Sunday night, a couple dined here and I'd like to talk to their server."

The man wasn't into chitchat. He strode to the reservation booklet on the podium near the door, flipped it open and said, "Names?"

"Turner Holland and Rebecca Zachau."

"Oh," he closed the book, and suddenly got more chatty. "What's the story?" He probably knew Turner was wealthy and had the same suck-up-to-the-powerful attitude as the newspaper's owner, Kit realized.

She gave him her most charming smile. Against his will he almost smiled back. In a lightly chiding voice she said, "I noticed you closed the book."

His smile faded and he said stiffly, "If you need information concerning Mr. Turner, you need to ask him."

"I just want to ask your server a few questions, off the clock, when it's convenient."

"Mr. Turner would never dine here again."

"He wouldn't have to know."

He just shook his head and gestured toward the door, and closed it firmly as soon as she stepped outside.

Oh, I hope this isn't going to be one of those days, she thought, and got out her phone to call her little brother John. He and Big Pat were her only sibs onshore; the other five were out commercial fishing.

"Johnny, who's the kid you skateboard with, the one with all the tricks?"

"Hi to you, too."

"Sorry, I'm on a story."

"No kidding? I thought you might be looking for skateboard lessons."

"As if I need lessons."

"You're rusty and out of shape, and you know it."

She did know it. "Okay, just humor your over-the-hill sister and tell me his name?"

"Freddie."

"He's a waiter at Silvers, isn't he?"

"Yep."

"I need to talk to him. Would it help or would it hurt if I claimed to be your favorite sister?"

"He already knows you're my *only* sister. He was checking you out the last time we were at the park."

"He's what? Still in high school?"

"And you're my sister. I told him to cut it out."

"Great, and now I have to ask this guy a favor. I really wish you hadn't told me that."

She could practically *hear* Johnny grinning into the phone. It happened to her a lot—young guys thinking she was younger than she was. It irked her, and Johnny knew it.

It seemed to be turning into one of those

days. She asked, "Where do I find him?"

"He's here now."

She knew where "here" was. When John wasn't working, he was at the skateboard park. "Can you call him over?"

"Freddie! It's my sister. She's got a question for ya."

"Hey Freddie," Kit said when he came on the phone, "you work at Silvers?"

"Hi, yeah, why?"

"Do you know who Turner Holland is?"

"He's got the Ferrari."

"Did you happen to work on Sunday and see him and his date, a blonde woman, come in?"

"Hey wait! I'll come with you." He said this to someone, and then came back on the phone. "Yeah, I was there Sunday." He went away from the phone again to shout "See you there!"

Kit wanted his undivided attention, if only for a few minutes. Being on the phone was not cutting it. "Can I come talk to you?"

"Sure!" he said.

When she got there, Fred was on his skateboard performing some complicated stunt she'd never even seen before, which confirmed that she was behind the times for sure. She spotted her brother Johnny off on the sideline but he didn't see her. He pulled a cigarette out of a pack, and was bending to stash the smokes in his sock. She came up behind and gave him a little sisterly goose.

He coolly ignored her as though his skinny butt was always getting grabbed—which they both knew wasn't the case. He wore no coat, and she noticed his cotton T-shirt showed every knob on his backbone.

"Hey," he said and slowly straightened up, unlit cigarette dangling from his mouth. He had fourteen inches on her, even though she was older by three years. "Got your lighter?"

"Where's yours?" she demanded.

He pointed to his coat, hung on the fence across the way so she dug her lighter out and handed it over. She didn't smoke but always had a lighter in her coat. Big Pat, who'd pretty much raised the bunch of them, had pounded it into them from an early age: never, ever forget to carry a fire-starter. They'd roamed in the wilderness constantly as kids, so it was a useful habit to form.

Johnny lit up and asked if she'd heard the weather report. She shook her head and he told her, "Storm's brewing out on the Gulf. Be here in a couple of days."

"Can't you just let me stay ignorant for once?" She waved his smoke out of her face. She always felt a little worry over the safety of her brothers and friends out fishing on the grounds, but an approaching storm made the worry much bigger. It wasn't a case of an inflamed imagination, either. Almost every season a gale thundered across the Gulf of Alaska, and it wasn't unusual for a boat to get thrown onto the rocks.

Johnny held his cigarette farther away from her and said, "Might chase everyone in, it's looking that bad."

This was actually good news. Instead of dropping anchor in some shallow indent along the Gulf coast, her friends and brothers would seek refuge in the harbor. And instead of being anxious for them, she and Clara would have a house full of laughter and men, and more fresh fish than they could eat for the next few days.

Freddie, a good-looking black-haired kid, finished his hotdogging and came over to talk.

"Whassup?" He flashed a grin.

"Turner Holland took my friend Rebecca out to Silvers Restaurant on Sunday."

"She's the one who died, right? I heard."

"Did you work that night?"

"Yeah. You think the Holland dude had something to do with it?"

She shrugged. "He might have seen her last, is all. Did you happen to wait on them?"

"No, but I can find out who had them. Let me have your number, and I'll call you." Then he gave her a sexy little wink.

After she gave him the number and he left, she growled to her brother, "Tell him how old I am." Johnny just laughed.

~~~

As soon as Elise walked away, Quinn sat down on the edge of the mall's central fountain, thinking that speed walking had to be the stupidest activity he'd ever come across. He put the envelope with the SeaLab advance in his coat pocket, and checked his email. He had one from Nate saying that he'd secured a boat.

He dialed Kit's number. "You still want to play cop over on the island this afternoon?"

"Definitely. What time?"

"Meet me at the harbor at three o'clock, slip B-fourteen. You're okay with piloting us over to the island?" People in Nipntuck were some of the best mariners around, and he guessed that Kit was no exception.

"Roger. How do we play this?"

"If there's any local insignia on the uniform, better remove it. We're going to say we're on special detail from Anchorage." He hesitated. "The bad news is, Turner won't be at the lab."

"But I wanted to –"

"You'll get your shot at talking to him," he cut in, "we'll find a way, but it can't be today. Today, we need to go look around and talk to anybody who's willing."

He was avoiding Turner partly because Elise had asked him to, but also because he felt Kit's small size was a problem. Anyone with half a brain would know she wouldn't qualify to be on any police force. Removing Turner, however, gave the uniform a greater chance of working, if only briefly.

"We'll say we're there to investigate Rebecca's death. We need to be cautious.

I may ask a few guarded questions about Marcus, but since we're not sure what's going on, we need to play it close."

"I hear you," she said.

"I've asked Nate to dig up a map of the grounds and a floor plan of at least the main building for us."

"I'm keen to see their facility. I haven't ventured over since they built the lab."

"You know the island?"

"This is my neighborhood, Quinn. I romped all over that island before those buildings were even a gleam in old Marcus's eye."

"Romped?" he said it in a teasing tone. For some reason he imagined rolling down a grassy hill—with Kit clasped in his arms.

"Things like hide-and-seek. Tackle tag. Camping out." There was a pause, and then she said, "Where is your mind?"

She said it sternly, but there was something in her voice. He wanted to imagine she was teasing him, flirting back. Or maybe she was truly chastising him. "Uh, right," he said briskly, "So I'll see you at three."

"I'll be the one in the cop uniform."

"The good-looking one." He winced.

Why couldn't he resist flirting with her? But then she laughed, and he felt encouraged.

"Yeah, that'll be me," she said mirthfully and hung up.

Putting away his phone, he stared at the sputtering, coin-littered fountain, thinking about his next move. He had a few hours before the trip with Kit to the island. He'd use that time to check out ESI, he decided, and meet William Leetham.

He purchased a cheap, ill-fitting leisure suit at the mall, and then drove to a nearby Radio Shack for two disposable cell phones. A cell phone could be left just about anywhere without raising eyebrows; for a quick and dirty eavesdrop, it couldn't be topped. He programmed the first phone's numbers into the second phone's speed dial and aimed the rental wreck over to ESI.

Although Elise had granted him permission to use the BMW, he was glad to have the rental today. It fit right in with the image he wanted to project.

Energy Systems Integrated, or ESI, was housed in a modern structure of glass planes and constant angles that looked imposing, but not very functional. *Some architect's wet dream, getting this contract.*

He entered the building and waved to the security guard, as though he was expected, and took the elevator up. Leetham's office suite took up an entire floor. He told the receptionist he had an urgent matter to discuss with William Leetham. He gave his name and said he was investigating for the IRS.

She asked him to sit down, but he stayed, looming over her, arms folded, legs spread in his best federal dude stance. Picking up her phone, she hunched forward over it and tried to speak quietly. Quinn heard a man's voice growl through the earpiece, "What? Speak up, girl!"

Finally she said in a normal voice, "There's a man here with the IRS, a Mr. Doug Quinn. It's urgent, he says." After a pause, she said, "I ah, can't tell him you're not here because he's standing right here." Leetham's response was so explosive she had to hold the phone away from her ear. *If this was a cartoon,* Quinn thought, *stars and asterisks would be shooting out of that phone.*

She hung up and said Leetham would see

him as soon as possible. Quinn gave her his warmest smile, which earned him a puzzled smile back. He sat down, and after a lengthy wait, Leetham came striding into the reception area.

Somewhat over fifty, Leetham was tall and had the florid good looks of a man with Mediterranean ancestry—dark eyes and coloring, a still-thick head of salt and pepper hair. His expensive suit claimed *wealth*, while his ugly tie and overbearing cologne said *tacky*.

Leetham shook his offered hand and led the way into a nearby conference room where he flipped on the lights and shut the door firmly behind them.

Quinn took the chair Leetham indicated, hiding his disappointment that they weren't meeting in Leetham's office.

"What can I do for you, Mr. Quinn?"

"I'm here to alleviate any concerns you might have, Mr. Leetham."

"Concerns?"

"Well," Quinn faltered. "To answer any questions you might have?"

Leetham's brow furrowed. "Why is the IRS asking if I have any questions?"

"IRS?"

"You told Shelley you were with the IRS."

"Oh gosh no, she must have misheard me—not her fault—I'm a consultant with I.E.R.S. International Energy Review Services, and basically I came to meet you personally and assure you that we are doing everything we can to mitigate the situation. And answer any questions . . ."

"What situation? You're not making any sense. Do you have a business card?"

"Of course, my apologies." He dug for his card, handed it over and said, "I guess I'm going about this wrong. You are aware of the threats they are facing over at SeaLab, and by association, the threat this may pose to your company? Ah . . . judging from the look on your face, I'm starting to think my boss, Chris Swayne, hasn't contacted you already?"

Leetham shook his head irritably. "What kind of threats?"

Quinn looked uncomfortable. "I'm terribly sorry. This is embarrassing. Someone should have briefed you on this. Chris is, by far, the best person to do so." He stood up hastily and offered his hand. "I had hoped I might be of service to you, but I'll have Chris contact you, and then I'll stop back by."

"Sit down, sit down." Leetham waved him back into his chair, and crossing his legs, said, "Start from the beginning."

"Could I—could I have some coffee?" He glanced at the conference room's cold coffeepot as he sat back down. "It actually helps to settle my—"

Leetham stood up, "There's a pot on upstairs. Let's go up to my office."

The executive suite was, unsurprisingly, spacious and expensively furnished. Leetham waved him to one of the two chairs positioned before a large, tidy desk. He took the coffee offered and watched Leetham settle into his chair.

"My girl makes a new pot every hour, no matter what, so it's fresh. Okay, now, fill me in. What's this you're saying about SeaLab? Threats? From who?"

Quinn leaned forward to set his coffee carefully on a drink coaster on his side of Leetham's desk. "You should have heard this from my boss, but I'll do my level best to sketch the situation out for you. Over at

SeaLab, there's reason to believe a saboteur is targeting their work and possibly threatening the personal safety of key personnel." Quinn preferred to stick to the truth as much as possible when he was lying.

"But this sounds serious. I'm sure I'd have heard about this."

"Me too. Maybe Chris called and spoke to someone else?"

"I mean in the news."

"Oh, right." Quinn picked up his coffee cup and took a sip, lifting his eyebrows as if impressed by the freshness. "Well, this hasn't been publicized because, as you know, the work they're conducting is at a very sensitive stage. But as you probably also know we are all obligated to respond in terms of the new international antiterrorism requirements, but at this stage—we're at level three—no one is obligated to inform the general public. Your knowledge is proprietary, of course, and so is mine."

"Antiterrorism? How do terrorists figure in? And for that matter, where does our company come in?" Leetham was trying hard to follow Quinn.

"Exactly," he said. "You see, I was brought down here from Fairbanks to assist Marcus Holland over at SeaLab, but now apparently he is, ah . . . out of the picture for a while. Something unexpected." He paused, to take in some coffee with a slurp.

Leetham didn't react to hearing that Marcus was out of the picture. He just kept staring at Quinn, his brow furrowing deeper.

After giving Leetham more than enough time to inquire about Marcus, Quinn plunged on, "Part of our service is to identify vulnerabilities, and because you're in the suspected target zone we wanted you in the loop. I guess that's all there is to say at this point, but you have my card should you need to call me."

"Why would we be in anyone's target zone?"

"Oh, well, because the work ESI is doing is very important. Everyone knows you're dedicated to enhancing and extending the sustainability of our earth's energy resources." He blithely parroted this portion of ESI's mission statement, then added, "SeaLab was targeted, we're all sure, due to that humdinger of an invention. That unveiling coming up will be interesting, you can bet."

"And what would you know about their project?" Leetham's eyes were pinned to Quinn's face.

"Oh, this and that," He did his best to look cagey. "Well," he finally said, gesturing with his coffee cup, "I've taken up enough of your time, so I should get back over to SeaLab. Although . . ." he gave a hearty fake laugh and looked around the plush office, "you do have a much nicer setup over here, compared to them." His eyes slid back to Leetham, "Too bad there isn't any . . . side consulting you need done. I mean," he coughed nervously, "who doesn't like to supplement their income . . . should an opportunity present itself, right?"

There was a long silence while Leetham studied him. This is where Quinn's cheap suit came in. "We have to be very careful who we hire," Leetham finally said. "I'll be in touch . . . perhaps."

"Okay, good." He placed his coffee cup down and knocked the drink coaster off the desk onto the floor. "Oh geez."

Bending to retrieve it, he placed one of

the disposable cell phones on the floor under Leetham's desk, and pushed autodial to make it call the other cell phone. As he straightened up, it rang in his pocket.

He pulled out the ringing phone as he strode for the door. Leetham had risen, intending to see him out, but Quinn didn't give him the chance. "No, don't bother, I know the way, and have to take this call. But we'll be in touch, okey doke?"

Phone pressed to his ear, Quinn strode off down the hall. As he expected, Leetham returned to his desk and made an immediate call. The planted cell phone under the desk picked up only half of the conversation, because Leetham didn't use his phone speaker, but even that much proved interesting.

Without preamble Leetham said, "Has this joker, Quinn, been over to see you?" A moment later, he said, "So that's the story he's giving you guys, eh? Well he just came over here and told me a different one. He says he's with some energy consulting firm. What a crock of shit." After another pause Leetham said, "No kidding—playing both sides can get a person hurt. Yeah, I'll use a couple of my boys. They're just hanging out downstairs, bored. Gotta throw meat to the tigers every once in a while."

Leetham paused again. "Sure, save your battery. Call me from a landline later. But trust me, he's going to be one sorry son of a bitch, guaranteed."

Quinn drove the rental car well under the speed limit, amused by the efforts of the driver in the Hummer trying to hang back and look inconspicuous while tailing him.

One, Leetham wasn't curious or surprised to hear that Marcus had unexpectedly dropped out of the picture. Two, judging from the phone call he'd made, he was chummy with someone over at SeaLab. Playing both sides indeed.

He got out his mobile phone and called Nate. "Elise told me SeaLab's development may eventually displace petroleum fuels."

Nate whistled. "Either this is big caca or it's bull caca."

"My thoughts exactly. Look, there's something I need you to do for me."

"Lay it on me."

He described his encounter with Leetham,

and asked if Nate could find out who Leetham
had called.

"Should be a snap," Nate said.

"You're a good friend to have."

"Remember that," Nate said, "the next
time I leave a salmon in your trunk."

"No next time!"

Nate just laughed and hung up.

Quinn parked at a bar on the edge of
downtown. Inside, the place was dark and
reeked of beer and urine. He positioned
himself on a bar stool with his back to the
door, and watched in the mirror behind the
bar as Leetham's "boys" came in and claimed
a table. They were both about three hundred
pounds, and wore ball caps pushed far back
on their fat heads. Quinn had a theory about
intelligence levels and how it related to the
angle of a ball cap a guy wore. These guys
looked special.

Like himself, they ordered the only thing
on the lunch menu, bratwurst, and he got a
chuckle when one of them seemed to find
something inedible in his food. They engaged
in a low-voiced argument; one was clearly
bent on complaining, the other one didn't

want to make a fuss.

The complainer's cell phone rang, and Quinn saw them share an unhappy look as they drew their heads together to listen to the phone. A minute later, they threw some money on the table and shuffled out the door.

He thought the "tigers" had been called away, but noticed, in the long mirror behind the bar, they were waiting outside, taking turns peering through the grimy front window to check on him.

He drank his Sprite. The bratwurst, lying on the plate before him like a sick snake, he ignored. He started to call Elise to get her thoughts about his encounter with Leetham, but paused. Could she be the one Leetham called? His gut told him no, but he decided to wait for Nate to call back with confirmation.

A few minutes later, Nate sent a text that he'd made it into ESI's phone system, but unfortunately the number Leetham called was blocked. If Quinn got him a list of possible phone numbers, Nate wrote, he'd go at it from the phone company side to learn which, if any, of those phone numbers had received a call by Leetham.

Quinn shot Elise an email asking her for a current list of mobile phone numbers for everyone working at SeaLab. She responded immediately, and he forwarded it to Nate.

While doing all this, Quinn paid attention to how often his two buddies waiting for him outside peeked through the window. It was about every two or three minutes.

He could surprise the two of them and give them an answer to take back to Leetham, but didn't see how that would gain him anything.

One of the guys peered in the window. As soon as he pulled his head out of sight, Quinn slapped money on the bar and exited the building through the side door. He made it to his rental car unseen, and drove as fast as he dared. He parked a block from the harbor, hopped out, cut through an alley, and got down the ramp undetected.

He quickly located the boat Nate had leased, bobbing gently in its slip. As he climbed aboard, he realized he was whistling cheerfully. The idea of going on a boat ride appealed to him, but what gave him the biggest lift was the thought of seeing Kit.

What's her story, he wondered, her personal

story? Waiting for her to appear, he thought about what he knew so far. She liked driving fast cars and negotiating with double-headed quarters. She was a good reporter. And she was determined to discover the truth about her friend's death.

Oh damn. He was watching a terrifically fat cop waddling down the ramp to patrol the harbor. *Kit's due any minute. If this cop sees her, there could be trouble.*

11

The fat cop walked straight toward Quinn, and it wasn't until she was a few strides away that he noticed she had Kit's blue eyes, and they were gleaming at him. Other than that, she was unrecognizable. Her disguise included a huge ass, a shelf of a bosom, and thick limbs that stuck out like a kid wearing a snowsuit. A bushy wig, a wart on her cheek, and an earpiece radio completed the makeover.

Smirking, she climbed aboard, and Quinn laughed at how easily she moved. "You look like a hippo," he told her, "but you move like a ballerina."

"Just wait until I get in character," she told him serenely. "I'll be all hippo."

He looked at her front, which pointed at him accusingly. Seeing the direction of his eyes, she said, "Stuffing. Pillows and balloons.

We added wire and duct tape for . . . extra shape." She proudly patted her missile-shaped boobs.

"Hmm," he said. "I could swear you said last night that the uniform was a perfect fit."

A sheepish look flitted across her face, followed by a defiant set to her jaw, followed by a charming smile meant to disarm him.

He reached for the papers Nate had left for them in the skiff. "The security staff at the island won't want to let us do anything until they check with Turner, which will be impossible. Elise promised to make sure he's in a dead cell zone." He showed her the search warrant. "Nate mocked this up for us. It shows an Anchorage number that's actually routed to him. He'll cover for us when they challenge it. Having a warrant will help, but getting into the facility is also likely to require some . . . assertiveness."

He spread out a map of the grounds and they studied it. Nate had made notations, showing where they'd dock and which was the main lab building, and inside the main building which was Turner's office, and also Marcus's.

"Nate's a man of many talents," she observed.

He pulled out a photo and handed it to her. "He got us a picture of Hamm."

She reached for it. "Hold up. This isn't Hamm."

"What?"

"This is Connelly, the six-pack guy I told you about. He's the one who picked up Rebecca's employee file for Hamm—" She stopped.

They stared at one another, and she said slowly, "So . . . he wasn't picking up the file for Hamm; he *is* Hamm?" Her eyes narrowed. "If Connelly is Hamm, who was the other guy in the sauna? The one calling the shots?"

He folded up the papers. "Excellent question. Once we get over to the island, we should have about thirty minutes. Elise said Hamm would be the one in charge with Turner gone. Let's go see what we can find out."

She steered them slowly past the breakwater, and then throttled up, heading southwest. She navigated primarily by sight, glancing occasionally at the electronic chart that showed their position.

Along the way he filled her in on his talk with Elise that morning, and also on his meeting with Leetham at ESI.

"So Leetham was going to have those guys hurt you. That shows a violent streak," she said. "He could be our second guy in the sauna."

"That's question one," he nodded. "Who was in the sauna with Hamm? Question two is the identity of Leetham's cohort on the phone."

As if on cue, Nate called.

"News flash," Quinn said right away, "Stan Hamm—he's Ted Connelly, the guy Kit followed into the sauna." He punched on his phone speaker so Kit could hear. "Did you find out who Leetham's in bed with?"

"I was able to check everyone off the list, except Turner. My friend at the cell company can't access records for his phone."

"Why not?"

"When people move here, sometimes they keep their carriers down in the Lower 48 until their contract term ends, and that's the case with Turner's phone. My contacts are all in-state, unfortunately."

Quinn said, "Can you find another way to determine if he got that call?"

"I can try. If I had the hardware, Turner's phone itself, it would help."

"The next time we see him, we'll ask him to hand it over."

"Do that, will you?"

"Thanks for checking in, bud." Quinn signed off.

Kit steered the skiff around a trio of small islands and pointed ahead. SeaLab's dock had come into view. Rocks rose sharply out of the water everywhere and Quinn watched, impressed, as she eased them forward, making constant corrections based on their immediate surroundings, plus what she read on the depth sounder and the illuminated chart.

Suddenly a muscular speedboat roared away from the dock up ahead, cut between the intervening rocks and swooped up to them. *SeaLab Security Patrol* was lettered on its side and it carried two men in camo coats and mirrored sunglasses.

"Help you?" The driver barked this out, his face expressionless behind his shades.

Before Quinn could say anything, Kit put her hand on her hip and announced, "We're investigating the death of Rebecca Zachau and require your absolute cooperation while accessing this facility, having obtained, per request, the appropriate paperwork. Go ahead and escort us in." She waved her hand commandingly at him.

The two men in the patrol boat looked at her, unsure what to say.

The driver cleared his throat. "You need to talk with our boss, Turner Holland. He's in a meeting over on the mainland."

She shook her head emphatically, then put her finger on the wart on her cheek. Quinn realized she was checking to make sure it hadn't moved.

"I understand you have your protocols," Kit told the men sternly, "but I have mine. Your boss's presence isn't required. We are entering SeaLab's facility with—or without—your escort."

The patrolman stared at her. He was going for a hard look, but she just kept glaring at him, chin and bosom thrust out as far as they could go, until uncertainty twisted his mouth.

The second one shifted nervously in his seat.

In an easygoing voice, Quinn said, "This is just one of many stops we need to make on this case. We can be in and out in no time."

Kit growled, "Unless we have trouble obtaining cooperation."

The driver hesitated. Finally he cranked the wheel on his boat, said, "Follow me," and gunned the vessel into a tight turn.

Quinn received a glance from Kit that made him want to laugh and simultaneously clutch his head in worry. Most people in this situation would be a little tense—he was, himself—but her eyes were sparkling with pure enjoyment. *Was she especially pumped today,* he wondered, *or was she like this every day?*

She landed the skiff with casual ease behind the patrol boat and they followed the patrolmen up a path to a large, salmon-colored building. They went past two security men and entered a bright atrium, which reminded Quinn of a roomy botanical garden. As they strode down a wide paved path by a gurgling fountain, birds chirped from all sides.

They passed into a spacious lobby and crossed to the other side where three more security guards stood sentry at a set of steel doors. They were instructed to wait there.

A door snicked open and through it came a bald man with an ape's sloping forehead and squat build—Hamm, a.k.a. Connelly. Kit moved in so tight Hamm had to retreat a half-step to keep from being jabbed by her gigantic breasts. "We're investigating the potentially violent death of Rebecca Zachau, an employee of SeaLab, Inc. And we expect your full cooperation."

Lip curling, Hamm said, "I never heard anything about this."

She drilled Hamm with the same stare she'd laid on the patrol boat driver. Quinn felt a tightening in his testicles. *How does she do that?* Something about that stare, and her jutting front, he guessed.

Hamm turned sideways to her, took out his phone and made a call. Quinn presumed he was calling Turner.

Hamm left a mumbled message, then hung up and turned back to face Kit. "We have a deal with the Nipntuck Police. It's a . . . security . . . uh . . . partnership." He pushed on, "If my boss didn't talk to me, that means NPD didn't talk to him, so uh, you can't go in."

"Anchorage has this case," Kit fired back, "—not NPD. And this is a search warrant, so obviously calling ahead isn't part of the procedure." Without taking her eyes off him, she put her hand out. Quinn gave her the warrant, and she thrust it at Hamm. "If you have any questions, call Anchorage." She stepped around him toward the security door.

He tried to grab her arm, and she wheeled on him. "You are attempting to obstruct justice, Mr. Hamm."

He stared at her, legs spread, jaw thrust forward, his breath rasping in and out noisily.

She nodded at the warrant. "Call the number, pal."

Hamm called the number on the warrant. He argued for few minutes, then angrily hung up.

"She committed suicide," he told Kit sullenly.

"We intend to conduct our business in short order. Stand aside, or you'll have to explain to *your* boss why *my* boss can have this place shut down for the next three months, should he decide your lack of cooperation provides sufficient reason for a more thorough investigation."

Hamm took the heat of her stare for another minute, then turned angrily and went to stand before the retinal scanner. The door clicked open.

Before moving through the door, Kit put her hand to her earpiece and appeared to listen. To Quinn she said quietly, but loud enough, "The rest of the team is almost here. They'll stay outside and look over the grounds."

Hamm nodded at the guards, held up four fingers, and pointed outside. Four men peeled off and went outside.

Quinn suppressed a smile. Now they were down to Hamm, plus one other guard. Damn, she was good.

The room they entered was a circular hub of substantial size, with doors on the outer edge leading to offices, meeting rooms, and storage areas. Workstations filled the center of the room; some were surrounded by cubicle walls, others were open tables. People were everywhere. They hurried along, absorbed looks on their faces, and stood in groups of twos and threes, talking earnestly.

Quinn knew from the building map that Marcus used the office straight across from this entry. As soon as they entered the hub, he split off and walked straight toward Marcus's office. He attracted the fellowship of the second guard, while Hamm stayed behind to shadow Kit.

Quinn reached Marcus's office and said, "Open it."

The guard turned to see what his boss was doing. Kit was in Hamm's face, obviously pressing him with questions. Hamm's arms were crossed, his lips were sealed tight, and he wore a frown on his face as he stared over her head, ignoring her.

Quinn's guard unlocked Marcus's office and stood next to the door, mirroring Hamm's stance, including the frown. Before entering, Quinn gestured up to the security camera mounted in the ceiling corner. "That's not working, is it?"

"What do you mean?" The guard said, "Of course it is."

"I've always thought that would be a pretty boring job, watching TV screens of people working. Gum?"

"No," the guy waved the stick away, but he uncrossed his arms and stuck his fists in his pockets. Rocking back on his heels, he said, "Well yeah, everybody hates that shift because you have to stay in one room, the screen room, instead of moving around. But somebody's gotta do it."

"Yeah, you got a room with a bunch of screens," Quinn said sympathetically, "and not one of them has a football game on it."

The guy snorted, "Yeah, but it's alright to make phone calls and such. As long as we watch the monitors at all times."

Quinn nodded. "And even if you missed something, isn't it being recorded?"

"Yeah, you bet."

Quinn made mental note to ask Elise for last Friday's recording. "Did you work last Friday night?"

"Yeah, why?"

"Anything unusual go on?"

"Same old." The guard shrugged and crossed his arms back across his chest.

Quinn went into the office and looked around. No coat graced the coat rack, and there was no briefcase to be seen. As Elise had predicted, every available surface was covered. A desk and two adjoining chart tables held drawings and notepads thick with scribbles. Stacks of books, flagged with notes, lay around and two filing cabinet drawers were agape. Also as predicted, coffee rings dotted the papers on the desk and drafting tables. The only coffee cup in view, however, was washed and sitting upright in the sink dish drainer. He went to the desk and tapped the mouse. The computer was powered down.

A curse rang out. Through the open door Quinn spied Hamm charging across the room, knocking people out of his way like a crazed quarterback. He reached the guard standing in the doorway of Marcus's office and shouted in the man's face, "You're supposed to be guarding him, shithead!" He shoved the man toward Kit. "Go guard her, I'll take him."

He moved in close, pressing his chest against Quinn's elbow, breathing raggedly. Quinn realized Hamm wasn't winded; he always breathed this way.

"So Hamm," he said, "What's going on

with Marcus? Any theories?"

Hamm just stared at him, his eyes defiant.

One more question, just a little prod, Quinn thought, *to see if I provoke something.* "I can't help wondering if Rebecca's drowning," he watched Hamm's face closely, "is related to Marcus's strange disappearances."

Hamm just remained stony faced and mute. Quinn wanted to probe further and bring up the name Joan, whom Hamm had mentioned in the sauna, but instead, he kept his mouth closed. *Until you know Marcus is safe,* he reminded himself, *step carefully.*

~~~

Right after Hamm charged off to hassle Quinn, a woman approached Kit. "I'm Lou," she said and extended her hand. "I overheard you asking about Rebecca."

Lean and tall, she had a careless haircut and a firm grip. "I was asked to clean out Rebecca's desk, but wasn't sure what to do with her personal things." She held up a tote bag. "Here they are."

Kit took the bag and asked, "Did you know that Turner Holland took Rebecca out to dinner the night she died?"

"He did?" Lou looked confused. "I didn't think she was his type."

"What makes you think she wasn't his type?"

A guard drew up to them, but hearing Kit's question, he rolled his eyes, and stepped back, looking bored. He thought they were just gossiping about men, Kit realized.

"Last week, I was under a desk running wires—I'm in information systems—and I overheard Turner and Mike, this other guy, talking about all the women here, going down the list, saying who's hot; who's not. Mike brought up Rebecca and Turner said she was too smart and had too much personality. It turned him off."

"He said that?"

Lou snorted. "I won't even tell you what he said about *me*. Anyway, Mike says, 'so you like 'em young and dumb' and Turner says 'yeah, why *work* for it?'"

"Hmm," Kit said. "He took Rebecca to Silvers. The best restaurant in town seems a bit much for a guy who doesn't like to work for it—"

Suddenly the air in the room swirled, as

though stirred by something unseen. Kit and Lou looked over and saw a man silhouetted in the door. From the corner of her eye, Kit saw Quinn striding toward her, holding up his phone, saying, "I just heard from Anchorage; we're outta here."

The man at the door surged into the room, throwing his overcoat and briefcase down on a lab stool. He intercepted Quinn, and they squared off, chest to chest. The man said, "What are you doing here?" His voice was low, but it pulsed with anger. "What the hell is your game?"

Kit had no doubt that this was Turner. "Gentlemen," she said loudly, making both men turn to look at her.

Every ounce of her wanted to confront Turner, but Quinn was drilling a look at her that said clearly: *don't do it.* "We're finished here," she said.

She handed Quinn the tote bag of Rebecca's things, then moved her bulk past him toward the door. Over her shoulder, she told Turner, "You can take any complaints you have up with Anchorage—" Suddenly, her foot caught on the rug, and she tripped.

Arms flailing, she toppled, pulling the lab stool holding Turner's things on top of her.

Shocked by the crash, everyone in the room froze.

"I'm okay," she called out irritably. With a loud grunt, she shoved the stool off her and pushed herself up. The sight of her wide bottom made everyone look away.

Quinn reached her side and without exchanging a word, they turned and hustled out the door and through the atrium. They took the path toward their boat, with Hamm and three other guards following close behind. Turner stood at the atrium entrance, watching them go.

On the way back to the skiff, Kit felt increasingly pissed off. If she were taller, she could have faced off with Turner. But no— she was too short to make a convincing cop! She had to turn and run away like a scared little girl. How she hated being this size!

They got to the dock, and were almost to the skiff, when Hamm, following close behind, said the wrong thing to Kit. In a taunting voice, he said, "Hard to believe they let such short, clumsy fucks on the police force."

Kit didn't hear "clumsy" nor did she hear the cuss word. All she heard was his reference to her size, and without thinking, she spun around to say, "Listen up, baldy. You—"

At the word "baldy," Hamm let loose a guttural cry, and a flash of understanding came to Kit just before he punched her. He hated his bony head in the same way she hated being short, but he expressed it more violently.

His fist drove toward her solar plexus, but instead of flesh, he punched her balloons, and she shot backward, banging her head on a dock piling. Before anyone could move, she lost consciousness and slid sideways into the icy blue-green water.

12

Quinn dove after Kit. He reached her and quickly hoisted her limp body up on the dock and launched himself up beside her. He gathered her to his chest and climbed in the skiff, talking to her, feeling for a pulse in her neck, asking her to open her eyes. They fluttered open, and she let out a small moan.

"I hardly touched the bitch," Hamm cried to the other guards. None of them would meet his gaze. One of the guards picked up Rebecca's bag of belongings and set it on the skiff's passenger seat.

Quinn tucked Kit into the most protected corner of the skiff. She was wet and dazed, but conscious. He fired up the engine and pulled sharply away from the dock, but slowed immediately. Rocks were everywhere.

The console chart showed the exact course

they'd traveled to get there, so he steered along the line on the screen, passing between rocks jutting up like teeth on all sides. He called Nate, who said he'd be waiting to help him tie up.

Twenty minutes later he reached the Nipntuck harbor, swung into the slip, threw a line to Nate and scooped Kit up. He intended to drive her straight to the hospital, but through chattering teeth she managed to vow convincingly that she'd never speak to him again if he didn't drop the idea. She asked him to bring her to the *Blue Sea* and he reluctantly complied.

Nate quickly joined him on the *Blue Sea*. He, like Quinn, was trained in rudimentary CPR and without speaking they set about getting Kit warm and dry, while trying to assess whether she'd suffered a concussion. They stripped off her sodden costume, swaddled her in Quinn's warmest sweat suit, and put her on the wide couch in the main cabin. They rubbed her limbs to encourage her circulation. Quinn peered in her eyes and asked her what day it was, what town, and what year.

She answered calmly. Again, Quinn raised the prospect of going to the hospital, and she told him no. When he started to argue she stopped him. "I'm not concussed. I've had several before and I'm sure this isn't one. So I'm warning you: if you try to make me go to the hospital, you'll be sorry."

He shook his head. "You are a stubborn woman."

She nodded. "Yes, I am."

He quickly went to change out of his wet clothes and when he reappeared he checked her pulse again, and found it strong and even.

She asked to use the head, and he helped her to it. It was down some steps and around a corner. He said he'd wait and help her back to bed, but she shooed him away.

He returned to the front lounge Nate asked, "What the hell happened?"

Quinn paced as he talked. "Turner came back before he was supposed to. It looked like we were going to avoid trouble and simply leave, but Kit's fuse proved too short, and Hamm's was even shorter." He related the taunts Kit and Hamm had exchanged and how Hamm, with spooky suddenness, had lost control and punched Kit into the water.

He stopped his pacing and sat down at the table. "I should mention, though, aside from the episode with Hamm, she's unbelievably cool under fire." He told Nate about her bone-chilling stare, her authoritative cop act, and the lines she delivered, like: "I understand you have your protocols, but I have mine."

"Wish I could have seen it," Nate said, wearing a half-smile. Then he gestured toward the cop outfit crumpled in the corner, and his smile faded. "Good thing she had all those balloons surrounding her, or she'd have gone under." His eyes met Quinn's. "We'd have lost her in the current."

Agitated, Quinn rubbed the back of his neck and jumped up to pace again. "I keep thinking about that," he said. "Finding Marcus and catching Rebecca's attacker, those things are important, but keeping Kit safe is the thing that's . . ." he paused.

"Not going to be easy," Nate finished the thought.

~~~

Kit didn't feel terribly bad, but she didn't feel very good either. When she returned to the main cabin, Quinn took her arm to help her back to bed, and wearing a little smile, she let him. He piled blankets all around her and supplied her with three pillows from the berths below, and checked her pulse again.

"I think you're being overprotective," she told him, "but I sort of like it."

"If you still insist on avoiding the hospital, we should call Clara and let her know you're staying here tonight."

She'd left her phone at home, so she used his, which had luckily survived his unexpected dip in the water. Speaking quietly, she told Clara she'd bumped her head a tiny bit, and Quinn and Nate were going to keep an eye on her overnight. Clara asked what happened, and she said she would explain later.

Before relinquishing Quinn's phone, she called Juneau to get an update on Rebecca, and learned she was still unconscious, but holding stable. Then she called her own number. She cycled through her messages and hung up, frustrated that both the phone company and the state troopers had failed to call her back.

After giving Quinn his phone back, she suddenly sat up straighter. "Hey, did you find

Turner's phone?"

The two men gave her blank stares.

She addressed Nate. "You said it would help to have it. As I was leaving, I tripped, and just happened to snag Turner's cell phone. The cop suit has a secret pocket between the boob balloons."

Both men lunged toward the sodden cop suit on the floor. Nate got there first and reached his hand between the two pointy balloons duct-taped together. Nestled in there was a clever plastic pouch holding a cell phone. He pulled it out and exchanged a look with Quinn.

"I'll get right on this," he said, and hustled off to his workstation in the aft lounge.

Quinn said to Kit, "I thought you were just going for comic relief, the way you stuck your backside in our faces."

She grinned, "People were *compelled* to look away, am I right?"

He laughed. "Clever woman."

Suddenly, she asked, "Hey, you got anything to eat around here?"

"You feel like eating?"

"I almost always do."

He told her the yacht's fridge held little in the way of food, but there was chicken soup in the cupboard. She voted for that.

As he heated up the soup, they discussed their trip to the lab. Neither of them felt they'd learned much.

Kit said, "Basically, I got nothing out of Hamm. I asked cop-like questions about where he was late Sunday, early Monday, and what his relationship was with Rebecca. He refused to answer anything. But I did get some interesting insight into Turner's taste in women." She told him about meeting Lou. "Turner's attitude toward Rebecca was that she had too much personality and was too smart. If he likes dum-dums with bland personalities, his dinner invitation to Rebecca strikes me as odd."

He came to the bunk with the steaming bowl of soup, and she moved too quickly to sit up, and her head whirled. She closed her eyes for a second.

"Are you dizzy?"

Just a little, she told him.

"If you want, I'll hold the bowl for you."

She nodded, and he sat down beside her,

cradling the bowl while she wielded the spoon.

It took her about two spoonfuls to realize she was growing warm, and it wasn't the blankets. A keen awareness of Quinn had started washing over her. There was something about the pure solid size of the guy that she liked. It reminded her of something, and after a moment she knew what it was. As a kid, her favorite place to go was up in the branches of a big cottonwood tree. She'd climb up the rope ladder that her brothers had made and then forgotten about, and she'd nestle there, embraced and comforted by the sturdy, waving branches. It always made her feel like she was absorbing the tree's solid strength. Quinn was having that effect on her. She wanted to reach out and close the space between them, to feel his embrace surround her. She wanted to climb *him*.

The thought was funny and unsettling at the same time. Nervously, she dropped the spoon into the bowl and hitched herself up a little straighter.

He waited until she rearranged the pillow behind her back, and then asked, "So is there a boyfriend?"

She couldn't believe it. He was asking her if she was single. *Could the feeling be mutual?* "No boyfriend," she blurted.

"You're kidding." He said it happily.

"What about you?"

"No one." He raised his eyebrows at her. His eyes were smiling.

How good it would feel, she thought, to wrap her arms around his neck. She had never made the first move on a guy before, but there was always a first time. It felt like it could even be seconds away. She clasped her hands primly over her stomach and nodded at the bowl in his hands. "Thanks, I'm done."

He stayed where he was, looking at her. Even though neither of them had moved, she felt like *things* had suddenly begun to move very quickly. Heart things. Male-female electricity. Whatever it was.

She gave him a blushing look. It seemed wrong that she would have these feelings. The attack on Rebecca needed to stay front and center in her mind. A dangerous situation was on hand, and it demanded that she keep her wits.

She cast around for something to say that

would take the charge out of the air, but couldn't think of anything. She was surprised at the feelings Quinn had managed to stir up in her, just by sitting beside her and feeding her soup. Criminy!

Finally, all she could do was stammer, "Uh, I think I'll . . . um . . . go to sleep now."

Quinn's eyes held hers with a look that was intense and unbearably warm. "Are you sure you're feeling okay?"

"Just sleepy," she told him. *Stop pounding*, she ordered her heart.

~~~

Quinn rose and went to put the bowl in the sink. *That heated look she just gave him*. He should have done something—admitted that she intoxicated him, told her how gorgeous she is, or maybe even kissed her right then. He probably should have, gauging from that look. But he wanted to take her on a date first. He didn't want to skip that part. Call him old-fashioned, but he wanted to court this woman, and then kiss her.

Nate stepped into the cabin. Seeing that Kit's eyes were closed, he gestured Quinn over to the table. "Check this out," he said quietly, and held out Turner's phone.

The display held a photo. It was a shot of Georgette, going into a house. Nate tapped the arrow and another picture came up of Georgette's Seville driving away from the same house.

"Okay," said Quinn, "That's Marcus's wife. What about it?"

Nate shrugged. "I thought you'd take one look and shout 'case solved!'"

Quinn figured Nate was playing him, holding out on the real find. "So what about the call history? Did Leetham call this phone?"

"I don't know," Nate scowled. "The phone's locked up with some damn encryption method I've not come across before. The photos were in a phantom file I found only because they were recently sent to a printer. But everything else . . . it's going to take some time."

He drummed his fingers on the table. "Today I tried digging deeper on Turner but found very little—suspiciously little—other than the basics I gave you already. As for Hamm a.k.a Connelly, I found no record of the Ted Connelly who had the six-pack incident. The archives of the newspaper show no trace of that article Kit mentioned, and the police also say they have no record of the arrest. You'd never know Connelly and Hamm were the same guy, unless someone told you. You and I both know it's possible to erase one's real identity, or at least smoke screen it, and that's what this feels like to me, regarding both Turner and Hamm."

Nate stood up. Surprising Quinn with the abrupt shift in subject, he said, "I'd better walk Flotsam again." He grabbed the dog's leash and clipped it on Flotsam's collar. The dog gained his feet, but turned sad eyes up at Nate as if to say, *Please, buddy, take yourself for a walk.*

"I don't think he wants to go out," Quinn said. "You walked him already today?"

"Yeah, a few times."

"How many?"

"Uh, four."

Taking advantage of Nate's split attention, Flotsam laid back down with a relieved look.

Nate really wants to go for a walk, Quinn realized. Maybe it was distress over Kit's run-in with Hamm. Quietly he asked, "What's up?"

Nate glanced over at Kit and saw that her eyes were closed. In a low voice he said, "Walking Flotsam earlier, I saw a woman over on the next float walking her dog. She's got the nicest body I've ever seen. I can't stop thinking about her."

"Ah." Quinn said. The bruises circling Nate's eyes had faded to faint yellow smudges; apparently he was ready to get back in the game.

Nate got a dog treat from the box on the counter. He cajoled Flotsam up, using the treat, but after gobbling it down, the dog laid firmly back down on his blanket.

Quinn laughed and said, "Why don't you just go for a walk without the dog?"

"She won't talk to me, not without the dog. Flotsam's the way, man, into her heart."

"It doesn't sound like it's her heart you're trying to get into."

"Cynic," Nate muttered as he unclipped the leash and hung it back up.

13

～～～～～～～～～～～～～～～～～～～～

Kit's eyes opened to bright sunlight streaming into a very quiet yacht, and the sight of the golden rays made her groan. Nipntuck was getting its first sunny day in weeks, and she was in no condition to enjoy it. She felt like one of those cartoon characters—after they'd been run over by a steamroller and before they peeled themselves up.

The clock by the window read 7:20. She closed her eyes and breathed deep, trying to ignore her splitting headache. Some important idea was skittering around the edge of her brain, but she couldn't seem to coax it forward.

After laying still for fifteen minutes, her sluggish brain finally corralled the thought. At the lab yesterday, Turner's haughty tone had sounded familiar. He had only said a few words, and then she'd taken her spill onto the floor, and Turner's words were directed at Quinn, not her, but he had spoken in a terse, low voice, and that was the type of voice she'd heard in the sauna. It seemed very possible he was the one who had been in that steam room with Hamm. The one who said, "It's been taken care of."

She shivered, despite the mound of blankets covering her. Even if Turner was the person who met with Hamm in that steam room, she still didn't know how any of it fit together. SeaLab and Marcus and Rebecca and Turner and Hamm. And also Leetham, who had sent those men to follow Quinn yesterday. Rebecca had stumbled into the middle of something—that was the only thing Kit knew for sure.

Her mind circled back to Marcus. If he was tied in somehow—and she believed he was—the venerable scientist could be in serious trouble. To say she was going to track down Rebecca's would-be murderer was one thing, but in truth, she needed to stop flailing around and figure out what to do.

She needed an opportunity, a chance to

talk to Turner and hear his voice some more, and to ask some questions. But her approach had to be nonthreatening, because Marcus's safety may be at stake.

It struck her that the chance could come that very night: the Cancer Society was holding their silent auction and dinner benefit. It was a Who's Who sort of occasion, so Turner would certainly be there.

The thought propelled her out of the bunk, an act she instantly regretted. Her headache, which had been a ten on a scale of ten, shot up to fifteen. With a groan, she slumped down at the galley table.

On the table lay a file with her name on it and a note from Quinn: *Here's your copy of the background Nate collected on our key players. He has found a suspicious lack of information on Connelly a.k.a Hamm, and also on Turner.*

Also, here are two photos Nate found on Turner's phone, of Georgette Holland. Nate and I are both wondering what they could mean. Any ideas?

Please rest easy. I'm on a run with Nate, but will be back soon with pastries and coffee.

She studied the photos of Georgette, but drew a blank. She didn't even open the file with the information Nate had provided. She felt groggy, and not up for reading any of it yet.

She was staring into space, rubbing her temples, when she realized she was staring at the tote bag Lou had given her of Rebecca's belongings. It was on the floor by the door.

She picked it up and tipped its contents onto the table: peppermint lip gloss, a wad of single dollar bills, lemon cough drops, pictures of Flotsam, and Rebecca's soft yellow sweater. She picked the sweater up. It bore a hint of the papaya-scented body soap Rebecca favored. *Oh Rebecca*, she thought, pressing it to her face.

Something crinkled in the fabric of the sweater and she flipped it around to find a zippered pocket. There was a letter inside the pocket, from Rebecca's mom. It had been postmarked only the week before.

She tugged Bev's flowered stationery out of its envelope and began reading.

Hi, Honey. Having our phone conversation cut short was annoying! It made me miss you so, so much!

I hate how unreliable the phones are here, but I guess the isolation is also what makes this place interesting.

Where else would you get 90 percent of the population joining the volunteer fire department—even the Russian sailors who rowed into the harbor a few weeks ago, their mast snapped by a storm, have joined. Our meetings are better attended than anything else we have going on, with a potluck spread to die for.

You asked how the diet's going. Crummy, to be honest. I'm trying to eat more fish, but I just don't like the stuff. Sam brings me one now and again, which is nice. You remember my redneck friend Sam? Well, he's sort of keeping company with me these days, off and on. (Off when he's drinking; on when he isn't.)

You were telling me about your handsome friend at work when we got cut off. Some years ago, there was a boy living here named Turner, but I'm sure he's not the same one. He wasn't handsome. He had orange and green spiked hair and was a mess of a person.

Well, I imagine we'll talk before this letter gets to you—they're saying we'll have our phones back any minute, but then again, they always say that.

You know it already, but I love you very, very much.

xxxxxxxoooo, your mom

Kit covered her face. It was so obvious where Rebecca got her gushy style. She would never tease her about it again. She blinked back tears, and read the postscript:

PS: It's probably crazy to even think it, but here's a photo of Turner. I took it on his birthday, August 18, six years ago, now. (Lord, how time flies!) If it's the same boy, I need to know right away.

Love you honey

Kit looked in the envelope, in the sweater's other pocket, and checked the bottom of the tote bag but found no photo. Her first reaction was that it wasn't the same Turner. How could

Rebecca's mom, all the way out in Saluda, know Turner Holland? That would be too far-out. But then again, unlikely connections between people happened all the time in Alaska. Some peculiar force field seemed to exist throughout the state, linking people together despite enormous physical distances. Alaska was a big state that functioned like a small town, people were fond of saying.

She picked up the letter again and skimmed it. It was a heck of a leap, though. Orange and green spiked hair just didn't go with the man she'd seen at the lab yesterday. Nor did "mess of a person." Not at all. He was as slick as they come. But then Kit thought about Connelly and how he changed his name to Hamm. *Appearances, like names, are malleable* she reminded herself. *Both can be changed.*

The thought made her palms itch. She needed to find that photo—it was probably somewhere over on Rebecca's boat.

She stood up to look for something else to wear. Quinn's running suit, though warm, was so gigantic she couldn't take three steps without floundering. The cop suit, crumpled in the corner, was a damp, salt-stained mess, so that wasn't an option. She picked up a man's bulky sweater draped over the back of a chair. She grew up with a bunch of brothers so the first thing she did was give it a cautious sniff. But it smelled wonderful, like fresh rain and something else, dark chocolate perhaps. *Quinn's,* she couldn't help thinking.

Shrugging off his oversized sweats, she pulled on the sweater's comforting weight. It went to her knees, which allowed her to skip looking for pants. The soggy leather cop boots were unpleasantly clammy on her bare feet, but they would get her home. On the bottom of Quinn's note, she wrote: *"Thank you for the breakfast offer, but had to get going. Borrowed a sweater to wear home. Pls. call me."*

She picked up the file of information that Quinn had left for her and stepped out on deck. Wincing at the bright sunshine, she walked slowly over to Rebecca's boat.

First, she looked at the photos Rebecca had tacked up over her bed, to make sure none had been added. There was a picture of Rebecca, a proprietary arm slung around the rotting mast of the *Valiant.* And a recent shot of Kit and Rebecca on the Mt. Edge trail, stuffing salmonberries in their mouths. And there were several shots of Rebecca's mom, Bev. Her smile was so like Rebecca's, Kit knew who it was without having to ask. But no shots of a wild-haired man. She searched all around the boat, hoping to turn up the photo, but didn't find it.

Giving up, she made her way home slowly. Clara wasn't there but had left ginger scones arranged in a heart on the cooling rack. Raising one to her mouth, Kit absentmindedly rearranged the remaining scones into a gap-toothed smile. She checked messages and had none, so she called the phone company. She kept punching zero. After suffering multiple rounds of computerized prompts, she finally got a person, who gave her to another person, who put her on hold for eight minutes until finally, a gruff male voice came on.

She asked about the interrupted phone service in Saluda.

"Yeah, long distance is out. Lost the signal."

"For the entire town?"

"Yeah," he said. "All twenty-three phones."

"I don't suppose there's any cell phone

service out there?"

"No towers reach."

"Internet?"

"Nope."

"What happened to the signal?"

She heard him take a gulp of something, perhaps his day's first cup of coffee. Whatever it was, it gave him the ability to speak in full sentences. "There's a polar bear hanging around causing problems."

She waited.

"Rubbing his back on the microwave tower and biting the tower's stay wires. Sixty knot winds screaming up there right now. Either the bear or the wind, or both combined, moved the tower off position."

"Oh," she said.

"Nobody can get close enough to work on the tower, and nobody's been able to get authorization to shoot the bear. They're protected and all that. Our new guy up there doesn't know enough to look the other way while one of the locals shoots the damn—" he fell silent for a second. "Uh, so . . . to sum it up, we're pretty much on the bear's schedule."

She thanked him for the information, then she went to take a shower to scrub the sea salt off. Afterward, still headachy, she curled up on the couch with another scone, and read the background information Quinn had provided.

Right away she noticed that Turner's birthday in the file, September 12, did not match the one Rebecca's mother had mentioned in her letter, August 18. She read on. Turner got his pre-law degree from a Hawaiian university and his law degree from UCLA. His transcripts were included, and his grades were excellent. Nate had written in his summary that there was no solid information available before Turner hit his mid-twenties—not one address, nor any record of employment or purchases with credit cards, nothing.

There was also a copy of the article that had run in the *Nipntuck News* about how Turner— his last name used to be Davis—had arrived in Nipntuck, surprising Marcus with the news that he was a father.

Finding that she had reread the same sentence several times without comprehension, she closed the file. It was hard to concentrate.

One reason was the thudding behind her eyes. But also, being on Rebecca's boat had made her heart ache. She wanted to go to Juneau, to see her.

Frustrated, she went and got a third scone and ate the thing without really tasting it. She usually adored her hometown, but not now. Leaving the island wasn't easy or cheap under normal circumstances, but with the ferry cancelled for the week, the most expensive option—flying—was her only option.

It was then that she remembered the credit card Jean-Philippe had dropped into her purse. She grabbed up her phone and rang his desk at work.

"You are in Seattle?" he asked, his voice hushed. "Please say yes."

"No, I'm at home."

"Oh," he said unhappily.

"I might need to go to Juneau, though."

"Yes!" he cried. "I made you an authorized user on the credit card, so please! Go!"

"Right." She hung up before he could ask how long she'd be gone. He wouldn't rejoice quite so much if he found out she planned to return later that day.

She was able to secure a seat on the jet but had to hurry to get to the airport. She jotted a note to Clara and fifteen minutes later was jumping into Buddy's cab.

Buddy pretty much had the taxicab market cornered on the island. A couple of other people ran cabs, but they weren't motivated, and that made them undependable. With Buddy, you could count on him being there, as much as you could count on being overcharged. She just smiled and handed him the credit card.

~~~

Quinn returned from his run, saw Kit's note and called her. She was about to board a plane to go see Rebecca. He promised to call the security guard who was posted at the hospital and let him know she was coming. "When's your flight back? I'll pick you up."

"I wish you could, but I scheduled a cab ride both ways, with Buddy. I don't dare cancel."

Quinn, puzzled, said, "Why don't you dare cancel?"

"Nobody cancels on Buddy. If you're a guy,

he'll track you down, walk right up and punch you—smack, down you go. Old, young, it doesn't matter. And if you're a woman, it's worse."

"Worse how?"

"He starts rumors. The last woman who cancelled on him had to leave town. I'm sure he made up what she was doing with that schnauzer. But still, I couldn't even look at her after that."

"This town," he said, laughing.

"I'll call you as soon as I get back."

Quinn wanted to confer with Elise, and realized he could still catch her at the mall if he hurried. And the timing would be good, since it would be toward the end of her walk.

He found her there, and when he caught up with her, she gave him an immediate apology for letting Turner surprise him at the lab the previous afternoon. "We've only had the whirlybird since June and I completely forgot to figure that in. He left our meeting and flew back to the island instead of boating over."

"He mentioned to you that we tangled?"

"Oh, I caught an earful about it. He can't

understand why you are showing so much interest in Rebecca, and is convinced you're imagining a crime where there isn't one. He said you hired somebody to wear a cop uniform to help you gain access? Actually, he said 'you hired some clown.' Is that true?"

He smiled. Turner wouldn't be calling Kit a clown if he realized that she'd lifted his cell phone.

"I can tell from your expression that it's true," Elise said. "So what's the report? Did you find anything of interest?"

"I took a look around Marcus's office and found everything in turmoil, as you predicted. No briefcase, no overcoat, so Marcus took those with him. Coffee rings everywhere, too, like you said. Although I did notice his coffee cup was washed and in the dish drainer."

"Well, he certainly didn't do that."

"A yellow coffee cup?"

"That's his. I've never known him to wash it. He just dumps out the old coffee and pours in new. It's disgusting." She shook her head. "Housekeeping probably had to take a pressure washer to the thing."

Quinn, determined not to let speedwalking

get the better of him two days in a row, was observing her technique, and was doing his best to copy it, when she said in a clipped voice, "Quinn, I know you went to see Leetham yesterday. Why would you neglect to tell me about that? I told you to keep me informed of your actions."

"How did you know I went to ESI?"

Her eyes locked onto his. "I asked a friend of mine to keep an eye on you."

"You had me followed?" Silently, he chided himself for not noticing.

"The memo from Marcus tells me that you've been hired, but for all I know, you approached him and not the other way around. It's entirely possible you have your own agenda." Her voice carried an edge. "So tell me Quinn, what's going on?"

He was amused by their mutual wariness. Before trusting her, he had waited until Nate confirmed her cell number wasn't the one Leetham called. And now here she was, looking at him with distrust in her eyes.

He filled her in on his encounter with Leetham and explained why he'd waited to tell her.

Accepting his explanation, she asked, "Did you find out who Leetham called?"

"We eliminated every number on your contact list," he continued, "except for Turner's—it's taking longer because his phone is ultra-secure."

"That's not surprising. He's like his father that way."

Thinking about the scant information Nate had found on Turner, Quinn asked, "When he showed up out of the blue, did Marcus confirm Turner was actually his son?"

She nodded. "If he'd come here wanting anything, money, for example, from Marcus, I imagine there would have been a DNA test immediately. But for someone so young, Turner is very independent-minded, and he's astonishingly wealthy. It was obvious he came here only to introduce himself, and to give a letter to Marcus from his birth mother."

"What did the letter say?"

"Turner's mother wanted to apologize to Marcus for leaving, and not telling him she was pregnant."

"The letter was authentic?"

"Marcus has no doubt about it. Oh, and

Marcus told me Turner has a way of tilting his head when he's listening, a very distinctive gesture, and very much like Polly Lynn, his mother."

"So Turner helped put his father back in touch with Polly Lynn after all these years?"

"Well, that's the sad part. Apparently Turner found Polly Lynn in some California backwater, and she was in rough shape—cirrhosis, sadly. They didn't have much time together. It was after she died that Turner came to meet Marcus and deliver the letter."

"What was Georgette's reaction to Turner's arrival on the scene?"

"I guess she didn't have any particular problem with it."

"Do she and Turner get along?"

"As much as anyone can get along with—" she stopped, then added quietly, "her."

Nodding, he said, "Her behavior toward me was . . . uneven. First, she acted blasé about the disappearance of her husband. Then she begged me to look for him. Next, she acted furious and told me I'm fired. Is this what you'd consider normal for her?"

"She . . . likes to be contrary."

"As a matter of fact," he said, "It was after I mentioned you and Turner had declined my help, that she hired me. She'd do that just to be contrary?"

She gave another shrug. "Georgette has . . . her own way of being."

"Okay, let's say she hired me to be contrary. But why did she suddenly get angry and fire me? Turner had apparently been out to see her. What the hell did he say to make her so angry at me?"

"I'm not sure. But she's the one who originally told you that Marcus was missing, right?"

He nodded.

"Maybe Turner went there to press her to keep things quiet. Maybe she was angry at Turner, but took it out on you."

It's possible, he thought. "I happened across some photos of Georgette—shots of her coming and going from a house. Do you know anything about . . ."

She shook her head.

He started to inquire about the relationship between Marcus and Georgette, but paused as Elise slowed down to pat an elderly man on the shoulder as she went by. The man beamed at her and called out hello.

Quinn waited until they couldn't be heard, then said, "So Marcus and Georgette, what's the deal—"

She stopped, catching him by surprise. "Juice?" she asked.

He was more than happy to stop speed walking, he told her.

She touched his arm. "This way."

The stores in the mall had just begun to lift their gates and admit customers. She led him past the fountain over to the corner of the mall where they found an Orange Julius.

"I haven't had an Orange Julius since I was a teen," he said. "I forgot how much I like them."

"Mmm," she agreed, sipping on hers.

He was aware that she'd interrupted him twice as he tried to inquire about the relationship between Georgette and Marcus. Was her timing just a coincidence? "So Georgette and Marcus. What's their story?"

She sighed, wearing an uncomfortable look.

Not a coincidence.

Finally she said, "Georgette and I do not . . .

get along. In fact, we do everything possible to avoid speaking to one another. So I'm not the best person to ask."

When he realized that was all she had to say, Quinn put down his drink. "Elise, you have exquisite manners. I understand that a conversation like this goes against your nature, but from the outside I might see things you're too close to see."

When she still didn't speak, he prompted her. "It appears that they're not even *in* a marriage, they lead such separate lives. Is there some bond I'm not seeing that keeps them together?"

Her expression was serious and sad. In a low voice she said, "It goes against that man's nature to break a promise, and marriage is a promise. He'd agree to a divorce if she wanted it, but she doesn't. She's perfectly happy, being unhappy."

Suddenly it dawned on him that there could be another reason, aside from her good manners, that made her reluctant to talk about Marcus's rocky marriage. He drew in a breath. "Of course, you'd be right to tell me to mind my own business," he shifted on the hard plastic stool, "but are you and Marcus . . ."

From her amused expression, he knew he was going down the wrong track before she even spoke. "At least you have the decency to ask," she said. "Everyone else just looks at my salary and assumes we're fooling around, never mind the work I do." She eyed him for a moment. "Marcus and I have been dear friends for a long, long time."

He nodded.

"And considering the vision we share, not to mention a shameful passion for eating Häagen-Dazs and telling dumb jokes after work, you can bet the temptation exists. But we've never stepped over that line." She sipped her drink, and giving him a half-smile, added wryly, "And it isn't because I'm the principled one, either."

The more he talked to her, the more Quinn liked this woman, and the more he wanted to find Marcus.

~~~

At the same time Quinn was meeting with Elise, and Kit was on her way to Juneau, Nate was trying to remain calm while taking repeated punches to his ribs.

He had been sitting at the table, chanting "come on, baby, come on," hoping the password-guessing software he wrote during the night would do the trick on Turner's stubborn phone, when three fat-fisted bozos stormed onto the yacht. He only had time to stand up before two guys were holding him for the third to use as a punching bag. Hamm was the one hitting him—Nate knew from the photo he'd found for Quinn and Kit. While Hamm let fly with his fists, he told Nate to deliver a message to Quinn: go back to Fairbanks or more people would get hurt.

Hamm signaled for the two goons to release him. He sagged down against the table while they got busy tossing his and Quinn's belongings off the yacht, sending half of it into the water.

Nate wasn't half as hurt as he appeared, and when he saw his chance to get a shot back at Hamm, he took it, and the impact made Hamm reel back in pain. The other two guys pounced on him, and threw him off the boat onto the dock.

Then Nate heard a surprised yelp, and Hamm stepped out on deck, dangling Flotsam by his back legs. Swinging his arm in an arc, he hurled the dog off the boat.

Nate managed to catch the pinwheeling dog, and noticed that Flotsam's body felt rigid against his chest. *Damn, he's injured*, he thought, and set him down on the dock. The thick-muscled dog remained stock still, legs spread wide, staring hard at the yacht with a peculiar look in his black, runny eyes. Nate realized it wasn't pain that Flotsam felt. It was rage.

Using his sleeve to wipe the blood dripping from his nose, he limped around and picked up what hadn't floated away or sunk, and then he got almost as mad as Flotsam. Not only did he get beat up and lose his computer, but most of what got flung into the water was his stuff. Quinn's duffel bag had landed on the dock.

He stashed everything on Rebecca's boat, including the still-furious dog, and then laid down on the bunk, arms folded under his head. Turner's phone was history—he'd watched it go hurtling into the salt water. Countless hours spent, with nothing to show for it. He was pissed. Not to mention computerless, homeless, and still bleeding from the nose. He shut his eyes. At least the password program he'd written was safe, stored on a flashdrive that was tucked in his pocket.

Though Turner's phone was now at the bottom of the harbor, its secrets undiscovered, it had prompted him to write that password-guessing software. And now that the phone no longer had his attention, something even more interesting beckoned. Why not take another look at SeaLab's ultra tight network? The brilliant software he'd authored, nestled in his pocket on that mini-drive, could be just the key he needed to break in.

14

As soon as Kit reached the Juneau hospital, the doctor initiated a brief meeting in which he confirmed what she already knew: it was a wait-and-see situation. Then he walked her to Rebecca's room, introduced her to the burly security guard by the door, and with a nod and a kind smile, left her.

Kit had tried to prepare herself, had tried to imagine what Rebecca would look like, unconscious and confined to her hospital bed, but when she saw her it didn't seem possible that this was even the same person. The Rebecca that Kit knew moved through the world with vitality, radiating so much contagious glee that people said yes before they even knew what the adventure was. The person in the hospital bed looked small as a child, and was as still as a stone.

The pressure in Kit's chest felt unbearable. She was grateful Rebecca was alive, but the truth was impossible to ignore—she may not regain consciousness or, if she did, she may never be herself again.

She sat down and placed her hand on Rebecca's, finding it warm and dry. Her fingers automatically moved to find a pulse, and the steady rhythm had a bracing effect on her. She studied Rebecca's face and found it composed. Slight movements under her lowered eyelids made it seem as if she was dreaming.

"Hi honey," she said hoarsely.

She thought she felt Rebecca's pulse strengthen very slightly, but it was hard to tell.

"I'm here with you. I know you can hear me." Though her eyes were brimming with tears, she spoke in a calm, clear voice. "I wish we could talk." The pulse did feel stronger, but Kit realized she might be feeling her own heartbeat in her fingertips, matching Rebecca's rhythm.

"I wish . . ." she paused. She wished with all her heart that Rebecca could tell her what had happened. But she also wished to steer clear of heavy words. "I wish . . ." she said, "that we were sitting at the Eat-n-Git." She settled in her chair, getting more comfortable. "You would get the chili. Because you always do. And I would order the bread pudding, extra cream." She started out speaking slowly, but then the words began to come easier. "I'd order that to console myself, because my nasty landlord raised my rent. While we ate, we could brainstorm all the ways he might suffer as a result of his own rotten karma. Maybe an encounter with fire ants, or perpetual car trouble, or having grown children who refuse to move out of his house . . ."

Kit chatted on like this. She told Rebecca about Big Pat's halibut and other tidbits of news that came to mind. Eventually, she worked her way around to telling Rebecca she was doing her best to find out what had happened. She promised that she wouldn't give up until she knew Rebecca was safe.

It seemed unnecessary to say anything else because it seemed as though Rebecca already knew what Kit wanted to say, and much more. Feeling all talked out, she sat quietly. A nurse stepped in to look at something on Rebecca's chart. She smiled at Kit, but didn't speak before she bustled off again.

Kit looked at her watch and discovered it was almost time to catch her return flight. She didn't feel quite so suffocated by grief as she did when she first walked into the room, but still, her throat tightened at the thought of leaving Rebecca alone.

Her fingers found Rebecca's pulse once again, and she bowed her head. She knew the machines humming around this bed were all doing their specific, life-saving tasks, just as the hospital staff and the security guy outside the room were doing their particular jobs. In the meantime, Rebecca had her assignment— fighting her way back. And Kit had hers— tracking down the truth.

She kissed Rebecca's brow, telling her quietly that she was loved and was not alone.

While waiting to board her flight back to Nipntuck, she finally heard back from the trooper's office up in Nome. The trooper apologized for the delay in returning the call and asked her what she needed.

She asked his help conveying a message to Bev Watterson, in Saluda, that her daughter

Rebecca had been hospitalized in Juneau and was in serious condition. She gave the trooper the hospital's number, plus her own, and an urgent request that Bev call her, day or night, as soon as she reached a working phone.

The trooper said shortwave radio should do the trick, or if not he'd figure something out. Then Kit realized she shouldn't wait until Bev got to a working phone to find out what she knew about Turner. "When you reach her on the radio, can you call me back and set up some kind of relay? So she and I can talk with your help?"

He said he'd arrange it, and they hung up.

On the flight home, she pondered what to do about Turner. The auction benefit was that night. It would be her chance to encounter him, but she wanted it to be more than a passing chance.

Just as the jet landed, she got an idea. Tickets to the event were sold in groups of four, and each party had its own table. Marcus was missing, so there was probably a spare seat at SeaLab's table, where Turner would be sitting.

One of the event's organizers had been

a crew member with Kit years before on a fishing boat. His back had gone out and she'd pulled double duty, no complaints. She called him to say she needed a favor, and explained she needed him to escort her to Turner's table, pretend that there'd been a mix-up with her seating arrangement, and ask if the SeaLab party would be kind enough to include her. He said no problem.

In Nipntuck, people rescued one another all the time, whether acquainted or not, so the ruse would probably work. And that way, she'd spend the entire evening with Turner.

Buddy swung onto her street. When Kit saw the blue BMW parked in front of the house her heart did a little dance under her ribs. A month ago, she wouldn't have dissected the feeling, but given her recent romantic train-wreck involving Jean-Philippe, after the cab left, she paused before going inside the house, and forced herself to think rationally about the impact Quinn was having on her.

Living in Nipntuck all these years, it was easy to gather intelligence on any local guy who caught her eye, but what invariably happened was that she'd find out too much, and her romantic leanings would straighten right up.

Jean-Philippe had lacked any history here, and his newcomer status created a sort of vacuum that made it possible for her to find him attractive. Thinking about how that turned out, she shuddered. Not knowing someone could be more thrilling than actually knowing them. She understood that now.

So her attraction to Quinn . . . how much of it was because he wasn't a local? She had no idea. She only knew that she found him dizzily, knee-knockingly attractive. But she was determined to avoid making another mistake like the one she'd made with Jean-Philippe.

But, she realized, there was another way to look at it. Because Quinn was only visiting, if she made a mistake with him it wouldn't be in her face as it was with Jean-Philippe.

But on the *other* hand, what if she really fell for Quinn? He didn't live here! Give her heart to a man just to have him break it when he left? That was a problem she sure didn't need.

All this rational thinking seemed to confuse her more, rather than help. It was like trying to wrestle down an octopus. She was eager to see him, that much she knew for sure. With a smile, she decided that was enough, for now,.

As she went inside the house, she heard Quinn in the kitchen, asking Clara what kind of therapy she did. *Maybe charming Quinn can extract the information from her*, she thought. But Clara just laughed airily and said, "Oh, I do consultations."

Kit joined them and Clara, giving her a hug, said, "I got your note. You saw Rebecca . . . ?"

The image of Rebecca, so diminished in that hospital bed, made Kit sit down and take a deep breath. In a low voice she said, "You know how she never, ever stops moving? I've never seen anyone laying so still." Clara's eyes filled with tears. "But . . ." Kit said, "she's going to be alright. Something in me knows it."

Quinn asked, "Has phone service been restored? Is her mother en route?"

"The phones are still out, but the troopers up north are going to arrange a radio relay." She told them about the polar bear and then a knock on the door announced the arrival of Clara's next client.

Clara left the room, and that was when Kit spied a wicker picnic basket and folded blanket resting on a chair beside Quinn.

"What's this?" she peeked inside.

"It's two things: a reward for getting us onto SeaLab island yesterday, and a bribe."

"Bribe for what?"

"I'll explain outside." He rose and led her out the back door. Thanks to the sunny weather, he had on just a thin T-shirt. Walking behind him, Kit's eyes drank in the sight of his back, shoulders and arms: smooth, undeniably gigantic, and tanned by the Interior sun.

He spread the blanket under the old twisty mountain ash tree. She arranged herself comfortably and he settled onto the blanket next to her.

"Hungry?"

"Not yet. I had peanuts on the plane. And three scones for breakfast. Bribe for what?"

"We can eat in a little while, then."

Instead of satisfying her curiosity, he leaned over and picked up a twig. The twig had what appeared to be a tiny wooden cup stuck to it.

"Bird's nest fungus," she murmured. "You have it up in Fairbanks?"

"Not that I've seen."

She reached over and dipped her pinky in the tiny hollow—the tip of her finger fit exactly. "Sometimes you find them with their spores sitting in the bottom, looking just like miniature bird's eggs. They're really splash cups, so when a raindrop hits one, the walls are shaped specially so that the little eggs go flying."

He was studying it now with a closer eye, and she considered telling him that old-timers warned if you found one in August, especially on a *sunny day* in August, you needed to dance the twig in counterclockwise circles over your head and say a certain rhyme to make bad luck stay away.

She'd be making it up, of course, just to tease him. In her family, teasing like this was a form of affection, but, knowing that not everybody was raised to think so, she resisted the temptation.

Quinn set the twig down and leaned back. Crossing his long legs in front of him, he leaned back on his elbows, studying her.

She found herself smiling at him, not a thought in her head, except how good-looking he was. Then she remembered the letter she'd found in Rebecca's sweater pocket. She pulled it out. "I found this in Rebecca's sweater pocket."

While he read it, she watched the ravens collecting and clucking in a nearby spruce tree. Ravens had uncanny memories, and Kit believed at some point in ancient history, a raven must have scored some food from a picnic basket and told his buddies about it, and they told their raven babies, and it became one of those things ravens just . . . knew. So now the shiny black birds were assembling as if they had been expressly invited to the picnic.

Quinn put the letter down and asked, "No photo?"

She shook her head and asked, "Did Marcus confirm that Turner is his son?"

Quinn said he'd asked Elise the same thing that morning. "Apparently Turner came to Nipntuck bearing a letter from his mother, which appeared authentic, identifying Marcus as his father, but no DNA test has been done."

She nodded and said, "As soon as the troopers put me in touch with Bev, I'll ask her what she knows about him. Meanwhile, I'll cozy up to Turner and make some inquiries."

"Kit." Quinn's voice was tight. "I want you to keep your distance from Turner." He gave the splash cup one last look, then tossed the twig at a raven that was preening and squawking hoarsely. "This picnic is to thank you for yesterday, but it's part of a plea."

Ah, Kit thought, *we're getting to the bribe part.*

He continued. "I want you to let me take it from here. I don't want to worry about your safety. Yesterday at the lab we saw Hamm's violent temper. And considering what happened this morning . . ."

"This morning?"

"I was gone, meeting with Elise. Three goons stormed the boat and roughed up Nate. They wanted him to give me a message: if I go away, no one else gets hurt."

"They beat up Nate!?"

"He's alright. But he does have two black eyes again. And a purple nose."

"Oh no," Kit said, agitated. "You should have brought him over here. Clara makes this special cottonwood balm. You wouldn't believe how soothing it is."

"Oh yes," he replied, "I would." He gave her a smile, and then his expression changed back to worry. "So the message, loud and clear, is to back off, and you're talking about doing the opposite—cozying up to Turner."

"How do we know Turner ordered the attack on Nate? You tangled with Leetham as well." She leaned forward. "Did Nate describe the guys? Were they the ones who followed you when you left ESI?"

"He did describe them. Hamm was one of them."

Kit said. "What about the other two?"

"They weren't the same bozos who followed me, but they were cut from the same mold."

"So Hamm could be answering to Leetham," she said.

He was looking closely at her. "But Kit, Turner took Rebecca out to the Silver on Sunday night, remember?"

She remembered, alright.

Quinn, seeing that his words had the opposite effect he'd intended, shook his head.

"Please. I'm asking you to reconsider. Don't try getting close to Turner."

"I'll consider it."

"You'll consider reconsidering." He didn't look happy.

"Can we eat?" She clasped her hands pleadingly at him, going for cute. He handed her a paper plate, but the look on his face told her he wasn't finished with the topic. She spooned a glob of tortellini salad onto her plate and reached for a chicken leg.

"Kit, look, you must feel it too—there's something twisted going on here."

He was right; she did feel it. Returning his sober look, she said, "Quinn, Rebecca is my friend. I'm extremely loyal to my friends. But on top of that, if I don't do something to counter this horrible act, I'll walk around feeling afraid, maybe for the rest of my life. And last but not least, this is what I do for work—I smell a bad smell and try to figure out what's rotten. I won't be able to breathe again until I do."

His forehead was etched with worry lines.

"Here's the thing," she said. "Everyone has their panties in a bunch over you.

Nobody's worried about me. Why not give the impression that you're leaving? Just do it for one day. Then everybody relaxes, and maybe I can find out something useful."

He was shaking his head.

"Nate didn't find any suspicious background on Turner," she said, "right? At least, I didn't see any in the file I read."

"What Nate found was suspiciously little on the man," he corrected.

"All the more reason for me to follow up," she argued, "and ask Turner a few friendly questions!"

She could feel him radiating disagreement, so she played her trump card.

"You know . . . it's possible, just by being here with me right now, you could be putting me in danger."

To allow time for this to sink in, she peeked in a white paper sack, and her heart leapt. He'd brought chocolates. She ate a dark chocolate chunk with pecans followed by a spoonful of coleslaw. It turned out to be a great combination. She followed up with another chocolate, one with a gooey caramel middle, licked her fingers, and said,

"I'd probably be safer if you gave everyone the impression that you were going back to Fairbanks."

After a long look, he finally said, "Now would be a good time to tell me that you're some sort of karate expert."

She took this as a sign he might be seeing things her way. "I don't know karate, but I am very good at dodging."

"Dodging?"

"I grew up with seven devilish brothers. A childhood spent trying to avoid getting caught will develop quick reflexes in a person." She was smiling, but her smile faded. "Especially since once a person gets their hands on me, it's . . ." She hesitated, and then plunged ahead with the truth. "Once I'm caught I fall into a panic, and become sort of . . . paralyzed."

She watched the ravens in the branches above. They were personable birds, posturing and tilting their heads as if listening and then sending down clucking noises and squawks like they were contributing their comments. "You probably don't know what it's like to be overpowered, but it's horrible."

"I know what it's like to be overpowered,"

he said, smiling, "by a certain pair of blue eyes."

She flashed him a look, and then dropped her gaze. She had kept her mind pretty well on track until this moment.

He said, "I'd like to propose something."

Yes, she thought. *The answer is a definite yes.*

"After lunch," he said, "can we go over some self-defense basics? It would make me feel better, anyway."

"Sure," she said, "if you agree to lay low. Just for a day. One measly little day."

He wore a grumpy look. "I'll think about it," he said.

They fell into a silence, nibbling a bit here and there until neither of them moved for a while. Eventually Kit stirred, stretched, and began stacking the empty containers. She stood up and brushed crumbs off her jeans, causing four ravens to hop down from their overhead perch. They stood nearby, eager to begin their crumb buffet.

Quinn stood as well, and shook the blanket, which sent the ravens hopping away, but not too far. "There are two questions I hope you can answer," he said. "Nate wants to take temporary refuge on Rebecca's boat. The harbormaster said moorage and electric are due next week. Nate'll pay that, and in the meantime he'll watch the dog and make sure the bilge pump keeps working."

"I think that would be a big help," Kit watched him fold the blanket carefully. "What's the other question?"

"Clara mentioned there's a room for rent in your house. I'd like to rent it."

Kit hadn't seen this coming.

"For a month, maybe longer," he added.

"Do you think it'll take that long to find Marcus?"

"Nipntuck is starting to have . . . other attractions for me." He wore that warm smile.

Her heart started doing some crazy gymnastics at the implications, but she hesitated, wanting to think about it before telling him yes. *She wanted to think about it before telling him yes?* That lacked logic. Suddenly she could picture Rebecca, hooting with laughter and saying: *logic-smogic! Just say yes!*

She decided to buy herself a little time. "Do you still want to go over some self-defense moves?"

His gaze lingered on her face. "I'm trying to figure out if that's a yes," he said.

Demurely, she said, "Maybe."

Stepping closer he took her hand and opened it flat, laying it on top of his. "This *L* . . ." He ran his finger along the curve that ran from her index finger to her thumb. "You can jab it into an assailant's larynx, and buy yourself a split second." His finger, tracing her skin lightly, made her bare arms break out in goose bumps. She forced herself to focus on what he said next. "I doubt this is news to you. But necks are big, relative to this striking surface." He was referring to her small hand. "So precision is important."

He lifted the web of her hand against her own windpipe. "Right here," he pressed it against a spot low on her throat, "where your trachea meets your larynx. This is the spot you need to know about."

The immediate gagging sensation Kit felt was weirdly reassuring. *It doesn't even take that much pressure*, she thought, *if you know the right place.*

He released her hand and said, "See if you can find it on me."

He raised his chin and she moved her hand against his throat. "Up a little higher," he said.

He's so serious and businesslike, Kit thought. *So sexy!*

"Good," he said briskly. Then he moved behind her so that they were both facing the same direction, looking at Mt. Edge. His hands went to her upper arms, and he gripped her firmly, leaving a couple of feet of space between them.

"If someone grabs you from behind, you have a couple of options. Try to pull away."

Instead of pulling away, she took a step backward. She couldn't see his expression, but felt something like surprise coming down his arms into her shoulders.

"Like that," he said quietly, "but more."

She took one more step backward he was drawing his arms around her, holding her to him. His chest was hot against her back. She closed her eyes and leaned back against him. They stayed still for a long moment, breathing together. To Kit, it felt exquisite. Then slowly, he eased her around to face him, and she was facing him, cradled in his arms, he leaned down and brushed her lips with his.

It was only a fleeting kiss, but the way his mouth felt on hers gave Kit a sense of vertigo, like she'd experienced a tremor that foretold an earthquake. A bolt of heat flared in her, making her want ten, then fifty more kisses. Instead, she buried her face against his chest, overwhelmed, thinking dizzily, *I can't. I go there. Not right now.*

~~~

Quinn had an unusually powerful reaction to the touch of Kit's lips. He always enjoyed the subtle and varied sensations of a first kiss, that heightening of awareness and desire. But when her lips met his everything in him wanted to pick her up and undress them both, while running with her somewhere, anywhere, as long as it was private. He understood that was not exactly a logical wish, since it was impossible to run and undress two people while carrying one of them. He understood, also, that the situation called for a little more finesse.

"Let me take you to dinner tonight."

Kit tipped her head, smiling up at him dazedly. "We just had lunch."

He wanted to dive back onto her mouth,

but restrained himself. "So dinner, tonight?"

They still had their arms entwined and were wearing punch-drunk smiles when suddenly Kit's face clouded over. "I can't. I just remembered." She slowly took a step away. "I'm busy tonight. I'm attending a Cancer Society fund-raiser."

"I'll take you." He wanted her to stay close, wanted to keep holding her.

"Tickets sold out a month ago."

"If it's a fund-raiser, you'd think they'd sell me a ticket."

She was looking away and answered in a subdued tone, "The hall holds only so many people."

Seeing how distracted she was, Quinn wondered if she already had a date to the dinner. He tried teasing, "And you can actually bear to go to this function without me?" She gave him a smile but didn't say anything. He decided two things: he wouldn't push, and he would be at that fund-raiser.

She murmured that she had to pick up some new shoes before the stores closed. He offered to drive her, but she declined, and together they walked around the house to his car.

By the car he hesitated, wanting to take her back in his arms again, but he could see the mood wasn't right. He climbed in behind the wheel. His bag in the backseat prompted him to ask her to let him know soon about renting the spare room.

This got him another distracted look. "I'll talk it over with Clara and let you know," she said.

As he drove away he called Elise. It was time to speak frankly with her, about Hamm, and about Rebecca, and he wanted to mention a funny feeling he had about Turner. And he wanted to ask if Marcus had bought a ticket to the auction.

Unfortunately he didn't get a chance to talk to her about any of it. She answered her phone in a rush, telling him she was juggling a couple of things right then with Turner. "He's helping me with—oh, hold on a second." She put him on hold briefly then came back. "I'm setting up a telecast so that media from elsewhere can tune into the unveiling, live, and—oh! There's my callback from the *Washington Post*. Can we talk later?"

He swung the car around and returned to

Kit's house, realizing Rebecca probably also had a ticket that might be available. As he pulled up, the front door swung open and a man bounded out the door and down the front steps.

Clara waited at the door, smiling, as Quinn parked and walked up to her. Curious, he asked, "What kind of consultations do you do?"

"Why, therapeutic ones, of course." She gave him a pert smile. "Kit's out somewhere, but you're welcome to come in and wait."

"I understand tickets to the fund-raiser tonight are sold out. Is there a ticket for Rebecca I could buy?"

She went to the rolltop desk in the front room. "She loses things all the time, so I said I'd hold it for her." She came back and placed the ticket in his hand. "I've been dreading Becca's empty seat at our table tonight. And Jean-Philippe is at our table, which'll be awk—" She stopped and gave him a radiant smile. "I'm so glad you can join us."

15

On her way to pick up her new shoes, Kit mulled over her plan for the evening and her decision to exclude Quinn from it. When he expressed interest in attending the auction that night, she considered telling him that he could have Rebecca's ticket, but then didn't. She had a feeling that things with Turner would go smoother if Quinn stayed out of the picture.

She got to the store and her new shoes were waiting for her. After months of far-from-subtle hinting, her brothers got together and bought them for her birthday present. The things were ridiculously expensive, added four inches to her height, and were so pretty she felt like crying when she saw them.

To make sure of the fit, she tried them on at the store. They fit fine, but they made her feel like she was teetering around on stilts. Looking in the mirror, she thought about how Rebecca should have been there, laughing at her clumsy walk, and a rush of sadness washed over her. She changed into her regular shoes, and walked slowly home.

Clara was in the kitchen, mixing up lemon bars. Kit sat down heavily and watched as her housemate slid the pan into the oven, set the timer, and then turned with a smile to say they'd be ready in twenty.

This sequence of tiny acts by Clara—the innocent domesticity they represented— made Kit close her eyes for a moment. She'd never understood how precious, and fragile, life's tiny moments could be.

She opened her eyes, and Clara, who was watching her face, said softly, "Things will get better, sweetie."

Kit sighed. "So much about life has turned upside down. I hate that Rebecca's attacker is walking around free. I hate that Rebecca's alone in that hospital. I hate that Bev has to travel so far to be with her daughter." She paused to take a breath, and to slow herself down. "And on top of all that, we're not going to make rent this month. I'm afraid we're going to get kicked out, and then what? Are we going to become bag ladies?"

Clara held up an envelope and said, "Starting with the last problem first, Quinn suspected you wouldn't take any acting wages for yesterday, so he entrusted them to me." Her tone grew stern. "He told me you were knocked, unconscious, into the water. How frightening, Kit! Do you realize—"

Kit felt she needed to lighten the moment or she'd start crying. "But I stayed afloat," she said. "My balloon boobs came to my rescue!"

Clara didn't laugh, and Kit felt herself succumbing to a sudden rush of tears.

Immediately Clara was holding her, rocking her. "I know, sweetie," Clara said softly, "I know . . ."

After a few minutes, Kit wiped her eyes, annoyed with herself. She could cry after she caught Rebecca's attacker.

Clara asked, "Would you rather skip the auction tonight?"

Kit sat up straight. "Are you kidding? The only thing that will make me feel better is to *do* something."

Clara smiled, "Like getting dressed up, and going out to have a good time?"

"Well, actually . . ." She filled Clara in on her plan to sit at Turner's table. "I'm sorry because that means I won't be sitting with you. Rebecca won't be there, so you'll be stuck with Jean-Philippe, by yourself."

"Oh, I'll be fine." Shooting Kit a teasing look, she asked, "So . . . the picnic with Quinn went well?"

"He's trying to convince me to stay away from Turner. That's what the picnic was . . ." she cleared her throat, "mostly about." She wanted to tell Clara all about the kiss in the backyard. But these next few hours were critical. She needed to get her emotions under control. Her sadness, her fear, and the jittery excitement that filled her when she thought about Quinn.

Clara brought up Quinn's request to rent their spare bedroom, and said, "With him here, at least we wouldn't have to worry about rent next month. But I'll leave it up to you to decide."

"I'll tell him yes." Kit called and left him a message. Then she ordered herself to stay

focused on Turner, not Quinn, for the rest
of the evening.

~~~

Quinn had pictured a small venue when
Kit told him tickets to the Cancer Society
benefit had sold out. So he was surprised to
see, arranged in the center of the large hall,
enough tables to accommodate hundreds of
ticket-holders.

Long, white-clothed tables lined the walls
of the dining hall, and upon these tables, the
art was displayed: highly stylized infrared
photographs, woodblock prints, landscape
paintings, black-and-white portraits, ceramics,
abstract art, textiles, and sculpture. Each
piece was accompanied by a description of
the work and its artist, an estimated value, and
a sheet for diners to write in their silent bids.

He especially liked one piece, a carved
cedar box, resting atop a tall pedestal. A
warm buttery color, it had been etched with a
sweeping design that managed to convey both
strength and grace, qualities that reminded
him of the women he'd met upon coming
to Nipntuck—Rebecca, Elise, Clara, and
especially Kit.

It occurred to him that the carved box might appear even more lovely because it was next to a piece of abstract art—a yellow and black crayon drawing—that did very little for him. Actually, he did have a reaction. Rather than leaving him cold, like most abstract art, it triggered a warm flush of suppressed laughter. It didn't look like art at all, but more like a smear of butterscotch-chocolate ice cream that had been erroneously included in the auction.

He wrote in a bid of eleven hundred for the cedar box, then scanned the room and spied Kit walking in the door. She had on a beautifully cut turquoise dress and very high heels that seemed to cause a slight hesitation in her step. To his eye, all the artwork in the room dimmed in brilliance compared to her.

Clara was with her, and after they handed off their coats at the coat check, the two women were engulfed in a group of friends. Kit hadn't seen him yet.

He was about to start over when she stepped away from her friends and went to speak to one of the organizers of the event. Quinn swore internally as he watched the man lead her to a table and introduce her. At the table were Turner, Elise, and a distinguished-looking gentleman who appeared to be escorting Elise.

Eyes narrowed, he watched as Kit demurely shook hands around the table. Then she bestowed upon Turner a shy, appreciative look as he rose and held the fourth chair for her.

Damn, Quinn muttered. Back across the room, Clara had seated herself at a table with a couple he didn't recognize. The table had one empty chair—his, apparently.

He strode to Clara's side, and she turned a dazzling smile on him. "Hello there!" she said, and took his arm to draw him into the seat. She seemed truly glad to see him, but Quinn was too agitated to return her smile. The others at the table introduced themselves: a twitchy Frenchman named Jean-Philippe and his wife, Frasia, a large woman with a vacant, round face.

Frasia announced she needed more water. "Why more?" Jean-Philippe said impatiently. "I gave you my glass, and you finished that?"

"I like to drink a lot of water. We need a carafe."

He ignored her, so she went to ask a waiter to bring one. As soon as she walked away, the Frenchman stared over at Kit, and hissed urgently at Clara, "Why is she here?"

Clara leaned toward him, asking softly, "Who?"

His eyes dove down into her cleavage. "I thought Keeet went to Juneau," he said to her breasts.

"She did," Clara said sweetly.

The wife returned to the table, followed by a waiter bearing a water carafe. She lowered into her seat, turned to her husband and began berating him about something in a low, hissing voice.

Quietly, Quinn asked Clara what was going on.

She whispered that Frasia was a surprise at their table. Jean-Philippe, under the impression that Kit was still in Juneau, had brought his wife and insisted that she was supposed to have Kit's seat.

Quinn was only half listening. From where he sat, he had a chance to observe Kit, and he didn't like what he saw. Turner spoke animatedly while she listened, her eyebrows lifted in an impressed arc. He leaned toward Clara and growled, "I don't like what Kit's up to."

"She's stubborn," Clara whispered softly back. Then giving him a little smile, she added, "I'm glad you're here."

He nodded, but didn't stop frowning.

~~~

After sitting down at Turner's table, Kit was surprised to find her cheeks heating up with self-consciousness. The ticket mix-up had been explained, the open seat at their table had been cordially offered, and introductions had been made, and now Turner was smiling at her. Gone was the taut, arrogant man she'd seen yesterday at the lab. Instead she felt a disconcerting warmth radiating off him.

First, she told herself, *check what he says about his background. Keep an ear out for unanswered questions or contradictions. Then bring up Rebecca when the time is right. And keep in mind what you learned about his taste in women—don't show much personality.*

She took a deep breath and started asking

the usual get-acquainted questions, trying as smoothly as possible to check the scant information Nate had provided on Turner.

Turner confirmed he'd attended law school at UCLA. *So that piece checks out.* "Where did you go for undergrad?"

He smiled. "I studied on my own to get into UCLA."

"Really?" Kit's curiosity shot up. *Why would he want to hide the undergraduate degree Nate listed for him at the Hawaii school?* "You honestly didn't attend undergraduate school?" She found that by ending her sentences on a high note, it made her eyelashes flutter. *I'm batting my eyelashes*, she thought.

Laughing, he shook his head. "I'm telling you the truth, little lady."

Calling her little anything was a bad idea, but she found the phrase, "little lady," especially irksome. She imagined giving him an unladylike jab in the throat, right where Quinn had shown her, and that helped her keep smiling.

Turner went on, "I needed to have an undergraduate degree for the sake of appearances, so I paid for one. There are

Hawaii schools that dole out degrees based on a couple of ridiculous tests you can take through the mail."

Oh, okay, she thought.

"Admittedly, I'm an anomaly." Turner watched to see if she knew what that meant and she obligingly looked uncertain while thinking: *so he wasn't in Hawaii . . . but he had to be somewhere, hitting the books, getting ready for law school . . .*

She was about to pose the question when the caterers arrived with the first course, halibut and smoked eel with horseradish and beetroot salad. She hoped it tasted better than it looked.

After the waiter withdrew, she asked, "Where did you live before you went to UCLA?"

"I've been to a lot of places," he said with a modest wave.

"Have you been anywhere else in Alaska?" She watched him closely. *As in . . . Saluda?*

"Not yet, he said.

She couldn't seem to get any traction with this guy.

"I assure you I've never lived anywhere as

pretty as this town." He followed this with a pause. Kit understood he expected her to do what locals loved to do: talk about Nipntuck's natural beauty. Instead, she stifled a yawn and flicked her eyes over his shoulder. She wanted him to keep talking.

It worked. "You see," he leaned in, "I've just never stayed in one place very long."

She didn't have to feign her interest. "Oh? Tell me some of the places you've been."

He said quietly, "My adoptive parents were transients. It wasn't . . ." A pained look crossed his face. "We moved around, but it wasn't pleasant. I never belonged anywhere."

Disappointed in the lack of detail, she asked, "You've never felt at home anywhere?"

"Not really." He was thoughtful. "I like the urban environment, but no particular place has that special appeal, that feeling of home, to me."

They paused while waiters brought the main course, breast of maize-fed chicken with roast pepper gnocchi and lemon butter sauce. Kit was glad the menu featured chicken. It was a welcome change from seafood. "So," she said, "if you prefer the city, why stay in this little place?"

"When my father asked me to stay, I hesitated to give up the city, but realized I was getting a shot at having a family." He looked away, embarrassed. "Family love wasn't even something I knew existed."

"I can't even imagine that," she said sincerely.

"You can't imagine it?"

Thinking about how she'd grown up in a puppy pile of brothers, she shook her head and said, "I come from a big family."

He laughed. "Then you're probably amazed to hear me say I'm so affected just by having a father. One other person isn't much of a family. Except, to me it is."

She nodded.

"And it isn't like my life plan has been hurt by this move. It's still on track."

"And what's your life plan?"

"To become filthy rich."

"Filthy rich!" His audacity made her laugh. She had to remind herself not to get caught up in this conversation, and, even more important, not to be charmed by this man.

"I'm already rich," he said, laughing with

her, "so the next logical step is to become filthy rich."

"So how's that going?"

He reached for her hand and lightly traced her fingers. "Very well," he said softly.

Against Turner's long elegant fingers, her hand looked stubby and childish. She slid it away from him and put it on her lap. Laughing, she said, "So, tell me some of your secrets."

"There are no secrets," he said, "but there are rules."

"Oh?" she said, fluttering away.

"The thing about money is to remain unemotional about it." Turner took up his wine glass. "You must be extremely focused, without being attached."

"Don't let the money control you?"

"Precisely," he said.

"It's better to save the emotions for things money can't buy."

He delivered his line like a pro: "Like family."

A waiter stepped in and took away their plates, and then Kit resumed the conversation. "I remember reading in the paper that you found your mother first . . ."

"And that's how I found Marcus." Turner looked past her and gave a barely perceptible lift of his chin. Suddenly the waiter was at their side and their wine glasses were filled. Once the waiter moved on, Turner said, "So tell me about yourself."

Hmmm . . . she thought, *was that a little sidestep on the subject of his mother?*

"What do you do?" he asked.

Buying time, she took a small sip of wine. She didn't want to tell him much about herself, but an outright lie could boomerang back on her—small towns were bad that way.

Then he helped out. "Are you in school?"

She lowered her head modestly so he'd think that was a yes. "I'm in communications," she said lightly, "but sometimes I have trouble concentrating."

He smiled indulgently at this.

The guy was painfully condescending, but her bimbo act begged for it. Setting that aside, she had trouble imagining that such a polished man was capable of committing an act of rank violence. She decided it was time to ask about Rebecca. This far into their talk, she was confident she could work it in naturally.

But before she could speak, Turner's phone rang. He glanced at the number and said apologetically, "I better take this, please excuse me for a moment." He rose from his chair and answered in a low voice, while striding toward the hall's foyer.

Watching him go, Kit put a dismayed look on her face and told the other two at the table, "Oh! That reminds me, I'm supposed to make a call. Would you please excuse me?" An entirely lame move, but her companions at the table seemed to buy it. Digging in her purse, she moved swiftly to follow Turner, trying not to look like she was doing just that.

She didn't go into the foyer with Turner, but stood at its edge, holding her phone to her ear, and angling her body away from him, so if he turned around and saw her, she'd look like she was also on the phone. He went and stood by the doors leading outside, his back to her.

She worried that she wasn't close enough to hear his conversation, but his voice rang out in the empty foyer. "No kidding? Two out of three!" She was surprised to see him throw an excited punch into the air. "So how many hits?" He shook his head. "Fourteen? Well, two out of three's not bad." He listened for a moment and gave a laugh.

This display of boyishness conflicted with his polished demeanor and rounded him out in a way that Kit found irritating. She wanted confirmation that he was a potential bad guy, but here he was being Mr. Happy Sunshine Guy.

"Alright, good," he said.

She sensed he was getting ready to end the conversation, so she turned and ducked back into the dining room.

Instantly, her eyes landed on William Leetham. He stood nearby, swirling a glass of wine, surveying the art at one of the long tables that lined the room. She knew him by sight but had never met him. While she could not imagine Turner speaking those sinister words in the sauna, she had no trouble picturing Leetham doing it. He radiated pomposity, along with something else, something less than trustworthy.

She went over and viewed the artwork at the table where he stood, moving slowly toward him until they had to step around one another. She peered at him. "Well, hello, Mr. Leetham."

"Well, hello," he said slowly, letting his eyes flick down to assess her figure.

She gestured at the piece of art in front of them, a panoramic photograph of the northern lights. "I know so little about art." She sighed. "What do you think about this?"

"Well," he said soberly, "I think it is ridiculous."

"Oh? Why is that?"

He lowered his voice, just the thing she wanted him to do. "I think," he leaned in, "the photographer did this just to please himself. He wasn't thinking about art. He was just . . . you gotta admit . . . artistically jacking off."

"You think so?" she looked at the photograph quizzically. It was actually a stunning piece of work. "Is there anything here you like?" She gestured down along the table.

He leaned closer. "How do I know you won't bid me up?"

The reek of cigar mingled with his heavy cologne made breathing difficult. She opened her purse to let him peek inside. "Because I didn't bring any money." She forced herself to smile when she said it. It was a silly exchange, and she would have preferred to walk away without engaging him any further, but every time he spoke, it made her think he was probably the one she heard in the sauna, rather than Turner.

She added, "I'm only window-shopping, since I don't have a very good sense of what makes good art."

He moved even closer. Despite his age—twice hers—he dropped his eyes down to her breasts and winked. "Good art makes you want to take it home."

Eewww, she thought, backing away from him. "Good luck on the bidding, Mr. Leetham." She tried not to, but wobbled a little on her heels when she walked away.

Back at the table she found Turner engaged with the others in a conversation about the artwork. She kept looking for a smooth way to bring up Rebecca's name but couldn't find one. She wasn't worried though, because she and Clara had a backup plan. They'd prearranged for Clara to come over, get introduced, and then ask Turner, "Oh! Aren't you the sweet man who took Rebecca to Silvers on Sunday?"

Kit noticed Elise look at someone approaching, and turned with a smile, expecting it to be Clara. However, it was Quinn.

He went directly to Elise and took her hand in a warm grip. Leaning over, he said, loud enough for the others to hear, "Unfortunately, something's come up, and I need to fly home tomorrow. I'm sorry I won't be able to stay for the unveiling."

An announcement floated over the room that the auction would soon end, and final bids were being solicited.

Turner rose, dropped his napkin on the table, and asked his tablemates, "Will you excuse us, please?" Then he indicated the edge of the room, and said to Quinn, "A word?"

"Certainly," Quinn said.

~~~

Quinn wanted to check his bid before the auction ended, so he led Turner over toward the cedar box. Halfway there, a tall woman wearing a head scarf stopped Turner to ask if he'd seen the application her son had submitted for a job with SeaLab.

Turner asked a few congenial questions, and then suggested the son follow up his application with a phone call. She beamed at him and asked how he was finding Nipntuck.

"Beautiful," Turner said. Quinn noticed how he turned his eyes to look at Kit when he said it.

~~~

Kit was ticked. Quinn had a lot of nerve. He thought it was fine to just waltz up and cut in on her time with Turner, and take him away before she got her chance to bring up Rebecca. She did *not* appreciate it.

She decided to broach the subject of Rebecca with Elise, so when Turner came back, they'd already be on the topic.

She waited for a pause, and then mentioned quietly to Elise that she'd known Rebecca and was devastated by her death.

Elise nodded sadly. "She was such a sweetheart." A smile softened her face. "You know about the birthday cakes?"

Kit wasn't prepared for the sudden ache

this caused in her breast. Rebecca loved to make cakes to celebrate her friends' birthdays. She baked them with great gusto, covering her boat's galley with flour and gritty sugar, singing the Beatles birthday song, but substituting in her own lyrics, "I know it's your birthday! We're gonna have a wild time!" over and over. The cakes were always either undercooked or burnt because her boat oven couldn't keep a consistent flame, but people loved getting them.

Elise was saying, "Last Friday we had our employee picnic at Sandy Beach, and Rebecca brought a cake for Turner."

To distract herself and quell the lump rising in her throat, Kit looked around to see where Quinn and Turner went. She spied them in the middle of the room talking to some woman. Right then, Turner turned and met her eyes. He sent her a smile, and she automatically gave him an answering one.

Elise, wearing a small frown, said, "Rebecca happened to have the wrong day—Turner's birthday isn't until September—and Turner let that upset him, for some reason. He normally has such lovely manners, but he's been under a lot of stress lately . . . oh, hello!"

An acquaintance stepped up and engaged Elise in some chat, and Kit looked back at Quinn and Turner. They had continued on to the edge of the room, and were standing face-to-face. The sight made her want to groan. If Quinn hoped to convey the impression that he was about to leave town, tail tucked, he was blowing it. An air of combativeness surrounded his body like steam, and Turner's stance was no less aggressive. She wished she could hear what they were saying.

A hand touched her shoulder and there was Clara, at her side.

Perfect, she thought, rising quickly to her feet. "Let me introduce you to my charming dinner companion," she said and led Clara directly over to the men.

16

Quinn, after upping his bid on the cedar box, turned to Turner. In an even tone, asked, "What's up?"

Turner said, "Why the hell did you come to Nipntuck? What's your interest in SeaLab's business?"

Quinn asked Turner why he wanted to know.

Turner was working to keep calm. "Rebecca's accident holds some fascination for you. Why is that?"

"My fascination holds some fascination for you—why is *that?*" Quinn shot back.

The two men glared at one another until Turner said, "Answer my question."

Quinn suddenly felt like beating the crap out of Turner. Part of it, he realized, might be jealousy over Kit.

Suddenly her voice carried to them, soft and sweet. "Turner?"

The two men broke off their stare and swung around to watch Kit and Clara approach. The women were smiling, and each carried a crystal glass of after-dinner port. Quinn felt a rush of heat flood his chest as he watched them walk up. Kit looked stunning in that dress.

When she was two steps away, her ankle gave a sudden twist and she flung out her arms, trying to keep her balance. A big slosh of deep red port flew out of her wine glass directly onto the crayon drawing, while her other hand, flailing, smacked the cedar box off its pedestal and up into the air.

Quinn grabbed Kit to save her from falling. Then, for a frozen moment, everyone stared at Clara. She had moved astonishingly fast to pluck the cedar box out of the air, and now stood calmly with it cradled against her magnificent bosom.

"Whew," she said softly, and placed the cedar box carefully on its stand. She turned to Kit. "Are you alright?"

"Yes, but . . ." Kit looked over at the

crayon drawing, now in a crimson pool of port. "That's not." She untangled herself from Quinn and stepped closer to view the drawing's bid sheet. "Oh no," she whispered.

He leaned in to see the top bid on the crayon drawing, and was shocked to see it was $1,600. Who the hell would pay that for *that?*

Suddenly, a cow-like bellow split the air, and the Frenchman's wife came barreling up. Shouldering Clara aside, she lunged at Kit, smacking her backward with a two-handed push on the chest.

Kit's empty wine glass flew out of her hand and splintered against the wall. Glass rained down on top of the wine-soaked drawing.

"You're the one!" the woman hissed, her face blotchy with anger. "In the pictures."

"Pictures!" Kit gasped.

Organizers and caterers dashed up, drawn by the sound of breaking glass, and Clara seized the moment. Dramatically, she pointed to the drawing and cried, "It's ruined!"

Quinn admired her fast thinking. The drawing, originally ruined by Kit's splash, was now covered in shards of glass thanks to the Frenchman's wife.

Jean-Philippe appeared and tugged at his snorting wife, trying to pull her away. "We'll pay for everything, of course."

"Pictures!" Kit repeated, staring hard at him. He strenuously avoided looking at her as he dragged his wife away.

An announcement came, thanking everyone for participating in a lovely evening. High bidders were asked to see the cashiers at the back table to arrange for payment.

Kit and Clara excused themselves to use the ladies' room, and Quinn went to pay for the cedar box. It took some time and when he finally finished, he looked for the women, but didn't see them in the crowd. He hurried outside but they weren't there, either.

After searching some more, he decided they must have gone back to the house. But he got there and found they had not. He paced up and down the porch steps, dialing Kit's number repeatedly, and getting no answer. He suspected they had gone somewhere with Turner. He hoped he was wrong.

~~~

Turner had walked with Kit and Clara out

of the event. Kit, her face bright pink, kept thinking about how much she wanted to go after Jean-Philippe, bring him down with a tackle, and throttle the answer out of him: *What pictures!?*

Turner was smiling at Kit's heated face, apparently taking it for shy interest. He stroked her arm with one hand while pressing his business card in her palm. "Call me," he said, and with one last smile, he left.

Kit put the card away. Apparently she had come across suitably lacking in personality and intelligence to interest him. *Good.* She would call him, and ask directly about Rebecca. She was sick of pussyfooting around.

She and Clara went over to their favorite ice cream joint and ordered a double scoop each. The dinner had been nice, but not very filling, they both agreed.

Sitting down, Kit said, "Let's *not* talk about Jean-Philippe and his wife, and please let's not talk about any pictures. I can't handle it. For now, I just want to enjoy my ice cream."

Clara nodded thoughtfully. "So what about Turner, can we talk about him? Did you learn anything?"

Kit sighed, exasperated. "I could not pin the guy down about anything. He inferred that he'd been abused, and that makes it hard to press." She licked her pistachio ice cream, "Who wouldn't want to shy away from the subject of child abuse?" She thought for a moment. "He seemed reluctant to talk about his birth mother as well, but don't ask me why."

"Hmmm." Clara nibbled a piece of chocolate off the top of her mint ice cream.

Kit shook her head, frustrated. "I was batting my eyelashes like a toad in a hailstorm, but it was all for nothing."

She felt defeated. She had Turner's card, but that seemed to be all. Then she remembered the phone call he received. "Oh, there was this one thing. Turner got a phone call, and it was interesting how he reacted."

"What happened?"

"All evening he came across very sophisticated, Mr. Oh-So-Cool, but on the phone, his behavior changed." She described how excited he got.

"What did he say, exactly?" Clara asked.

"He said something about two of three.

Then he asked, how many hits, and the answer, I gathered, was fourteen." Kit's brow furrowed. "Do you think he was talking about drugs?" She had no experience with that kind of thing.

"He got really excited?" Clara asked.

"Yes."

"And you're the one with all the brothers..." Clara said teasingly.

"What do you mean?"

"Sports, sweetie. It's a betting pool on a baseball game. Guys bet on things like the exact number of strikes, balls and hits their hometown pitcher will throw."

Kit just looked at her.

Clara said, "He said something about two out of three? And then asked how many hits? I would guess that he won on guessing strikes and balls, but not hits." Then Clara scoffed, "With all those brothers, how could you not know this?"

"This is Alaska!" Kit said, a defensive squeak in her voice. "My brothers don't obsess over sports because they're too busy fishing and hunting—being real men!"

She started laughing along with Clara

because of the way she'd jumped to defend her brothers' virility. Growing serious, she said, "I never would have guessed that Turner, refined as he is, would get so excited over guessing some stupid numbers."

"You know how it is," Clara said, "Sports are the one thing boys are allowed to get emotional about. And they love to be right."

Kit snorted. "And he claims he's not emotional when it comes to money."

"Well, it's not so much about money. It's more about loyalty," Clara said. "He's probably been following that pitcher's career for years. A guy can move to a different city, or ten different ones, but ask him who he follows, and it's often his hometown team."

"Hmm," Kit said, "his *hometown* team, you say?"

Their eyes met.

Clara's eyebrows arched. "How many hits did he say? Fourteen?"

She took out her phone and dialed. "Honey Bun?" she said. "I have a baseball question for you. Now take your time. Which team's pitcher gave up fourteen hits in a game today? Well, that was quick," Clara laughed.

"Okay, then. Yes, me too, babe. Bye!"

She hung up and told Kit, "Seattle Mariners."

"Who was that?"

"My friend in Boston who just loves baseball," Clara said. "He always tells me: call anytime." She looked at her watch and gave a start, "Except, I forgot about the time difference. It's three in the morning there. Whoops."

Kit thought for a minute, and then said, "The University of Washington's a top-rate school. I can see Turner going there and getting infected with this thing for the Mariners. He claims he moved around a lot, but he could be lying."

"Is there someone who can do some snooping down in Seattle for us?"

Kit grinned. "You're not going to believe this, but I have a free ticket to Seattle." She told Clara about Jean-Philippe's credit card, still in her purse.

"Go," said Clara instantly.

Kit turned on her phone and called Alaska Airlines. The only seat available on the morning flight to Seattle was in first class.

She hesitated, but Clara mouthed, *"Go!"* So she took it.

She called Buddy and scheduled him to taxi her to the airport in the morning, and pick her up on her return. Noticing that Quinn had called multiple times, she suggested to Clara that they head home.

On the way, she told Clara, "Dashing down to Seattle feels a bit like a wild goose chase, but if nothing else, I'll eliminate the idea. That's what investigating is mostly, anyway—pursuing dead ends." She thought for a minute. "I have so little to go on. Turner's name was Davis before he came here, and I have his date of birth from a file Nate prepared on him."

Then she stopped and grabbed Clara's elbow. She'd been distracted by Quinn's appearance at the benefit, but now it hit her. Elise had mentioned that Rebecca made Turner a birthday cake on Friday. Kit got a buzz in her belly whenever she hit upon something of significance and she got that buzz now. Friday was August 18, the day the boy with the wild hair in Bev's letter had his birthday. *If Rebecca made him a cake on August*

18, then he's got to be the Turner in the photo her mom sent.

"Pay dirt," she whispered.

"What is it?" Clara asked.

She explained and Clara said, "Oh my."

They rounded the corner onto her street, and there was Quinn, waiting halfway up their front steps. Just from his rigid stance, Kit could tell he was not happy.

By the time she reached the bottom of her steps, she could tell his mood was more in the range of *pissed-off*, and in response to this, her own temper flared. On top of being bone tired, she was annoyed that she never got to bring up the subject of Rebecca with Turner. And why? Because Quinn stole him away. At the bottom of the steps, she met his glare with one of her own.

Clara slipped up the steps and went into the house with a quiet, "Good night, darlings."

Quinn was so tense he seemed unable to put a sentence together. It swept over Kit. She did not want to fight with him. It had been a long, difficult day, and all she wanted was some sleep. Coolly, she told him, "I'm going to bed. The spare bedroom is upstairs, second door on the left."

She would have taken the steps two at a time and sped directly to her room—conversation over—but her high heels made that impossible. Gripping the rail, she climbed carefully past him, trying for dignified.

"Kit," he touched her arm. "Wait." His voice was rough with emotion.

She turned to face him. Because she stood two steps above him, their eyes were level. She liked that. She drew herself up so she was even taller than he, and gave him the raised eyebrow treatment.

In a tight voice he said, "Bravado is admirable, but it can backfire. Can't you see—"

"Bravado," she cut in. "Is that what you think this is?"

"I just—"

"It's not bravado, it's desperation," she interrupted. "Ever since I saw Rebecca down in that harbor water," her voice cracked, but she didn't stop, "fear has consumed me. I don't feel safe, and I don't feel the people I love are safe. I'm in a fight to believe this world is a good place, Quinn, and if I lose this fight, I'm not sure what will happen to me."

He took a deep breath, and his shoulders slowly lowered. "I hear you. I do. But this entire hour, not knowing where you were, I kept thinking about what happened to Rebecca and . . . oh, hell . . ." He shook his head and touched her arm softly. "This hour felt like a year to me."

She placed her hand on his. "Clara and I went for ice cream, you knucklehead!"

He tilted his face up and addressed the night sky: "Can someone please tell me why I don't mind that she's calling me a knucklehead?" When he brought his gaze back to her, she expected him to be smiling, but his brow was furrowed. "Aside from worrying about your safety, I need to admit something. My worst male instincts woke up tonight. The way you kept looking at Turner, it was so . . ."

"Pathetic?" she supplied. This, finally, got him to smile.

"I was going to say convincing," he told her. "You really are the consummate actress. And your turned-ankle—that deserves an Oscar." He smiled. "So what's Turner missing now? His new phone?"

She stared at him in surprise. "Ah . . . guess what."

"Yes?"

"I tripped. Truly."

He threw his head back and laughed. "My God, you are a surprise!"

"Stop laughing." She gave him a little push. He was so big and solid, the effort had no impact on him; it just made her lose her balance. She grabbed him by the shoulders at the same time his hands went to her hips. Through her dress, his palms were searing hot. She shivered at how good they felt.

They stared at one another for a breathless moment. She loved that their faces were perfectly aligned.

It was a kiss that started out slow and savoring, but it built, and kept building, until they ended up in that place beyond frenzied.

Finally they broke apart, gasping for air, to gaze wide-eyed at one other. Kit was surprised to find that they were clutching one another on her porch rather than on a fluffy cloud with a big fat NINE stitched on its side. She was surprised their clothes hadn't just exploded off their bodies from the heat of that kiss, and that the boom of her pounding heart didn't cause people to fling open their doors and yell about the noise.

Quinn looked ready to sweep her into another kiss. She held up her hand. She was barely able to speak. "Ah . . . we need to . . . ah . . . I'll come to your room," she said faintly, and led him inside.

She was in her room, pawing through her clothes for something suitably sheer and inviting to wear while simultaneously brushing her hair, when her phone rang.

The screen showed the call was from the Juneau hospital and her hand shook as she answered. Sober-voiced and to the point, the nurse told Kit that Rebecca had stopped breathing. She had begun again quickly, but her vital signs were unstable, and she appeared to be failing.

Kit sank to her floor and sobbed, "No."

When she went to Quinn and told him the news, he held her close while she called Alaska Airlines to see about getting to Juneau. He said he would go with her, which made her feel better. But it turned out the morning jet was full, and only one seat remained on the noon flight. She reserved the seat.

Quinn made her tea and sat with her on the couch, holding her hand while she burrowed against him, filled with frustration and sadness. Not being able to jump in a car and rush to Rebecca's side made her grief even sharper.

A few minutes later, she got up to wake Clara with the awful news and the three sat together on the couch, holding vigil. An hour later when the phone rang, Kit answered, her voice thick with dread.

"Rebecca's vital signs have stabilized," the nurse said. "We're watching her closely, but it appears she's not in imminent danger."

Clara made breakfast while they discussed whether Kit should still go to be with Rebecca, or proceed with her plan to go to Seattle. They finally concluded that she should go to Seattle. From there she could respond quicker if Rebecca took a turn for the worse; more jets flew to Juneau from Seattle than from Nipntuck. She knew also that she'd worry less about Rebecca if she stayed busy.

"And you should go accept your press

award," Clara said. "Rebecca would want you to."

Kit thought about it for a moment, and then agreed. She could put in an appearance at the press awards. By lunchtime she'd have collected her award and could dedicate the rest of the day to thinking about Turner.

"I'll call you at lunchtime," Quinn said. "If I can't be there, I can at least be your sounding board on the Turner questions."

She went to pack. When she returned to the kitchen, Quinn said he'd drive her to the airport but she shook her head sadly. "I scheduled Buddy. He's bringing me to the airport, and also picking me up on my return."

She walked to the window to watch for her ride.

"The cabbie who terrorizes customers who cancel?" Quinn came up and put his arm around her.

"That's the one."

He lifted her hair away from the back of her neck and kissed her there, once, and then again. Goose bumps rippled all over her.

She turned to face him, wondering if he

could see how much she yearned to pick up where they'd left off on the porch. She felt like it must be blazing from her eyes. "I'll be home at eleven tonight."

"I'll be here," he promised, "waiting for you."

~~~

Quinn slept for a few hours, and by the time he woke he'd missed his chance to catch Elise at the mall. He went by SeaLab, hoping to find her alone rather than with Turner, but the yellow Ferrari was parked in the lot.

He was going to call Elise to request a private opportunity to talk, but before he could dial, Nate called and said he wanted to discuss something he'd discovered about SeaLab's network.

Quinn wanted to drop his suit off at the dry cleaners, which was next to the Sea Shanty, so he told Nate to meet him there for an early lunch.

As soon as the waitress brought them their food, Nate grabbed for the saltshaker. While he talked, he vigorously covered his burger, fries, salad, his lap, and half the table with white granules. "I've been poking around

SeaLab's network, and discovered that there are two networks, with one acting effectively as a screen for the other. I got suspicious because when I managed to—hey, you're not listening."

Quinn had been replaying the meaningful look Kit had given him when she said good-bye that morning. All he wanted to do was make the earth spin faster so that eleven p.m. would come sooner.

"Go on," he told Nate. "I'm listening."

Nate peeled the top bun off his burger. Setting aside the tomato and lettuce, he began to lay his french fries on top of the meat. "So I managed to penetrate the one network, the one that's more visible and it was all just up-front tidal power stuff—nothing sensitive." He crisscrossed a second layer of fries on top of the first. "So that made me ask, why so much security, right? Well, I kept poking and found a bunch of encrypted activity on another level. I'm pretty sure it means SeaLab has a second, hidden network, where some really juicy secret stuff could be happening."

He paused and put the lid on his burger. He took a bite and half of the fries fell out. "Damn." He set the burger down. "I overbuilt."

Their waitress came to ask how their food was and Nate grinned at her. "A little salty, but it might have been me."

Her eyes went to the salt sprinkled all over the table and she laughed uncertainly before walking away.

Nate shoved three long fries in his mouth, leaned forward and told Quinn, "She's new. I think she likes me."

A second later he gave Quinn a strange, bug-eyed look. For a second Quinn thought he was choking, but then Nate whispered something that sounded like, "Incoming."

She slid into the booth beside Quinn, snuggling against his shoulder while ignoring Nate. "Hi, there! I *just* got your message. I was out of town."

Quinn stared in surprise at his former fiance.

"Allie," he said. "Hi."

17

At the awards ceremony, Kit's former coworker McPhee gave her a gleeful greeting, and instantly demanded to know how long she was staying. When she told him she was returning to Nipntuck that night, he said, "No, you're not. You are staying longer. We need to party!" Twenty-six, with smiling green eyes and longish blonde hair, McPhee worked hard, and played harder. He was one of Kit's favorite people on earth.

She couldn't tell him about what had happened to Rebecca because the awards ceremony began and they had to stay quiet. When her name was called, she went up and received the award. Back at the table, McPhee gave her one of his attaboy shoulder punches. It gave her a wonderful feeling, to get the award, and to see him again. But it wasn't long before she began to tap her fingers anxiously.

Finally, she couldn't stand it. Even though they had another hour before the lunch break, she leaned over and whispered, "McPhee, I need your help with something. Want to cut out and go somewhere we can talk?"

"Before lunch?" McPhee was a good friend, but he was also thrifty, and lunch was included in the event fee.

Glad, once again, for the credit card Jean-Philippe had forced on her, she said, "I'll buy us lunch. Money is not an issue." She added ruefully, "You'll enjoy hearing the story why."

He ticked off his fingers as he spoke, "You're buying lunch. Money is not an issue. There's a story." Rising, he said, "Let's go."

~~~

Allie wore a new haircut that showed off her fine cheekbones, and a blouse that gave Quinn a peek of something lacy underneath. But it was her lips he always noticed. Her full, beckoning mouth pulled him in every time. He snapped his eyes back to meet hers. "How are you?" he asked.

"Sad," she pouted. Those lips again. "I can't stay long. I have to rush off. I just wanted to say hi."

"Sad about what?"

"Oh, it's a long story. We should get together for lunch later this week, or something."

"What are you doing right now? Where are you headed?"

Nate, who had been staring down at his plate, looked up at Quinn, and then away.

"Oh, my car started acting strange, and I made the mistake of bringing it to this one mechanic, and you know how it goes—the next thing I know, I have to get a new car or pay a fortune to have the old one fixed."

"What's wrong with it?"

She waved her hand, "Oh, I don't know, something mechanical." He ignored the ironic look Nate flicked his way.

Allie said, "I need to go see the mechanic about it right now."

"Want me to come with you? Take a look at it?"

Somehow she managed to make her entire body look pleased. "Would you?"

Quinn stood up to follow her out the door and Nate muttered, "Good luck."

"Thanks," Allie sang over her shoulder.

"I was talking to Quinn," Nate said.

When they got to the BMW, Allie climbed in and wiggled appreciatively. "Nice," she said, patting the dashboard.

He asked what she was doing after they conferred with the mechanic.

She had to run errands, then catch up on some paperwork at work.

"I'll run errands with you. You can ditch me anytime you want."

"I could never ditch you."

"You did once," he said quietly.

She rolled her eyes. "I'm crazy about you, Quinn, you know that."

"Just crazier about that blonde guy."

"Don't be mad at me, please."

He fell silent. He should be furious with her. Why wasn't he? He had moved from Washington, D.C., to join her in Fairbanks— at her invitation. After a year had passed, he wanted them to marry. He was ready to be her husband and start a family. She begged him to be patient, said she was almost ready to become his wife, but not quite.

Another year passed. Some rumors came his way that she was cheating on him. It drove him crazy because he was sure the rumors were false, but it forced him to confront her. He demanded to know if she was ever going to marry him. And she said yes, she just needed a bit more time. Almost another year passed, and she still wouldn't commit. Finally he gave her the ultimatum—or, as Nate called it—the ol' tomato. Marry him or he'd leave, he told her.

It took months but she finally said she was ready for marriage. Right away, she began planning a huge engagement party.

He didn't care for all the fuss that led up to being married, he just wanted to get going on their life together. But planning the engagement party, which was growing grander by the day, grander than most wedding receptions, made her happy. So that made him happy. He was happy right up until the day after their engagement party when she informed him that she was moving in with some other guy. She told Quinn she'd accidentally started sleeping with the man.

In shock, he asked her what that meant: accidentally sleeping with someone.

Tearfully, Allie told him she didn't know

what to say, it was just that her new lover didn't need much from her emotionally, and somehow that worked better for her.

Remembering this, waiting for Nipntuck's one traffic light to turn green, he took a moment to study her lovely profile.

Nate had tried to convince him that she was a cheat who used men for their money. He could see why Nate would think this, but he believed the problem really was that she was scared of love. Why else would you pick a lover who didn't want an emotional bond?

The light changed, and Quinn drove on, asking casually, "So where is lover boy, anyway?"

"Gone," she said, "and forgotten. I'm single now."

"Weren't you two engaged?"

"We broke up."

He wondered if it was before or after the engagement party, but the thought evaporated when she reached over and did that tickly itsy-bitsy spider thing of hers across his shoulder and around the back of his neck. "I wish you lived here," she said. "I've missed you."

He was thrown off by her words, especially

the last three. In the eight months since their breakup she'd given him no sign that she ever wanted to hear from him again.

They got to the auto repair shop, and the mechanic said her car was ready for her.

"You mean you went ahead and fixed it!?" she asked. "I just wanted an estimate."

"Lady, I gave you the estimate, and you said fix it."

"I did not!" Her red lips were open in shock. She looked at Quinn for help. "I did not!"

Shaking his head in disgust, the mechanic handed over the charge sheet for the work he'd done on her little Saab. The bill came to nine hundred dollars.

After looking over the charges, Quinn told her they looked reasonable.

Exasperated, she said, "My Visa was stolen on my trip. I'll have to come back with my checkbook." Then she moaned. "I just remembered, I'm all out of checks! This is so frustrating; I really need my car!"

"I'll cover this," Quinn said. "You can pay me back."

"I will," she said with a sincere nod.

"Don't let me forget." She brightened. "In fact, I insist on paying you back with interest! Remember my special massage? I'll do that dance on your back, like I used to! I know how to get those tight spots to relax."

Laughing, he agreed that she did, in fact, know how to get those tight spots to relax.

They went back outside, and she said, "I'm supposed to make an appearance at work, but you make me want to play hooky. Want to play hooky with me?"

~~~

McPhee suggested they eat at a place called the Speakeasy Pub in Seattle's University District. While they ate, Kit told him about Rebecca, and about Turner. McPhee said he had a friend in the UW records office who might help dig for information on Turner. "I can call now and see if she's working."

The call was brief. He hung up, telling Kit, "She's not even there anymore. Some guy I don't know is working today. Shall we go over and charm him in person?"

She paid for their lunch, and they headed over. In view of the news about Rebecca, McPhee forgot to ask why money was no object, and Kit was happy to leave that story for another time.

The student behind the desk at the records office wore polyester pants pulled too far up and a poop-brown, misbuttoned 1950s cardigan.

"Ow, my eyes," McPhee breathed.

"Be nice," she whispered.

Charming the guy ended up being unnecessary. McPhee gave his name and identified himself as a *Seattle Times* reporter, and the young man blurted, "I'm a journalism major. The sex ring involving animal sacrifice and tiddlywinks—you wrote that story, right?"

"Yeah," McPhee said. His voice was gruff, but Kit could tell he was pleased.

She explained to the clerk that they needed help on a story and he said, "Sure, I'll help."

"We're looking for information on a student who may have attended the university sometime in the last decade, possibly in pre-law. I have the first name Turner, and a possible last name of Davis, and two possible dates of birth. I know it isn't much . . ."

He frowned. "They've been saying all summer they're upgrading our computer system, but we're still on the old one and it's having problems."

Kit waited.

"But," he said, "write it down for me, and have a seat. I'll see if I can locate any records that have at least a couple of your parameters."

She gave it to him, and he went to a terminal. A little while later, he stepped back to the counter and handed her a printout. Shaking his head, he said, "I found plenty of people named Davis, and several people with the last name Turner, but none of them matched either of those birth dates."

She glanced the list over, but saw nothing intriguing. She was disappointed but not surprised. She cast around in her mind for another angle. "How about trying two other names for me? Can you try Ted Connelly?" She spelled it for him. "And Stan Hamm?"

"Birth date?"

"Not known."

"Also possibly in pre-law?"

She shook her head. "I doubt it. Can you check your entire enrollment?"

"It's going to take me a while. Do you want

to wait or come back?"

"*Beer*," McPhee mouthed the word at her. "We'll come back," she said.

They went to a bar nearby. McPhee went to order their beers and Kit called Quinn. He'd promised to call her around lunchtime, and it was already past two o'clock. She wanted to talk to him about her efforts regarding Turner, but mostly, she just wanted to hear his voice. Disappointed that he didn't answer, she left a message urging him to call.

McPhee came back to the table with two frosty mugs of beer. She took a sip and asked, "So how are you doing, anyway? You still miss the Devil Woman?" McPhee had been in a relationship—not a good one—before he left Nipntuck. The woman's nickname, openly used by everyone, even by him, was Devil Woman. And yet, after he moved, he was unable to resist buying her tickets so she could come see him in Seattle on the weekends.

"Bad woman, good sex," he said, when Kit called to question his judgement. Finally after several months, to everyone's relief, even McPhee's, the woman hooked up with a man everyone in Nipntuck called "Circus" because he had the look of a carnival worker. Circus and Devil Woman packed up their El Camino and left on the ferry, either to Ketchikan or to see the world, nobody was sure which.

McPhee stared at his beer. "How am I doing? I'm doing okay. I take a lot of walks."

Her eyebrows lifted at this. He'd always professed to hate walking.

He flashed her a grin. "I see women wearing miniskirts, and it helps."

She laughed. "I didn't realize Seattle women are that into miniskirts."

"They aren't, but you see them now and again, which is more than I can say for Nipntuck."

She laughed again. "True."

He raised his mug in a toast and drank. "So what about you? How's it going with Jean-Philippe?"

She told him how *that* had turned out, and he clutched his chest and laughed at her. He was the only one who could do that and get away with it; in fact, he made her laugh along with him.

"But I did just meet an intriguing man

. . ." Kit said, after they calmed down. Feeling a tug of hope inside, she added, "It could be something . . . special."

~~~

"What?" Quinn laughed at Allie. "You're kidding."

"No, really," she hugged his arm. "There's surfing in Nipntuck now. We can rent wetsuits and boards and go out to Sandy Beach. Let's go! You drive!"

Quinn helplessly agreed. He had zero desire to go surfing, but did like the idea of seeing her in a wetsuit. An hour and quite a bit of money later, they were paddling around on rented boards. The waves were small, and they were the only ones in the water, which he thought lucky. Allie looked like an Alaskan surfer babe, but he looked ridiculous in a wetsuit that was too small for him and had a camo design that was, for some stupid reason, purple and red. Neither of them knew how to surf, and they spent the day laughing because they couldn't seem to get the hang of it. Finally they just lolled around on their boards, talking idly, watching Arctic terns wheel around a blue sky.

Mostly Allie talked, replaying their past to him. She teased out details that he didn't remember, delighting him with their mutual story, making him happy all over again.

"Remember when we were in Hawaii, and you gave me those flowers? That you picked from that field? And we got yelled at because it was some special park or something? I still have one of them pressed in my diary."

He didn't remember seeing this sentimental side of her before, but he liked it.

They eventually called it a day and returned the gear. Outside the surf shop, she stepped into his arms and squeezed tight against him. "Quinn, I've been thinking about you constantly," she declared. "Seeing you just confirms it—I was crazy to give you up. Can you ever forgive me?"

18

Kit and McPhee got back to student records, and the counter clerk, looking pleased, announced, "I got two Ted Connellys, one in art school who graduated fourteen years ago, and the other in liberal arts. He dropped out six years ago, in the middle of his second year."

"The one who dropped out, he'd be, what, twenty-six now?" Kit said. "That sounds like the right age."

"He was in wrestling, it says here, and was about to get kicked out of the university for starting fights, but then he dropped out."

Her heart started pounding. "Really? Is there a picture of him?"

The student looked mournful. "There's a big red X where all the pictures should be. That's one of the problems we're having with the old system—the older IDs are causing some file incompatibility issue." He pointed to the screen on his computer. "But I can print you this summary page and probation report on him . . ."

The summary indicated Ted Connelly had earned a grade point average that hovered just slightly above a D. He'd been reprimanded repeatedly and then was placed on probation for violent tendencies. He dropped out just before he was kicked out.

She pointed to the words "violent tendencies," and told McPhee, "This could be the guy I know. He's about this age, and he's violent. I need to find a picture."

The counter clerk typed for a moment, then said, "You know, we're having trouble with everything right now, including our digital yearbook archives. Why don't you check at Dean Romero's office. That office has a library with old yearbooks, you know, like actual hard copies of them."

The dean was a handsome Hispanic woman who looked harried but proved pleasantly willing to talk with them. She said her yearbook collection had been phased out and now the only hard copy collection was over in the yearbook offices, but they were closed until the fall term began. "But you know," she said, "when it comes to remembering details about our students, my assistant Sylvia might be able to help you. Sylvia's been here forever, and it's amazing what she remembers."

Kit shared a glance with McPhee, thinking this was a lucky break, until Dean Romero added, "Unfortunately she called in sick today."

Kit slumped in frustration, and McPhee sent her an amused look. He liked to point out that her greatest downfall was patience, and she always shot back: I don't have *time* for patience.

The dean said, "Sylvia's getting up in years and is trying to pace herself, but she'll probably call later today to check in. If she's feeling up to it, shall I have her call you?"

They left McPhee's number because it was local and stepped outside. Kit's phone rang, and she fumbled for it, knowing it had to be Quinn. But the number displayed on her phone was unfamiliar.

"Hullo?" She asked, leaning into a gust of wind that came blasting down the street.

"Kit, it's me, Fred."

She blanked on the name for a minute, until she recalled that Fred was the skateboarder who worked at Silvers Restaurant. "I found out who served your friend last Sunday night. Her name's Willow. She's working tonight, so stop by if you want. I'm working too."

"Okay, I'm in Seattle at the moment, but I get in around eleven tonight."

"By that time the restaurant shouldn't be too busy, so there should be plenty of time to talk."

"Good. I'll come right from the airport. Say, what's the weather doing? Have they moved up the storm warning at all?"

"No, your flight should land fine. The gnarly stuff isn't predicted to start until tomorrow afternoon."

She hung up, and McPhee asked, "What next?"

"The record shows two addresses for Ted Connelly. It was years ago, but why don't we go check out where he lived."

On the way she dialed Quinn's phone.

To her disappointment, she was again sent directly to his voice mail. "Hey," she said. "Where are you? Call me, okay?"

Next she tried Clara, to ask if she'd seen Quinn. When Clara didn't answer, she left a message and called Nate, who didn't answer either. "Geez," she muttered, leaving him a message as well.

McPhee drove them to the first address listed on Ted Connelly's housing record, but it was now a Wendy's restaurant. When they reached the second address they nodded at one another. The house had a half-hearted paint job, neon beer signs propped in two windows, and a sofa spilling its guts on the porch. Still student housing, from the look of it.

McPhee's phone rang before they left the car. He answered, jotted down a number and hung up. "That was Dean Romero with Sylvia's home number. She recommends calling right away because Sylvia is about to take a nap."

Kit made the call, putting her phone on hands-free so that they could both hear. After six rings Kit was thinking guiltily, *maybe she's asleep already*, when a soft wavering voice said, "Hello?"

"Is this Sylvia?"

"Yes, who is this?"

"This is Kit Finnegan. The dean gave me your number and said it was okay to call you to inquire about Ted Connelly."

"Who?"

She couldn't tell if Sylvia's faint "who" was about who was calling, or who gave her the phone number, or who she was inquiring about. She said it all over, slower and louder this time, and Sylvia said, "Oh, yes, how are you?"

"Fine, thank you. I wonder, can you recall any student named Ted Connelly? He was enrolled in the liberal arts college, but only attended a year and a half before he dropped out, six years ago." Kit paused, and then added. "He was a wrestler?" She paused again. "I know it's a long shot . . ."

"Oh, I think I recall him. In fact, I'm sure I remember Ted. He had a brother, John Kennedy. There was something . . ."

"Excuse me Sylvia—not Kennedy, Ted Connelly."

"Oh yes, of course. Connelly. But I remember the brothers because their names were Ted and John. Like the Kennedy boys."

Throwing a doubtful look at McPhee, Kit said, "Oh, I see. So Ted Connelly had a brother who also went to this university?"

"Oh yes. John was older, though. What was the thing I heard about them? Somebody died in a car . . ."

Kit raised her eyebrows at McPhee and said gently, "Maybe you're thinking of Ted Kennedy and that famous incident? When his car went off the road at Chappaquiddick?"

Sylvia coughed, stopped, and then coughed again, sounding increasingly feeble.

Apologetically, Kit said, "I should let you go. But thank you for talking to me. I hope you feel better soon."

"Oh, I'm sure I will. Bye-bye now."

A stringy-haired young woman answered their knock at the run-down house and said, "I have no idea," when they asked about Ted Connelly. "But there's a wall with photos. Some are ancient, like five, six years old." She cracked her gum. "Maybe he's in one. I wouldn't know."

She led them to a long hallway and left them there. A few minutes into studying the wall of pictures, Kit said, "McPhee."

He stepped to her side. She put her fingertip on a photo. It was a black-and-white shot of Hamm—also known as Ted Connelly—in a striped shirt, grinning and holding up a beer. A buddy leaned on him, drinking liquor out of a bottle.

She looked closer. *Oh my God.* The person leaning on Ted Connelly was Turner. He was wild-haired and glassy-eyed, and a bottle of Wild Turkey half-obscured his face, but it was him.

She told McPhee, and they simultaneously spotted another photograph with the two men. They were seated at a table eating spaghetti messily, and this photo—it was in color— showed Turner's hair was not only spiked out everywhere, it was also neon pink, green, and purple. Something was scrawled in faded blue crayon on the border of the photo.

He pointed. "It's labeled 'The bros.'"

"So they are brothers," she said slowly. She was getting that feeling, the tickle in her stomach. "We thought Sylvia was rambling on about the Kennedy brothers, Ted and John, but she was giving it to us straight—telling us that Ted Connelly and his brother were students here." She grabbed his arm. "Ted and John Connelly. Turner's former identity must be John Connelly."

McPhee said, "Let's go see if our well-dressed friend can confirm it."

She slipped both photos into her bag, and they drove back over to student records.

"Well," the clerk said after a quick search, "I found several John Connellys, but this guy's got one of the birthdays you mentioned before. He graduated six years ago, early."

"What do you mean, 'early'?" McPhee asked.

"He zoomed through in three and a half years, finished his degree in December of that year, not June like everyone else." He looked back at the screen, and then up again. "Took honors in pre-med."

"Pre-med?" Kit asked. "Not pre-law?"

"Hey!" the records guy looked excited. "The December John Connelly graduated? That's exactly when Ted Connelly dropped out, six years ago."

"I want to go somewhere and eat," Kit told McPhee, "and think this out."

On their way back to the car, she got a return call from Nate. She told him about her discovery about the Connelly brothers. Then she said, "Hey, I left a couple of messages for Quinn, but he hasn't called back. Where is he? Do you know?"

He was silent for a moment before saying, "I'm not sure where he is—" He stopped short, then said in a rush, "Hey, just so you know, my main client needs a bunch of help from me, all night tonight, and probably part of tomorrow, but if you need anything, Kit, you can call me."

She took the phone away from her face to stare at it, thinking, what's up with him? There was an odd note in his voice, some curious undertone, but she couldn't identify it. She decided it was probably her imagination, and asked if he would help by looking for any online information to confirm that Turner had attended UW as John Connelly.

He told her based on how Ted Connelly's identity had been obscured, it was doubtful he'd find much. "Turner has probably done a wipe on his name, but I'll be glad to try."

Kit and McPhee went to a café and ordered sandwiches. McPhee said, "What the hell is Turner so desperate to cover up?"

Kit said, "My friend Walsh always says, 'Tell a lie on one side of Alaska, and it'll catch up with you on the other.' Something happened in Saluda, something Turner wants to keep hidden, and Rebecca found out."

On the table between them were the two photos she had of the Connelly brothers and the information they had from student records. She tapped the photos. "We need to go see Sylvia. We'll show her these and get confirmation that Turner is John Connelly."

She called Dean Romero to ask for Sylvia's address while McPhee went to check on their sandwich order, which was taking a while.

"You need to ask Sylvia for her address," said the dean. "She'll decide if she's able to have company. Call her later, once she's had a chance to sleep, or better yet, check with her tomorrow morning."

Kit hung up and tried Clara again. She answered, and Kit asked eagerly, "Have you seen Quinn? He isn't answering his phone."

"He said he'd see me here at lunchtime, but he didn't show."

When Clara said this, Kit got a bad feeling.

After disconnecting from Clara, she tried his cell phone again. Her shoulders clenched tight when she found that his mailbox was now full. Why would he let his mailbox fill up? And why hadn't he called her as promised? What was going on?

Suddenly, into her head popped the image of Quinn, beaten unconscious and left to die somewhere by a gang of thugs. She jumped up and pulled her sweater on. McPhee came back to the table, followed by the waitress, who was carrying their order.

Kit blurted. "We need the check. I need you to get me to the airport so I can catch an earlier flight."

McPhee got her to calm down enough to explain. When he understood that Quinn had neglected to call as promised, his phone messages were overflowing, and thugs had already beaten one person up, he agreed that her concerns weren't far-fetched. He insisted they wrap napkins around their sandwiches and take them along.

She slapped some money down, and they jumped into his car and screeched out of the parking lot. He wrenched them around a corner and zoomed onto the expressway. As they were weaving in and out of cars on I-5, he said, "I'll get with Sylvia and show her the photo, ask her to confirm that Turner is John Connelly."

She gratefully tucked the spaghetti picture in his pocket.

"I probably won't even be hung over," he said grumpily, "since you're not sticking around to party. All because your new boyfriend needs you to rescue him."

He was trying to make her smile. She patted his shoulder and said, "Oh, don't worry, you'll be hung over. There are dozens of other journalists to party with."

"Amateurs," he scowled, "compared to you."

He got her to the airport just in time, and she was able to grab a last-minute seat on the earlier flight. But then the jet stayed grounded on the tarmac for almost two hours while technicians tried to fix a cargo door that wouldn't close properly. She sat in the cramped plane, growing hot and then cold with worry over Quinn. Why didn't he answer his phone?

~~~

When Allie pressed herself against him and admitted she'd been wrong to give him up, Quinn had two simultaneous reactions. One thought was that he'd be smart to turn, walk away, and never look back. But on the other hand, people can change. They can grow up. It was possible that Allie had realized she'd made a mistake, and now wanted to correct it.

He'd spent three years madly in love with her, driven by visions of their future together. It had been a huge emotional investment. Now her words were making him wonder if, instead of being painful to him, those years could actually end up being the foundation for a long life together.

Allie took his hands in both of hers, and swinging them, she said, "It's already past eight. No wonder I'm starved. Are you starved?"

He nodded.

"I'll cook for you!" She squeezed his hands and let go to open the car door. "You've been so generous today, it's the least I can do."

He joined her in the car. "No, please," he said, "you don't have to cook."

She snapped the seatbelt on. "I know, but I want to!"

He fell silent. She was a disaster anywhere near a kitchen. He was pretty sure that hadn't changed. "I'll tell you what, I'll take you out."

"Quinn," she objected, "you're so sweet! But I want to cook you dinner."

"Please," he implored her, "let me treat you."

"If you insist," she said, giving him both a pout and a smile.

He brought Allie to her apartment, stopping on the way to pick up his suit from the dry cleaners. She disappeared down the hall to shower, and as soon as she left his sight, everything he'd neglected to think about all day came rushing to the front of his mind. Marcus, Rebecca, Kit. *Kit.*

He grabbed up his phone and saw that his voice mailbox was full. Several messages were from Nate. They were insulting to Quinn's intelligence and Allie's general character— she's a user, he bluntly stated. Quinn skipped ahead through Nate's calls until he got to several from Kit, asking him to call.

He definitely needed to talk to her; he owed her an explanation about Allie. He shook his head. But what explanation? He had no idea what Allie's words actually meant. She was crazy to give him up? That was flattering to hear, but what did it mean? And furthermore, did he even care?

Then it hit him. If he and Allie could talk about what had occurred between them, not just the good but the bad, he'd feel better about it all. He knew that was one thing he wanted—to make peace with the past.

Another thing he wanted was to pursue this special feeling that had sparked up between him and Kit. It felt far from trivial. It felt potentially wonderful, in fact.

His watch said it was almost nine. She was due back from Seattle in a few hours. Rather than try to get her by phone, he'd go to dinner with Allie, and put the past to rest. Then he'd get with Kit. The first thing he would do is apologize for falling out of touch all day. And then he'd—

Allie pranced into the room wrapped only in a towel. She took his phone out of his hand

and merrily turned it off. Then she pointed toward the bathroom, commanding, "Go get clean! I'm starving!"

When he came out of the shower, she was already dressed, and looked gorgeous in a gold brocade dress he'd never seen before.

He found himself thinking that even though she'd hurt him, everybody made mistakes. Maybe she was sincere, and really did want to correct hers. Then, inwardly he chided himself. Just the sight of her had the power to rattle his thinking. *Keep your head*, he told himself as she took him by the hand and led him out the door.

~~~

Kit's return flight back to Nipntuck ended up being one of those things that starts out bad and just gets worse. First, the cargo door problem kept them grounded in Seattle for hours. Then some electrical glitch forced them to make an unscheduled stop in Wrangell, south of Nipntuck, where they had to change planes.

She got into Nipntuck at ten, only an hour before her original flight would have landed. *This has been the longest day of my life*, she thought, and whipped out her phone to call Quinn. "Answer, Quinn, please," she whispered. But he didn't.

She had arranged for Buddy to pick her up early, and finding no one at the house, had him wait while she called Clara. Clara, with some theater friends for drinks, reported she still hadn't seen Quinn.

Swallowing back her fear, she called the police and the hospital to see if Quinn had turned up at either place, but he had not.

She had Buddy drive her to the harbor, and had him wait while she ran down to Rebecca's boat. It was dark, but she called out Nate's name and pounded on the pilothouse, in case he wasn't working for his client, but was sleeping instead. All she heard was Flotsam growling. Although deaf, he could feel the boat list and always growled when somebody climbed aboard. Kit slumped, unsure what to do next. She was so worried she felt sick. *Where was he?*

She decided to keep moving. It was either that, or going into a frozen state of panic. She thought about Fred's call, telling her about Willow the waitress. Maybe the restaurant would still be too busy, but Kit decided to go see. It gave her something to do, anyway.

Buddy drove her to the restaurant, and she told him he didn't need to wait. His fee, thanks to the multiple stops, his waiting time, and his taste for round numbers, amounted to three hundred dollars. She paid him with the credit card, and he roared off with a smile.

Kit stepped into the entry of Silvers and noted that the dining room was still very busy. The long summer days tended to delay the dinner hour and nice weather made people play longer and eat even later.

She saw Freddie standing at a table, holding up a bottle of wine like a pro, but made no attempt to catch his eye. She'd come back when things were slower, after the kitchen closed.

She turned to leave but froze. Just past Freddie, she spied Quinn at a table with a woman with bleached blonde hair. The woman was very pretty, and as Kit watched, she slipped a foot out of a high-heeled pump and slowly extended it under the table toward Quinn's lap.

Kit felt a flash of white, furious heat. It

was distressingly similar to the feeling she had when she found out about Jean-Philippe's wife. She whirled around and left.

19

Quinn could still feel where Allie's toes had clamped onto him. He'd forgotten how strong her feet were.

The whole dinner had been a fiasco.

Mistake number one. He had expressed himself. He'd explained how it bothered him, the way their engagement had ended so abruptly. Absolutely no closure, just shock on his part. He'd asked: How can two people be that close, for years, and be planning a future together, and then . . . nothing? Not be in each other's lives at all? He wanted some kind of relationship to be possible, he told her. But he was pretty sure it was friendship.

And that's when she slipped off her shoe and clamped onto him with her toes. She told him they would talk things over when they had more privacy. When we get home to bed, she'd said.

She must have noticed the look of distaste on his face because she laughed, a bit harsh, and said something about how he'd changed, and she wasn't sure she liked it.

He removed her foot from his lap and said, "Allie, I've met someone." Mistake number two.

She stared at him in surprise, and then color flooded her cheeks. She tried to put her foot back in his lap, but he fended her off. A competitive person, she spent the next fifteen minutes pursing her lips, wiggling, speaking baby talk, and generally trying to trigger any stupid male response in him that she could. It sickened him, but the feeling was directed mostly at himself and his determined blindness, more than at her.

The waitress dropped off their check, and Allie said, "I should treat you. I might have enough cash . . ." She opened her little velvet purse.

"No need." He reached out to stop her, and accidentally bumped her purse so that it spilled its contents onto the table. A Visa card skidded out and stopped at his fingertips. He picked it up, looked at it, and then at her.

It was only a second, but in that second, he caught a look of dismay on her face, followed by a quick look at his eyes, and then a guilty look away.

Snagging the credit card from his fingers, she stuffed it in her purse and said, "That one's expired." With a lame shrug, she jumped up to go to the ladies' room, promising to be right back.

When she returned, he stood up and politely escorted her to the door. He moved with studied calm, but his entire body was sweating. All he could think was: *what a fool I am!*

Outside, she let out a huge yawn and apologized that she was suddenly so tired . . . too tired for company. He drove her home and she slid out of the car, gave him a casual wave, and hurried inside the building.

He grabbed his phone and turned it back on, intending to call Nate and tell him: *you were right—she used me. I'm the worse kind of fool.* He saw he had two new messages. One of them was from Elise. She'd called a few minutes after nine.

"Quinn!" she said. "Marcus showed up!

I'm so relieved! He's unharmed. It was another drinking episode. Like before, he has no recall, can't remember where he was. He's exhausted, but wants to go over to the island and get right to work, which is ridiculous. The man needs a shower, and sleep, and time for the booze to leave his system. I told him that he's spending the night on the *Blue Sea*, and I will have my way because I grabbed the key to the Toad, and put it where he doesn't dare try to get it back." She gave a wry laugh. "I just wanted to let you know that he's back and is safe. I hope whatever drew you back to Fairbanks so suddenly is getting sorted out. Oh! That man is impossible—now he's trying to hotwire the Toad. I need to go!"

He looked at his watch. Just after eleven. Marcus was probably asleep. He felt like kicking himself. It was pathetic how he'd let everything slip from his mind all day because of Allie. He'd meant to discuss Hamm, and Turner with Elise, but hadn't. Plus, he'd acted like a jerk toward Kit—dropping out of touch all day.

He swung the car around and sped toward her house. It was after eleven, so she was back from Seattle. He could see so clearly now that his feelings for Allie had been entirely based on illusion. Whereas with Kit, illusions didn't stand a chance. One look from those blue eyes of hers, and you knew where you stood.

Along the way, he remembered his second phone message, and played it back. "Quinn," Nate's recorded voice was clipped. "I'm working for my client all night, and he's in a cabin over on Hamburger Island, so I'll be out of cell range. But listen up, this is important. The harbormaster had me empty Rebecca's mailbox because it was overflowing. There's a letter—Rebecca wrote it and mailed it to her mom, but it was returned, postage due. I decided to open the letter and I'm leaving it here on the *Valiant* for you. You need to read it. I could be mistaken, but it looks like—" Quinn heard a rustling of paper, and then Nate's message got cut off. Quinn's in-box had filled up again.

He tossed his phone down, disgusted with himself for letting Allie take his phone from him earlier and turn it off like that. He'd go get Kit, and together they'd go to the harbor to get Rebecca's letter.

He rolled to a slow stop in front of the house, perplexed by what he saw. His duffel bag sat on the sidewalk, and behind it, the residence stared at him, unlit and expressionless. His watch said 11:23 p.m. *What's going on?* he wondered. Could Kit be *that* mad he'd neglected to meet her at eleven sharp? Then he reminded himself about how he'd failed to call her midday as promised, and also that he'd let his mailbox fill up. She had every right to be pissed—he was a thoughtless jerk.

He went up the walk and knocked on the door. There was no answer. He looked back at his bag, huddled forlornly on the sidewalk. He called her phone and left a message. "Let me apologize," he said. "I need to see you."

After waiting a few minutes, he again knocked on the front door. Then he called her phone a second time. "Please answer, Kit. There's a letter Rebecca wrote. Nate left it on the *Valiant* for us and says it's important. Please answer the phone."

But he got no response. Reluctantly, after waiting another few minutes, he went to the harbor without her. On his way down the ramp, he noted that the lights on the *Blue Sea* were ablaze, and wondered if Marcus might still be up. He was eager to meet him, no matter what condition the man was in. First, though, he'd retrieve the letter from the *Valiant*.

He stepped onto Rebecca's dark deck. Nate was obviously gone for the night, but Flotsam was home. Quinn could hear him growling inside. He tried to go through the door and face the growling dog, but he couldn't make himself do it.

Instead, he went over to the *Blue Sea*. If Marcus was still awake Quinn could explain everything, and together they'd retrieve the letter. Marcus loved Flotsam, Kit had said. Or, maybe Elise was around if Marcus was asleep.

"Hello!" He swung open the door of the wheelhouse, and stopped in shock. The foul smell of a backed up toilet hung thick in the air. The floor of the main cabin was littered with pizza crusts, cushions were upended, and booze bottles were strewn everywhere.

For a split second he wondered if Marcus had somehow wreaked this havoc while on a drinking binge, but dismissed the idea. The thugs probably did this, he realized, after they tossed Nate off the yacht.

He retreated outside, the letter plaguing his mind. It was cowardly, but he could not make himself brave Flotsam's teeth to get at it.

Suddenly, he just wanted to go find a hotel. He'd hardly slept the night before, due to worry over Rebecca. First thing in the morning, he'd find somebody to help him get that letter.

He called the nearest hotel, then the next closest, and so on, until a tired hotel manager informed him why everything was full. "Nipntuck's annual blueberry festival," the man told Quinn. "I'd be shocked if you found a bed anywhere."

He was about to go spend the night in the BMW, when his eyes fell on the Toad, tied next to the yacht. He peered under the bow and saw a bunk. He crawled over some gear and fell onto the thin mattress, ready for this rotten day to be over.

When his eyes opened, pale dawn showed through a tiny skylight. The Toad was rocking from the weight of someone who had come aboard. He started to sit up and call out a greeting, but heard a ringing phone and paused.

"Yeah," he heard Turner say. "You heard right. He's gone."

Still groggy, he thought Turner was telling someone Marcus had disappeared again. He snapped awake when Turner said, "Ran back to Fairbanks."

Turner continued, "Those new hires fucking trashed the yacht. I'd be pissed as hell about that, except he's getting blamed for it, which is convenient. Hey, I gotta go—"

A beat later Quinn heard him say, "Morning, Dad. There's coffee in the thermos." Turner's voice had a warm note Quinn hadn't heard him use before.

"Good morning, son. I'll take some more coffee, you bet."

Quinn wanted to jump up and confront Turner, but waited, hoping to hear more. He didn't have to wait long.

"So Dad," Turner said. The motor turned over and the Toad began to move. "I'm surprised you hired Quinn. If you're worried that our security is insufficient, why didn't you talk to me about it?"

Marcus spoke slowly, as if being careful with his words. "I wanted to meet him before

I introduced you two. I . . . wanted to get a feel for him . . ."

With a snort, Turner said, "Well, do you have a feel for him now?"

"I'm afraid I do. That mess on the *Blue Sea* can be cleaned up, but the same can't be said for his reputation, unfortunately."

Quinn watched out the tiny porthole as they threaded their way slowly out of the harbor. Once past the breakwater, they picked up speed, and Turner spoke loudly so his voice could be heard over the roar of the twin outboards. "So what did you want Quinn for? What are we not already doing?"

"I'll level with you, son." The boat curved between two islands, and the wind noise dropped, allowing Quinn to hear clearly. "I feel we didn't know the entire story about Hamm, but you tried to convince me otherwise. I took that as a sign that you simply can't think about one more thing. You're spread thin enough. So I was going to have Quinn examine Hamm's credentials. Investigate, if you will. But I wanted to make sure you two had decent chemistry, so you didn't feel your toes were getting stepped on. The last thing I wanted to do was send you a vote of no confidence. So, putting all this about Quinn aside, we need to address the question of Hamm."

After a silence, Turner said, "I should have listened to you. I'll debrief Hamm and let him go immediately. You can stop worrying about it." He followed this with the sudden question, "Do we seem bow-heavy to you?"

"Something's odd," Marcus agreed.

Quinn tensed.

"Play with the trim a bit," Marcus suggested. A moment passed. "There, that seems better."

Only a moment or two later, the boat slowed, and Quinn realized they were weaving through the many rocks that marked the approach to SeaLab's dock. Turner said, "Elise and I did our best to smooth over your absence, but the team will be relieved to see you. We only have time to say hi to everyone, and touch base with the team leaders briefly. Then we'll need to get back downtown for our meeting with Elise."

The two men secured the Toad and left. Quinn uncurled his legs and flexed them, hoping to get his circulation back to normal. Since it was a brief stop, he would stay hidden, and see if the return trip yielded more information. He was more than ready to confront Turner, but he'd hold off until they reached Nipntuck.

Keeping a wary eye out for anyone approaching, he dialed Elise.

She picked up and immediately said, "Oh Quinn, please tell me you didn't leave that mess on the yacht. I convinced Marcus to sleep on the *Blue Sea* last night, but then we found it in that state."

Anxious to clear his name with her, he said, "I didn't make that mess. I hate to tell you this, but Turner sent his thugs to the yacht and they beat up a friend of mine—"

"So it was your friend? Well, they were right to kick him off." A phone jangled in the background.

"Elise, wait, no, Nate didn't do that to the *Blue Sea*. Turner is actually to blame for it. He—"

She cut in, an edge in her voice, "I know for a fact that Turner wouldn't do that to our company yacht. He won't set a glass down unless there's a coaster under it." The phone in the background kept ringing, insistent. "Look, I have to take this call. I'm upset now, because instead of apologizing it sounds like you're trying to duck blame."

"Wait, Elise. I have to tell you some things—"

"I know we need to talk more about this, but it needs to wait until after the unveiling tomorrow. I'm sorry but I have to take this call." She hung up.

He took a deep breath and called Kit.

"What." Her voice carried a distinct lack of warmth.

"It's me."

"I know. What do you want?"

"To apologize. I'm—"

"Don't bother," she said.

"I should have called you back yesterday, and I'm sorry I got back to the house after you."

"That's your apology?" He could *hear* her eyes narrow.

"Kit, please. I'm sorry. I'll make it up to you, let me—"

"Look," she drew in an angry breath. "You tell me you're not involved with anyone. You throw the charm around and start putting the moves on me . . ." Her voice began to rise.

"You think it's cute to play with me like this, but I happen to know you *are* seeing someone, and you're doing it *right* under my nose! I saw you on a full-blown *date* at that *restaurant*."

His heart fell. She'd spied him eating dinner with Allie. At the same time he realized this, he noticed Marcus and Turner were approaching. He withdrew back onto the cramped bunk. "Kit," he said urgently, keeping his voice low, while making sure he was not visible from on deck, "Did you hear my message about the letter—"

Furious, she cut him off. "*Don't* change the subject. I saw what she did to you with her foot, and I almost *threw up!*"

He tried to muffle the phone into the bunk as the men approached. "In fact, you're making me want to *throw up* right now with your—"

Wincing, he turned the phone off just before the two men climbed onto the boat.

20

Kit couldn't believe it—he hung up on her. She flopped down on her bed. She had actually considered him attractive. Not to mention strong, kind, and smart. *Get. Out. Of. My. Head.* She punched her pillow on each word. *You. Are. Banned.* She jumped up to pace around.

"He calls *me* and then hangs *up* on me," she said, getting angrier by the minute. She wanted the last word.

She dialed Quinn's phone, but he didn't answer. Then she saw, in addition to the messages he had left the previous night—which she'd ignored—that Nate had called as well. She felt the burn of humiliation remembering the way Nate had hesitated yesterday when she asked where Quinn was. That odd undertone in his voice—it was *pity*. She'd been made the fool, and Nate knew it!

She threw the phone down.

The phone rang, and she dove on it, ready to yell at Quinn some more. But it was Walsh, her trooper friend, finally responding to the message she left for him on Monday.

Gruff as usual, he got right to the point. He was back in Nipntuck, but would be in town only a few hours. He'd gladly meet with her, but it needed to be right away.

His office was several miles out the road. She put on her running garb and set out at a fast pace. Normally, she'd drive, but the parking tickets littering her backseat had caught up with her, and her car was at the impound lot. She was ignoring the situation. And running more.

It was sunny for the third day in a row, but the rays were thin, filtered through muggy air that foretold a change in the weather. As she ran, she shoved thoughts of Quinn to the back of her mind. Rebecca was the subject she wanted to keep front and center.

The night before, she'd returned to the Silver at closing time. Fred had brought her over to Willow, who was counting her tips, and introduced her.

Willow confirmed she'd served Turner and Rebecca on Sunday night, and Kit asked, "Did you notice anything about them? Their conversation, their manner . . . anything at all?"

Willow said, "When I saw them, my first thought was, what a good-looking couple. I don't mean couple-couple—more like a first- or second-date couple. They had that alert, private look people get, like when they're just getting to know one another. Compared to the bored look couple-couples have when they've been together too long."

Good, Kit thought, *a waitress who keys into people.*

"New couples are usually good for tips," Willow said, "because the guy will want to seem generous, even if he's really not. So after they ordered drinks, I was keeping an eye on them, you know? He said yes to another round of drinks, no to appetizers, and after that I made sure to keep in the background—ready, but not pushy. But it started looking more and more like he wanted no food, just drinks. Which is disappointing, you know? It ties up a table all night, and I make hardly anything."

"Could you hear what they were talking about?"

"Not really, except when I went to fill their water glasses this one time. He was asking her, 'Where did you get this? Who gave it to you?' He stopped talking when he saw me come up with the water carafe. He covered their water glasses and just waved me away."

"Did you see what he was talking about?"

"He had something in his hand. It looked like a photo."

"What was his tone of voice?"

"I don't know . . ."

Kit waited. People automatically said 'I don't know,' but given a moment, they sometimes did know.

"I guess there was something intense about the way he asked."

"What happened next?"

"The woman, Rebecca? She was shaking her head, not saying anything. She had this deer-caught-in-the-headlights kind of look. You know that look?"

Kit's throat tightened. She did know that look.

"I went and took care of another table, a normal one, where the people actually wanted to eat something."

"Then what?"

"He waved me over and all the tension in him was gone. Rebecca seemed relaxed, as well. He gave me a charming smile so I knew their stressful moment had blown by. It made me hope that they'd finally order dinner. But he wanted the check. I thought he'd at least leave a good tip for me. But guess what?"

Kit answered, "He stiffed you."

"Bingo."

~~~

Quinn hated to hang up on Kit, but he had no choice when Marcus and Turner climbed back aboard the Toad. Father and son commented on the calm-before-the-storm feeling in the air, and then once they were up to speed, because of the wind direction, Quinn only heard the occasional word they said. At one point, Turner mentioned Georgette's name, and eager to hear better, Quinn raised up on an elbow. In his hurry, he cracked his skull against the a brace directly above his head.

"Did you hear that?" Turner said, throttling

down suddenly.

Quinn fully expected to see Marcus look under the bow and find him, but instead Marcus said, "It sounded like a deadhead."

"Deadhead?" Turner asked.

"A submerged log," Marcus explained. "That didn't sound like a bad one, compared to the one I bumped last week."

The boat sped up and they raced across the water for another ten minutes, before slowing down again. Quinn turned his head carefully to look out the porthole. He expected to see them back at the *Blue Sea*, but they weren't. Turner had pulled up to the service dock on the opposite side of the harbor.

The boat rocked, and there was a thump as someone jumped aboard. He began unfolding himself out of his hiding place, determined to confront Turner and redeem himself with Marcus. Then he heard Marcus, from a distance, say, "And also get your diver to check the hull. Last week I thumped a deadhead, and today we found another one."

Quinn realized now that Marcus and Turner were walking away. He struggled to get out of his tight quarters, but discovered both his legs had fallen asleep.

By the time he crawled out onto deck, and surprised the mechanic who was changing the Toad's engine oil, Marcus and Turner were nowhere to be seen.

Quinn limped away from the fuel dock, searching futilely for a glimpse of the two other men. He turned his phone back on and called the number for Marcus, but got no answer. He swore when he saw Nate had left a fresh message while his phone had been turned off.

Nate sounded worried: "I'm at Rebecca's boat, but I need to get back over to Hamburger Island again. I've tried calling Kit about this letter, but she isn't answering. And obviously you didn't come by for it last night. I'm going to assume you're not dead in a ditch somewhere, and you're just being stupid over Allie. Really fucking stupid."

"Great," Quinn scowled. Everyone was disgusted with him—his oldest friend, two powerhouse women, and the scientist he was trying to help.

One thing at a time, he told himself. He needed to grab the letter off the *Valiant*.

And he needed to look for something to eat—his stomach felt like it was chewing on him from the inside out, as though it was mad at him, too.

"Nice Flotsam," he said, easing inside the door of the *Valiant*. The dog kept up a steady, menacing growl, as it came out from under the table and took a bowlegged stance.

Quinn cautiously slid his front foot forward. The letter was on the table, only a few steps away.

"I'm just here to get this letter . . ." he said, pointing and reaching for the letter.

When Flotsam sprang, he didn't snap at Quinn's leg, instead he came at his face. Quinn threw his arm up to ward off the attack, and Flotsam fell back onto the floor, a scrap of coat sleeve clamped in his jaws.

Covered in a cold sweat, Quinn spun around and burst back out the door. He went straight to the BMW, climbed in and slammed the door shut. A feeling of relief washed over him. A nice car didn't solve all the world's problems, but it did offer a quiet refuge in the middle of a shitstorm.

He sat there trying to shake off the traces

of his sweaty dog-induced fear. When he stopped wanting to take a fire hose to Flotsam, he realized had no idea what to do next, but decided that taking a drive in the Beemer might help improve his mood, while he considered his options.

Out the road, the bay glimmered in the hazy sunlight, looking dreamy and serene. After six miles, when the pavement ran out, he pulled down the slanted concrete boat ramp and stopped a few feet before it disappeared into the water.

Though this region of Alaska was pretty, Quinn preferred the arctic's open whiteness. In the far north, because often ice and sky were barely discernible from one another, some people found it disorienting, but he liked it. The uninterrupted space helped focus him. But here, hemmed in by sky-sucking mountains, and trapped by a road that went nowhere, it was harder for him to think, harder for him to stay on balance.

What the hell was Turner up to? He considered it convenient that Quinn was being blamed for trashing the *Blue Sea*, but why? Who had he been talking to on the phone?

Leetham? Hamm? Someone else? Quinn had no evidence linking him directly to the attack on Rebecca, or Marcus's problems. Quinn didn't even have any solid reason to doubt Marcus was suffering a drinking relapse, but he felt certain there was more going on.

Marcus should be drug-tested immediately, he realized. If he had any drugs in his system, the window for detecting them could be fast closing. He had been tested before, down in Seattle, but just going to Seattle had created a time lapse. One that may have been crucial.

He called Elise and left her a message about it, but realized after he hung up that Elise and Marcus were distracted by the unveiling, and they were also convinced that the problem was a drinking problem and nothing more. He had to convince them of the importance of getting Marcus drug-tested immediately. But it complicated things that his credibility was at an all-time low, thanks to the mess on the yacht.

It occurred to him that if he made a show of good faith, Elise and Marcus might listen to him. The envelope with the check Elise had given him for seventy-five hundred sat in his coat's inner breast pocket, still unopened. He could give it back, which might help. He should also relinquish the BMW. He could leave it at Marcus's house, where it had been originally.

He had a plan. Nothing brilliant, he knew, but something was better than nothing. He'd leave the car off at Marcus's house, and get a taxi back downtown. He'd go straight to Elise and give her the check. And then he'd make her listen to him, even if it took going down on bended knee.

He turned the car around and called for a cab to meet him at Marcus Holland's house.

"We're giving you Buddy," the dispatcher warned, "don't cancel."

"I won't," he said.

He got to the house and Georgette answered the door with a sneer. "What do you want?"

"I'm leaving the BMW here with you." He handed her the keys. "A cab will be here any minute to take me downtown."

Her mouth twisted angrily. "So how much did she pay you?"

On the basis of her having a drink-fogged brain, he excused her blunt question. Indicating the check in his coat's inner pocket, he just said mildly, "I'm returning the check, uncashed."

Her eyes glinted and before he could stop her, she snatched the check, tore the envelope open and pulled out the check. She stared at it, and then at him. "Don't tell me you did it for fun."

"Did what for fun?"

"You took pictures of me."

"I took no pictures of you. I saw some shots of you on Turner's phone, though. What's the deal with them?"

She glared at him through narrowed eyes. "Why didn't you cash this check? That seems stupid to me."

He shrugged. "I didn't do anything to earn it. Marcus showed up on his own."

"He's back?" Georgette's eyes narrowed even more.

"He showed up yesterday—"

With surprising strength, she yanked him inside and slammed the door shut. They heard his cabbie honk out in the drive. She reopened the door, screamed "Cancelled!" and slammed it shut again.

Quinn heard his ride peel out of the drive.

Georgette was making herself a cocktail. "Want one?"

He could now add psycho-cabbie to the list of people pissed at him. Sure, he told her, a drink was just what he needed.

He was joking, but a moment later she thrust a tall cocktail at him.

Studying his face, she swigged down some of her drink. "Elise hired you to gather information on me."

Quinn shook his head. "What information? Did Turner tell you that?"

"Well, either Elise hired you, or she hired someone else to take those pictures."

Without thinking, Quinn took a drink, and then studied the glass, wondering what she'd concocted. It seemed strong.

With a huffing noise, she pushed herself upright and said, "Turner lied to my face. The bastard's double-dealing me, I just know it."

"Double-dealing you how? What are those pictures about?"

"Wait here." She left the room, and Quinn heard her rustling papers in the study. He tried his drink again and liked the taste better this time.

She finally came back in the room with a large yellow envelope. Sealing it, she handed it over. "Give this to Marcus."

He set down his drink, surprised to note the glass was nearly empty. "What is it?"

"It's the truth. You can tell him that."

"What truth?" When she said nothing, he tried to give it back to her. "Tell him yourself."

She refused to take it back, and instead held up the keys to the BMW. "You can have the car—I mean *have it*—if you do this for me. My name is on the title, not his."

Yeah, right, Quinn thought, taking the keys from her. He went out and climbed in the car, tossed the envelope on the seat and started the engine. He had no interest in helping Georgette out. But he was glad to have the car to get back downtown. And he'd certainly look and see what was in the envelope when he got there.

He'd gone only about a mile when he heard "*Whooop! Whooop!*" and a cop was on his rear bumper, flashing lights and tooting the siren. *Observant*, he chided himself. At least he hadn't been speeding.

He pulled over and rolled down the window. Holding out his license, he asked genially what the problem was. The cop took his license, while a second cop stood a few paces back, hand on the butt of his holstered firearm.

"Leaving town?" The cop eyed the duffel bag that Quinn had rescued off the sidewalk in front of Kit's house.

"No, just in between places," he said. "What's the problem, officer?"

"This car has been reported missing."

Elise and Marcus thought he was back in Fairbanks, so they couldn't know he was the one who'd taken the car. He started to explain this to the officer, but stopped when the cop suddenly leaned closer to sniff suspiciously at his face.

Putting one hand on the top of his billy club, the cop stepped back and ordered him to step out of the car.

Quinn expected to be told to walk the line or to get a breath test, both of which he knew he'd pass, but instead the cop told him to empty his pockets. He took away his phone and his wallet, then shoved him against the car and patted him down.

"What the hell—"

The cop yanked him back around and said a few lines about his rights while snapping cuffs on. He shoved him in the back of the patrol car as the second cop happily jumped into the BMW.

At the police station, they stuck him in a locked interview room by himself. Bile green walls leaned in on him while a glaring fluorescent light whined and flickered overhead. The room itself was nearly a form of torture. All they had to do was add some chimes, and he'd confess to anything.

He tried to think, but his mind just lumbered in circles like a jet trying to land: the letter from Rebecca he still hadn't seen; Turner's game, whatever it was; Kit's wrath toward him; Nate's disgust. He wanted to act on all these things, but first, he had the bozo cops to contend with.

A cop unlocked the door and stuck his head in, and with a grunt, started to retreat. Quinn jumped up, stuck his foot in the door and insisted he be allowed to make a call.

They gave him his phone back. "Kit—

don't hang up," he said when she answered. "I'm in trouble."

She didn't hang up, but she didn't say anything either.

"I'm being held at the police station. Marcus has reappeared. But he needs to be drug tested. And also, Nate found a letter. I haven't read it yet because Flotsam attacked me, and now I've been arrested . . ." He groaned. Clear as mud. He tried again, "There's a letter from Rebecca . . ." Damn! He couldn't tell her what it was about because he didn't know. So he just said, "Can you get me out of here?"

"One hour," she said and hung up.

~~~

Kit had just arrived at Walsh's building and was catching her breath when Quinn called. She was relieved to hear that Marcus had reappeared—it made one less gnawing worry to carry around. She wondered how Quinn had managed to get arrested, but pushed the thought aside. It was time to talk to Walsh.

"You ran here." He'd been expecting her, but not on foot.

Gerald Walsh was one of the smartest men Kit knew, but he had a mental block when it came to exercise. He couldn't believe people did things like running—voluntarily, that is. He was at least six two, and had a hard, round gut that thrust his khaki shirt out in front of him. He had a brush cut, an unevenly trimmed mustache, and from a distance looked like nobody special. But up close his brown eyes carried an alert, knowing light that said he probably knew the score. Kit had never known him not to.

"Your car's impounded again?"

She studied a strand of her hair for split ends, waiting for the subject to pass.

"I'd have driven downtown to meet you."

"Running clears my head, some days."

"It help today?"

Ruefully she shook her head. "I was hoping you could donate some brainpower."

"I heard about Rebecca."

"That's what I want to talk to you about."

"Thought so."

He opened his desk drawer and pulled out some car keys. "I'll drive you back home while we talk."

Once in the car, he looked at her, and then glanced away. "So how's Clara lately?"

"Good," Kit said.

Despite being seventeen years older than Clara—Walsh was fifty—he had a substantial crush going for her. He'd never married and had rarely dated. Kit used to think it was due to the demands of his job. Lately, though, instinct told her that this calm, dry-witted man, whom she'd never seen ruffled, might actually be shy when it came to love. Instinct also warned her that if she ever teased him about Clara, he would stop speaking to her.

They pulled up to the house and remained sitting in the car until she finished telling him everything that had happened. Then they went inside to have some coffee, and Walsh was visibly disappointed that Clara wasn't around.

"She's probably with a client," Kit said apologetically. She made coffee, and they sat at the table. As she hoped he would, he began distilling everything she told him down into a few sentences.

"Setting aside, for the moment, the funny business going on with Marcus Holland disappearing and reappearing, we have Rebecca hung off the side of her boat early Monday morning." Walsh ran a hand back and forth over his brush cut, a habit he had when he was busy thinking. "There's a suicide note you believe is in her own hand, but she couldn't have tied that knot herself and wasn't in the least suicidal. Her mother lives in Saluda and knew a man named Turner, and she wrote a letter wondering whether it was the same man Rebecca knew from work, photo enclosed, except the photo wasn't enclosed." He took a drink of coffee. "On Friday, August 18, Rebecca made Turner a birthday cake. It was the date mentioned in the letter. He denied it was his birthday and was rude and angry, out of character.

"On Sunday, August 20, Turner, who apparently didn't find Rebecca attractive, took her to Silvers for dinner, and was possibly the last person to see her before she was attacked. Their waitress said he was showing a photo to Rebecca, demanding to know where she got it, and Rebecca didn't seem to want to answer."

Kit nodded. Summed up like that, what she knew seemed terribly skimpy.

"And you think Turner, though he claims to be self-taught before he went to UCLA's law school, actually went to the University of

Washington, under the name John Connelly. And he's the possible brother of Ted Connelly, who works security at SeaLab under the assumed name Stan Hamm."

"I'm expecting McPhee to call any minute with confirmation that Turner is John Connelly."

"Nothing you've said so far implicates Turner in anything, except failing to disclose everything about himself. People do that all the time, for various reasons."

She nodded.

"What's needed," Walsh told her, "is a witness or a weapon."

"What if I just confront him? Tell him I know his story doesn't add up. Provoke him?"

"Kit," Walsh barked. "Don't be stupid. Take a step back and ask: What does this person want? Forget words; study behavior. Fact: he lied about his background, so we know he wants to keep that hidden. If he's hiding something serious, asking him straight out is a bad idea. That's dancing with the devil." He stared sternly at her. "Am I making myself clear?"

"Yes," she said, "but my gut tells me it's

time to press Turner." She looked at him, imploringly. "Will you help?"

"Of course I'll help. I'm flying back out to Edam Bay this afternoon. It's a sticky case, but it should wrap up shortly. I'll call you as soon as I'm back."

She countered, "What if I can get Turner to meet me for lunch today? Before you go back to Edam Bay? You could appear at our table and lay some questions on him, and I could remain the innocent bystander."

His eyebrow went up. "Questions like what happened when he was with Rebecca on Sunday, and whether he's ever been to Saluda?"

She nodded. "And what's his relationship to Ted Connelly who also goes by the name of Stan Hamm?"

"It would have to be soon."

"I'll call him right now." Retrieving the card Turner gave her at the auction, Kit dialed. Getting his voice mail, she left a message, asking in a soft, breathy voice if he would join her for lunch at the new Thai restaurant. "I'd really like to see you," she said, and hung up.

Walsh was shaking his head. "How do you

women do it?"

"Do what?"

"Put so much promise in so few words?"

She gave him a little knowing smile, and he pretended to shudder.

"Okay, kiddo," he stood up and moved toward the door. "If he calls back, let me know. It might work. I'm supposed to fly out at three thirty."

After Walsh left, she dialed McPhee's number and left a message asking if he'd had any luck getting with Sylvia yet. Then she remembered she was supposed to go bail Quinn out of jail.

21

As Kit walked toward the police station she tried to sort out her feelings toward Quinn. It pissed her off that he'd call needing her help, right after lying to her face. Underneath her anger was sharp disappointment, and hurt. She hadn't let him jump into her bed, like she did with Jean-Philippe, but Quinn had gotten into her heart, which felt even worse. What was it about her? Did she have some neon karma sign blinking on her forehead that said: Liars! Cheaters! Welcome. Stomp all over me, please.

She had to pull herself out of this losing streak—no one else was going to do it. *I'm going to walk straight up to Quinn and let him have it with both barrels. Then turn and leave.* She was walking faster now. *Let him call his nimble-toed girlfriend for help.*

Except when the cop led her down the hall and showed her into a vomit-green room, Quinn's eyes lit up with a look that stopped her short. Then he crossed the distance between them and held her so tight she couldn't even think straight.

She heard him say, "I'm sorry Kit. I know I need to explain."

"I don't want your explanation," she said, getting her mad back on. She put her hands on his chest to push away. "How dare you even touch me!"

Quinn looked down at her, his eyes unbearably warm, his hands resting lightly on her upper arms. With dismay, she realized she hadn't pushed against his chest so much as clutched his pecs—because she was a pathetic, feeble woman who had no control whatsoever.

She twisted away and backed up, pointing and ordering, "Stay there! Do not touch me." His touch was lethal. It confused her. He was a liar, and she needed to remember that.

Quinn said, "Please help me get out of here. There's a letter Nate left for us on the *Valiant*, and he says it's important. Rebecca wrote it. And also, I need to convince Marcus to go get drug tested."

She closed her eyes. She wanted to just walk away, and leave him here to *rot*.

Instead, she made herself go hold a little conference with the cop in command. He grumpily told her no charges had been brought against Quinn *yet*, but that was all he could tell her because he was very busy. *Very busy.*

He got less busy once she told him her family had lucked into a substantial amount of halibut. "More than we can eat," she said.

"Like about forty to fifty pounds more?" the cop in charge asked.

"Well, like ten to twenty pounds for sure."

"Thirty-five, forty pounds would sure be nice," he said.

"Fine," she said. *Greedy pigface.*

He pulled a form out of a desk drawer, signed it, and directed one of his underlings, "Go get Big Guy for her."

Quinn gathered up his belongings, including his duffel bag while she stood by in stony silence.

"Thank you," he said when they got outside.

She refused to look at him.

"Kit." He stepped in front of her so she

had to look at him. "You have every right to be mad, but here's what happened. The woman you saw—I was involved with her, engaged in fact, but it ended eight months ago, and we haven't spoken since. I left a message for her when I first got to town, before I met you. Yesterday she tracked me down. It was idiotic of me, but I thought I could salvage a friendship with her. But I guarantee you, it's completely over. I'm not going to see her again. There's no longer the slightest trace of romance between us. You have to believe me."

Kit just wished she could walk away, and not have this talk. She'd seen with her own eyes, the woman sitting with him at the restaurant, slipping off her shoe to reach for him *with her toes*. The image made it difficult for her to stand here and listen to what he was saying, let alone believe him.

Quinn continued, "We need to talk about this some more. But Nate left a letter for us on Rebecca's boat. He says it's important."

She immediately started toward the harbor, and Quinn shouldered his bag and fell in beside her. While they walked, he told her the few details he knew about Marcus's reappearance, and they agreed that finding Marcus, and getting him drug-tested, was critical.

They discussed Turner next. She quickly sketched out what she'd learned in Seattle, and he filled her in on what he'd overheard on his ride in the Toad.

They found Nate on the *Valiant's* deck, flipping salmon steaks on the barbecue. As they walked up, Kit noticed that he gave Quinn a long, pointed look.

"I'm cured," Quinn told him. "You should see the bill."

Nate grunted. "I'd get a certain amount of pleasure in that."

She didn't understand the exchange, but forgot all about it when Nate handed her a letter and said, "Rebecca wrote this to her mom and it got returned, postage due. She wrote it the night Marcus disappeared."

She and Quinn bent their heads together over the letter. Rebecca had dated the letter August 18. A PS was at the very bottom, and then a PPS was scrawled sideways on the page.

Dear Mom, it's almost 3 a.m. Friday night (actually Saturday morning!) and I can't sleep. In fact I'm pacing around my boat right now. I feel like such an idiot and really, really wish we could talk. I wish the darn phones would stop cutting out!

Okay, I'll slow down and tell you what's going on. I got your letter with the photo, and of all the crazy things, it is the same Turner! He's changed, though, very clean-cut now and is super smart— he's very high up in SeaLab.

But I feel like such a dummy. You know how I always make birthday cakes for everyone? Well, you said in your letter that Turner's birthday is August 18. So I baked him a cake and brought it to our employee picnic today. But he got really mad and said I had the date wrong, which seemed like such a little thing to get upset about.

So a bit later I made a little joke about his punk rock days—I just wanted to tease him, get him to lighten up a little—but he just stared at me and said, "What?" So teasing still, I said, "Oh, I know all about your past." Right then someone came up to talk, and he just left. Because it's such a busy time at work for all of us, I assumed he just wasn't in a joking mood. But then I finally realized what was going on—I shouldn't tease him about his past or expect him to celebrate birthdays—I'm pretty sure he was abused as a child. And here I am, throwing bad memories in his face.

I'm going to apologize first thing Monday. Anyway, my hand is cramping up from writing this so fast. I'm going to try to get to sleep now. Thank you for listening!

Lots of hugs and kisses ~ XXXOOO Your Rebecca

PS: Oh, Mom! I just heard SeaLab's little commuter boat—called the Toad— pull up. Usually it's my boss who drives it, but it was Turner, so I rushed out to say I was sorry. He wouldn't even speak to me! In fact he couldn't get away from me fast enough. He went inside the company yacht and wouldn't even answer my knock.

Quinn pointed to this PS about the Toad. "Rebecca wrote this on Friday—the same night Marcus disappeared. Elise thinks Marcus brought the Toad back from the island, but it was Turner."

Kit turned her head sideways to read the final words Rebecca had added in the margin.

PPS: I'm going to write an apology and stick it on the door of the yacht so he'll see it tomorrow. I feel so bad—I hope he forgives me!

A cold chill swept over her Kit. Her voice shaking, she said, "Rebecca wrote that note of apology to Turner . . . I think he tore off the bottom of it and used it as . . ." She saw Quinn turn the letter sideways to read Rebecca's final words, and then he looked at her, stunned by the same realization.

"The suicide note," he said, "was part of the apology Rebecca left for Turner."

Kit's phone rang, and she fumbled to dig it out. McPhee, she reasoned, calling to say he had confirmed that Turner was John Connelly.

But it wasn't McPhee, it was Turner.

She answered, goosebumps prickling her arms.

Turner said he'd be happy to meet her at one o'clock, at the new Thai restaurant.

She looked at her watch. "Can we make it one-thirty?" She needed time to reach Walsh and make sure he got to the restaurant ahead of them.

"I'm sorry, my schedule's packed today," Turner said. "But I'd really like to see you. Would it help if I came and picked you up?"

I need to make this work somehow. Her heart was thudding, but she managed to speak calmly. "Actually, one o'clock will work. I'll meet you there." She hung up.

Quinn, seeing her face, asked "What is it?"

"Excuse me," a voice made them all turn.

A stocky gray-haired man walked up to the *Valiant*. "I'm Marcus Holland," he said somberly. "I just heard about Rebecca."

Kit felt a rush of relief when she saw Marcus. Whatever twisted game Turner was playing, providence had brought Marcus right to them. She closed her eyes and sent a thank-you out to the universe. Now Quinn could get Marcus in for drug-testing, while she and Walsh rounded Turner up.

It was showdown time.

Marcus asked, "Does anyone know if a service has been planned for Rebecca?"

"I'm Rebecca's friend, Kit Finnegan," she responded, "I've been trying to reach Rebecca's mother, and when I do, I'll make sure she contacts you."

"Thank you," Marcus replied. "Are you Kit Finnegan, the reporter?"

She liked it when people said that. "I am." She moved toward the rail. "I'm sorry to rush off, but I have a meeting."

Quinn put his hand on her arm. "Kit. I want to make sure you understand—" he stopped. Obviously he wanted to continue pleading his case to her, about that blonde woman, but knew this wasn't the right time.

"I need to go now, Quinn. I'm meeting with my trooper friend, Walsh. I have to catch him before he leaves town again."

She stepped off the boat, taking the hand Marcus offered her. She clasped his palm for an extra moment. "Mr. Holland, Rebecca has said many times how honored she . . . has felt working alongside you."

"It was mutual," he said, his voice catching. *In a minute, Quinn will explain it all,* she thought, *and you'll know she's still with us. But then you'll have to learn the terrible truth about your evil son.*

Hurrying away, she dialed Walsh, who answered promptly. She told him lunch was on, for one o'clock. She started to tell him about the letter, but he interrupted, "Listen, Kit, I'm in a tight spot here. I can't make it to the restaurant ahead of you, but I should just be a few minutes after one o'clock. I don't want you with this guy, unprotected, for even five minutes. You need to have someone with you."

"I agree," she said emphatically.

He said. "I'll get there as soon as I can."

~~~

Quinn introduced himself to Marcus, and the older man eyed him coolly. "Out of respect for your late father, I will merely say I'm disappointed in your conduct, and leave it at that. Good day." He turned to leave.

"Mr. Holland, I wasn't the one who left the *Blue Sea* in that condition."

Marcus, who had been keeping a somewhat

neutral expression, now looked upset. "Elise told me you tried to suggest that Turner is to blame for that mess. Did he also make you drink, and then drive my car?" He spun on his heel to leave.

"Mr. Holland," Quinn said quietly, "give me one minute before you go—"

Marcus turned back around, impatient.

Quinn said, "I understand why you would have trouble finding me credible, but please put that aside for a moment and listen to me. I think it's critical that you get into the hospital to get tested for—"

Marcus interrupted, "I've promised Elise I will check myself into the hospital, right after the unveiling tomorrow. Now you need to excuse me; I'm under an impossible deadline." He started to turn away again.

Quinn plunged on, "Mr. Holland—last Friday night, do you recall leaving your lab office, walking down the path, getting in your boat? What's the last thing you remember?"

Marcus rubbed his temples. "I don't know, son," he said tiredly. "I just know the biggest event in my company's history is tomorrow, and I have a week's worth of preparation to do before then."

"You didn't leave the island under your own power. I believe you were overcome, very possibly drugged. The lab's security tapes may show us something. But more importantly, you need to get your blood tested. Samples of your blood may offer proof of what's going on, but those traces could be fast disappearing. Time is of the essence."

"Time is of the essence," Marcus said wryly. "That's what I'm trying to tell you."

"I can prove you did not bring your boat downtown."

Marcus stared at him. "What?"

"You don't remember getting in your boat Friday night."

Marcus had a curious expression on his face. "I don't," he agreed. "The last clear memory I have is working at my desk."

Quinn picked up Rebecca's letter, and seeing Georgette's envelope in his coat, he handed them both over to Marcus, saying, "Rebecca wrote this letter, the night you disappeared. The other envelope, underneath it, could be relevant, as well."

Marcus took them but froze when he recognized the handwriting on Georgette's envelope. "This is from my wife?"

"She said to tell you it's the truth, or something along those lines—"

"I know what it is," Marcus's voice shook with anger. Without another word, he strode to a nearby waste bin and slammed the envelope into the basket, throwing away Rebecca's letter with it. Then he turned on his heel and walked away.

Quinn hopped over the *Valiant's* railing and went after him to explain he had no idea what Georgette had put in the envelope, but Marcus didn't give him a chance. He went directly to the Toad, started it up and pulled away, with only these parting words: "It confounds me, Quinn, that you would join her efforts to ruin me."

He disappeared around the breakwater, and Quinn walked back to retrieve the papers from the waste bin. Slitting Georgette's package open, he pulled out a sheath of legal papers. A glance told him that they were divorce papers. Quinn felt a blood vessel thudding in his temple. *I don't understand how he sees this as ruination, and not salvation, but I don't understand a lot of things.*

He went back to the *Valiant* and told Nate they needed to do some damage control. He explained about getting blamed for the mess on the *Blue Sea*. "Was there anyone around that day, anyone who saw those assholes having their party, who could vouch for me?"

"I saw the guy with the obnoxious chimes around, but he's in a snit because of what you did."

"What I did?"

"Yeah the whole harbor knows: you duct-taped his chimes. You're a hero to everyone except him."

"Listen, I need to go find Elise. In the meantime can you try to butter up the chimes guy? Make my apologies or something?"

"I can try."

Quinn put Rebecca's letter into his coat pocket and climbed off the boat. Noticing his frayed cuff, he stopped. "Are you feeding Flotsam?"

"Sure, why?"

"He seems different."

"Ever since Hamm threw him off the boat, he's been in a bad mood."

"Terrific," Quinn said. "A dog who holds

grudges."

"He's sensitive," Nate said.

Quinn had to look twice to be sure, but Nate was in earnest. *Yeah, a sensitive, vicious, creepy, ugly canine*, he thought as he left.

At SeaLab, he saw that someone had brought the BMW over from the police station and parked it in the lot. He touched its fender for luck before going inside the building.

To his relief Elise was in, but she refused to meet his eyes. He asked, "Do you know where Turner is?"

She shook her head.

"We need to talk," he said.

"I'm terribly busy, Quinn."

"Give me a task. I know you have a lot to do before tomorrow."

She said, "No, but thank you," and disappeared down the hall juggling an armload of what looked like press packets.

His phone rang, and Nate said, "I'm here with the chimes guy. The deal is this: I vouch for the chimes guy, and then he'll vouch for us."

"You'll vouch for him?" Quinn said.

"To his chick. We're stepping over to her

boat right now to patch things up."

"Patch what up?"

"Long story. Heartbreak, bad timing, dirty blonde. Gotta win back the woman."

"The dirty blonde?" Quinn asked.

"No, we're all trying to forget her. That was a mistake."

"I can relate," he said. "Okay, do whatever it takes, just keep him there. I'll kidnap Elise if I have to." He hung up.

"Excuse me?" Elise had returned to the reception area and was standing, hands on her hips, frowning at him.

He said, "You're coming with me over to the harbor. There's someone who will explain about the *Blue Sea*. And then I need to share some information with you. It's critical."

"About what?"

"It concerns what happened to Rebecca, and what's happening with Marcus."

She studied him for a moment, and then sighed. "Fine. Kidnap me. But make it snappy."

He held the door for her. "I know a fast car we can take."

~~~

The last thing Kit wanted was to be alone

with Turner at the restaurant. The idea made her whole body turn cold. As she raced home to change out of her running clothes, she called around, seeking someone to accompany her, at least until Walsh could arrive. Unfortunately, no one she called even answered—including her brothers, Johnny and Big Pat. She left messages in case they were screening calls. Then she considered stopping at the Shanty to recruit someone, but she was already running late.

At home, she threw on what she considered the most innocently tarty outfit in her wardrobe: short shorts and a top that rode up on her belly just a bit. Then, looking in the mirror, she tore it all off and dug through her closet looking for something else.

Finally she found it—a soft, bust-hugging sundress she had not worn since high school. The kind of thing a person kept in their closet because they liked the material, not because they ever expected to wear it again. It made her look thirteen. With a woman's boobs. It wasn't her—and it was just right.

Walking rapidly toward the restaurant, she tried to think of anyone who might be close by and could join her. Just as she got there, she thought of Nate. Quinn had to stay with Marcus, but Nate could peel off and join her. She'd have to explain things to Nate, and then wait for him to arrive. Maybe she had time; it was possible Turner hadn't even arrived yet.

She glanced in the window of the restaurant and immediately saw Turner, and he looked decidedly impatient. Before she could pull back out of sight, he saw her through the window and stood up. She had no choice but to go in.

22

At the door of the restaurant Kit hesitated, aware that the sun backlit her in the flimsy dress. She paused, not for effect, but to swallow back the terror bubbling up in her throat. She was barely able to breathe as she stared across the room. This man, she now had reason to believe, had tried to kill Rebecca.

Please get here quick, Walsh, she thought, and made herself go forward. As she walked toward Turner, his eyes glinted in a way that told her the baby-doll look was working. She took a seat. Their waiter arrived with menus, and she asked for a Thai iced tea. Her mouth felt like a desert.

As soon as the waiter departed, Turner spoke. His words, though they sounded casual, made Kit's skin prickle. He said, "At the art auction, you told Elise that you were friends with Rebecca."

Kit nodded emphatically. "Yes." She didn't like the careful way he was watching her. "I miss her."

"I miss her, too." Turner said. "Did you two meet through your work at the newspaper?"

Kit took a sip of water, buying a moment to think. Clearly Turner was playing some cat and mouse game, and she was the mouse. Shaking her head, she said through dry lips, "Mutual friends." She fought to keep her expression as bland and innocent as she could, while waves of panic rolled through her.

"I took Rebecca to dinner the night she died," Turner said.

A drop of sweat threaded down her back as she tried to think of some response. "She was really taken with you." Surprisingly, the words came out sounding genuine.

The door opened, and she shot a look that way, hoping it was Walsh, but it wasn't. She needed him to arrive. Now.

Suddenly Turner's phone trilled. He answered, and exclaimed, "He's what?" His eyes snapped wide. "Obviously. Call everyone together for a meeting. I'm leaving now." He listened for a moment.

Kit couldn't believe it. Turner was leaving. Before Walsh could arrive.

He hung up his phone, pushed back his chair, and announced that he had to resolve a crisis at work.

Something made her suspect Turner was taking flight, and not just from the restaurant. The thought made her blood race. She wanted to stop him, accuse him, do *something*.

"Turner," she said softly.

He'd risen from the table and was about to leave, but stopped.

"You should know . . ." she looked at him with all the sincerity she could muster, "you were in Rebecca's thoughts those days before she died."

He nodded impatiently.

"I know because I ended up with some of her personal things, like her . . . diary."

He eased back down into his chair. "Oh?"

She slid her hands, which had started to tremble, onto her lap, feeling as though she'd just stepped out on a high wire.

She forced herself to keep going. "When I opened it, I just started to cry, and I couldn't even see the words . . . but I saw your name everywhere." She shook her head.

Turner leaned in, his eyes pinned to her face.

"You have this diary?" His lips were a thin line. "Do you have it with you now?"

"I don't have it with me right now, but I was wondering . . ." she took a deep breath. "Maybe we could do something symbolic with it, together? Something in Rebecca's memory?"

He stared into her eyes. Nodding slowly, he said, "I recently came across an article about a midnight mourning ceremony, a Tibetan tradition. Let's do that."

She broke her eyes away from his hypnotic stare. "Okay," she mumbled, staring down at the table.

He leaned closer and stroked her arm. Though desperate to pull away, she forced herself to sit still. Gently, he said, "Don't read the diary; you shouldn't do it alone. We'll remember her together. Tonight. At midnight."

"How about nine or ten?" Her voice came out sounding faint. She cleared her throat. "Earlier is better for me."

"I would, but I'll be in meetings until late. We're scrambling to pull together our big unveiling tomorrow."

His fingers, still stroking her arm, were cold metal rakes. *I'm going to scream if he doesn't stop touching me.*

"SeaLab has a yacht moored downtown," he said, "the *Blue Sea*. Let's meet there, at midnight."

She nodded, wordlessly.

He stood back up, told her the boat's slip number, and a second later he was gone.

~~~

Quinn and Elise walked up to the plywood houseboat. The chimes were nowhere to be seen. Nate was inside with the boat's owner, who turned out to be an okay guy named Henry.

He poured them all cups of sludgy coffee, and then gave Nate a sort of thumbs-up and turned to Elise. "I guess you want to know how your yacht got all messed up." He paused, his head bobbing thoughtfully while they all waited.

"Well, what happened was I was working on my boat . . . and these three big dudes came along and they went on the yacht." He waved his cup in the direction of the *Blue Sea*, sloshing coffee on the floor without seeming to notice. "And they went inside, and I heard some stuff."

After gazing out the window vacantly, he swung his gaze back to Elise. "There was, like, these bumping noises and kind of a yelp—" he laughed, accidentally dribbling some saliva. He wiped his chin. "Sorry man," he said to Nate, "but it sounded like you yelped."

They all looked at Nate, who shrugged, and then turned back to Henry, ready for him to go on, but he didn't. Finally, Quinn said, "What happened then?"

"What? Oh, yeah. After they threw him off, the three guys left, and things were quiet for a while, but then two of the guys came back later, and man, the party started. There was music, crashing sounds, yelling. And once . . ." But he turned to look out the window again.

"Once . . . ?" It was Nate's turn to prompt.

Henry's eyes swung back. "Um, yeah, this girl with an awesome Mohawk brought a whole load of beer and pizza, and she stayed in there a long time, man." He blinked slowly and finally grinned. "So that's the deal, you know." He stood there swaying and nodding his head.

"Thank you, Henry," Elise said.

Henry considered her words before giving her a happy nod. Then he pulled Nate aside to whisper something.

"Wish I had some too," Nate said.

Walking back to the car, Elise told Quinn, "I'm sorry I even thought you were capable of such a thing. Things are so crazy right now, with Marcus showing up, and the unveiling . . ." She opened the door of the BMW and climbed in.

Quinn joined her in the car. "I know you're focused on getting ready for the unveiling. And you're happy that Marcus is back, unharmed. But Marcus is not out of danger." He started the car and aimed them back to the office. "Do you have any idea where Turner is?" he asked.

"I'm not sure. He fitted his father with one of those locator devices, so he might have let Marcus out of his sight. What danger is Marcus in?"

He parked in SeaLab's lot and turned to

Elise. "Turner is not who you think he is." He reached in his pocket and pulled out the letter. "Rebecca wrote this letter last Friday, the night Marcus disappeared."

Elise read the letter and then reread it. She murmured, "Rebecca saw Turner bringing the Toad into the harbor at that hour, instead of Marcus? I don't understand. Why would Turner tell me Marcus brought the Toad back that night?"

He pointed to the part on the page where Rebecca vowed to write a note of apology and leave it for Turner. "There was a note on her boat, staged there to look like a suicide note. It was taken from this apology note Rebecca wrote to Turner."

Elise was shaking her head.

Quinn said gently, "Elise, it looks like Turner is the one who attacked Rebecca, and it's very possible he's Marcus's abductor as well. You cannot trust him, nor Hamm."

She stared at him. "I can't believe . . . why on earth . . ."

Quinn was struggling with the same question. *What did Turner want?* Into his head popped Nate's pithy phrase: follow the money, sonny.

He asked, "What are your liquid assets right now?"

"We have about fourteen million readily available."

Quinn felt a prickling on his scalp. "Can just one company exec draw from the account?"

"Up to a certain amount, but for substantial amounts, a second signature is required."

It made sense that the firm's cash reserves were accessible only through double approval. He should have guessed that would be the case. He stared at Elise, thinking, *What could Turner be up to?* He felt like he was in a race, in the pitch black, without any idea how the course turned or what the prize was.

"I'm not sure what's going on," he told her. "But we need to get Marcus in for blood tests. If he's been drugged, it would be very telling—like finding a weapon. We need to do it quickly, but here's the critical part: we need to do it without Turner knowing. I need you to call Marcus right now, and if you reach him, let me speak to him. If he doesn't answer, leave a message that you need to see him, and it is urgent. But say nothing more than that.

Alarming Turner right now would be a serious mistake."

She called and Marcus didn't answer. After she left the message as instructed, Quinn said, "I'm going to arrange to have the testing expedited at the hospital. I should only be a few minutes, and then I'll come right back. If you see Turner or if you see Hamm, call me and don't say anything, just hang up. I'll come immediately. If Marcus shows up here alone, call right away and let me know."

Elise, though pale, spoke evenly. "What you're saying about Turner . . . it seems mostly based on conjecture."

Quinn said grimly, "I'm working on that. Just promise me: if you see Turner, or Hamm, or Marcus, you'll call me."

~~~

After Turner left the restaurant, Kit started shaking. She pressed her iced tea glass to her forehead and tried to calm herself.

Walsh arrived a moment later and she felt a flood of relief. But from the way he walked toward her, she could tell he had concerns of his own. "What is it?" she asked.

"The storm's moving faster than predicted. The pilot's waiting for me, has the engine running already. Either we go now, or we wait until after the blow."

She looked outside and saw their sunny day had changed to gray and gusty. From the look on his face, she knew his case probably hinged on him leaving immediately.

"You'd better go," she urged.

"What happened here? Is Turner late, or did I miss him?"

"He's come and gone. I'll fill you in as soon as you get back. Don't tempt your pilot to cancel the flight."

"If the weather allows, I'll be turning right around with my suspect." He gave her a stern look. "You came alone to meet with Turner?"

"Go." She waved at him to hurry.

He turned to leave, but paused. "Kit. When I get back, we'll tackle this thing. Don't do anything rash."

"I won't." She said this automatically because her mind had gone blank. She had no idea what she was going to do—rash or otherwise.

The waiter came to take her order and Kit,

distracted, pointed at some soup on the menu. It came quickly but just sat in front of her, untouched. Her stomach was heaving with stress. Then McPhee called, and what he told her made her stomach hurt even more.

"I tried yesterday afternoon, and last night, and again this morning, but couldn't get a hold of Sylvia so I called Dean Romero. She said Sylvia went to the hospital last night with pneumonia."

"Oh no."

"She's stable, so they just now allowed me, her long-lost grandson, to see her. I showed her the picture of "the bros" and asked if she remembered them. Well, the poor lady was out of it, mumbling and all, and she mentioned the car thing again. But you know how we thought she was confused, and remembering Ted Kennedy's car crash at Chappaquiddick? Well, this morning, she mumbled something about car exhaust, and said something about suffocating."

"Carbon monoxide."

"Yeah, and guess what? I searched on that, and I got a hit. It was the parents. Patty and Ben Connelly. The article said they were found dead in their car in the garage—suicide. Survived by sons John and Ted."

"Oh God."

"Yeah. It wasn't in Seattle, it was up near Bellingham, in a little place called Kurk Falls."

"Never heard of it."

"Yeah, tiny town. Apparently they just got their archives scanned and put online, which is why Turner missed it when he was doing his background purge. I found another article. It was written years ago about some community service award the family got, and there's a picture. They're our boys. I emailed you both articles. I also dug up the number for the Kurk Falls police."

"I'll take it."

He gave it to her. "Look, I gotta get some sleep. But call me later to let me know what goes down. And Kit—"

"Yes?"

"Stay safe."

She opened McPhee's email containing the articles about the Connellys. The first was a brief mention of the parents' death. The incident happened in December, six years ago, and was called a tragic double suicide.

As McPhee said, the couple was found dead in the garage, car running. From the sound of it, the Connellys were model citizens. They were survived by their sons, Ted and John.

The second article was older, written about ten years ago, and was a long puff piece, recognizing the Connellys for their many years of community service. It listed good deeds ranging from hosting church fund-raisers to volunteering at the animal shelter. The article ran to a second page, and on this second page there was a picture of the family. It showed the parents with their three teenagers: John, Ted, and Joan.

Kit's mind flashed back to the sauna, and how Connelly had inferred some sinister act involving someone named Joan. She gripped the edge of the table trying to calm herself, as she realized that in the more recent article about the parent's suicide, Joan hadn't been mentioned as one of the survivors.

She called the number for the Kurk Falls police and asked for the person in charge.

The man who answered said, "You got him," and introduced himself as Chief DeSmet.

She introduced herself and said she had some questions about a family who lived there some years ago.

"Sure," he said cheerfully, "fire away."

She asked if he'd been involved in the Connelly case.

"Oh, yeah," his voice saddened. "That one was a real shocker."

"Mr. and Mrs. Connelly were good community members?"

"Oh, they were, ma'am. They sure were."

"I hope you don't mind me asking, but do you think there was any possibility of child abuse in the family?"

DeSmet said, "You've got them mixed up with some other family, miss, I'm sure of it. Patty and Ben were crazy about those kids. They adopted them, you know, maybe that's one reason they treated them like that."

"Like what?"

"Well, gave them lots of spending money since they were tots, and bought them cars as soon as they turned sixteen, and allowed them all the freedom they wanted." He paused, and added, "Maybe too much freedom."

"What do you mean?"

"By high school the boys were starting to turn into little toughs, and even worse in college. My Lord, when they came back for the holidays, we couldn't believe how the city changed them—the older one, spiked-out hair; the younger one, saying rude things. But it wasn't Patty and Ben's fault. They were softhearted is all. And once kids leave home, what can you do?"

Swallowing around the hard place in her throat, Kit asked, "And Joan?"

"Oh, she was a sweetheart."

"Was?"

"That's why her parents did it—killed themselves—everyone figures. They were devastated over what happened to her."

"What happened to her?"

"Drugs. She overdosed. She was living in Seattle. Nobody here even knew she was into drugs. Her parents took it hard, for sure. Then, a month later, at Christmastime, the boys, home for the holidays, found their parents in the garage. You know how holidays can be the hardest when you've lost someone, especially a child. And she was such a bright, pretty thing."

Kit's throat was so tight she could hardly

breathe.

"Say, what's this about anyway?"

"There's been an attempted murder and the Connelly brothers might have been involved."

After a silence, DeSmet said slowly, "You say you're with the press? Shouldn't the police be asking these questions?"

"I'm helping the police look into this. I have a personal interest in it. The woman who was attacked is my friend." She told him about finding Rebecca, and summarized quickly what had happened.

When she finished, he remained quiet. She wished she could see his face. Some cops didn't mind talking to a reporter, but others did. She took a deep breath. "I know I've taken a lot of your time, but could you tell me if there was any reason to doubt that the Connellys committed suicide?"

After a pause, he said, "Not at the time, ma'am." Then he let another silence fall.

She wondered if his silences were because he was thinking or because he was shutting down on her.

"Was there a large inheritance?" she asked.

"The Connellys were wealthy, that much

I know."

Kit waited.

He cleared his throat. "I could look back over the file, think about this some more." She breathed a sigh of relief. It sounded like he was willing to work with her.

"You know," his voice was quiet. "It's a nice town we live in . . ." he paused. "People here do bad things, don't get me wrong—I see it all the time. But this kind of thing . . . the mind doesn't even want to go there."

Kit found it hard to speak. Finally, in a low voice, she managed to say, "I agree."

~~~

Quinn went to the hospital to see Allie. The desk nurse told him she was on break, probably across the street at the cream puff place.

He found her just coming out of the bakery. She looked surprised to see him, and then pleased. "Hi there," she purred, stepping close. She pulled a cream puff out of a bag and brought it to her lips. Watching him over the top of it, she suggestively licked its edge. "Want some?"

He declined her offer, keeping his voice friendly. "Are you due back at work soon?"

"Unfortunately," she pouted.

"I'll walk you back."

Quinn knew once they stepped into the hospital, she would straighten up. She was serious about her work, and that was what he needed.

"Okay." She linked arms with him and took another slow lick of her cream puff.

~~~

Kit was on her way home from the Thai restaurant. She happened to glance across the street and stopped in shock. Quinn was standing with that blonde woman from the restaurant. They stood arm in arm outside the cream puff place, and from where she was, Kit could see the woman's *tongue* mauling a cream puff.

She turned and ran home. Storming up to her room, she dove onto her bed and clamped a pillow against her face.

He'd lied when he swore it was over. She let out a long, low moan.

There was a rap on her door. "What!" she shouted.

"It's Clara."

After a pause, she said in a subdued voice,

"Come in."

Clara entered and sat on the bed. Kit rubbed the wet corners of her eyes angrily. She knew the situation with Turner was what mattered. She had to tell Clara about Kurk Falls, but the words got stuck behind the lump in her throat.

Clara reached out and took her hand, and in a rush, Kit went ahead and told Clara about Quinn and that woman.

When she finished, they sat quietly for a while. Clara was staring down at Kit's hand, apparently lost in thought. But then her lips curved into a little smile. She pointed at Kit's palm and said, "Oh my."

"Oh my what?" Kit asked.

"My auntie taught me to read palms, and yours is like nothing I've ever seen before . . ." she gave a soft laugh.

"You read palms—for real?" Kit spread out her palm flat, and they both stared at it. "What does it say? What's weird about it?"

"I didn't say it was weird. But it does practically shout out that you're in for a wild ride, especially when it comes to heart matters."

Kit groaned. "Don't say that. I just want my love life to settle down!"

Clara gave her an amused look.

"What else do you see? If it says I'm going to take a vow of poverty and also that I'm going to make a lot of money working in international finance, then we're looking at some crossed signals, right?"

Clara studied her hand. "Honey, the signals aren't crossed at all. I've never seen so many converging signs." With the lightest touch, she traced a line running deep and curved across Kit's upper palm. "Your heart line is here. It says: ardent, vivid, dynamic."

She pointed to the fleshy pad of her palm by the thumb. "This area's called the mound of Venus. Venus, you probably know, is the goddess of love, the mother of Cupid. See all these lines running across here?"

Kit leaned in to look. "What do they mean?"

"They're influence lines, and goodness, look at all of them. Each one represents a person who will influence you in love."

Kit's brow furrowed. "Like lovers? All these lines mean a different lover?"

Laughing, Clara said, "They appear in

Venus, so I doubt they mean brothers."

"I don't want a lot of lovers! I just want one! Just one decent man!" Her voice was high and agitated. "Is what you're telling me supposed to help?"

"Don't be mad at *me*," Clara said. "I just thought it might help to know that you're probably going to be in love more than once." Then she rubbed Kit's hand briskly and said, "There, doll, now you've had a little session. I hope this satisfies your curiosity."

It took Kit a second to understand Clara's reference to a session, then she clapped a hand over her mouth. "All the men parading through the house—you're reading their palms?" She couldn't believe this was the therapy Clara provided. "But why just men? And why act so secretive!"

Clara shifted so she could lean back against some of Kit's many pillows. "I decided to concentrate on men because they get fewer opportunities to talk. They mill around all day with their chests puffed out, but honestly, they're just dying to get somewhere safe so they can blab. They come in to see me, place their hand in mine, I make a few observations, and it's like a floodgate opens."

Kit leaned in. "What do they talk about?"

"Same as women," Clara smiled. "Hurt feelings. Confusion. Guilt. Fears. Lovers, parents, best friends . . . you name it."

"Holy moly," Kit said.

"As for being secretive . . . it was my auntie's method. Men like telling their buddies to just come see me for a 'session.' The less said, the easier for them to avoid the stigma of going to see a palm-reader."

As soon as she stopped talking, they heard a faint knock on the door downstairs.

"A client?" Kit said, but Clara shook her head that she wasn't expecting one.

Kit ran downstairs and opened the door. A woman was sagging against the porch post. Grief had etched deep shadows into her face, but Kit recognized her from the photos she'd seen on Rebecca's boat.

"Bev?" she gasped, reaching out to grip Rebecca's mother by the hands.

23

~~~~~~

As Quinn expected, Allie became serious once they got back inside the hospital. She had her shortcomings, but one of them wasn't her work. She oversaw the staff of nurses caring for patients suffering from Alzheimer's, and was, herself, an excellent nurse.

Quinn walked her to her office, where he handed her the slip of paper he'd prepared. "I added up what you owe me. You said to remind you."

Allie looked shocked. "But I don't have it right now."

"That's okay, I just wanted you to have the total."

She looked down at it, and back at him, hurt all over her face. "You're giving me a bill? You were never stingy like this before." With a glance toward her office door, she dropped her voice suggestively. "Why don't you come over tonight. I'll make you dinner . . ."

"I'll tell you what," he said, taking it back from her. "I'll tear this up if you take care of something for me. My associate needs his blood drawn for some very specific testing. It needs to happen quickly and it must be done carefully. I'd like you to oversee it."

She looked confused. "Why me?"

"You could run the lab downstairs if you wanted, considering the years you put in spinning blood in Anchorage. I remember you once told me the date rape drug has a mean little brother drug that makes people not only loopy, but it makes them forget, sort of like your Alzheimer patients. We're looking for traces of something along those lines, or anything that might cause an otherwise healthy man to be unable to recall what's happened to him." He held up the piece of paper. "And then we could forget about this. Friends helping out friends, that kind of thing."

She agreed with that last part. He could tell.

"Okay," she said. "I'm friendly with the techs down there, so it shouldn't be any problem. Just call me when you're ready."

~~~

Rebecca's mother had shoulder-length blonde hair, streaked with gray, that was pulled back with a single yellow rubber band. She wore no makeup and carried one small, flowered overnight bag, which could have been from the 1970s. Her face, like Rebecca's, was beautiful.

When Kit saw the anguish on Bev's face, she feared the worst—that Rebecca had died. But then Bev asked tearfully, "Do you know where my Rebecca is?"

Quickly Kit said, "She's in Juneau, in the hospital. The troopers didn't reach you?"

"She's alive?" Tears were running down her cheeks. "Oh thank God. I've been traveling for four days. I thought I came too late—" She couldn't speak for a moment.

"Becca is alive, but . . . come sit down. "

She gently steered the shaken woman into the front room and helped her take a seat. Bev grew pale while Kit told her about finding Rebecca in the water. Meanwhile, Clara called the Juneau hospital, and put Bev on the phone with the nurse there.

Kit got on her phone to arrange a flight for Bev to Juneau. While she was on hold with

Alaska Airlines, she saw an incoming call from Quinn. She let it roll to voice mail. The first seat available for Bev was in the morning, and she made the reservation.

Bev finished her conversation with the nurse, hung up, and began to sob. In a strangled voice, she said, "Our phones went out and I started worrying about Rebecca so bad I couldn't stand it. It took me a couple of days before I could get off the island, but finally I flew over to Nome, and called, but she didn't answer, and then I knew something horrible had happened. I came as quickly as I could." She paused, clenching and unclenching her fists. "That bastard."

Kit and Clara looked at one another. "Turner?" Kit asked.

Bev nodded.

"What do you know about him?"

"I should have been more specific when I wrote to Becca about him . . ."

Kit said gently, "What do you know about Turner? What is he covering up?"

Bev took a shallow, shaky breath. "I moved to Saluda about eight years ago, when Becca went off to college. Turner's mother, Polly

Lynn, befriended me, and we became very close."

Kit sat up. "Turner's mother lived in Saluda?"

Bev nodded. "One day, he showed up on her doorstep. This was about six years ago. He was this . . . punk. Neon-colored hair, slouchy posture, messy clothes. But he seemed to care about her, and Polly Lynn was absolutely nuts over him, and very, very proud because he was studying law and all.

"When she started to get sick, we were all especially glad she had him." She stopped and closed her eyes to hold back tears. Clara jumped up and poured her a glass of water. Bev took the glass, but put it down without drinking any. "I visited her almost every day. One day, I stopped over earlier than usual, and saw what he was doing." She was white and trembling and trying not to cry.

"What did you see? What was he was doing?" Kit whispered.

Bev said, "Polly Lynn never said anything about needing shots."

"Shots?"

"He was stabbing her with a needle. Here,"

Bev touched her thigh. "I walked in on him, and I started to ask him what the shot was for, but he looked at me and something was wrong with his eyes. They were black inside. Have you ever seen a bear up close? It was like that. He was completely mute, but somehow so full of threat. I got so scared that I just left."

She took a nervous sip of water. "I couldn't stop thinking about it. I was going to ask Polly Lynn but Turner said she'd taken a turn for the worse and wasn't able to have company. So I tried to bring it up to a friend, but she refused to listen.

"When everyone thinks a person is so wonderful, it's virtually impossible to fight that, even in your own mind. I let my friend convince me that Turner was just giving Polly Lynn something for the pain."

She was crying now, her face lifted to the ceiling, her fists clenched in her lap. "Polly Lynn went into a coma and I never spoke to her again. A few days later she was dead." She wiped her eyes with the tissue Clara gave her.

"I couldn't even go to the funeral. He went to it, of course, and while he was gone, I snuck into her house and searched. I left all the needles in case he counted, but I took this little bit of powder." She pulled a small ziplock baggy of yellow powder from her case and placed it on the table.

"But then I didn't know what to do. We have no police in Saluda. We'll call the troopers sometimes and they fly out to handle a drunk on a rampage, or when some girlfriend starts shooting at her man. But this—" she poked the bag, "how could I explain this over the phone to some trooper? I stole it from another person's house. I don't know what it is. Then, before I could figure out what to do, Turner left. Nobody knew where. So I did nothing."

"Was there an inheritance?"

"She left him everything," Bev said quietly. "She worked all her life, saved all her life, and didn't have any other children. When he showed up, she gladly put him in her will. Not that she expected to get sick and die. She was simply thrilled to have someone to name in her will."

She looked at the two other women, her face white. "I know he killed her. It must have been for her money. And then he tried to kill Rebecca because he didn't want his past to catch up with him—I shouldn't have sent her that photo of him!" She crumpled over in grief.

Clara wrapped her arms around Bev. After a while, she suggested gently, "Would you like something warm to drink?"

"I'll make us tea," Kit offered. While waiting for the tea water to boil, she thought about the bag of powder Bev had shown them. When she saw Quinn earlier, he'd been right near the hospital, probably waiting while Marcus got drug-tested. Miss Cream Puff had been in a nurse's uniform, something Kit hadn't registered in the heat of the moment. He's taking care of Marcus, she thought angrily, while having a *really* nice time himself.

The kettle whistled, and Kit rose to make the tea. She wanted to forget she ever met Quinn. But she had to inform him about what had happened in Saluda. And in Kurk Falls. He needed to know just how dangerous Turner was. He had to be sure to keep Marcus safe.

If she spoke with him now, she would lose her cool and either yell, or cry, or probably both. She hated to lose her dignity, any more than she already had. *Nate*, she suddenly thought. *I'll call him. He can tell Quinn.*

Nate answered on the first ring and told her excitedly that he was seconds away from learning the nature of SeaLab's project. She stopped him and said she had critical information about Turner. She told him what she'd learned about Turner from Bev, and from Chief DeSmet, and in a small voice she concluded, "Quinn needs to know all this, but I'm . . . having difficulty talking to him."

"I'll take care of it," Nate said, immediately. "He and Elise are getting Marcus into the hospital for blood testing. I'll call Quinn and tell him everything you just said."

Kit joined the others in the front room. After she poured out the tea, she sat down, took a deep breath and told the other two about her conversation with Chief DeSmet, and what had happened in Kurk Falls. When she finished, a horrified silence hung over the room.

She broke the silence, concluding sadly, "Marcus was so happy to discover he has a son. And now he's going to learn his son's a monster."

"Except." Bev cleared her throat. She

looked at them, and then looked back down, smoothing her skirt. "Polly Lynn told me before she died: Marcus may not actually be Turner's father."

~~~

Quinn went back to SeaLab and found Elise distraught. Turner had just sent her a text asking if she'd seen Marcus, and when she replied no, he wrote that the locator device on Marcus has gone off-line and he feared Marcus was missing again. "He texted that I should keep my spirits up, and continue preparing for the unveiling, while he searches for Marcus."

"Text him back and ask where he is," Quinn urged.

She did so, and Turner texted back after a minute. "I'll find him. Don't worry."

They looked at each other for a long moment until Quinn said, "I suggest we go look for both of them."

In a low voice she said, "Yes."

They went to the harbor and saw that the Toad was still gone. Elise said even though the weather was worsening, the *Blue Sea* would get them over to the island alright. They boarded—a cleaning service had restored it to order—and she fired up the twin engines.

As she steered past the breakwater, she said, "Marcus disconnected the autopilot when he bought this boat. He's old-school—claims that autopilots make people inattentive." She deepened her voice to imitate him, "Either you're steering or you're not!"

A moment later she murmured, "I'm trying to believe that he just lost track of time." She looked over at Quinn. "He dropped his phone in the toilet bowl once, and didn't notice it was missing for six hours. Most of us would notice if our cell phone didn't ring, or at least go to use the bathroom in the space of six hours, but not him. He said it was a very peaceful six hours." She looked ahead, checking their course. "I'm babbling, aren't I?"

"Not at all," Quinn said. "Marcus is an unusual man, isn't he?"

"Unusual doesn't begin to cover it," she smiled ruefully. After a moment's silence, she said, "I want to tell you about our project."

She paused to steer them around a kelp wad before continuing. "Marcus has developed an ultra-battery. He's collaborating with a team of scientists back at this secret lab he built in California. The science is beyond me, frankly, but it involves nanotech, and is also based on some big discovery he made concerning the seawater up in this northern latitude." She gave Quinn a small smile. "Tomorrow at the unveiling, he will explain it all, so I won't even try to tackle it myself right now."

"So tidal power isn't part of it?"

"Actually, it is. But it's also serving somewhat as a cover. We wanted to draw Leetham off the scent of our nanotech work. From SeaLab island, Marcus can 'work alongside' his colleagues in California. The set up is really quite amazing. He employs a sophisticated network hookup with a virtual reality component."

His phone rang, and she paused while he took the call. It was Nate, saying, "Kit learned a bunch of bad shit about Turner."

Quinn tensed. He'd left Kit two messages. *She'd called Nate, and not him.*

"But first I have to give you the good news." When he got revved up, Nate's voice squeaked, and it squeaked in Quinn's ear now. "I got into SeaLab's secret network. You're not going to believe how cool their secret project is. There's a clandestine group of nanotechnicians who are working on what I can only describe as a kick-ass battery. These batteries are bendable and lightweight, like film, and reusable. An entire house could be powered by one of these babies, for a month.

"When the battery runs low, it's just switched out with one that's fully charged. The run down battery gets mailed to SeaLab to be recharged—using tidal power—and gets mailed back to the customer. You know how Netflix pioneered sending DVDs back and forth through the mail to customers—it'll be like that. Marcus has figured out a way to circumvent the electric grid altogether and deliver power straight to the people! Power to the people!"

Nate rushed on, "And in the not too distant future, these batteries will end our dependence on oil because they're going to power our cars! And trains and jets. That's why ESI is freaking—they can see the writing on the wall. Marcus is a genius! Is he still with the doctors? If not, put him on the phone. I gotta talk to him."

"Marcus is missing again," Quinn said.

There was a silence, and then Nate said in a voice so low Quinn barely heard, "No." Then his voice surged through the phone. "This is really bad."

"I know."

Nate's voice carried an oddly hollow note. "No, you don't know. I mean, it's worse than you think." He paused. "Rebecca wasn't Turner's first victim."

He could feel Elise watching his face and put the phone on speaker. She immediately throttled down so that she could hear. By the time Nate had finished telling them about Turner's mother dying a slow death in Saluda, and about Mr. and Mrs. Connelly in Kurk Falls, and Joan Connelly in Seattle, Elise had her face covered with both of her hands.

Quinn hung up his phone, and lacking any words, just reached out to place his hand on Elise's shoulder. She made a visible effort to collect herself, and a moment later, her face taunt with anxiety and determination, she resumed steering.

Twenty minutes later she brought the yacht up against the island's dock, and he had to hustle to secure the tie-up lines before the gusts could shove them away.

She stepped onto the dock beside him, and Quinn said, "Keep in mind that Turner isn't the only one we have to worry about. Hamm is a threat, as well."

They walked rapidly through the atrium and into the facility, which was oddly quiet, with only a few people present. Elise asked the first person they encountered, "Polly, have you seen Marcus?"

"A few hours ago. He came into the building and went straight in there." Polly pointed to the room that lodged the security screens.

They went to the door, and Elise raised her eyes to the retinal scanner. The door clicked open.

A security guard was leaning back in his chair with his feet up on a desk, talking on the phone. He hung up quickly and came over. "Hi, Elise," he said.

"Dale, we're looking for Marcus. It's urgent."

"He came in a few hours ago, wanting to see last Friday's recording. Mr. Hamm came in right after."

"And?" Elise asked. Her face had gone pale.

"Mr. Hamm said they needed extra security by the entrance, and sent me there."

Elise swallowed, and Quinn took up the line of questioning. "Did you see Marcus or Hamm after that?"

"I saw Mr. Hamm. I was stationed at the entrance only a short while, maybe twenty minutes, and Mr. Hamm called everyone together for a meeting. It was right after Mr. Holland, junior, arrived in the bird."

"What was the meeting about?"

"Good question," Dale said, and then he hesitated, throwing a worried glance toward Elise.

"Why do you say that?" she nodded encouragement for him to continue.

"Mr. Hamm herded all of us, security, techies, everybody, into that big conference room. I thought we were going to get a preview of what's coming tomorrow. But instead he gave us some handouts we'd already seen and said something about setting up a film for us, and left, but that never happened. Nothing did. It seemed a bit . . . unorganized, you know what I mean?"

"What happened next?" Elise asked quietly. "Did you see Turner or Marcus?"

"Neither of them. I heard the bird take off, though, while we were in the meeting."

"What time was this?" Quinn asked.

"A little after two this afternoon."

"Then what?"

"Finally Hamm came back into the meeting, and told us a storm was coming and everyone should go home while the catamarans could still make the trip safely."

Quinn and Elise exited the screen room, and once they were alone, Quinn summed things up somberly, "Marcus wanted to see Friday's recording and apparently that prompted another abduction. Hamm probably called everybody into a meeting so that Turner could get Marcus into the chopper and leave without being seen."

Looking pale, Elise said, "I need some air."

He took her arm. "Let's go search the grounds and discuss our options."

~~~

Kit stared at Rebecca's mom. Stunned, she repeated Bev's words. "Marcus may not be Turner's real father?"

Bev nodded sadly. "No one knows, except me. When Polly Lynn told Turner the identity of his father, she said what she *wished* was true—that Marcus was the father—rather than the actual truth."

"What truth?" Kit and Clara both exclaimed.

Bev sighed and took a small sip of tea. "It's a very, very unhappy story. Polly Lynn and Mark—she called him Mark—were sweethearts. He was a professor at Stanford—and one night while he was working late, his friend Bill, who was also a professor, showed up at Polly Lynn's place, drunk. Bill forced his way in and raped her."

Kit and Clara stared at her, wide-eyed.

"She grew deeply depressed, and wasn't able to talk to Marcus about it. When she learned that she was pregnant, she disappeared and gave the baby up for adoption. She never knew for sure who the father was—Mark or Bill."

She let a brief silence fall, and then continued, "Polly Lynn struggled all her life over the question of whether to contact Mark and tell him everything. She was able to keep track of him because of his career—both Mark and Bill ended up prominent players in energy development—but she didn't have the courage to face him."

Something clicked in Kit's mind. *The men were at Stanford, and both went into energy development.* "The man who raped Polly Lynn. His name was Bill?"

Bev nodded.

"William Leetham!" Kit said. The resemblance seemed clear to her now. Though Leetham had fifty pounds on Turner, they were built alike, and had the same coloring. And the timbre of their voices, including a certain arrogant note—no wonder she'd been confused by which of them may have been in the sauna, talking to Hamm.

Her phone rang, making them all jump. It was Chief DeSmet, and Kit quickly told him what Bev had revealed about Turner and his birth mother in Saluda.

"Holy cow," he muttered. "I've reopened the file on Patty and Ben Connelly and we're looking at that as a possible double homicide. Also, I contacted the Seattle police about Joan, the sister. It turns out two of their guys never believed Joan's death was accidental. They were about to come out and question her brothers when the tragedy with Ben and Patty happened. Their superior officer, who thought they were on the wrong track, said wait, don't interrupt the family while they're in mourning. Then the brothers disappeared without a trace. The case was dropped, but never closed."

"The Seattle guys are making arrangements to fly to Nipntuck to question the brothers about Joan, and I'm coming also, with questions about what really happened to Patty and Ben."

"The sooner you get here," Kit said, "the better."

After she hung up, she took a deep breath and told Bev and Clara there was one more thing she had to tell them.

When she told them about her lunch with Turner, and how she'd agreed to a midnight meeting, both women reacted with shock. "That is crazy, Kit!" Clara said. "You are not going to meet him."

Kit's fists were clenched into balls. "He thinks he's going to silence me, but I'm going to lay a trap for him."

Both Clara and Bev started to object strenuously.

"Wait," she overrode them. "I have a plan, a good one. It involves a lot of muscle power." She thought for a moment. "And firearms."

24

Quinn escorted Elise outside the SeaLab's main building and they began walking. He saw her struggling to compose herself, and wished he could say something to help. A construction area fanned out from the side of the main building and as they walked by the perimeter, he paused.

"Looks like somebody goofed." He kept his voice light, hoping to divert her thoughts from Marcus, if only briefly.

He stepped over to a row of white poly bags. They were about the circumference of a child's swimming pool and were filled thigh-high with gravel.

"Why do you say that?" Elise asked.

He directed her attention to holes torn in the bottom edge of several of the bags. The foundation-leveling gravel had been airlifted into the remote site by helicopter, and the bags had accidentally been set down atop a row of rebar spikes. "Nobody on the ground guiding the delivery," Quinn shrugged. "It happens."

Elise worked up a weak smile to show she appreciated his attempt to offer the diversion, and they walked on. They covered the grounds and stepped through the many outbuildings, but found nothing out of place.

Just as they climbed aboard the *Blue Sea*, a powerful gust of wind leaned the boat hard to port. They looked at one another and without speaking, Elise cranked the motor, while Quinn quickly undid the lines.

Once they were under way, he suggested Elise send Turner another text. "Tell him you're running into problems making arrangements for the unveiling, and you urgently need his input. Maybe he'll respond in a way that gives us a clue as to his whereabouts or his plan."

While they waited to see if Turner would respond, Quinn told her about his odd encounter with Georgette that morning. "She was drinking and, actually, so was I," he said, "so the entire conversation seemed pretty insensible. But she apparently thinks you hired me to gather information on her."

Elise looked annoyed. "Why would I do that?"

He added, "She also seemed to think Turner was double-dealing her." He pulled out his phone and called the Holland's house. When Georgette answered, he turned on his speakerphone and asked, "Are you interested in how Marcus reacted to getting that envelope?"

"Tell me," Georgette said. Her voice sounded odd to Quinn. Smug, with a note of something else.

He said, "First, you tell me how Turner's involved in all this."

"I can't decide if . . ." They heard what sounded like ice clinking. "If . . . Turner's a liar," *clink-clink* went her ice, "or a prick," *clink-clink* ". . . or a lying prick."

"What's the story, Georgette?"

"Okay honey, I'll tell you my little story." After an extended gulping sound, she said, "Turner came to see me and told me what Elise is up to."

"What is she up to?"

"She hired someone to spy on me to get those pictures."

"What pictures?"

"Of me at my boyfriend's house."

Elise clapped her hand over her mouth.

Quinn said slowly, "Why would Elise want those pictures?"

"To pressure me into resigning from the firm."

"I didn't realize you had a role with SeaLab."

"Chief communications officer. It's a title Marcus saddled me with at the beginning, trying to get me to pitch in and help him with his stupid company." There was more clinking of ice and another gulp, and then she continued. "So, first Turner came out to ask me to resign, all nicey-nice, but when I told him to get lost, he came back and showed me the pictures and said if I didn't take myself off the company letterhead, Elise was going to tell Marcus about my boyfriend."

At a loss, Quinn just said, "Why did they want you to resign?"

"Because SeaLab is about to be in the public eye, mister, and the whole world will be calling up to arrange interviews, asking to speak with the chief communications officer—in other words, me. Elise wants to keep the company image squeaky clean, and I don't exactly fit that image, do I?"

"So why would Elise make Turner act as intermediary?"

"She and I haven't talked in years."

Quinn didn't understand what made Georgette suddenly want to blab and convey all this information, when she'd been so edgy and close-mouthed before, but something had shifted. She sounded almost delighted to be talking to him.

"Turner *strongly advised* if I wanted to keep the status quo, and continue enjoying my boyfriend's company, I should just resign. He said he would make sure those photos got destroyed, and we would all live happily ever after."

"And what did you say?"

"I told Turner nobody is going to tell me what to do, least of all that bitch, Elise." She laughed, but it turned into a cough. "But it did get me thinking, and I realized I was sick of that man."

"Turner?"

"Marcus, you fool. I got my lawyer to draw up the divorce papers, and called Turner to say I'd quit the company formally, but I'd only do it face-to-face with Marcus, and it had to happen the minute he reappeared. I didn't tell Turner what I really wanted, which was to see my husband's expression when I told him that I was leaving him, and why.

"But this morning, when you told me Marcus was back, I realized that little fucker Turner wasn't following my instructions. And if I didn't act fast, Elise would have her fun telling Marcus I've got a boyfriend. Give her that pleasure? Not a chance. So I thought, screw the face-to-face meeting, and dashed off a lovely letter to go with the divorce papers, things I've been wanting to say to him for years. So tell me, how did he react when you gave him the envelope?"

Quinn asked, "Have you seen Turner today?"

"He can go to hell," she said.

"Is that a no?"

"Yes, that's a no," she snapped, sounding more like her old self. "Now tell me, when Marcus got the papers, what did he do?"

"You should be fine," Quinn said neutrally.

"I'm always fine," she yapped her laugh.

"At least, that's what my boyfriend tells me."
She disconnected abruptly.

The weather was getting worse, and they
were running too hard against the waves. Elise
reached for the throttle and slowed the boat
down. She said, "I think I know, now, what
Turner is maneuvering for." The boat rose
steeply on a wave, and then crashed down,
burying its bow into the next wave. She slowed
down even more.

"He wanted Georgette's resignation
because that left three majority shareholders.
Me, him, and Marcus." She looked at Quinn.
"If Marcus dies, Turner will inherit his father's
share of the company. He gains undisputed
control of the company."

She paused to steer around a reef marker.
"When he couldn't pressure Georgette into
resigning," she continued, "he came to me
with a different story."

"What story?"

"He said Georgette was going to release a
statement to the press exposing the fact that
Marcus had a drinking problem."

"You believed him? Why would she'd do
that?"

"She hates the company, she hates me, and sadly, she hates Marcus. Her favorite thing to do is cause strife. Even if she didn't actually follow through, the threat sounded enough like her. Turner *strongly advised* we remove her title. At least that way, if she made any public statements concerning Marcus they would be coming from a drunken wife, not an officer of the company."

"But," Quinn said, "to remove a company officer, even one who is inactive, surely Marcus would need to sign off on that. And he wasn't here to do that."

She nodded. "Except, when Marcus returned after the first episode, we told ourselves it wasn't going to happen again, but just in case, he had Turner revise our bylaws to stipulate that should Marcus be unwell, or absent, his duties and rights transferred to his remaining executive officers. So, when he disappeared the second time, Turner and I, collectively, possessed the power to terminate Georgette's role with the company."

"So what did you do?"

"I refused to sign. Turner made a faulty assumption. He thought I would enjoy taking away Georgette's title. But I just kept saying, 'Marcus is going to turn up any minute. We'll let him handle it.'"

"So," he said, "Marcus showed back up last night."

She threw him a pained look. "This morning we had a meeting. Marcus agreed with Turner that Georgette is a wild card, and took away her title."

He nodded. Now he understood one small thing, at least. Marcus believed his wife wanted to ruin him, and that was why this morning, when Quinn handed him the envelope from her, he'd thought it was a statement she'd prepared for the press, to expose his drinking. Marcus had no idea Georgette wanted a divorce.

They entered Nipntuck's harbor and despite the gusting wind, Elise expertly guided the large yacht into its slip.

She cut the engine, and said, "The police here are astonishingly inept, but we should notify them—" she stopped. "No, I have a better idea. Let's go talk to the state troopers."

They found only one person at the state troopers office, a trooper-in-training named

Blount who happened to be staying late. He had no authority to open an investigation, he told them, only Gerald Walsh could do that, and Walsh was out of town. But Blount said he could at least meet with them to discuss their situation.

The recruit led them to a closet-sized office where they all squeezed in and sat down. Elise introduced herself and Quinn, and then summed up the situation.

As soon as the young man—he couldn't have been twenty—heard the word "abducted," he asked them to wait because he wanted to call the state troopers' regional office in Juneau and request a phone conference with Chief Trooper Sills, the man in charge of investigations. When Sills came on the line, Blount turned his desk phone so that the speaker faced Elise. "Go ahead," he said.

Elise explained, and when she was done, Sill's voice came back, "How long has Mr. Holland been missing?"

"Since noon," she said.

Quinn looked at the wall clock, and then exchanged a glance with Elise. It was six.

"You say no money is missing?"

Quinn and Elise both frowned. She said, "That is correct. But . . ." She sat forward and spoke into the phone, "I cannot stress how urgent this matter is. I insist you take this seriously." Her voice was strident, her face ashen.

After a pause, he said he was taking her seriously, and promised to get back to them after he made some calls.

She sat back in her seat and covered her face with her hands.

They waited. Blount asked if they wanted coffee. They both said no, and the silence stretched out for several minutes. Finally the phone rang, and Sill's voice came over the speakerphone: "If Mr. Holland isn't back by first thing tomorrow morning, check to see if Gerald Walsh is back to that office. If, for some reason, he isn't back, it means his case in Edam Bay hasn't wrapped, and then I'll do my best to get authorization to send somebody down there."

Elise stared at the speaker on the phone. "But we need action now—" her voice broke.

Regret in his voice, Sills said, "I wish I could authorize that, but tomorrow is the soonest we can act. I understand you're telling me about a situation that could be very serious."

She had tears on her cheeks now, but she spoke calmly, "Tomorrow could be too late."

"I'm sorry, ma'am, it's the best we can do."

After they left the state troopers' office, Quinn and Elise sat in the car, sharing a frustrated silence. She checked her phone and discovered that Turner had texted her back. She read aloud: *Still searching, Marcus will want us to carry on with the unveiling no matter what.*

Angrily, she said, "What about my urgent message that I needed his help? I should tell him the unveiling is off, and see what he does."

Quinn began driving. "Let's think about that for a minute. It sounds like he wants the unveiling to occur. It might be our chance to catch him, provided he shows up. By that time, we'll have the troopers' cooperation."

He stopped the car at a crosswalk to let a throng of pedestrians cross the street. They moved quickly, coats and packages flapping in the wind.

As they rolled forward, Elise said softly, "It's ironic." She was staring out the window, lost in thought. "We were so worried about

Leetham, we completely overlooked where Marcus is most vulnerable."

Quinn waited.

"Family," she said, throwing him a look full of sadness. "Marcus always dreamed of having a big family . . . kids, grandkids, and he ends up with just one person . . . a wife who—" she shook her head. "Anyway, when Turner walked into his life, all his hopes were rekindled. Not only did Marcus suddenly have a son, but what a son Turner seemed to be." She pressed her palms to her eyes tiredly. "We should have been more on guard, but we weren't. Turner found the place of despair in his father's life, and he filled it with hope. Nobody can see straight when that happens."

He pulled into a drive-through coffee kiosk, ordered two coffees and pulled back out. His mind kept returning to what Elise had said about being blinded by hope. Considering the way Allie had strung him on for a number of years, all he could do was agree, and sympathize with Marcus and his particular vulnerability to Turner.

He turned the car around, telling Elise, "There's a stop that I need to make."

~~~

Kit phoned Nate. She'd forgotten to tell him about the midnight meeting she'd arranged with Turner. He answered, but before she could say anything, he told her Marcus was missing again.

It was as though a hand suddenly clamped onto her throat and would not let go. She kept swallowing, but it didn't help. The tears needed to come, and she had to let them.

"Can I call you back?" she choked out.

But immediately after she hung up with Nate, there was a pounding on the door, and suddenly, her house was filled with men. She'd summoned her brothers, who were on shore to avoid the looming storm, and they had come, ready to help, and they'd rounded up some friends.

Within an hour, everyone was crowded into the kitchen; some were seated, some stood, a few milled around, and everybody was wolfing down giant pieces of Clara's homemade seafood pizza.

They made their plan, and Kit felt better. At midnight, she was not going to step one foot onto the *Blue Sea*. She wasn't going to speak a word to Turner. Instead, the guys would capture him, and the first thing they would do is force him to reveal where Marcus was. She refused to think that midnight would be too late.

~~~

Quinn pulled up in front of Kit's house, but he didn't go up to the door. The kitchen windows were thrown wide open and he could see her inside. She had her back to the window, and men were milling around her—a lot of men— and more often than not, one of them had an arm around her. As he and Elise watched, two more guys hustled up the steps and went in with a hoot and bang of the door.

Quinn knew he should respect that Kit didn't want to speak to him. She'd surrounded herself with men, so it wasn't like she was in any danger. He yanked his phone out. He wanted to be one of the guys surrounding her. He should be.

To his relief, she answered, but then she immediately said, "I don't want to talk about personal stuff. I can't do that right now. Tell me what's happening. Nate said Marcus is missing again."

Quinn told her everything he and Elise had done and discussed. When he finished, he couldn't stop himself. He told her he wanted to see her. "I'm outside your house."

There was a silence during which Quinn tried to assess what she might be feeling. Her next words gave him a pretty good idea. "I can't see you. I just can't." She stopped, and then said, "Don't press me," and hung up.

By nine o'clock, both Quinn and Elise were moving like zombies. They had continued driving around, talking intermittently, but mostly sharing a silence.

They ended up back on the *Blue Sea* where they split a can of soup and some crackers. Turner had remained silent in response to several pleas that Elise had sent to him, asking him to meet.

Trying to reassure her, Quinn said, "We'll go see the troopers again, first thing in the morning." She still looked so dejected that he took her arm and said, "Come with me."

He led her over to the *Valiant* and introduced her to Nate, who offered them each a glass of scotch. Quinn declined, but

Elise agreed to half a snifter.

They sat and talked for a few minutes. Rain started, then stopped, then started again. The wind blasted at the *Valiant* in frequent, hard gusts.

A silence fell, and Nate, in an obvious attempt to counter the heavy mood, asked if they wanted to see Flotsam's trick.

Quinn started to say no, thanks, but Elise, smiling tiredly, said yes.

Nate set Flotsam on the floor and stood over him. "Okay, show us your trick." Nothing happened. "Oh, I forgot. He's deaf. I'm supposed to go like this—" He pointed at Flotsam, and without hesitation the dog sprang up onto Nate's shoulder. The leap was so sudden, and so vertical, it seemed to defy multiple laws of physics. And as soon as he reached Nate's shoulder, the dog buried his tongue in Nate's ear, making him shout, "Ick!"

Quinn and Elise both burst out laughing, and laughed some more as Nate twisted and bucked, trying to dump Flotsam off. But Flotsam rode his shoulder, slurping Nick's ear for far longer than seemed possible, before finally falling off onto the bunk.

Nate grabbed a paper towel and dug it into his ear, saying, "It's like he uses his tongue to hold on!" and the other two broke out laughing again.

To Quinn, the levity felt like rain after a drought, and he could tell Elise welcomed it as well. Still wearing a slight smile, she put her glass down and said she was ready to go home for some sleep.

Quinn hated to turn serious again, but he felt compelled to raise a disturbing question: What if Turner's plan involve taking out all the SeaLab executives, including Elise?

Elise said she'd thought about the same thing. "But I think he'll consider me an asset, at least, for the time being. SeaLab will make him rich, but he needs me to make sure SeaLab functions successfully."

Quinn asked if she would agree to spend the night on the *Blue Sea*, with him as her bodyguard. Just for peace of mind.

She agreed that it was a good idea.

25

Kit paused at the top of the harbor ramp, gathering her nerve. The wind whipped at her coat while rain pelted her in the face. The rest of the troops had gone on ahead and stationed themselves all over the place. A few were visible, battening down boats against the storm or talking in twos and threes, while others hid in various boats. Earlier, they'd seen a light shining from *Blue Sea's* main cabin, and then it was extinguished, so the consensus was that Turner had come early and was lying in wait for her.

The minute she stepped forward to descend the ramp, he would have a line of sight on her from the darkened yacht. He'd know she was entering the harbor—and believe that she was entering his snare.

She planned to walk down the ramp, but stop immediately under the brightest cluster of dock lights on the main float, and wait there, as if confused about where to go. To get her, Turner would have to come off the yacht, and Big Pat and his deputies would pounce on him. If for some reason, Turner didn't allow himself to be lured onto the dock, the men would go aboard the *Blue Sea* and do whatever was necessary to learn where Marcus was.

From where she stood, she could see a light shining bright from Rebecca's boat, and remembered suddenly that she'd failed to tell Nate what was going on. Earlier, she'd called to tell him, but he'd broken the news that Marcus was missing, and then her brothers had descended on her. She wondered if she should include him in the plan, but realized she had plenty of help. She looked at her watch. It wasn't yet midnight, but she was ready for action, ready to go place herself in the pool of light on the main float.

Suddenly a hand gripped her arm. It was Turner, saying softly in her ear, "Did you bring Rebecca's diary? Am I going to be embarrassed?"

"No," she gasped.

"You didn't bring her diary?"

"You scared me, Turner! Yes I brought it!" She tried to twist away while she yelled this at him, expecting her protectors to hear, but the gusting wind tossed her words in the wrong direction as soon as they left her mouth.

His fingers stayed clamped onto her arm like a vice and a scream welled up, large in her throat, but got stuck there as the old terror— the one she'd fallen into since she was little— flooded her. Once someone had a hold of her, she became paralyzed.

She forced herself to stay calm. If she could move just a few steps down the ramp, someone would be watching for her, and would notice Turner was with her. Turner would be in the trap. She was just escorting him into the trap, she told herself. It wasn't like he'd pulled a weapon on her. They weren't fighting one another.

She took a step toward the ramp. That she was able to still move told her she'd be okay. Everything was fine.

But then, with stunning speed, he yanked her over to a car parked beside the ramp.

It wasn't his Ferrari.

"Where are we going?" She tried again to twist her arm free.

He flung open the door and pushed her in, slamming and locking the door electronically before he sped around and let himself in behind the wheel. She was shaking, simultaneously hot and cold with dread.

"Change of plans," he said cheerfully, and before she could say a word, he'd fired up the ignition, whipped out onto the main road and punched the accelerator. "Marcus took the *Blue Sea*," he said. "I didn't know he had plans for it."

Kit sat frozen in her seat. Her brain momentarily shut down.

Then an internal voice cut through the fog. It said calmly: *Don't give in to fear. Play along.*

"Where are we going?" she asked a second time. She had her hand on her phone in her purse. She would call someone with her new destination as soon as she knew it.

"It's a surprise."

Too soon, he swept the car into a turn. He had a remote in his hand, a gate opened, they went through, and the gate clanged shut.

He parked, came around to pull her from the car, and started walking her toward the dark hulking helicopter, his grip tight on her arm.

"Your helicopter," she said through dry lips.

"Yes," he said, still adopting a cheerful tone, still moving.

"Oh, how exciting," she said, and picked up speed as if eager to go with him. His grip relaxed slightly. "But gimme a sec, I have to pee!" she cried suddenly and twisted her arm free. She sprinted toward the nearest cover, a bulldozer parked off to the side. Turner strode after her, confident that she couldn't go far because they were in a fenced enclosure. She ducked behind the bulldozer and speed-dialed Clara, who picked up on the first ring. "We're taking the helicopter," she gasped.

"Kit? Is that you?"

"The helicopter!" she repeated loudly just as Turner rounded the bulldozer. She stealthily dropped her phone into her purse and patted her pants zipper. Addressing him, she asked, "Isn't it dangerous to go up in this weather?"

"We'll be fine," he said, quickly gripping her arm.

The tarmac was dark and still except for the swirling wind. There wasn't a soul around to help her. She prayed Clara had heard.

He pulled her over to the helicopter, and with frightening ease, belted into the passenger seat. She kept willing her body to fight but fear had frozen her limbs. He climbed in behind the controls and slammed the door closed.

Her cell phone trilled. "Give it," he said, holding out his hand. "It will interfere with the instruments."

She tried to answer the call while the phone was still in her purse, but his hand flashed out and he grabbed her purse before she could stop him. He turned the phone off and pocketed it, while also flipping switches and turning on the ignition. Then the helicopter was in the air.

Kit's mind was screaming. Everything was going too fast. She clamped her knees together to control her shivering body and told herself to pay attention.

Turner's profile, lit by the glow of the instrument panel, was calm. The wind and rain hammered at the windshield, and she couldn't see out the dark window, but the illuminated

GPS screen on the console was visible. She blinked in disbelief. They were nearly atop SeaLab island. How could they have traveled so fast? A moment later they were touching down in a construction site next to SeaLab's brightly lit main building.

Think, she told herself. *Get away from him. Watch for your chance.* Suddenly she knew what to do. *The throat jab.* Quinn had shown her that defense move, and now she was going to use it. She stole a look toward Turner's neck, thinking about where to strike, and tensed, waiting for her opportunity.

He flipped some levers on the console, and then turned to rummage in a pack he'd stashed behind the seat.

She remained still, thinking, *be ready.* He shifted his weight forward and she failed to see the needle he jabbed toward her shoulder, but she sensed danger enough to jerk away at the last minute. Liquid brushed her cheek like a cold kiss from death.

He swore and pinned her with his arm, and jabbed the needle home. She felt a hot spike of regret and tried to struggle, but she couldn't move. He muttered, "Half a dose will be enough for you."

Her mind screamed *"No!"* just before consciousness drained away.

~~~

His ringing phone snapped Quinn upright. He took a half-second to remember where he was—on the *Blue Sea*. He'd stretched out in the narrow hall outside Elise's stateroom, wishing to sleep, but also wanting to block access to her.

It was Clara on the phone. In a frantic rush, she told him about Kit's plan, and that it had gone awry. "At first I thought she said 'cops,' but then I heard her say clearly, 'helicopter.'"

He was up and dressing.

She cried, "Her brothers are stationed around the harbor, on foot and in boats. They were supposed to protect her. I don't know what happened!"

"I'll find her brothers, and we'll find her."

"Quinn!" A sob choked her. "Calm does not run in the family. I'm sure the boys are armed to the hilt. If any of them gets hurt, she'll never forgive herself."

"Who's the most level-headed?"

"The oldest, Big Pat. You can count on

him, for sure. And Johnny—he pretends to be a smart aleck, but he's—"she gulped, "—he's not."

"Call Nate," he told her, "tell him to meet me outside."

He roused Elise. "You shouldn't be left alone. Call someone, maybe get that new trooper, Blount, if you can reach him."

"I'll do that," she said, "now go!" Her voice broke. "Please find Kit."

He grabbed a headlamp off a shelf by the door and ran outside. Nate was flinging himself off the *Valiant* while still pulling on his clothes. There were men moving toward them from all sides—Kit's brothers, Quinn realized. He called out urgently, "Turner's got Kit. Where's Pat?"

After a surprised pause, several men pointed and the shout went up, "Pat! Johnny! Turner has Kit!"

A speedboat—it looked both fast and seaworthy—cut over to where they stood. Two men were on board. The driver had to be Big Pat—he was huge—and the other, apparently Johnny, was barely twenty, thin, with flashing eyes.

Rapidly Quinn explained about Clara's call, and Pat dispensed searchers by boat, heading north and south, and directed some men to drive to the airport in case the chopper was still on the ground. Pat said he'd take his boat over to SeaLab island; Quinn and Nate were aboard before he finished the statement.

Pat gunned the boat out of the harbor, and they began beating their way across Big Bear Bay. The storm made it hard going. They crashed along, taking wave after wave over the bow. More than an hour passed before they drew close to the island.

The island was dark, except for one small light. "Johnny," Pat said in a low voice, "get out the spotlight. Wait until I give the word."

The dimly lit screen showed rocks between them and the dock—a lot of them. In one particular spot, the rocks were so thick, Quinn realized they'd need to navigate some of it by sight.

All eyes were glued to the screen as the boat nudged forward in darkness, making a series of twists and turns. Soon they heard breaking waves ahead, and then on all sides. Their prop dinged against a rock and Pat said urgently, "Now."

Johnny aimed the beam ahead. They were momentarily blinded by light reflecting off spray lofted into the air by the half-dozen rocks surrounding them. Pat yanked the boat around a rock about to stop them dead. Through the spray they could see the reflectors on SeaLab's dock ahead. Pat said tersely, "Off now."

They eased along in the dark until they rubbed up against the bumpers of SeaLab's dock. Quietly, they secured the boat. Pat and Nate had shotguns, Quinn held a rifle, and Johnny gripped a pistol.

The four men stepped out of the boat onto the dock. Ahead of them, a high-powered spotlight blazed on. When the light hit their faces, they instinctively threw up their arms to cover their eyes. Invisible behind the spotlight, Turner barked, "Drop the guns."

Simultaneously Pat and Johnny shifted forward. "Move forward again," Turner said sharply, "and you'll die. Drop the guns. Now."

There was a moment where nobody moved. Pat glanced at Johnny and inclined his head slightly. They bent and set the guns at their feet. Very close to their feet, Quinn noticed.

He and Nate followed suit.

Turner said, "Step back into the boat. Leave the firearms. Do it now."

Rushing Turner, or the place where his voice came from, simply wasn't an option, Quinn told himself. The damned light cast their surroundings into deep blackness. It was likely Turner was armed and had other men with him. But none of these facts stopped him from wanting, with every cell in his body, to charge.

Turner said, "You're trespassing. Leave now, or you will be shot." Quinn could feel the tension in the men standing alongside him. They all wanted the same thing—to get at Turner.

It was Clara's plea to keep Kit's brothers from harm that convinced Quinn to turn and reluctantly climb back in the boat. Slowly, the others followed.

The spotlight stayed trained on them as they pulled away. When they were some distance away, Pat spoke quietly. "On the other side of the island there's a tiny lagoon that's protected. I'll land there and we can hike back."

"Too bad about the guns," Quinn muttered.

"We have more," Pat said.

"A lot more," Johnny confirmed.

~~~

Kit stirred. A sharp pain throbbed across the back of her head. Foggily she noted that water was running into her eyes. She tried to raise a hand to wipe her face but couldn't. She was too tired to move, and cold. Something kept jerking her around, jabbing her shoulder.

For a moment, she thought her brothers were playing one of their mean games on her, but then she remembered: she wasn't a child at the mercy of her brothers—Turner had her. He had wrapped her in something. But what? She heard a whooshing sound—wind? She thought she recognized the pungent smell of spruce pitch in her nostrils, and though it made absolutely no sense to her foggy brain, she had the sensation she was swinging in a tree.

Several violent gusts of wind hit. Her body whipped one way; then the other. Whatever had been wrapped around her loosened, and then on the next gust, it released her altogether. She plummeted downward, kicking and flailing—then jackknifed violently to a stop.

Gagging and groaning, she explored frantically with her hands, and determined she had dropped onto a branch. She really was in a tree. It was a fat branch, as thick around as her leg, but even so, it waved and bucked in the wind. Icy rain drove at her as she began to pull herself along the branch, moving toward the tree's center.

Finally she had its solid trunk in her arms and there she clung, trembling and gulping with fear. Terrified glances downward revealed only darkness. She couldn't tell if she was up ten feet or one hundred feet.

Her muscles began to shudder and she realized her grip wouldn't last long in this cold. She made herself move. With the bracing smell of resin in her face and the rough bark tearing into her hands, she began to work her way downward.

Finally, after what seemed like a long time, she ran out of branches. The ground was somewhere below, but there was no way to tell how far away. Dread filled her, but she forced her fingers to let go.

She fell only a short distance before she landed with a hard jolt. She collapsed against the hard earth, blood pounding in her temples. She was alive. It was pissing rain, the wind was screaming, and she couldn't see her hand in front of her face, but she was alive.

Shakily she rose to her feet and took a couple of faltering steps, but then her feet slid and she fell at the edge of some body of water. She tasted the water; it was fresh.

Think, she ordered herself. The last thing she knew, she had been flying in the helicopter next to Turner. No, they had landed on SeaLab island—the building had been lit up, she could see it now in her mind's eye. Then, the needle. And somehow she'd ended up here.

Though she felt far from sure, she decided this must be the lake near the middle of SeaLab island. To believe this was the case gave her some sense of being oriented. If she could move away from this water, keeping to one straight direction, she would eventually reach the island's edge. Once daylight arrived, she'd be able to flag down a passing boat.

She tried to execute her plan, but quickly found that walking in any direction, much less a straight one, proved impossible in the dense dark. The island had been carved, very roughly, by a receding glacier, and everywhere she put her feet, they twisted over rocks, tree roots, and boggy hollows. She tripped so many times that she finally stayed down and just crawled along.

Cold rain was falling in sheets, and she was in danger of becoming deeply chilled. But she never doubted that Clara would send help. She only had to stay in motion to keep herself from freezing, and not tumble over one of the island's many cliffs.

Which is exactly what she did a moment later.

~~~

After finding the lagoon on the back side of the island, the four men secured the skiff with beach lines. Each carried a light and a firearm as they began working their way in the direction of the SeaLab facility, now on the opposite side of the island. Pat had a handheld GPS and that gave them confidence as to which direction they needed to go, but without daylight to show them the lay of the land, they were stymied by impassible gullies, deep bogs, and tangles of windfall. It took them two hours to reach the island's approximate middle, which was marked by a lake.

They were skirting the lake's edge when Quinn heard an odd flapping overhead. He shone his light in an arc and spotted something white hanging high in one of the trees edging the lake. Then his flashlight landed on an object on the ground.

Recognizing Kit's purse, he pounced on it. By the time the other men came to his call, he was halfway up the tree. The tattered white object, he discovered, was a gravel bag like those he and Elise had seen at the construction site adjacent to SeaLab's main building.

Resting his head against the spruce's trunk, Quinn tried to reconstruct what had happened. Turner must have put Kit in the gravel bag and slung it by helicopter to the lake. He'd released it, expecting it to plummet straight down, unaware that the rebar had punched a hole into the bag's bottom and allowed the gravel to pour out along the way. Carrying so little weight, the bag must have hung back in the fierce wind, hidden by the dark, and upon release, had lofted like a kite to become snagged up in the tree on the lake's edge.

The image of Kit's body tumbling through

the air tried to enter Quinn's mind, but he pushed it away. He was not going to consider the possibility that she'd done anything other than climb down from the upper branches of this tree under her own power. She had to be on the island somewhere, alive and waiting for daylight.

~~~

When Kit fell off the cliff, the wind was knocked out of her, but it could have been worse. She could have landed on bone-cracking granite, but instead hit a much softer, mossy deer bed. She knew it was a deer bed because she was surrounded by the unmistakably pungent smell of a season's worth of deer droppings.

Groaning, she rolled onto her back and tried to peer into the night, but it was like she had no eyes. Gradually, though, she did discern a faint glow on the cliff face above her. She blinked to be sure, and laughed out loud because she knew what it was.

One of her brothers had painted some whimsical words on the rock during their games here as children. The lines were from the book *Where the Sidewalk Ends*, by Shel

Silverstein, and this many years later, they had to be illegible, but she knew them by heart:

If you are a dreamer, come in.
If you are a dreamer, a wisher, a liar,
A hope-er, a pray-er, a magic bean buyer . . .
If you're a pretender, come sit by my fire,
For we have some flax-golden tales to spin.
Come in—Come in.

Oh welcome words! Now she knew exactly where she was. She started to pull herself upright, and her legs almost gave out. Her body was quickly becoming too chilled to move.

She pushed herself into motion, feeling her way along the base of the cliff until her hand touched the cold concrete of the World War II bunker.

The front entrance to the bunker had been boarded over decades ago, but there was a back way in. The cliff that abutted the bunker's rear wall wasn't flush along the bottom, but jogged inward, creating a natural tunnel low to the ground between the cliff and the bunker. Ten yards along that tunnel, there was a hole in the bunker's crumbling cement which allowed entry if one was small enough to wiggle through.

Kit and her brothers had always kept a stash of homemade torches—sticks smeared with spruce pitch—at the start of the tunnel. She bent and felt around, wondering if one could possibly still be there. Her hand found a piece of sticky wood, and she let out a glad cry. Of course the wood was rotten, but it was dry, and pitch always burned.

She dug the lighter out of her coat pocket, and it took her shaking hands a dozen tries before the makeshift torch caught. A visceral relief filled her when the light pushed away the oppressive black.

As a child she had slithered along the tunnel with room to spare, but now she was just able to squeeze along while bent almost double. She was tired, so tired. She thought about lying down as soon as she was out of the rain, but the harsh wind was whipping through the tunnel, and she knew it would wick away the rest of her warmth while she slept.

Ten paces in, she found the hole in the

bunker wall. She could smell the bunker's air, the distinctly metallic odor of old, packed earth. She thrust the torch in ahead of her and wiggled through, and then stood, torch in hand, blinking to clear her head.

A glow shone from across the bunker, and she stared at the sight, dizzy and confused. Her torch should have been the only light. Then her eyes made out a small kerosene lantern, and a cot. And someone was lying on the cot, underneath a mound of blankets.

Heart pounding, Kit crept forward and gasped when she saw the person was Marcus. The cot was the sort that would be found in an ambulance, and he was strapped in. His eyes were closed. His chest lifted the blankets in a reassuring rhythm. She touched him softly, and then more insistently, while saying his name. He stirred slightly, but she couldn't get him to open his eyes. Turner was holding his father captive in this bunker. Kit tried, but her tired mind could not begin to fathom why.

Holding up her torch, she worked her way around the bunker and discovered that the front entrance was blocked with new plywood.

She tried, but could not move it from the inside.

She went back and stared down at Marcus, pondering what to do. Her pitch torch was almost burned out. To take the kerosene lantern would leave Marcus in the dark. What if he awoke and went into a panic? Daylight, just an hour or two away, would make every difference. She'd go for help as soon as it grew light outside.

Marcus's topmost blanket had slid off onto the concrete floor. She pulled it around herself and huddled on the floor beside the cot, trembling with fatigue and cold. Soon, she nodded off.

26

The men had traversed the island and were almost to the lab, when they heard the chopper lift off from the facility. Daylight was just breaking. They took cover and watched it fly over, going back the way they had come.

A moment later they heard it land behind them, somewhere near the lake, and without a word all of them began sprinting back in that direction.

~~~

Kit jerked awake. The whopping of a helicopter, close by outside, screamed in her ears, and then stopped. A loud thud at the front entrance launched her upright. She tried to run, but could only hobble stiffly in the direction of the back wall. She was about to go through the hole but froze. Her pitch torch lay on the floor by the cot.

Outside, a nail squawked in protest as it was pulled from the plywood. She ran and snatched up the torch while another nail, and then a third screeched out of the wood. She returned to the hole, dove through, and turned to watch, barely breathing. The day's early light beamed into the cavern. As she dreaded, and expected, Turner stood outlined in its glow.

He strode to the cot and opened a bag he carried. He stared down at his father, and then in a low, furious voice, he spoke. "Fucking shit keeps happening." He rummaged around in the bag and extracted a syringe. "First, you start snooping around, wanting to view that security tape." Kit could see spit spraying from Turner's snarling mouth. "Then that bastard Quinn comes looking for Kit. And now my shit-ass brother has anchored the *Blue Sea* somewhere without a signal, so I can't reach him." He loaded the syringe using a vial, tapped the needle, and pushed it into Marcus's thigh.

When he stabbed the needle in, Kit clamped her arm over her mouth to keep from crying out. *Did she just watch Turner end Marcus's life?* The horrific thought made her head swim.

Then Marcus stirred, and her heart, which

had nearly stopped, began to thump again.

"And before this batch of shit," Turner spat. "I had all that trouble with Georgette. That twisted bitch *enjoys* conflict."

From his bag he pulled out several cans of some kind. He unclipped the cot's straps and jerked the older man up into a sitting position. Marcus's eyes were open but he was mumbling incoherently. Turner opened a drink with an impatient pull and handed it to Marcus who tipped it back and drank thirstily.

Turner threw the empty can in his bag, pushed Marcus down on the cot and refastened the straps. Marcus shifted his head restlessly from side to side while Turner readied another needle.

"Everything better go smooth at the unveiling, no more fuckups." Turner's tone was softer now. "But if it doesn't go smooth, you, dear father, will be my bargaining chip."

He squirted some liquid into the air, shoved the needle in, and Marcus grew still.

~~~

Quinn and the other men were almost to the lake. Since they weren't sure exactly where Turner had landed, they were forced to move slow and stop frequently to listen. Suddenly, his voice low and urgent, Johnny said, "I know where to go." He turned to Pat. "You remember the bunker? The one we used for a fort?"

Pat shook his head.

"Just us younger kids used it, I guess," Johnny said. "There's a flat, open space right there. I'll bet that's where he landed."

Quinn asked, "Are we close?"

"I think so," Johnny said. And then, not far away, they heard it—the chopper's motor fired up.

~~~

Kit listened to the chopper move away, fading to a distant stutter. She felt the tunnel pressing close around her and realized she desperately needed fresh air. She hauled herself along the tight passage, reached daylight and dropped to her knees, gulping oxygen as though she'd been under water.

Then she heard a thrashing in the woods. *Bear!* she thought. It was very close, charging right for her, and all she could do was curl up in a ball and cover the back of her neck—

where bears usually bit first.

"Kit!" Suddenly she was being picked up. It was Johnny, and he was squeezing the air out of her.

Johnny released her, and Pat swept her up. As soon as he set her down, there was Nate, fighting tears as he wrapped his arms around her. A second later she was in Quinn's arms. She stayed pressed to him so long the others got embarrassed and started shuffling their feet and clearing their throats.

"Marcus is in the bunker," she finally gasped.

They rushed to the blocked-off entrance and tore a piece of plywood off. Without wasting any time, they wrapped Marcus in a blanket and started traveling back to the lagoon as quickly as they could.

Along the way, Kit told them about the needle Turner managed to stab into her, and how she'd woken up in the tree. "I was in some kind of white plastic. I have no idea how I got there."

Quinn told her what it was, and sketched for her his impression that Turner had tried to drop her into the lake, but had instead landed her in the tree.

Kit felt sick at the thought. Then she felt even sicker and clapped her hand to her mouth. "Turner must have seen the gravel bag in the tree when he flew over just now! And now he's looking for me!"

No, Quinn quickly reassured her, they'd cut the bag out of the tree and buried it before continuing their search for her. But there was a related concern, he said. Turner might go back to the bunker and discover they'd rescued Marcus. The hospital would be the first place Turner would go, if he went looking. "I suggest we take Marcus to your house," Quinn told Kit. "Allie can meet us there to advise us about his condition, and take a sample of blood for—"

"Allie?" Kit wheeled around and glared at him. "You mean *Miss Cream Puff*?"

Looking confused, Quinn said, "She's a nurse."

The other men had stopped to listen, but Kit gave them an annoyed stare until they took the hint and continued on.

She turned back to Quinn, but before she could say anything, he stepped close and said, "Kit, here's the bottom line: I have no romantic feelings for Allie whatsoever. When I came down to Nipntuck, I wasn't sure how I felt, but I am now. I was a fool for having spent even a minute in her company. You have to take a leap of faith here, and trust that she and I are over. Please." Without a trace of defensiveness, he added, "The only reason I was with her at the cream puff place, and brought up her name just now, is because she's the best person to help us with Marcus."

Kit felt at a loss for words, which was rare. He seemed sincere, but a person can sincerely *want* to be over an ex-lover, without actually *being* over them. But whether or not she could trust Quinn's declaration, one thing was clear: they had to do the best thing for Marcus.

"Fine," she said huffily. "Call her."

She went ahead and caught up with Nate. Reaching his side, she blurted, "How well do you know Quinn?"

"Better than I know my own brother."

"What's his deal with the nurse?"

Nate stopped and faced her. "He's been blind about her for years. But this week he woke up."

"Define 'woke up.'"

"He sees her, for real. I'm—" Nate paused.

"You're what?"

"Relieved. Because I've never seen a woman who's a better match for him."

Angrily she turned and resumed walking. "If she's such a match for him, then why can't he admit it."

Nate put his hand on her arm and stopped her. "I'm talking about you, Kit. You and Quinn." His eyes were fixed earnestly on hers.

Quinn joined them but before anyone could speak, Quinn's phone, which was still in his hand, rang. He glanced down, and handed it straight to Kit, saying, "It's Clara."

Kit answered and told her right away, "Everybody's okay. And we found Marcus, but Turner's still loose."

Clara, her voice breaking, said she also had good news, about Rebecca. In the middle of the night, she had surfaced to semiconsciousness for about an hour, but then slipped back under. Clara sounded joyful, but for some reason, when Kit heard this, she felt frightened, rather than hopeful.

Clara added, "Rebecca's mom is on the flight

to Juneau. She's about to land any minute, and promises to call us with any news."

Kit described their plan to bring Marcus to the house and Johnny, who stood nearby, waved his arms to get her attention. He clasped his hands together imploringly and said, "Tell Clara we're starving."

Kit relayed the message, and Clara promised she'd have food ready for them.

Even though the wind and rain had abated, the chop on the bay was huge, and the trip back in the skiff was long and bone-jarring. When they finally got to the house, as promised, Clara was ready with plates piled high with food. A gratifying sight, Kit thought, with only one thing marring the picture. That Allie woman sat at the table, glowing and fresh in her nurse's uniform, sipping on a steaming cup of coffee.

Over the last twelve hours Kit had been stabbed with a needle, thrown in a gravel bag, and dropped in a tree. She'd crawled through the woods in a storm, and fallen off a cliff onto a poopy deer bed. Then she'd slept, sitting up, in a concrete bunker.

She wasn't at her cheery best.

Clara wrapped her in a hug, and said she'd been keeping a lavender-scented bath warm for her. Kit knew this was the right order of things, but stared longingly over her shoulder at the mounds of French toast, eggs, and bacon, as Clara led her away.

After her bath, Kit zoomed back to join the others. The Allie woman was gone and so were her brothers and Quinn. Nate stood staring out the window, and Marcus sat at the table, his head folded down to his chest. He appeared to be asleep. Clara was tucking a blanket around him.

Nate turned from the window. His face was stark white. "Quinn went to look for Elise. She isn't answering her phone." He swallowed, "And the *Blue Sea* is gone."

~~~

Elise wasn't answering her phone because she couldn't. She was gagged, bound hand and foot, and duct-taped in a chair.

The night before, after Quinn raced off to look for Kit, she had tried to rustle up some protective company, as he'd suggested. But Blount, the trooper-in-training, had an unlisted phone. She'd tried several other people, but couldn't raise anyone. She went to lock the door of the yacht, knowing it was symbolic more than anything, and noticed Flotsam was sitting out on deck.

Even though she'd held the door open to invite him in, he stayed where he was. "Okay," she told the dog, "Nate mentioned you're deaf, but deaf or not, I feel better knowing you're standing guard." Feeling only slightly paranoid, she got a big knife from the galley and put it on the floor beside her bed, and then slowly, fitfully, drifted off to sleep.

Her eyes opened in the dark; she'd been startled awake by some noise. A split second later a hand slapped adhesive tape down across her mouth. More tape got wrenched around her hands and feet and suddenly a pillowcase was over her head. It happened so quickly she saw nothing of her assailant's face.

He threw her over a shoulder and carried her up to the main cabin. She struggled, but her bound hands and feet made her nearly helpless. He slammed her down. Again the sound of adhesive tape ripping, and then she was being strapped into what felt like one of the pilothouse chairs. She fought to keep herself from being bound tight against the chair.

She heard her assailant, breathing raggedly, move around, closing the curtains, and it hit her that he wasn't breathing ragged from exertion. Her assailant was Hamm.

A moment after she realized this, he pressed a rag smelling of something bitter against her nose, and then everything had turned black.

It was her ringing phone, over on the table, that had brought her back to consciousness. The phone rang a few more times and then fell silent.

In the next moment she realized four things: First, the boat was sloshing around uncomfortably. *Why?* she wondered foggily. Her ears told her that the *Blue Sea*'s engine, though running, was out of gear.

Second, she couldn't hear Hamm. Third, the tape over her mouth had come unstuck. Her last realization was why the tape had come loose—she'd drooled. Falling asleep in an upright position always made her drool. It was an embarrassing tendency in church and on planes, but this one time, it happened to be a wonderful thing. With her mouth free, she could lean over and bite the tape away from her wrists. Once her hands were free, she fumbled to remove the pillowcase from her head, and then she looked wildly around.

Hamm was nowhere to be seen. She unbound her feet and freed herself the rest of the way from the chair, and looked out the front window. What she saw made her lunge for the controls. The *Blue Sea* was mere seconds away from being tossed up on the reef off Hamburger Island. She reversed hard, and got some distance from the reef, before putting the boat back in neutral. *What happened to Hamm?*

She peeked out on deck and gasped. He was out there, laying crumpled on deck, a dark pool of blood by his head. And Flotsam sat beside him, looking around with an alert air, like a lion guarding his kill.

She locked the door, returned to the wheel, put the yacht in gear, and headed full speed toward Nipntuck.

~~~

Quinn was driving out to the state troopers when his phone rang. Seeing it was Elise, he wrenched the car to the side of the road.

"Where are you?" He asked in a rush. "Are you safe?"

"Hamm attacked me, but Flotsam got him," she said. "I'm bringing us in on the *Blue Sea*. He's unconscious on deck." She paused. "I realize I may not be making complete sense."

"Where are you?" Quinn asked.

"I'm north of town. Fifteen minutes out."

"I'll meet you at the harbor. I'll stay with you on the phone until you reach the dock."

"Good," she said. "I must admit I'm starting to shake a bit."

He told her that Marcus and Kit were both safe.

After a sharp inhalation of breath, she said, "Tell me what happened."

~~~

Kit got a call from Quinn, telling her he was with Elise, and that Hamm had been caught. Quinn surmised that Hamm had stepped out on deck for one reason or another, and Flotsam surprised him with his trick. The violent version of his trick, Quinn said, judging from the way Hamm's ear was torn to shreds. "It looks like Hamm panicked, cracked his head on something and knocked himself out. He's locked up at the trooper's building, until the Seattle police can question him. We moved the *Blue Sea* over to the Coast Guard service dock. It's hidden from view so there's no chance Turner will see it."

Kit asked, "Where are you now?"

Quinn said he and Elise were almost back to the house.

"Good," Kit said. "The unveiling is in less than an hour. We need to make a plan."

27

The high school auditorium had a capacity of about three hundred, and it was already packed by the time they got there. Kit had found a couple of hooded sweatshirts for both Marcus and Elise to wear, decreasing the likelihood that someone would recognize them.

Marcus had opened his eyes only twenty minutes before and was moving slowly, but at least he was moving. They helped him into the back row where he slumped between Kit and Elise, his head listing sideways, while Quinn and Nate took seats on the aisle.

All of them were edgy, except Marcus who had no idea what was going on.

Kit's brothers had staked out the building and its surroundings, and Pat was going to call and alert her as soon as Turner was spotted. A moment after she sat down, her phone rang. *Here we go*, she thought. But it was Chief DeSmet from Kurk Falls calling to say he and the Seattle cops had landed.

She told him the state troopers were holding Ted Connolly, alias Stan Hamm, for questioning. More importantly, she said, John Connelly, who was going by the name Turner Holland, was still at large, but was expected to appear any minute to speak onstage at the school auditorium.

DeSmet said, "We're minutes away."

She hung up and her phone instantly chimed. It was a text from Big Pat: *Turner just arrived. He's about to take the stage.*

The lights suddenly dimmed, and the crowd grew quiet. After a perfectly timed pause, Turner strode onto the stage, radiating confidence.

Kit's fists balled in her lap, and she leaned forward to look at Quinn, who gazed back calmly at her. Their plan was to lay low at first, to see what Turner did. The Seattle police would show up any minute, and in the meantime there were plenty of able-bodied men scattered around, inside and outside the building, determined not to let Turner escape.

Turner greeted the audience energetically, and everyone in the room seemed to lean forward into his presence. "I have some surprises for you," he said, "the first being a schedule change." He held up a copy of the schedule Elise had prepared for the event.

"Actually," he coughed, "there's been a lot more than a change of schedule." Giving the audience an open-faced, apologetic look, he said, "To be honest, I'm in a bit of a shock myself about what I'm going to tell you."

He paused and seemed to brace himself. Everyone in the room held a collective breath. "My father Marcus Holland, the principal executive and founder of SeaLab . . . is not able to join us today. Nor is our . . ." he paused, "our Elise who, as many of you know, has been with the firm for more than twenty years."

Kit sat forward. *I bet he's going to say that they went down in the storm on the Blue Sea.*

"I regret to inform you that Marcus and Elise have . . ." Turner paused. He repeated, "Marcus and Elise have . . ." He gave an embarrassed cough and said, "run off into the sunset together—"

Kit and Elise both let out surprised gasps.

Turner held out his palms and gave a charming sort of shrug while the crowd rumbled with questions. He spoke over the noise, "I wasn't privy to this news until this morning and must admit I am reeling from it."

"What about his wife?" called a reporter in the front while flashes from cameras began popping.

Turner waited for the noise level to subside, and then said, "I'd like to finish this statement, and then I will be happy to answer any questions." He gave a firm nod and said, "Marcus arranged for me to assume all executive responsibilities at SeaLab. He made this a permanent arrangement." The audience rumbled louder at this.

He held up his hands to quiet the crowd. "While this is a tremendous vote of confidence by my father, upon reflection I have made an important decision. SeaLab is at a critical point in its existence. I feel the responsibility keenly. The work of my father and our hard working staff of experts must not only continue, it must be nurtured."

Turner paced a few steps forward, and opened his palms to the audience, "I've pondered the question of how best to proceed in light of my father's quite unexpected retirement. And so, I'd like to ask Mr. William Leetham to kindly join me onstage. Mr. Leetham will help me tell you about the exciting course we've set for SeaLab's future."

Quinn, Kit, and Elise all sat without moving, mesmerized by Turner's performance. Then Marcus, who had fallen asleep, gave a little snort. Elise poked him. "Marcus," she whispered sharply, "pay attention. I mean it."

He obediently turned dazed eyes to the stage. When he saw Leetham bound up onstage, he sat up, suddenly more alert.

Turner met Leetham halfway and shook his hand warmly. They walked over to the podium together, and Turner swung to face his audience. "This morning I was charged with the daunting task of running a corporation on my own. Now, acting in SeaLab's best interests, I've decided to effect a union between SeaLab and ESI, a giant in the energy field. We have here before us an agreement drawn up by our lawyers this very morning, establishing an alliance that promises to ensure SeaLab's proud work will continue."

There was a confused smattering of applause as some people reacted to his confidence-inspiring tone. Turner brandished a pen and signed with a flourish. He seemed to expect applause, but instead a reporter yelled out, "Mr. Holland! Considering the relative size of ESI and of SeaLab, your choice of words—union, and . . ." he consulted his notes, "alliance—are interesting, but this is basically a takeover, is it not?"

Another reporter jumped to her feet. "Are you saying that SeaLab is to become a subsidiary? Or will it disappear altogether within the research arm of ESI? And what is the purchase price?"

"What about jobs?" called someone in the audience. "Will our jobs be cut?"

Quinn gave Kit a nod, and Kit returned it, seeing what he'd seen: the Seattle police had arrived and were taking covert positions on both sides of the stage. Quinn and Nate began moving toward the front of the room at the same time Kit launched up from her seat.

"Turner Holland," her voice cut through the crowd clearly, "your father's right here, and I think he has something to say about this deal you're trying to swing."

Everyone in the room turned. Half of the people stood to see better, and there was a collective gasp as Marcus pulled himself upright next to Kit.

On the other side of him, Elise rose to her feet. She flashed a look at Kit before announcing loud and clear, "I, too, have an opinion on this matter."

The room rumbled with excitement and confusion while Turner froze, rooted to the stage. Kit turned to Marcus and asked loudly, "Mr. Holland, did you run off with Elise?"

"No," Marcus answered firmly. He looked straight at Elise and said quietly, "Though I would very much like to." Elise blinked, and blushed bright pink.

Kit forged ahead. "Mr. Holland, is your son in a position to sign any agreements with ESI?"

Marcus's voice rang out. "I DID NOT authorize—" Here he allowed a full measure of wrath to enter his voice, "any dealings with ESI, and DO NOT, henceforth."

At this, Turner burst into a run, heading for the steps leading off the side of the stage.

He flew down the steps and ran solidly into a Seattle police officer. Leetham dashed off the other side of the stage, sputtering, "I know nothing!" and another cop was there to grab him.

Kit sped out into the aisle and down to the front of the hall, intent on witnessing Turner's capture. She was almost there when a shout rang out, and the police officer holding Turner staggered back. Kit was horrified to see a needle sticking out of his neck.

Turner leapt back up onto the empty stage. It looked like he intended to jump off the back and make his escape that way. Quinn launched himself up onto the stage and caught Turner in a flying tackle. The two men hit the stage with a thunderous crash.

Then Kit felt a whoosh of wind and realized it was Nate, flying past her. Turner started to lift himself up on one elbow but Nate's knee landed on his chest and smacked him back down. Nate punched Turner's face twice, fast and hard. "That's for Rebecca!" he cried. "You rat bastard!"

~~~

The police took Turner and Leetham away,

but the hall remained full of people milling around, rehashing the drama that had just unfolded.

Kit spotted Jean-Philippe standing nearby with his back to her. She thought about the pictures, and was about to go confront him about that when someone touched her arm. It was Quinn, and Nate was with him. Her heart flooded with warmth at the sight of them.

Before any of them said a word, Buddy, the cabbie, came stomping up to them. "Which of youse is Quinn?" he demanded, jabbing his finger angrily at Nate and Quinn. "I axed Georgette Holland, and she pointed over here."

"There," Kit pointed to Jean-Philippe, who stood nearby, still facing the other way, unsuspecting. "That's him."

Buddy didn't hesitate. He spun Jean-Philippe around and delivered a single blow, low and hard. The skinny Frenchman sailed back several feet before crumpling on the floor.

Buddy stalked away, and Kit walked over to gaze down at Jean-Philippe. "You will destroy those pictures," she told him calmly.

He clutched his gut and moaned.

"If you don't," she continued, "your pain is just starting. My brothers will come after you—"

"I'll do it, I swear!" he moaned, "I'll destroy them!"

~~~

A few hours later, Kit had nearly everything she needed to write her story. She'd spoken with the Seattle police and DeSmet, and had obtained quotes from Elise and Marcus.

She had also read the agreement between Turner and Leetham. It was complicated, but in the end Turner would have walked away with SeaLab's fourteen million in liquid assets, plus another forty-five million dollars from ESI for the acquisition.

ESI wanted exclusive rights to SeaLab's breakthrough technology. The winners? Big Oil. They were in position to quash the technology and ensure the status quo. The losers? They were too many to count, but generally speaking, the entire world population.

Kit knew she couldn't put it that bluntly in her story, but the stage was now set for a series of follow-up articles. She would dig in and do her research, and with the help of a lawyer friend who had vetted her investigative piece on the Holy Roller tax-evaders, she'd do everything possible to expose ESI.

She had only a few more questions to pursue before sending today's breaking news piece to her editor. One of them concerned Ted Connelly a.k.a. Hamm, who was at the troopers' office being questioned by the Seattle police. She rang the troopers' office, and Walsh picked up.

Perfect, she thought, and asked eagerly if he'd been briefed on all the developments.

Walsh just said quietly, "Kit."

Her entire body tensed up as she realized what was coming. *He's going to yell at me, tell me what a fool I was. He'll point out how easily I could have ended up dead.*

But Walsh didn't yell. In a low voice, he said, "Is there anything I can say to make you promise you will stop getting tangled up in this kind of shit?"

"No, sir."

He was silent for minute, and then told her, "We're going to talk about this later."

She stared at her notes, blinking back tears.

A lot of people told her that she shouldn't do the things she ended up doing, but Walsh was the one who mattered. He was smart, and had survived countless situations that would have crushed a lesser person.

They would talk later, and when they did, he would calmly drill her about her own mistakes. For example, when Turner captured her at the top of the ramp, it was because she and her brothers had jumped to the conclusion he was already on the *Blue Sea*, lying in wait. Walsh would remind her of the trap we create for ourselves when we make assumptions, and he would point out about ten other ways she hadn't used her head. He would quietly scare the tar out of her—that was how he showed he cared.

She swallowed. At least he was willing to wait and do it later. "Can you give me the lowdown on Ted Connelly?"

He told her to hold on for a moment. When he came back, he was all business. He told her that Connelly had refused to talk at first, claiming he couldn't remember anything because he'd hit his head. But after learning the police had found a single plane ticket to

Antigua in Turner's pocket—and no second ticket for him—Ted Connelly broke down and started punching things—the table, the walls, and finally, his own head.

Then the police said they'd found references to an offshore account, and inquired whether he knew anything about that. Ted Connelly asked if there were two names on the account or just one. When he heard there was just one, he spilled everything.

Much of what he confessed, Kit already knew. But he did fill in some important blanks. When Turner stabbed her shoulder with the needle, whatever he shot her with, it wiped her out. But everything that happened right up to that point, she remembered clearly. So if Turner had given Marcus such a shot, even if Marcus didn't feel the actual needle, he'd remember Turner was with him right before he stopped remembering anything. She couldn't figure out how Turner managed to abduct Marcus without his awareness.

Turner, Walsh reminded her, had medical training. He had a way with needles, but that was only part of his method. He had a serum he used to sicken his mother in Saluda, and another he used to drug Marcus when he poured him a coffee at opportune times. He had also concocted a vapor—it was on the rag his brother used to render Elise unconscious on the *Blue Sea.*

This reminded Kit of another question: What had Turner planned to do with Elise and Marcus?

His ultimate plan for Marcus and Elise, Walsh replied, was to raise the alarm in a few days, saying that they hadn't called to check in with him while on their romantic trip, as promised. Their bodies were going to turn up, along with the shipwrecked *Blue Sea,* on a reef near Pt. Couverton, outside Juneau.

"Unbelievable," Kit said. "Turner murdered his birth mother in Saluda, and also killed his adoptive parents and sister. He thought he pulled off two more—Rebecca and myself. Plus he abducted Elise and Marcus with the intent to murder. Did he really think he could keep killing people and just . . . get away with it?"

Walsh said, "I can give you my opinion, but it's off the record."

"Off the record, then."

Walsh said, "He gauged a few things correctly. Like the trust Marcus Holland would extend to him, and that he'd be asked to stay and join the company. He counted on the embarrassment Marcus would feel about his past drinking, and how it would make him want to hide what was happening.

"Turner also calculated correctly that Leetham would pay big money to own the rights to SeaLab's new technology. He played all that very smart. Plus, he's an expert at disappearing. He knows the old maxim is true—the trail gets cold, fast."

Kit said, "But all of it was so convoluted, and complicated, and parts of it were not even really very smart."

"Yeah, true, there were some things he didn't gauge very well. Georgette and Elise gave him trouble. And they were nothing compared to you, Miss Little Sundress." Kit blinked, surprised he even knew the word *sundress*. She wondered if he was going to make a comment about ornery women, but he didn't.

He continued, "When things didn't go his way, he got sloppier and sloppier, never thinking he could be making a mistake. It's classic bad guy arrogance. A guy gets away with murder, literally, and thinks he's very smart, and everyone else is easily fooled."

Walsh had to put her on hold for a second, and she had a chance to think about it all. Rather than guns, or fists, Turner used legal knowledge, and medical tricks to accomplish his awful deeds. And, in the digital arena, he'd shown considerable skill at erasing his trail. Except, no matter how good he'd proven to be at erasing information digitally, he had failed to erase the truth. People, and what they know, were outside his control. The letters Rebecca and her mom exchanged; and the memories recalled by the dean's assistant Sylvia; and everything Chief DeSmet in Kurk Falls shared with her over the phone. If any of these pieces had failed to fall into place, Turner might have succeeded.

Walsh came back and Kit had one more question. "So, would Turner have pulled the business deal off? Was it even legal for him to do what he tried to do?"

"Apparently after Holland reappeared the first time, he directed Turner to rewrite

SeaLab's bylaws. The new bylaws stated that if Marcus became unable to perform his duties as head executive, the remaining executive officers would assume his powers. In the end, Turner thought he had arranged to be the only executive officer left standing."

Walsh said he had to go. "Any more questions, text'em to me."

"I think I have what I need. At least, for today's story."

~~~

Afterward, gathered around in Clara's kitchen, Kit, Quinn, Nate, and Elise took turns filling Marcus in on all that had transpired.

Marcus had completely shaken off his drug-induced stupor, and was giving Kit a wide-eyed look of disbelief, having just learned that Turner was not his son.

"Turner had no idea," Kit informed him, "so his actions weren't even tied to some sick sense of loyalty to Leetham. He was simply acting out of greed."

Marcus said knowing Turner was not his son gave him a measure of comfort, but still, he felt deep chagrin over how he'd been so easily manipulated. "How could I have been so blind?" He buried his head in his hands. "Turner was always pouring me coffee. I made it easy for him to drug me. Holy hell, I invited him to join the firm. Where was my judgment?"

No one seemed to know what to say for a moment, until cheerfully, Nate said, "You were doped *and* you were duped."

The comment made everyone laugh and wince at the same time.

Marcus had many questions, and as they talked, Clara baked. She plied them with scones and then key lime pie and then brownies. Everyone was in agreement that the morning's events—the week's events, actually—called for deep, guiltless indulgence.

While they talked, and ate, the air was charged with vast relief that Turner had been captured, but an undercurrent of grief over his deeds also weighed on everyone. They talked about Rebecca, and how close Kit came to dying, and also, Elise's narrow escape. Marcus reached over and took Elise's hand. "Ellie, I don't know what I would have done if . . ." his voice trailed off.

Kit felt a little tug in her heart at the way

Marcus called her *Ellie*. Quinn gave Kit a look that said he caught it as well. She leaned over and asked him softly if Marcus knew, yet, what Georgette had actually put in that envelope for him. When Quinn shook his head, Kit whispered, "I think now would be a good time to clue him in."

Quinn cleared his throat. "Marcus . . . I gave you an envelope yesterday morning, when I met you in the harbor."

He got up and retrieved the envelope. "I think you might want to take a closer look at it."

Marcus pulled the papers out. When he realized he was looking at divorce documents, he blinked in shock, and then an odd expression came over his face. Kit realized it was the look of a man who had just been pardoned from a life sentence. Very slowly, moving with great deliberation, he got out a pen and signed the papers. Then he raised his gaze and looked directly at Elise.

If there was ever a marriage proposal in the air, it was at that very moment, Kit realized with tingle, watching as Marcus reached out to take Elise's hand. But before he could say a word, suddenly the loaded silence was broken by a ring from Kit's phone. "It's Rebecca's mom!" she said and hit answer.

Bev was crying so hard she couldn't speak. Kit stood up slowly and turned her back to everyone. She knew she should leave the room to take this call, but was too heartsick to move.

Suddenly Bev choked out the words, "Becca's awake . . . and she's herself!"

~~~

The house was quiet. Quinn and Kit were entwined on the couch in the front room, watching the fire burn low in the fireplace.

Kit had written up everything and emailed it to her editor at the Nipntuck News. She wrote a note saying she'd give him first crack at running the story as long as he paid her for the week and gave her full rein to do any follow up articles.

His email back was a terse, "Alright."

She'd taken that as a sign that her job was secure—for the time being, anyway.

She shifted on the couch and moved Quinn's arm so that it rested more comfortably across her shoulders.

"Hey," she said sleepily a few minutes later,

"Quinn?"

"Hmm?"

"You really are over that nurse?"

"I am very much over her."

"You'd better not be lying to me . . ."

"I'm not."

"Good. Because my brothers would squish you."

"I believe you."

"I'm glad we have that straight." Kit snuggled against him. "Now, here's another question—"

He turned to her and cupped her face in his hands, "I'm falling ridiculously, helplessly in love with you."

She laughed deep in her throat. "That wasn't my question, but it's good to know. I actually wanted to ask if you believe in . . . palm reading."

"What?"

"Do you think our futures can be read in our palms?"

He took her hand and looked at it for a moment. When he raised his eyes to meet hers, something in his gaze made her heart flip. He said, "If your palm says I'm going to kiss you, sweetheart, then, yes."

She leaned forward to glance at her palm, then raised her eyes to meet his. "It says a million kisses, actually."

He drew her to him and said, "You just described the perfect future."

A Note from Carole Gibb

Dear Reader, feel free to look me up online and drop me a note to say hello.

If you've enjoyed this book, tell your friends about it. This is a homespun effort, and word of mouth is my best hope for finding an audience.

ACKNOWLEDGMENTS

It's my great fortune to be in a writing and editing cooperative with three fabulous writers: Arlene Springer, Kelley Beebe, and Leslie Barber. What amazing women. The hours we've spent sharing revelations and encouragement have been priceless to me. I simply can't thank you enough.

Many friends were kind enough to edit copy and/or provide support, moral or otherwise.

Evelyn Heaton, you are my angel neighbor.

Brad Swanson, my hero, always.

Richard Webster, I have you to thank for so much, but especially for the showdown scene.

Donna Denno, what can I say? Our walks and talks have been central to my life, and also to this work.

A hat tip to the Fremont Brewing Company, especially for their Interurban IPA, and also to Phillip for introducing me to it.

I stole the name *The Big Skinny*!

Thanks Lou Seapy, wherever you are.

And, speaking of thievery, Jane Roodenburg, I hope it's okay I copped your idea for a restaurant named the Eat-n-Git. And Tom and Minnie, I'm sure you recognize the nickname you gave your skiff, once upon a time, in a land, far, far away!

Generous help with editing came from Gery Rudolph, Pat Halsell, and Charles Dyer, and also from family members Mary Lou Healy, Sue Zitterman, Mary Healy, and Kitty Carrico-Carpenter.

Kind readers and advisors also include Mary Bowen, Anne Reilly, Alice Salcido, Deborah Alexander and Lori Perry. Quique Olvera, gracias, mi amigo, for your website advice.

Tim and Lorelie Olson, that lovely retreat at Shady Grove, surrounded by dogs and books and tall pine trees was pure heaven.

Toni Carrington and Paul Olson, I adore you for many reasons, but especially for adopting me on my first

Thanksgiving in Seattle.

Shel Silverstein, I wish I'd had a chance to meet you in person before you left us. Thank you for giving us such beauty in the work you did. You rule.

Thanks, also to the hardworking Bhamipuri family at the 7-11 in Seattle at 36th St. N. Your graciousness has been lovely in the midst of many late nights.

Geri Rudolph, graphic designer, your eye for beauty and your high standards made this book a visual wonder.

Paul Watkins, you are the sweetest tech savvy-dancer-photographer-cyclist in the whole world.

And last, but not least, Radhika Sharma, the closing scene was inspired by a joke you told me a long time ago. I'm still laughing.

ONE

WHEN THAT FIRST SALMON, one hundred feet below, bit the hook and began darting to and fro, it rang a little bell fastened up in the boat's rigging. I engaged the hydraulics and spooled the wire aboard, drawing the fish up toward the surface.

I was on a forty-foot wooden boat, commercial trolling along the jagged, fish-rich coast of Southeast Alaska. While the skipper steered the boat, trying to get our hooks and lures in front of the fish, my job was to bring the fish on board, one at a time, treating each one with care.

A few years shy of forty, I liked my comforts. I was an inexperienced mariner and being around machinery scared me. But people often do things for money that they wouldn't do otherwise.

My plan was to live on this boat July through September, work relentlessly, and walk away at the summer's end with eight, maybe ten thousand dollars. I wanted this wad of cash to help finance a long-deferred dream, which was to write a mystery novel.

There it was. A shadowy shape, cutting back and forth just below the water's surface. A silver salmon.

Seeing it gave me an unexpected thrill. I swung the fish on board and stared at it in wonder. Just one fish was all it took. Some primal part of my DNA started to sing.

I thought my attraction to catching fish would be the big surprise of the summer, but it was just the first.

~~~~~

Dear Mary,

Logged eighteen hours on the ocean today, but somehow we managed to catch only forty-one silvers. Each fish earns us under three dollars, so you can imagine the disappointment.

We'd anchored for the night in a natural cove along the rock-strewn edge of the Gulf of Alaska and I was tucked into a corner of the boat with my notebook, writing to Mary, my sister.

Mary was unlike me in every way imaginable—a financial analyst who lived in Atlanta, she was married to a cop and had three kids. But we shared a sweetness of understanding that allowed us to speak our hearts to one another. And better yet, we got each other's jokes.

Fishing will improve, I'm sure. And meanwhile the ocean provides some good entertainment. This morning, I cleaned a salmon and there was a little fish inside, wiggling with indignation— apparently just swallowed. I scooped it overboard and watched it hurry away. I can see the little guy catching up with his buddies and saying, *You're not going to believe what just happened*.

Then we had a humpback whale surface fairly close to the boat.

Massive, I thought, when I saw it. Seeing all that latent power gliding along so smooth made my entire body tingle. But then it angled toward us and dove, and the tingles changed to a crawly feeling on the back of my neck, since it looked like it might pass under the boat.

We turned to give it some room, but even so it resurfaced uncomfortably close. It came up and blew, *whooooosh*—and the misty breath floated right onto me.

Cool, you might think. Well, think again, because it smelled putrid. Somebody should tell that whale to brush its baleen!

Until this stinky whale breath incident I never appreciated how, even though we're dealing with fish blood and guts all the time, the boat just smells like ocean and air. Never even a whiff of that rank fishy smell. That smell apparently occurs when fish oil oxidizes, which is why I'm constantly hosing down the deck and, at the end of the day, scrubbing with bleach.

Speaking of guts I'd like to state for the record that the goo inside a fish is squishy, but less messy than one might expect. It's arranged in this sensible package—you make three quick slices with a well-placed blade, grip and pull, and the works come out in a sort of balloon. Overboard it goes, all in one motion. Well, ideally anyway. I have flung guts pretty much all over the boat because I get excited and lose focus.

Today, we quit around ten p.m. and charged to one of the little semi-protected indents that dot the Gulf of Alaska coast. Charging means going top speed, but a troller's top speed is only about eight knots (a hair over eight mph), so it's not like restraint harnesses are required.

We negotiated around a bunch of rocks to enter this little cranny in the coast called Peril Cove. Tom dropped the anchor and cut the engine. When it humped out its last cough it was as though my ears had been hot and thirsty all day, and the silence settled on them like a deep, cold drink.

Glad to be off duty, I played with the dog, Fidget, tossing a carrot around the deck for her to fetch. She's a graceful dog, with a silky black body and a tan face, chest, and legs. Tom recently rescued her from the pound and though I've never been around dogs much, or even cared to be, she's pretty sweet.

Ocean-caught fish for dinner. You'd think eating so much fish would get boring, but it's gorgeous food and my body seems to know it. I'll go further and confess that eating wild fish makes me feel sort of wild myself, inside. Fidget chases her tail out of sheer giddy happiness, and sometimes Mary, I swear I feel like doing the same.

Okay, my eyelids are drooping. I'll write more later!

xxoo

Carole

PS: You asked how it's going with Tom. Things are good. We're working out well on the boat.

In her last letter she'd inquired about me and Tom. It was an apt question since couples often have trouble working together. But he and I had been sweethearts for years and ours was a comfortable, elastic relationship. He was a stocky, smiling, huggable guy, although when fishing started he turned more serious, less huggy. Past summers I'd remained in Juneau while he went fishing, and I hardly heard from him. It was a normal part of the commercial fishing life and I didn't take it personally. When the season is open, romance falls off the radar. So whether I was in Juneau or beside Tom on the boat, I knew the drill: it was work now, play later.

~~~~~

Deckhands, especially new ones, can get nauseous in the fish hold and my first time down in the belly of the boat, I understood why. My body was getting jerked back and forth as though I'd fallen inside a washing machine. The waves against the boat's hull made a sloshing sound that echoed in the cave-like space, worsening the sensation.

The wild salmon we caught were destined for fine restaurants and upscale fish markets, which meant that after landing and cleaning fish we had to get their temperature down quickly, but it had to be done without marring their surprisingly tender scales. So I faced the task of gently layering our catch on ice, one by one, and sprinkling ice around each one.

I sat there, fighting nausea, telling myself I was on an amusement park ride, but was getting paid for the thrill. My bottom kept sliding a bit to the left, then to the right, but after a few minutes, I'd melted a tiny hollow in the ice and stopped moving so much.

I took a salmon into my gloved hands. Maybe it was the backdrop of the glittering white ice, but I noticed something I hadn't seen before. The scales of these fish were truly beautiful. Though primarily silver, they also glinted with jewel-like flashes of purple, aqua, and green.

Wild salmon hatch in a fresh-water stream, live three or four years out on the ocean, and return to their origin stream where they spawn once and die. The dry scientific facts are simple.

But written on those colorful scales, I saw the story of a life, a story that began before this fish even existed. Four years ago, in the spring, the snow melted and rushed off the mountains. It swelled the streams and put out a scent, calling mature salmon in from the wide ocean. After a harrowing trip upstream, past eagles and bears, otters and fishermen, a pair of salmon spawned. Minuscule eggs buried in the stream gravel started to grow. And this particular fish, the one now in my hands, emerged months later from the gravel as a fry. It grew up to live a free and fishy life, roaming all over the sea.

And when the time was right, some drive inside the fish, combined with that hint of spring snowmelt in the ocean, drew it back toward the fresh water stream of its birth.

It comforted me that we caught these salmon at the end of their life cycle, right before they were going to die anyway. And I liked that fisheries biologists and a state advisory board ensured that a healthy percentage of fish got through to spawn, and kept the cycle going, before we were allowed to take our share.

Sitting in the fish hold, growing numb from the cold, a little hope bloomed in my heart that whoever ate this fish would do so with a special kind of pleasure. Even if they gave no conscious thought to its life story, maybe some part inside of them would thrill to the wildness that formed it.

~~~~~

Those first few weeks I was deeply happy to be fishing. The work touched a chord inside me. But there were a couple of clouds smudging the horizon.

The price per pound we got for our silvers was well under a dollar; the lowest Tom had ever seen it. Apparently, it had to do with farmed fish flooding the market. The price was expected to go up—it always did as the summer progressed—so we could count on better wages ahead. But those first weeks our earnings were painfully meager.

Compounding this was another issue. We couldn't seem to catch many fish.

The state fish and game bureau does a thorough job of managing commercial fisheries, so we knew the cause wasn't depleted stocks. Tom said he wanted to determine if other boats were doing poorly, or if it was just us. If other fishermen were also experiencing low catch rates we'd know the fish were just running late, or had shifted slightly north or south to travel in currents that were more feed-rich.

Finding out how other boats were performing, though, wasn't as simple as just asking.

Dear Mary,

We're on our way to anchor up. There wasn't much scrubbing to do since we hardly caught anything. It poured all day, plus there was a steady wind with a bite to it. In July.

I ducked inside the pilothouse to thaw out every few hours. Tom's not much into conversation lately, so mostly we listened to the "VHF." This is what he calls the marine radio. I'm trying to remember to call it that too, but I accidentally keep saying "VHS" instead.

"VHF, very high frequency," he patiently says.

"Oh, right," I nod as if that means something to me, while secretly thinking, *very happy fruit fly*, and *virile hunky flirt*, trying to lodge those letters V-H-*F* into my brain.

So the reason we're listening to the radio is to pick up hints on whether nearby boats are catching. The thing is, fishermen don't like to disclose their catch rates, or how deep they fish, or what type of lures they favor, or what they had for breakfast, or when they last changed their socks, or how they feel about cauliflower. In other words, they're secretive, these fishermen.

Certain skippers, the successful ones, have coding partners—other successful people with whom they share catch data via the VHF. But since everyone monitors the radio, hungry to learn where the bite is, partners must be wily. Their secret codes can sound funny. One guy will say, "I have a few more than a . . ." There will be a rustle of paper while he refers to his key sheet of codes, and he'll finally say, "smoky brown cow." Then his partner will say, "I've got a candied ham," and the first guy replies, "Sounds good with eggs."

Other fishermen hide their codes in casual conversation. Rather than saying, "I have a such-n-such fill-in-the-code-name," they sneak code words in on the sly. Tom told me about a couple of guys who talked gardening all last season and nobody knew whether they were using it for a cover, or really liked gardening, or both.

We're not coding with anyone, but some friends invited us to a barbecue tonight on their boat, so after we "set the hook" (that means anchor, matey!) we'll row over in the dinghy. We'll get dinner, but we're also going to get the scuttlebutt. I'll let you know what we learn.

xxoo

Carole

Unfortunately, the scuttlebutt indicated that we *were* doing poorly compared to other boats. I fretted to Tom that it was me, jinxing us. Maybe the salmon could sense my desire. Maybe my lust for catching fish was traveling down the wire and radiating off our hooks, and that made the fish veer away, as though warned off by a bad scent.

Tom said I wasn't jinxing us.

Then I wondered if my lack of experience was causing the trouble. I tripped and hit my head a lot. Maybe my head-thunking scared the fish off. Tom reassured me head-thunking happened on boats all the time, and fish didn't seem especially sensitive to that.

The weeks stacked up and we tried not to buckle under these two stresses—few fish and a distressingly low price. We worked harder, we changed areas, we stayed in the same spot, we asked advice, we kept to ourselves—we tried it all—but nothing seemed to help. Despite the long days and unflagging effort, we were barely making enough to cover fuel.

Dear Mary,

I can handle the wet, the cold, and how few fish we're catching. The worst part, I've discovered, is how hard it is to make a fashion statement out here.

Every day, I waddle around in the same outfit: rubber rain bibs, oversized rubber raincoat, and XtraTufs—the rubber boots everybody wears. They come to the knee, have a good tread on slippery decks, and are excessively clumpy. I think BF Goodrich makes them.

Footwear made by a tire company. Now do you see why I feel somewhat less than chic?

I tore the page out of my notebook and crumpled it in a tight ball. The happy mood of the initial weeks on the boat was gone. I had managed to write a letter pretending otherwise, but couldn't send it because it was a lie. Letter-writing always required one thing from me: that I dig down and try to speak the truth.

Hey Mary,

The money sucks . . . but at least the hours are long.

This single sentence, this tiny touch of honesty, made it impossible to pretend there was much hope for my goal for the summer, which was to get ahead financially.

The real problem, though, ran deeper than money. My interest in the fishing life had become stronger than I even knew. Wanting something that makes emotional sense but goes against logic spells trouble.

But it can also raise some interesting questions. What constitutes wealth, aside from money? What's true security? If you always have to whisper *righty-tighty-lefty-loosey* when using a screwdriver, does that mean you're dense?

Questions like these loomed ahead of me, but when I wrote this single line, this wry lament to my sister, I had no idea. I was just trying to get at the truth. But the truth has a peculiar power, a sort of momentum to it. One truth leads to another, and that takes you to the next. It's the kind of thing that can be disruptive to plans, especially if the plans have to do with arranging a calm, tidy life.

33732270R00333

Made in the USA
San Bernardino, CA
09 May 2016